NANCY Drew DIARIES®

#3

"The Fake Heir"
and
"Mr. Cheeters is Missing"

Based on the series by
CAROLYN KEENE
STEFAN PETRUCHA • Writer
DANIEL VAUGHN ROSS and **SHO MURASE** • Artists
with 3D CG elements by **RACHEL ITO** and **LUIS LUNDGREN**

PAPERCUTZ™
New York

Nancy Drew Diaries
#3

"The Fake Heir" and "Mr. Cheeters is Missing"
STEFAN PETRUCHA – Writer
DANIEL VAUGHN ROSS – Artist, "The Fake Heir"
SHO MURASE – Artist, "Mr. Cheeters is Missing"
with 3D CG elements by LUIS LUNDGREN ("The Fake Heir")
and RACHEL ITO ("Mr. Cheeters is Missing")
BRYAN SENKA – Letterer
CARLOS JOSE GUZMAN – Colorist
MICHAEL PETRANEK – Associate Editor
JIM SALICRUP – Original Editor
BETH SCORZATO – Editor
JIM SALICRUP
Editor-in-Chief

ISBN: 978-1-62991-054-3

Published by arrangement with Aladdin Paperbacks,
an imprint of Simon & Schuster Children's Publishing Division.

Printed in South Korea
October 2014 by We SP Corp.
2F, 507-8 Munbal-dong, Gyoha-eup
Paju City, Gyunggi-do
Seoul, Gyeonggi-do 413-756

Distributed by Macmillian
First Printing

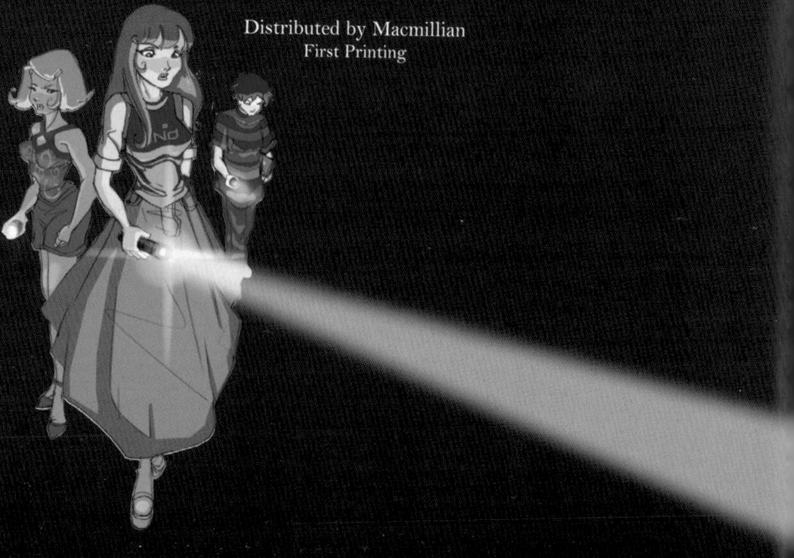

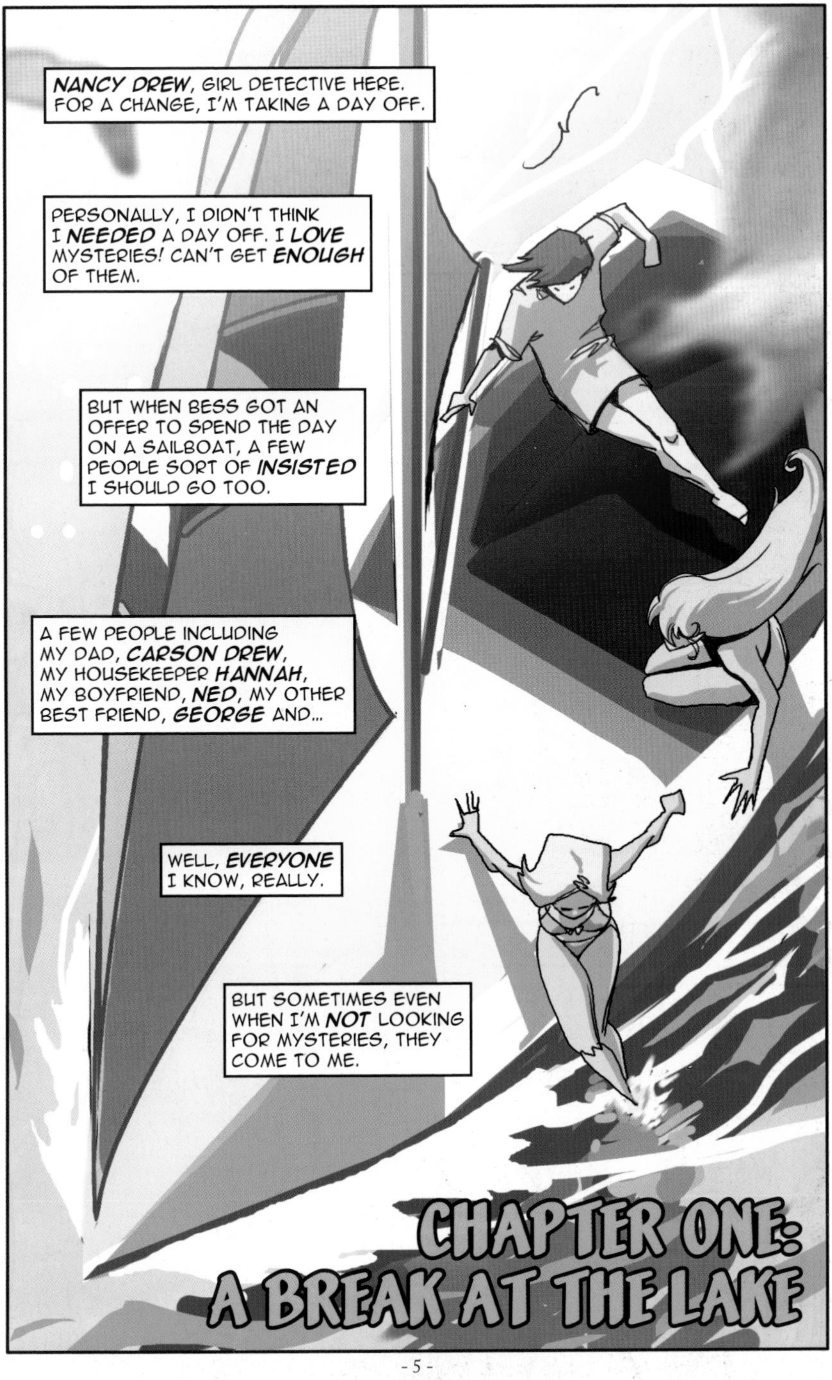
NANCY DREW, GIRL DETECTIVE HERE. FOR A CHANGE, I'M TAKING A DAY OFF.
PERSONALLY, I DIDN'T THINK I NEEDED A DAY OFF. I LOVE MYSTERIES! CAN'T GET ENOUGH OF THEM.
BUT WHEN BESS GOT AN OFFER TO SPEND THE DAY ON A SAILBOAT, A FEW PEOPLE SORT OF INSISTED I SHOULD GO TOO.
A FEW PEOPLE INCLUDING MY DAD, CARSON DREW, MY HOUSEKEEPER HANNAH, MY BOYFRIEND, NED, MY OTHER BEST FRIEND, GEORGE AND...
WELL, EVERYONE I KNOW, REALLY.
BUT SOMETIMES EVEN WHEN I'M NOT LOOKING FOR MYSTERIES, THEY COME TO ME.
CHAPTER ONE: A BREAK AT THE LAKE

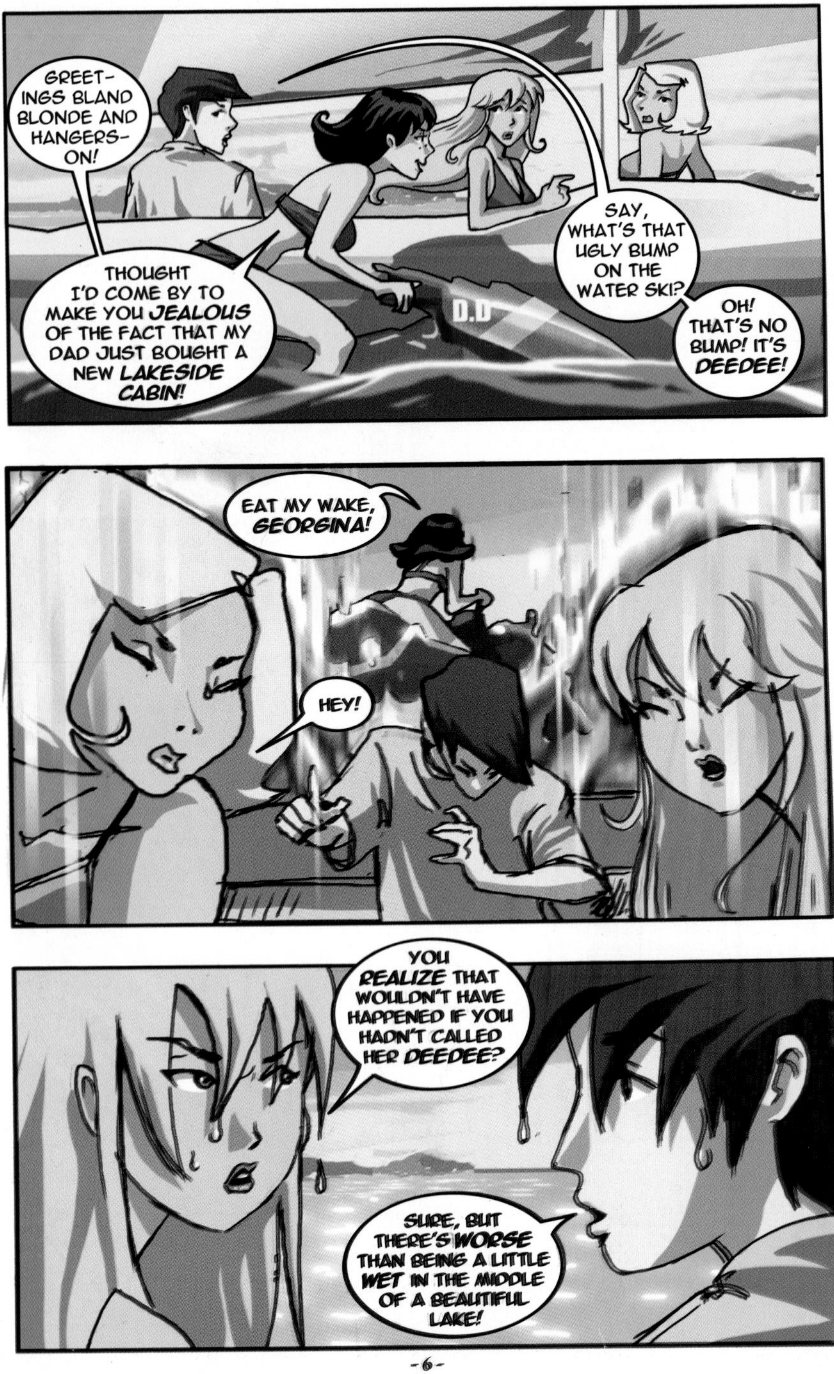
GREETINGS BLAND BLONDE AND HANGERS-ON!
THOUGHT I'D COME BY TO MAKE YOU JEALOUS OF THE FACT THAT MY DAD JUST BOUGHT A NEW LAKESIDE CABIN!
SAY, WHAT'S THAT UGLY BUMP ON THE WATER SKI?
OH! THAT'S NO BUMP! IT'S DEEDEE!
D.D
EAT MY WAKE, GEORGINA!
HEY!
YOU REALIZE THAT WOULDN'T HAVE HAPPENED IF YOU HADN'T CALLED HER DEEDEE?
SURE, BUT THERE'S WORSE THAN BEING A LITTLE WET IN THE MIDDLE OF A BEAUTIFUL LAKE!

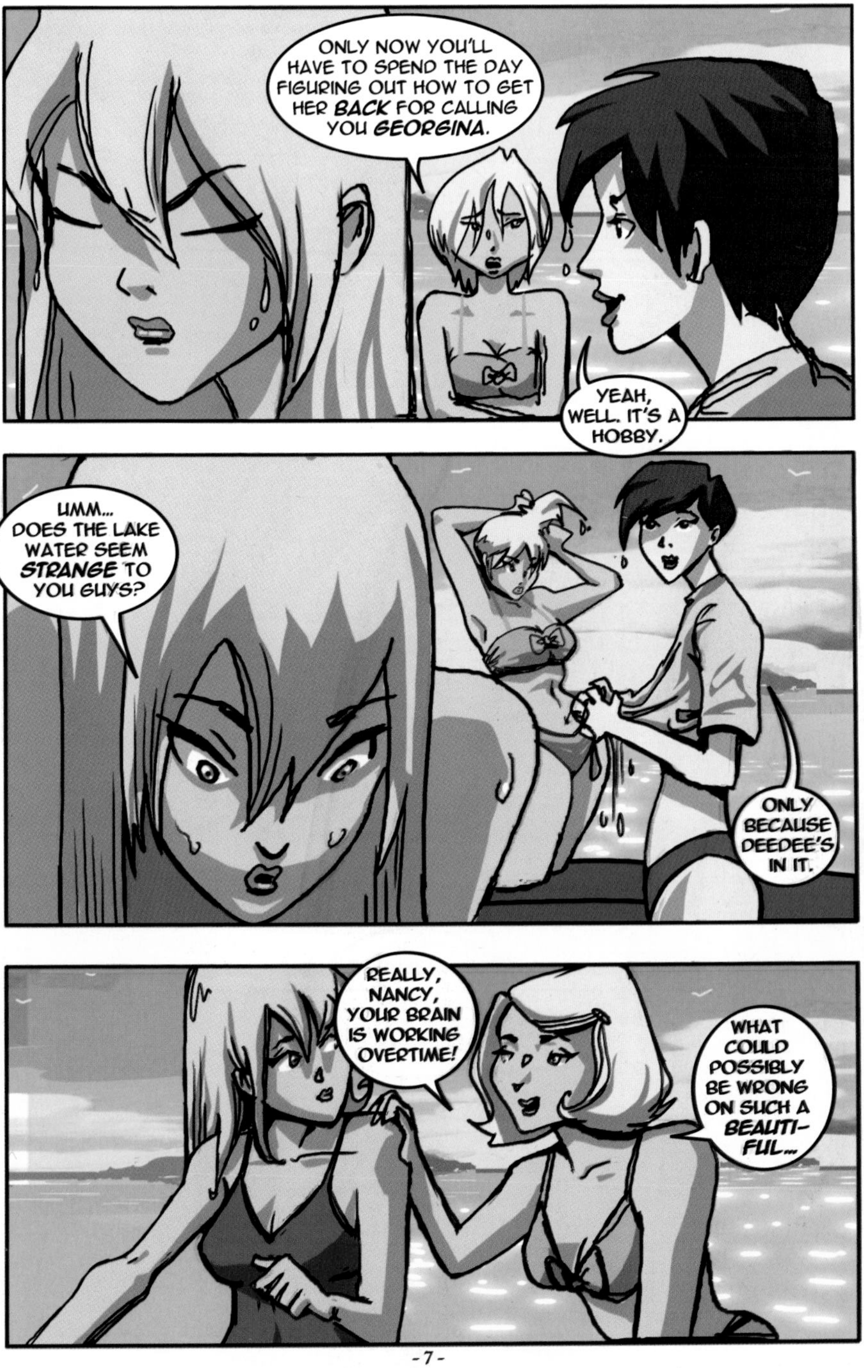
ONLY NOW YOU'LL HAVE TO SPEND THE DAY FIGURING OUT HOW TO GET HER BACK FOR CALLING YOU GEORGINA.
YEAH, WELL. IT'S A HOBBY.
UMM... DOES THE LAKE WATER SEEM STRANGE TO YOU GUYS?
ONLY BECAUSE DEEDEE'S IN IT.
REALLY, NANCY, YOUR BRAIN IS WORKING OVERTIME!
WHAT COULD POSSIBLY BE WRONG ON SUCH A BEAUTI-FUL...

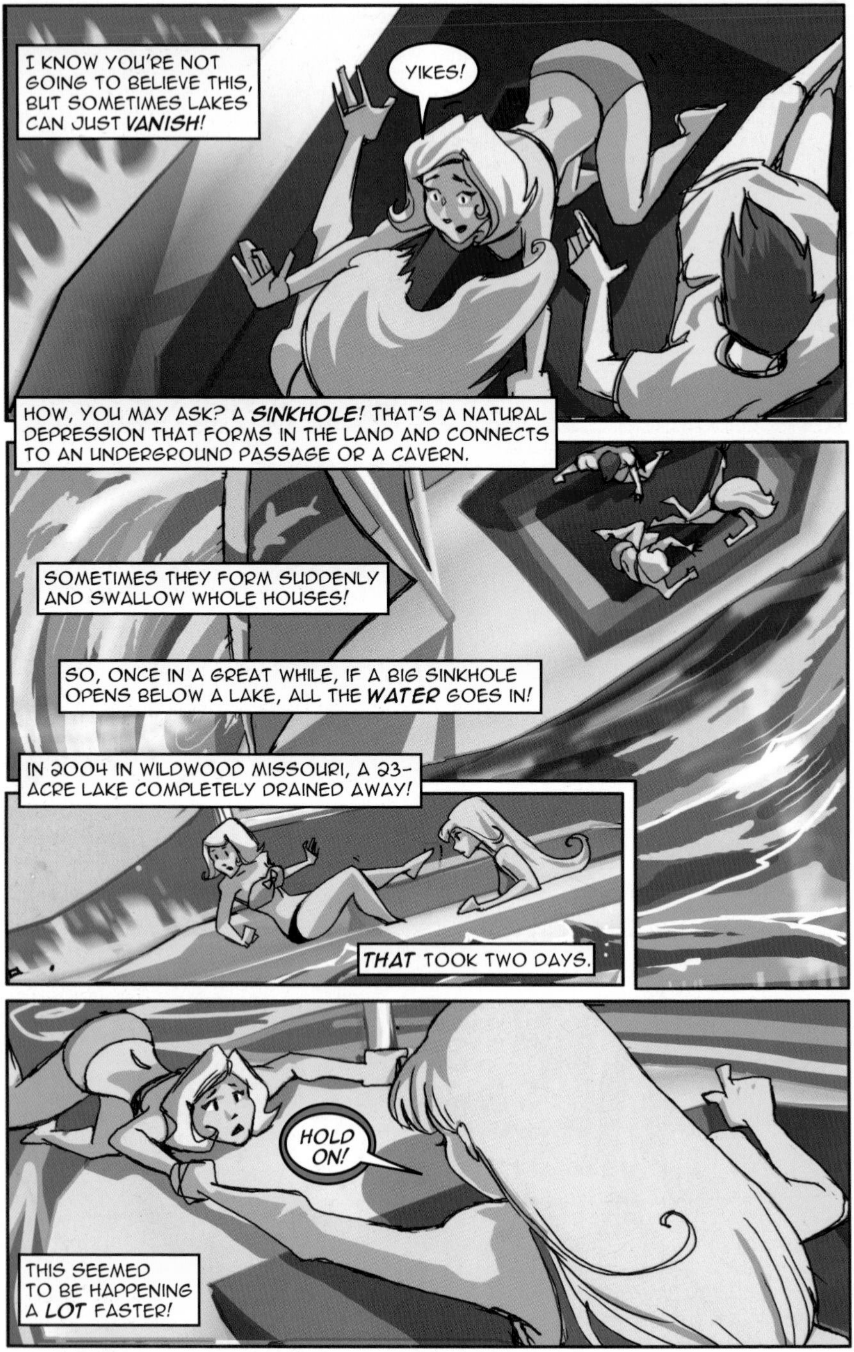

I KNOW YOU'RE NOT GOING TO BELIEVE THIS, BUT SOMETIMES LAKES CAN JUST VANISH!
YIKES!
HOW, YOU MAY ASK? A SINKHOLE! THAT'S A NATURAL DEPRESSION THAT FORMS IN THE LAND AND CONNECTS TO AN UNDERGROUND PASSAGE OR A CAVERN.
SOMETIMES THEY FORM SUDDENLY AND SWALLOW WHOLE HOUSES!
SO, ONCE IN A GREAT WHILE, IF A BIG SINKHOLE OPENS BELOW A LAKE, ALL THE WATER GOES IN!
IN 2004 IN WILDWOOD MISSOURI, A 23-ACRE LAKE COMPLETELY DRAINED AWAY!
THAT TOOK TWO DAYS.
HOLD ON!
THIS SEEMED TO BE HAPPENING A LOT FASTER!

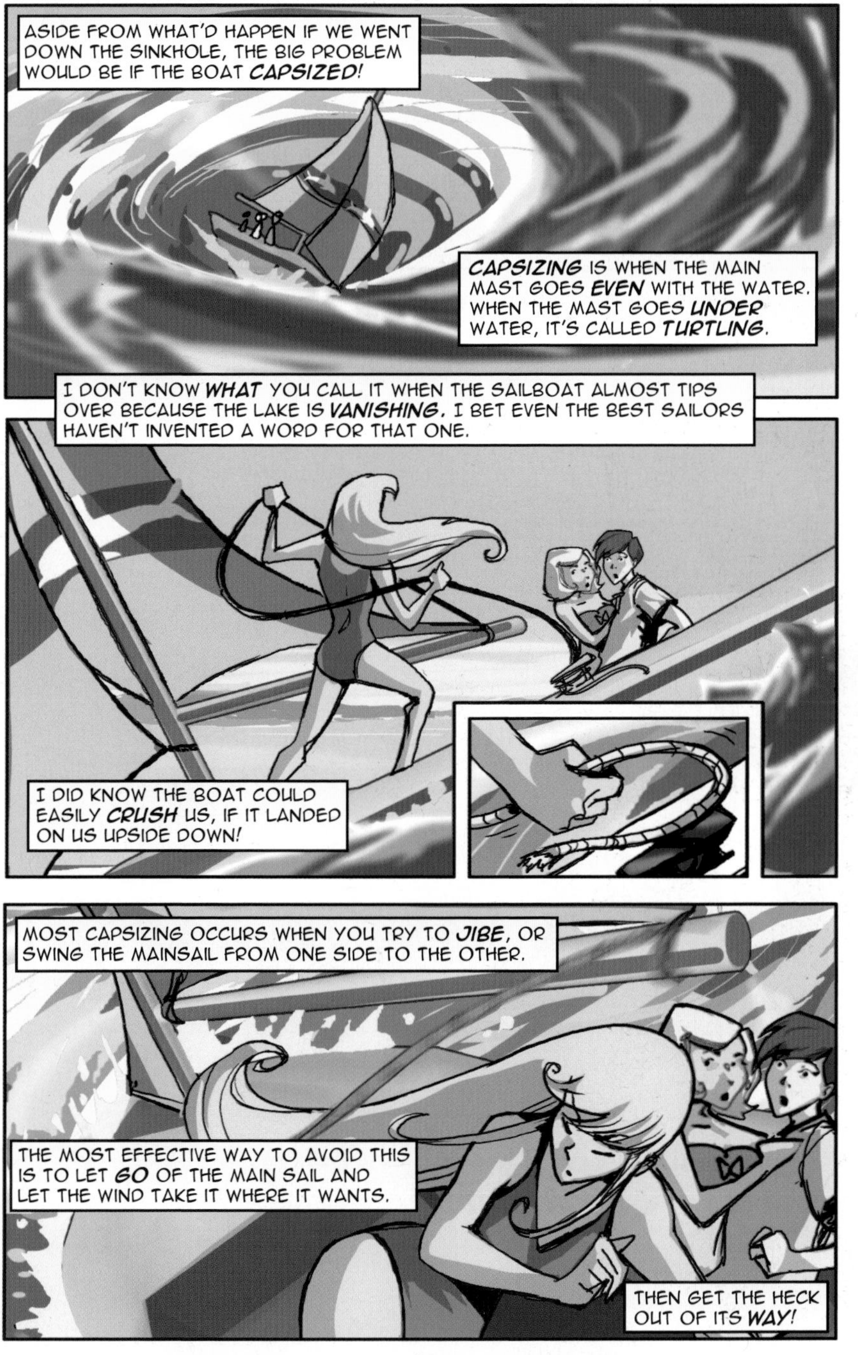
ASIDE FROM WHAT'D HAPPEN IF WE WENT DOWN THE SINKHOLE, THE BIG PROBLEM WOULD BE IF THE BOAT CAPSIZED!
CAPSIZING IS WHEN THE MAIN MAST GOES EVEN WITH THE WATER. WHEN THE MAST GOES UNDER WATER, IT'S CALLED TURTLING.
I DON'T KNOW WHAT YOU CALL IT WHEN THE SAILBOAT ALMOST TIPS OVER BECAUSE THE LAKE IS VANISHING. I BET EVEN THE BEST SAILORS HAVEN'T INVENTED A WORD FOR THAT ONE.
I DID KNOW THE BOAT COULD EASILY CRUSH US, IF IT LANDED ON US UPSIDE DOWN!
MOST CAPSIZING OCCURS WHEN YOU TRY TO JIBE, OR SWING THE MAINSAIL FROM ONE SIDE TO THE OTHER.
THE MOST EFFECTIVE WAY TO AVOID THIS IS TO LET GO OF THE MAIN SAIL AND LET THE WIND TAKE IT WHERE IT WANTS.
THEN GET THE HECK OUT OF ITS WAY!

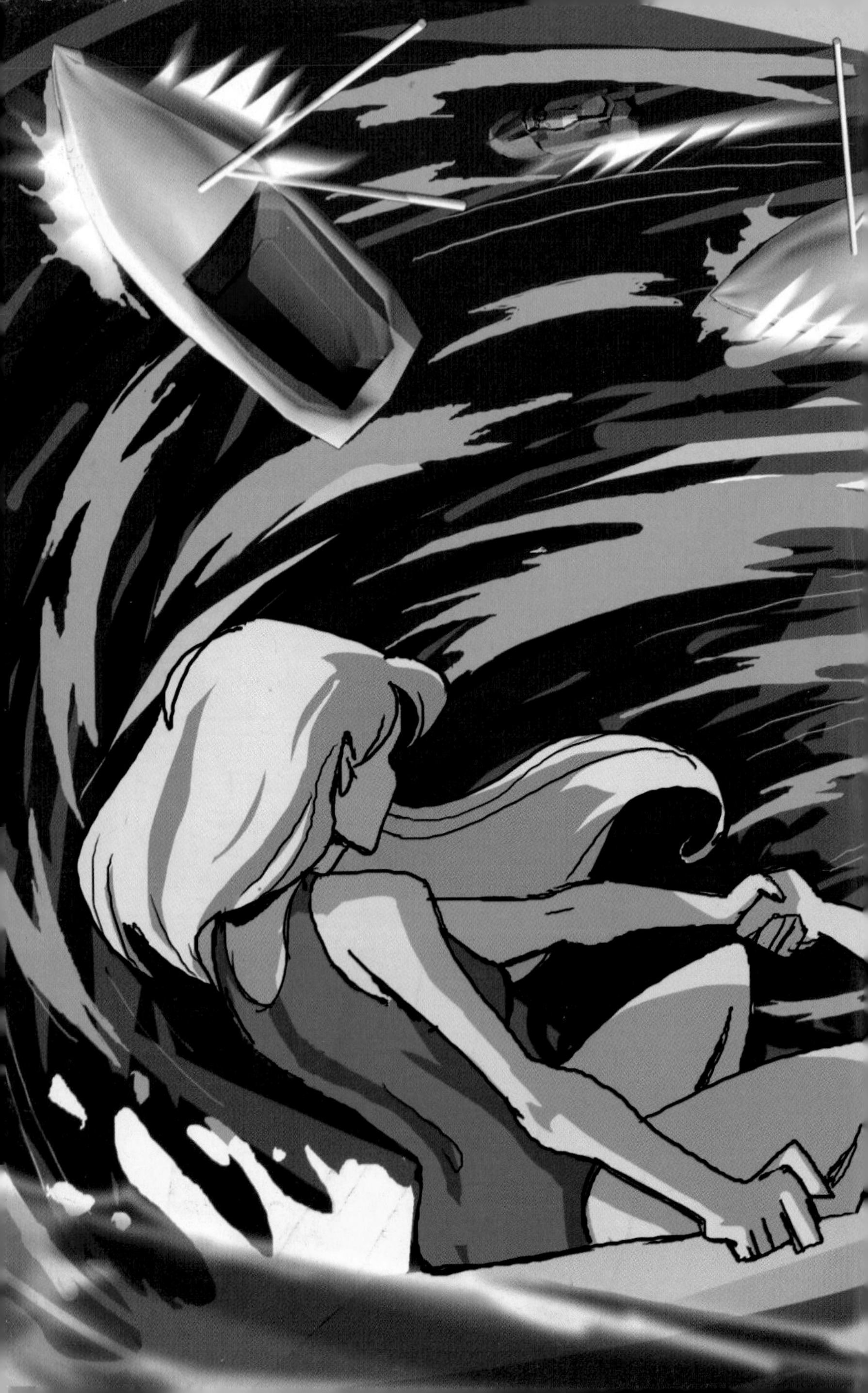

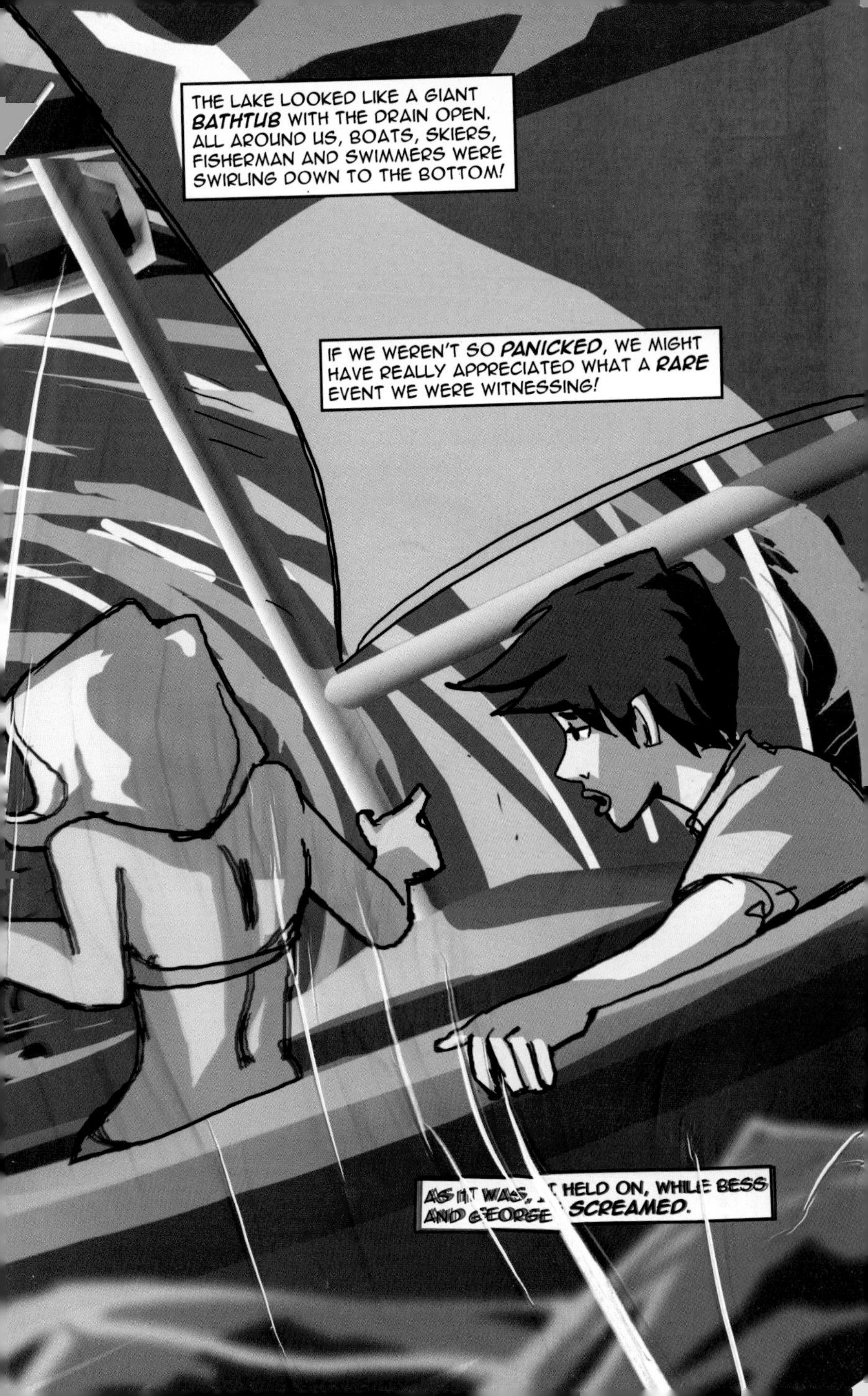

THE LAKE LOOKED LIKE A GIANT *BATHTUB* WITH THE DRAIN OPEN. ALL AROUND US, BOATS, SKIERS, FISHERMAN AND SWIMMERS WERE SWIRLING DOWN TO THE BOTTOM!
IF WE WEREN'T SO *PANICKED*, WE MIGHT HAVE REALLY APPRECIATED WHAT A *RARE* EVENT WE WERE WITNESSING!
AS IT WAS, I HELD ON, WHILE BESS AND GEORGE *SCREAMED*.

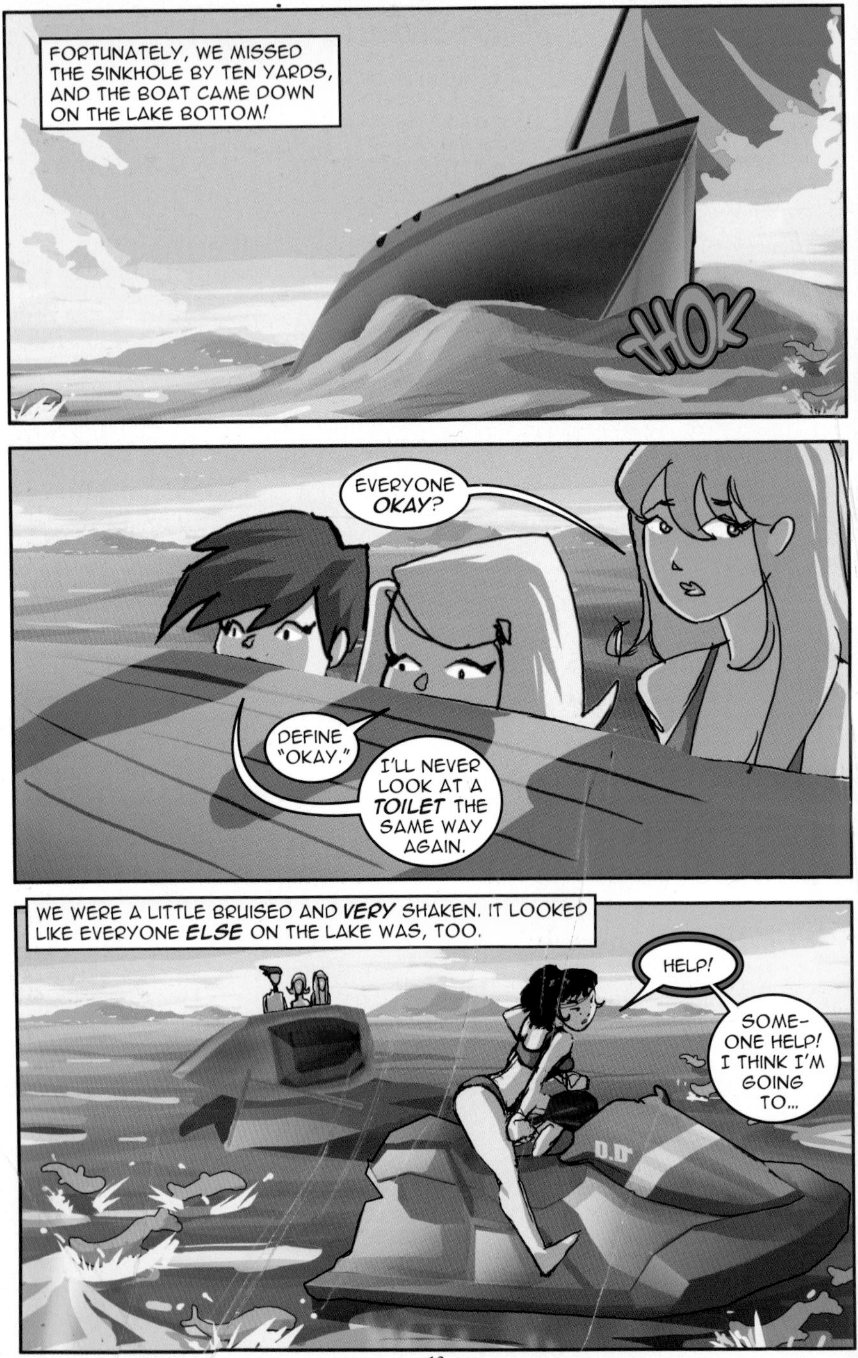
FORTUNATELY, WE MISSED THE SINKHOLE BY TEN YARDS, AND THE BOAT CAME DOWN ON THE LAKE BOTTOM!
THOK
EVERYONE OKAY?
DEFINE "OKAY."
I'LL NEVER LOOK AT A TOILET THE SAME WAY AGAIN.
WE WERE A LITTLE BRUISED AND VERY SHAKEN. IT LOOKED LIKE EVERYONE ELSE ON THE LAKE WAS, TOO.
HELP!
SOME-ONE HELP! I THINK I'M GOING TO...

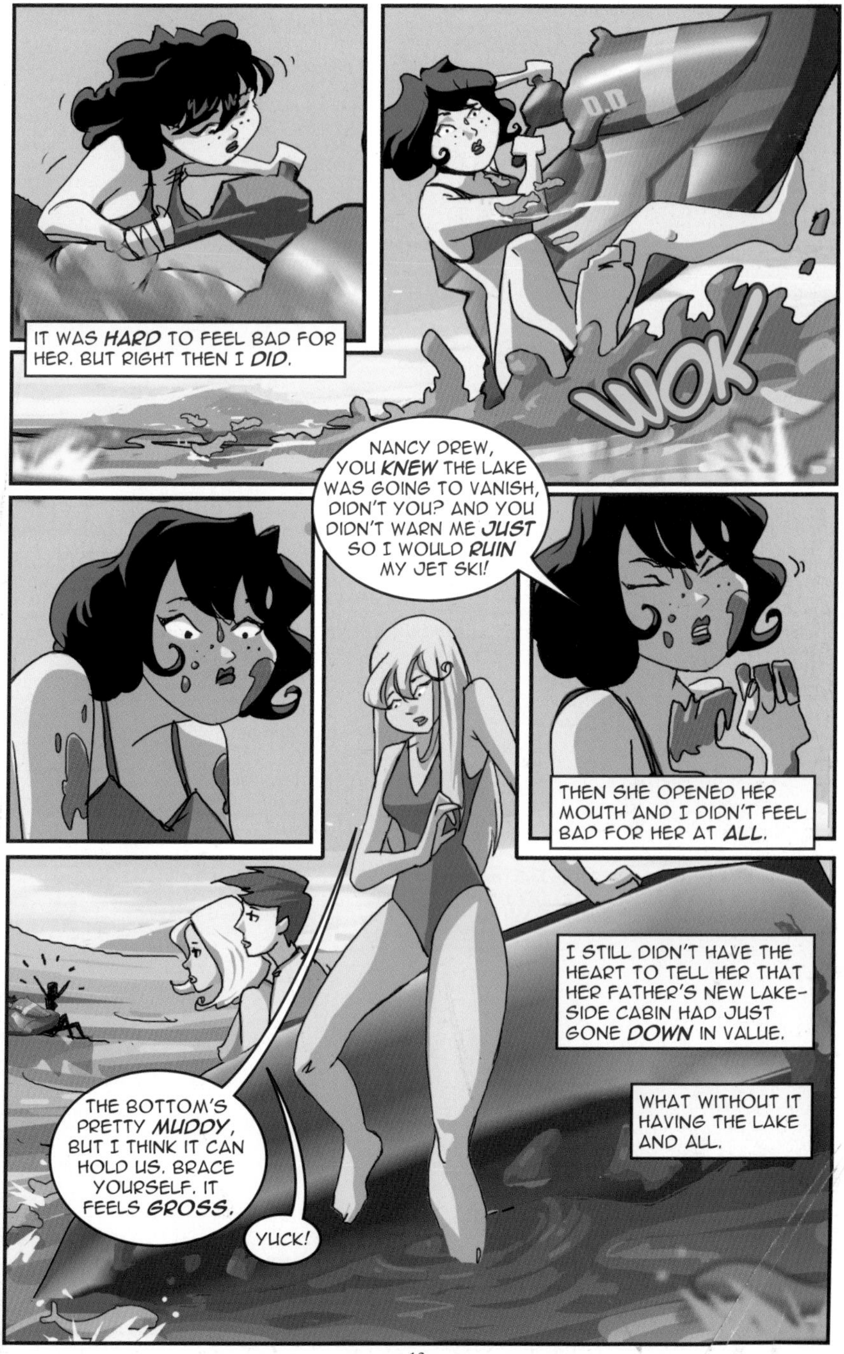
IT WAS HARD TO FEEL BAD FOR HER. BUT RIGHT THEN I DID.
WOK
NANCY DREW, YOU KNEW THE LAKE WAS GOING TO VANISH, DIDN'T YOU? AND YOU DIDN'T WARN ME JUST SO I WOULD RUIN MY JET SKI!
THEN SHE OPENED HER MOUTH AND I DIDN'T FEEL BAD FOR HER AT ALL.
I STILL DIDN'T HAVE THE HEART TO TELL HER THAT HER FATHER'S NEW LAKE-SIDE CABIN HAD JUST GONE DOWN IN VALUE.
WHAT WITHOUT IT HAVING THE LAKE AND ALL.
THE BOTTOM'S PRETTY MUDDY, BUT I THINK IT CAN HOLD US. BRACE YOURSELF. IT FEELS GROSS.
YUCK!

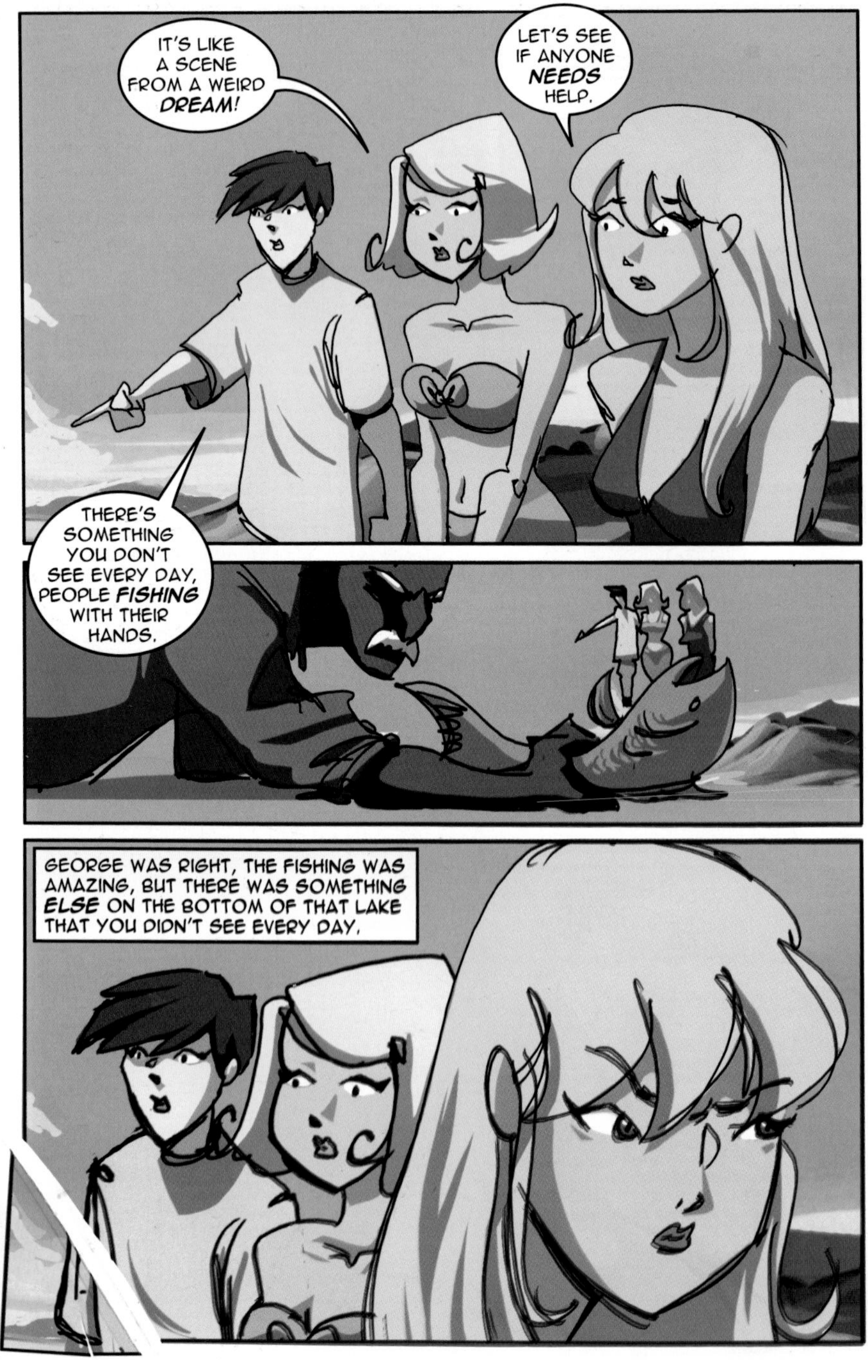
IT'S LIKE A SCENE FROM A WEIRD DREAM!
LET'S SEE IF ANYONE NEEDS HELP.
THERE'S SOMETHING YOU DON'T SEE EVERY DAY, PEOPLE FISHING WITH THEIR HANDS.
GEORGE WAS RIGHT, THE FISHING WAS AMAZING, BUT THERE WAS SOMETHING ELSE ON THE BOTTOM OF THAT LAKE THAT YOU DIDN'T SEE EVERY DAY.

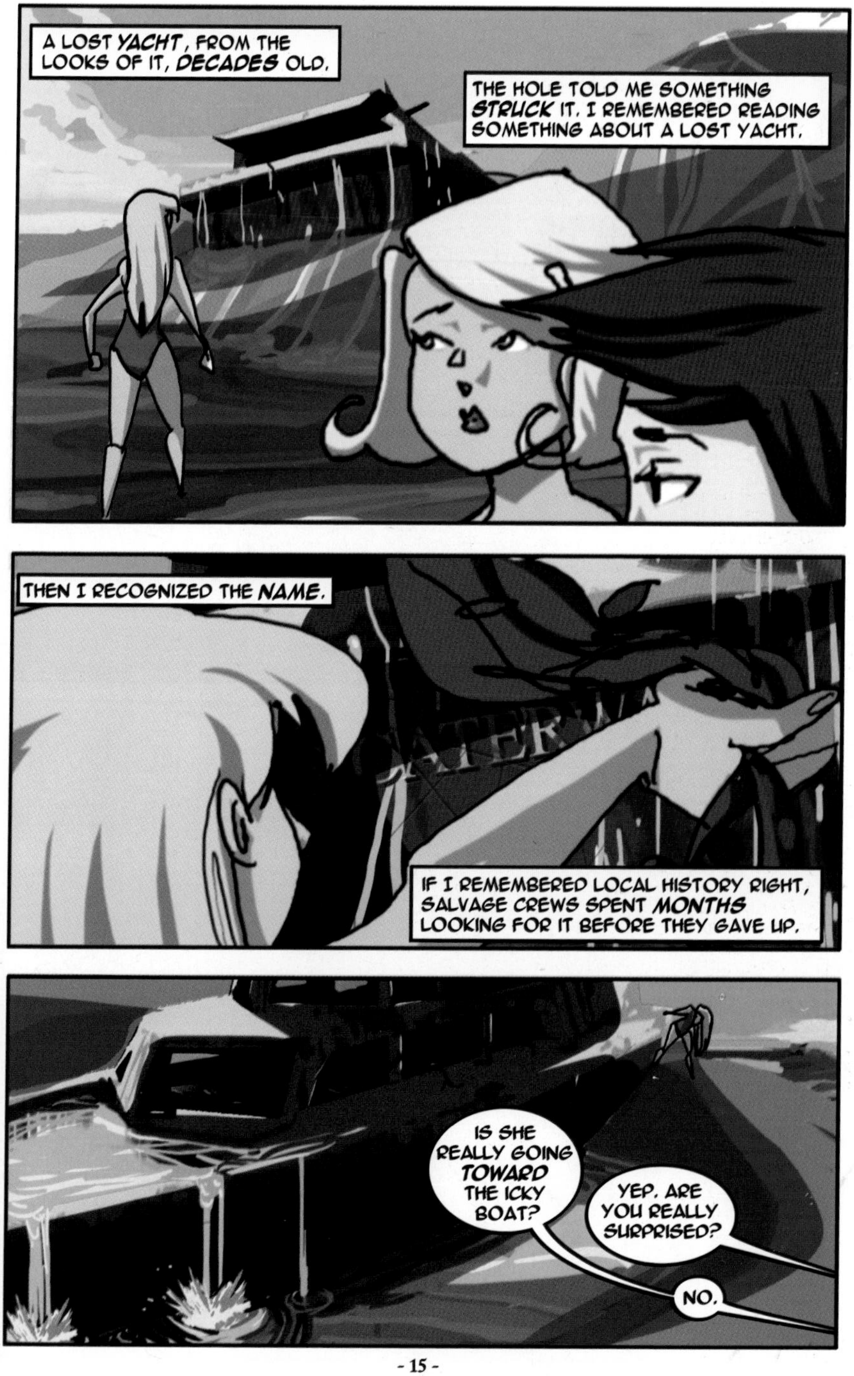
A LOST YACHT, FROM THE LOOKS OF IT, DECADES OLD.
THE HOLE TOLD ME SOMETHING STRUCK IT. I REMEMBERED READING SOMETHING ABOUT A LOST YACHT.
THEN I RECOGNIZED THE NAME.
IF I REMEMBERED LOCAL HISTORY RIGHT, SALVAGE CREWS SPENT MONTHS LOOKING FOR IT BEFORE THEY GAVE UP.
IS SHE REALLY GOING TOWARD THE ICKY BOAT?
YEP. ARE YOU REALLY SURPRISED?
NO.

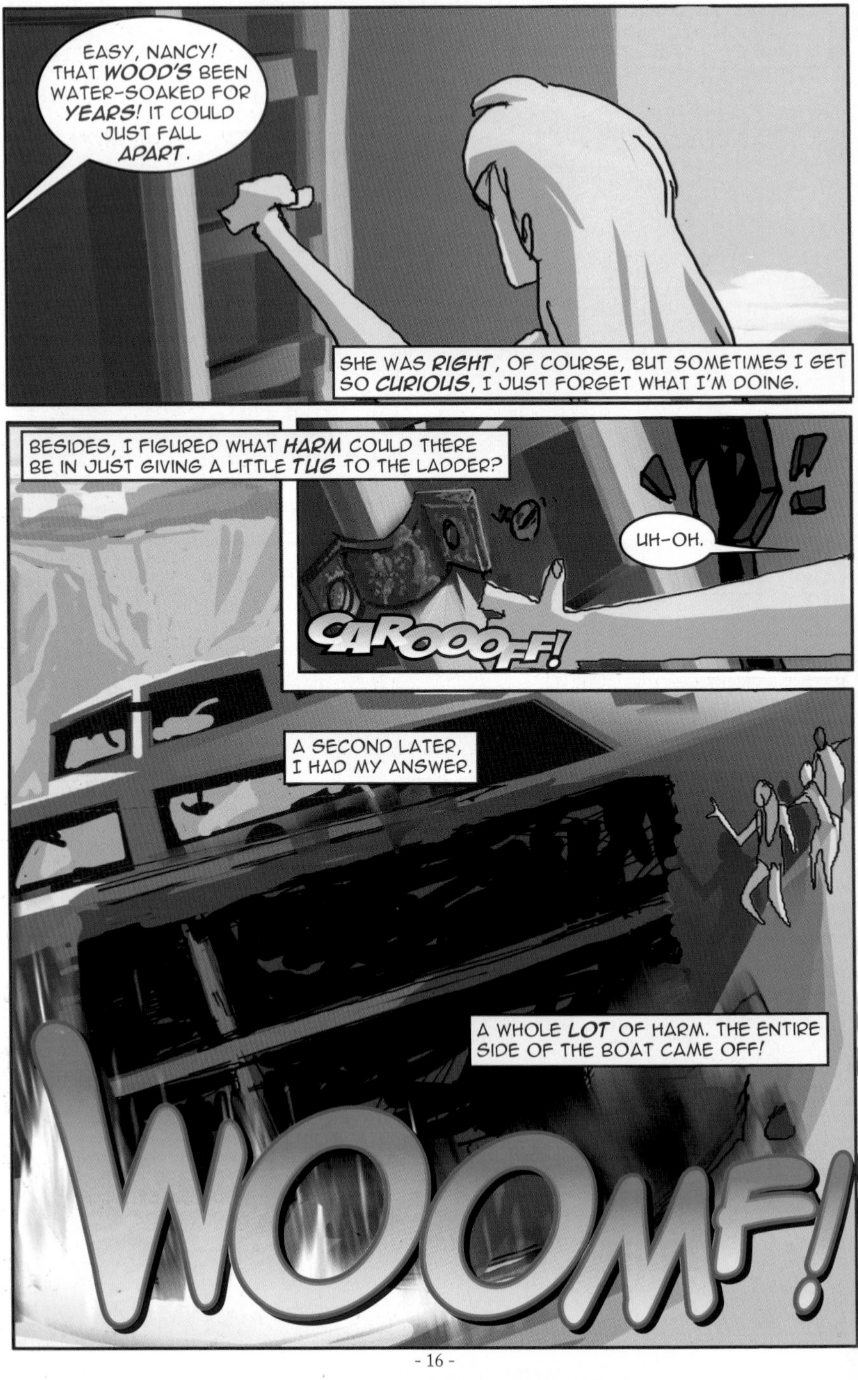
EASY, NANCY! THAT WOOD'S BEEN WATER-SOAKED FOR YEARS! IT COULD JUST FALL APART.
SHE WAS RIGHT, OF COURSE, BUT SOMETIMES I GET SO CURIOUS, I JUST FORGET WHAT I'M DOING.
BESIDES, I FIGURED WHAT HARM COULD THERE BE IN JUST GIVING A LITTLE TUG TO THE LADDER?
UH-OH.
CAROOOFF!
A SECOND LATER, I HAD MY ANSWER.
A WHOLE LOT OF HARM. THE ENTIRE SIDE OF THE BOAT CAME OFF!
WOOMF!

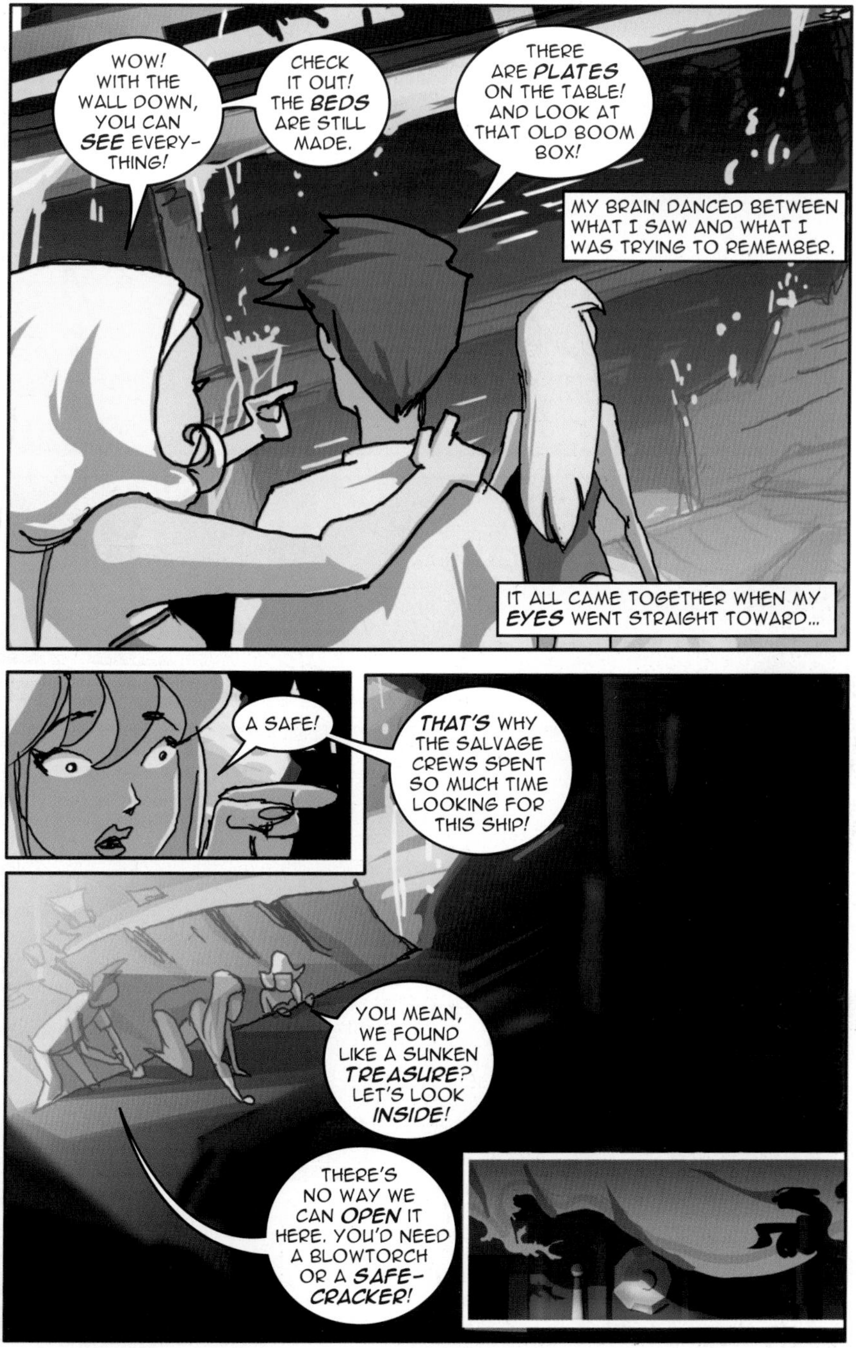
WOW! WITH THE WALL DOWN, YOU CAN SEE EVERY-THING!
CHECK IT OUT! THE BEDS ARE STILL MADE.
THERE ARE PLATES ON THE TABLE! AND LOOK AT THAT OLD BOOM BOX!
MY BRAIN DANCED BETWEEN WHAT I SAW AND WHAT I WAS TRYING TO REMEMBER.
IT ALL CAME TOGETHER WHEN MY EYES WENT STRAIGHT TOWARD...
A SAFE!
THAT'S WHY THE SALVAGE CREWS SPENT SO MUCH TIME LOOKING FOR THIS SHIP!
YOU MEAN, WE FOUND LIKE A SUNKEN TREASURE? LET'S LOOK INSIDE!
THERE'S NO WAY WE CAN OPEN IT HERE. YOU'D NEED A BLOWTORCH OR A SAFE-CRACKER!

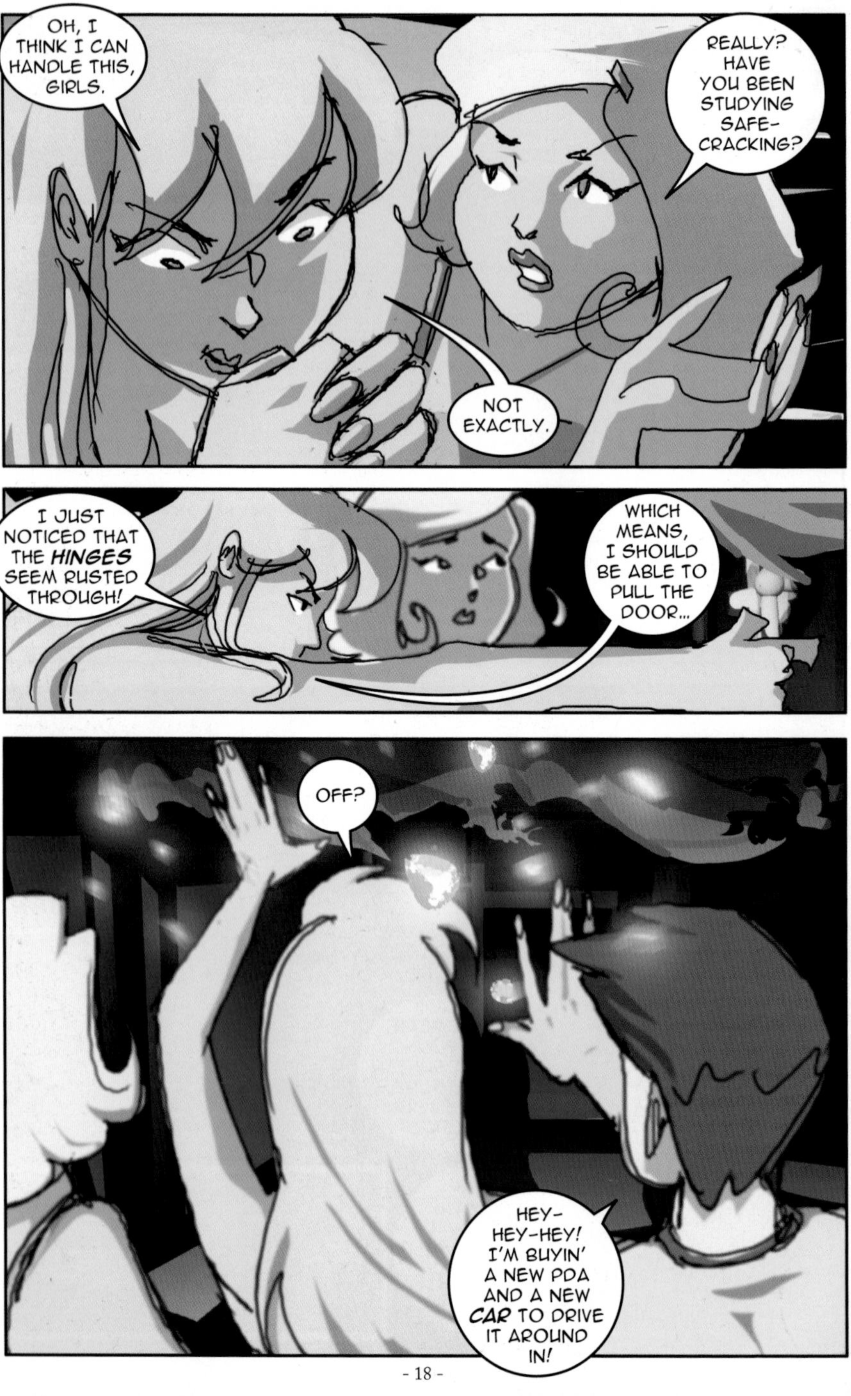
OH, I THINK I CAN HANDLE THIS, GIRLS.
REALLY? HAVE YOU BEEN STUDYING SAFE-CRACKING?
NOT EXACTLY.
I JUST NOTICED THAT THE **HINGES** SEEM RUSTED THROUGH!
WHICH MEANS, I SHOULD BE ABLE TO PULL THE DOOR...
OFF?
HEY-HEY-HEY! I'M BUYIN' A NEW PDA AND A NEW **CAR** TO DRIVE IT AROUND IN!

I HATED TO BREAK IT TO GEORGE, BUT I FIGURED OUR TREASURE WAS *ALREADY* SPOKEN FOR.

A QUICK CALL TO MY DAD, ATTORNEY CARSON DREW, CONFIRMED THE SS CATERWAUL WAS OWNED BY HIS LATE CLIENTS, *JACK AND AMELIA DRUTHERS*.

IN LESS THAN TWO HOURS, A TEAM WAS RECOVERING THE WRECK AND THE SAFE.

I DON'T KNOW WHAT'S MORE *AMAZING*, NANCY, THE LAKE VANISHING OR THAT YACHT TURNING UP!

JACK AND AMELIA PERISHED IN THE STORM, BUT AS THEIR ATTORNEY, IT WILL BE *MY* JOB TO SEE THAT THE JEWELS GET TO THEIR SURVIVING *HEIRS*!

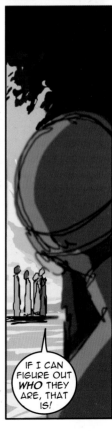

IF I CAN FIGURE OUT *WHO* THEY ARE, THAT IS!

- 19 -

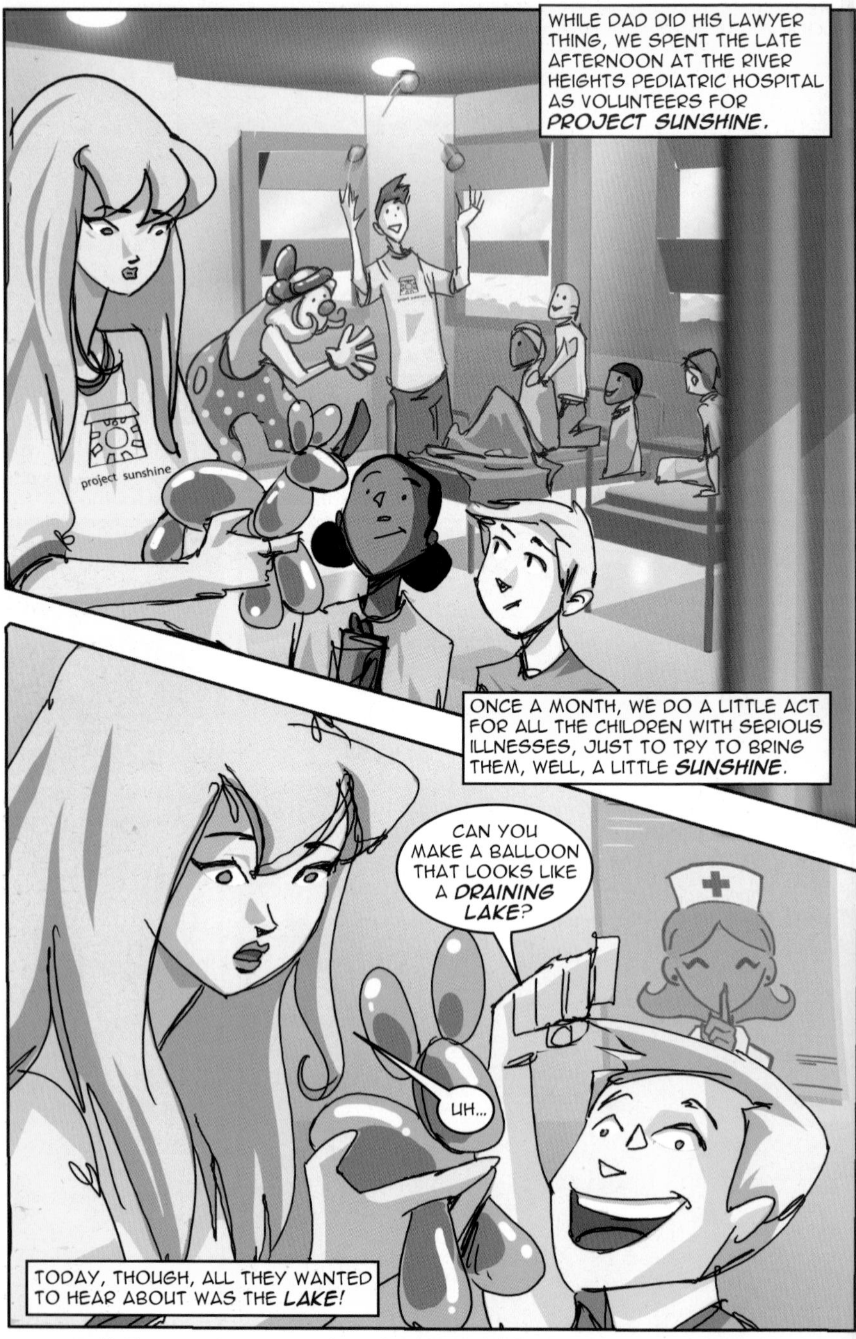
WHILE DAD DID HIS LAWYER THING, WE SPENT THE LATE AFTERNOON AT THE RIVER HEIGHTS PEDIATRIC HOSPITAL AS VOLUNTEERS FOR *PROJECT SUNSHINE.*
project sunshine
ONCE A MONTH, WE DO A LITTLE ACT FOR ALL THE CHILDREN WITH SERIOUS ILLNESSES, JUST TO TRY TO BRING THEM, WELL, A LITTLE *SUNSHINE*.
CAN YOU MAKE A BALLOON THAT LOOKS LIKE A *DRAINING LAKE*?
UH...
TODAY, THOUGH, ALL THEY WANTED TO HEAR ABOUT WAS THE *LAKE*!

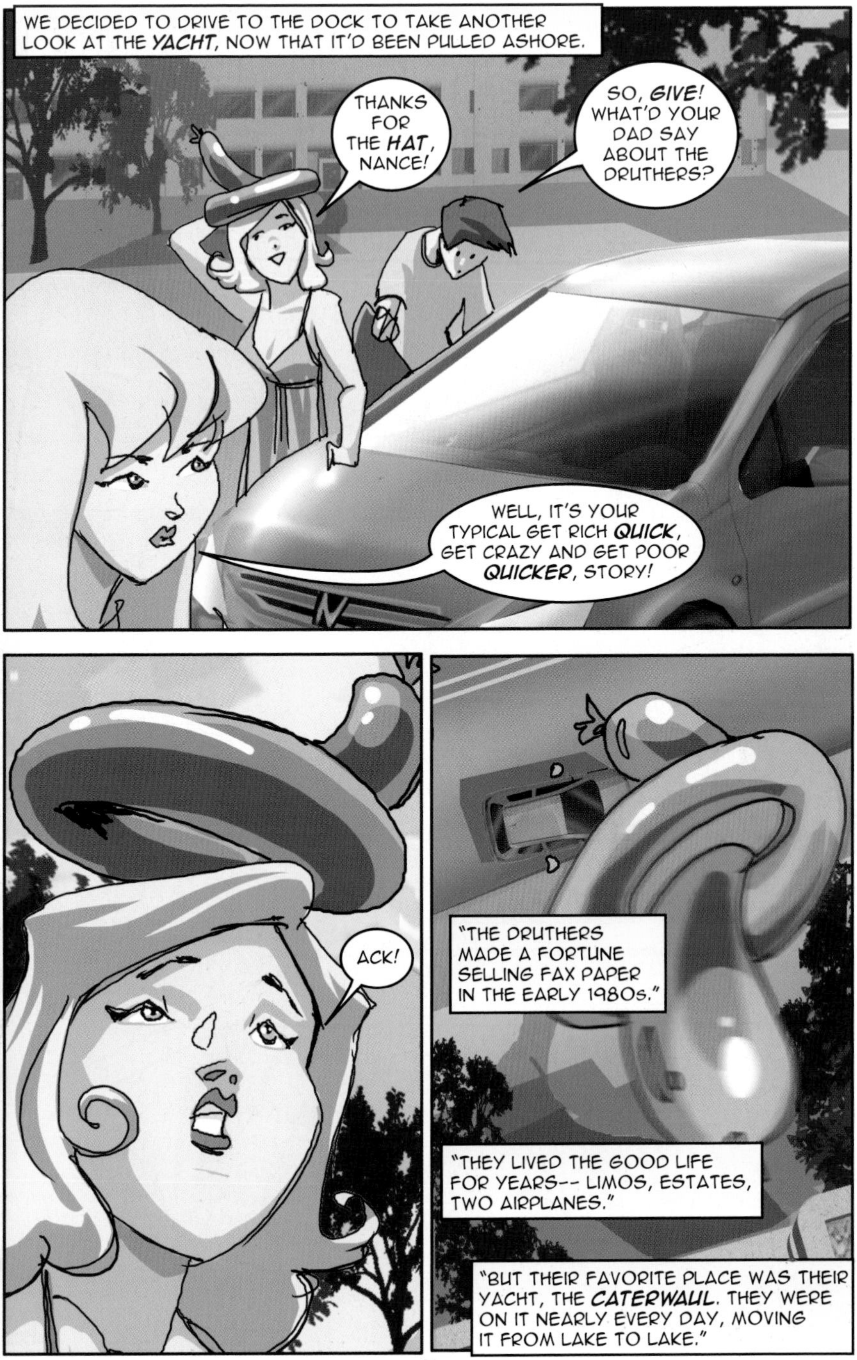
WE DECIDED TO DRIVE TO THE DOCK TO TAKE ANOTHER LOOK AT THE YACHT, NOW THAT IT'D BEEN PULLED ASHORE.
THANKS FOR THE HAT, NANCE!
SO, GIVE! WHAT'D YOUR DAD SAY ABOUT THE DRUTHERS?
WELL, IT'S YOUR TYPICAL GET RICH QUICK, GET CRAZY AND GET POOR QUICKER, STORY!
ACK!
"THE DRUTHERS MADE A FORTUNE SELLING FAX PAPER IN THE EARLY 1980s."
"THEY LIVED THE GOOD LIFE FOR YEARS-- LIMOS, ESTATES, TWO AIRPLANES."
"BUT THEIR FAVORITE PLACE WAS THEIR YACHT, THE CATERWAUL. THEY WERE ON IT NEARLY EVERY DAY, MOVING IT FROM LAKE TO LAKE."

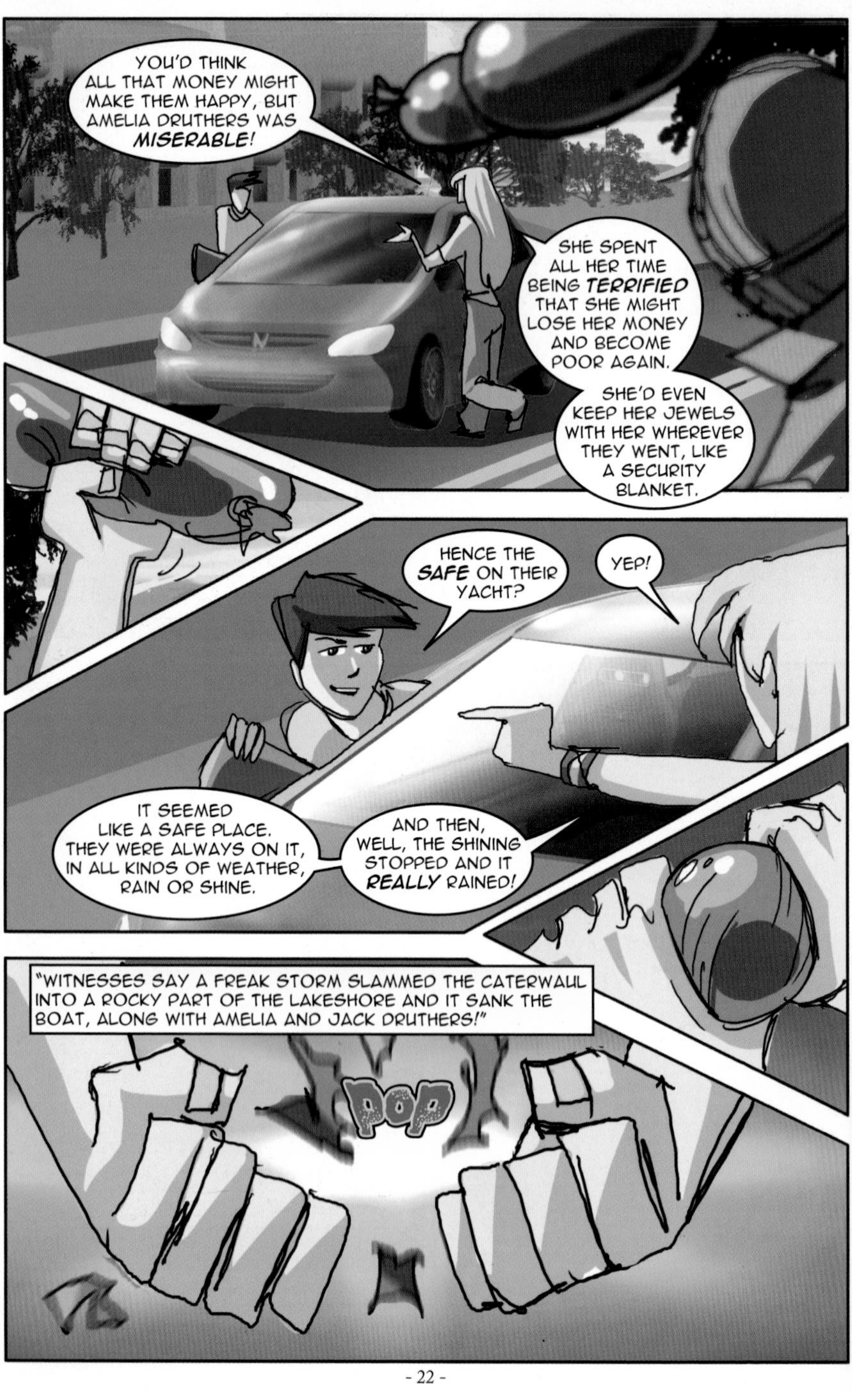
YOU'D THINK ALL THAT MONEY MIGHT MAKE THEM HAPPY, BUT AMELIA DRUTHERS WAS *MISERABLE*!
SHE SPENT ALL HER TIME BEING *TERRIFIED* THAT SHE MIGHT LOSE HER MONEY AND BECOME POOR AGAIN.
SHE'D EVEN KEEP HER JEWELS WITH HER WHEREVER THEY WENT, LIKE A SECURITY BLANKET.
HENCE THE *SAFE* ON THEIR YACHT?
YEP!
IT SEEMED LIKE A SAFE PLACE. THEY WERE ALWAYS ON IT, IN ALL KINDS OF WEATHER, RAIN OR SHINE.
AND THEN, WELL, THE SHINING STOPPED AND IT *REALLY* RAINED!
"WITNESSES SAY A FREAK STORM SLAMMED THE CATERWAUL INTO A ROCKY PART OF THE LAKESHORE AND IT SANK THE BOAT, ALONG WITH AMELIA AND JACK DRUTHERS!"
POP

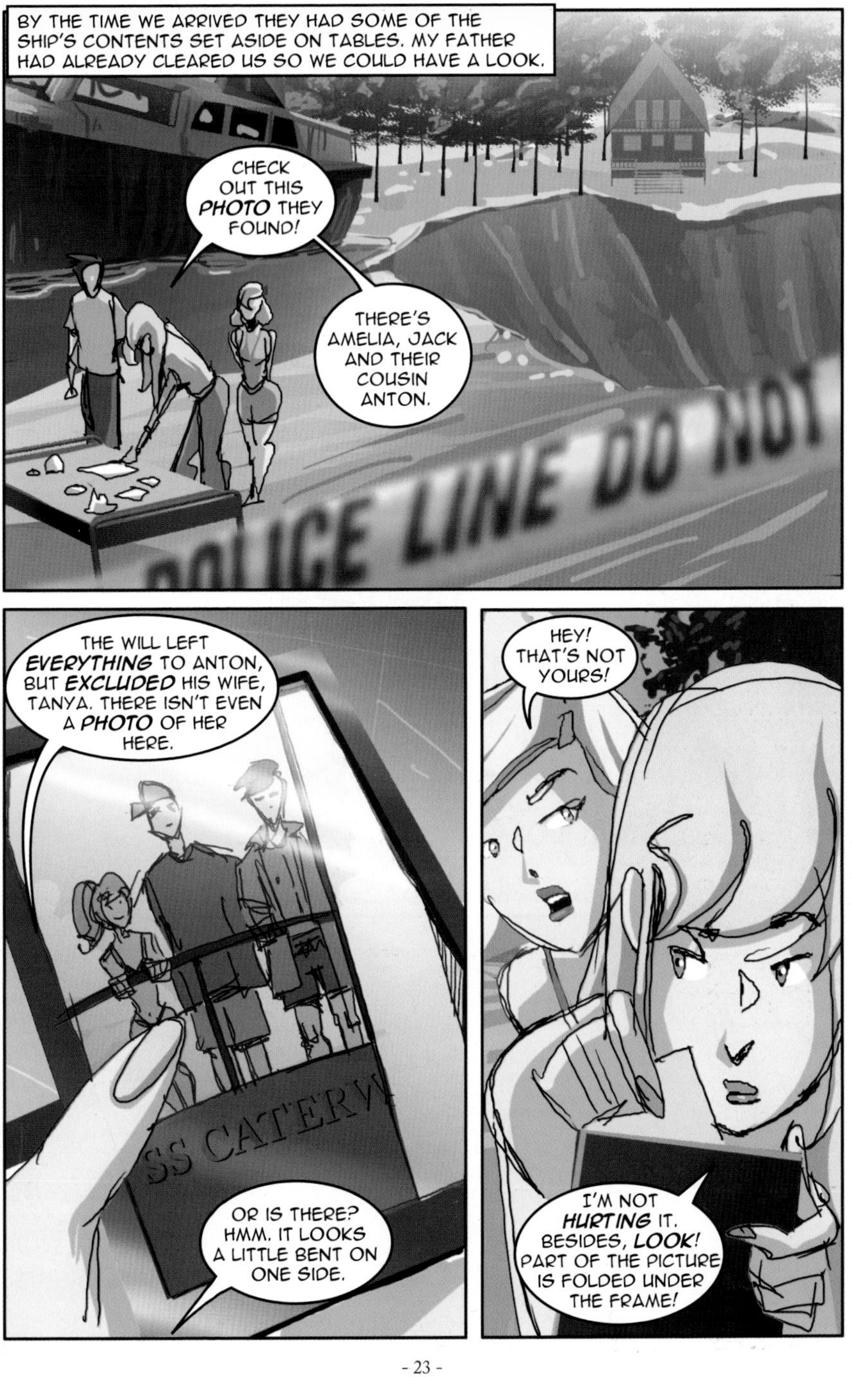
BY THE TIME WE ARRIVED THEY HAD SOME OF THE SHIP'S CONTENTS SET ASIDE ON TABLES. MY FATHER HAD ALREADY CLEARED US SO WE COULD HAVE A LOOK.
CHECK OUT THIS PHOTO THEY FOUND!
THERE'S AMELIA, JACK AND THEIR COUSIN ANTON.
POLICE LINE DO NOT
THE WILL LEFT EVERYTHING TO ANTON, BUT EXCLUDED HIS WIFE, TANYA. THERE ISN'T EVEN A PHOTO OF HER HERE.
SS CATERY
OR IS THERE? HMM. IT LOOKS A LITTLE BENT ON ONE SIDE.
HEY! THAT'S NOT YOURS!
I'M NOT HURTING IT. BESIDES, LOOK! PART OF THE PICTURE IS FOLDED UNDER THE FRAME!

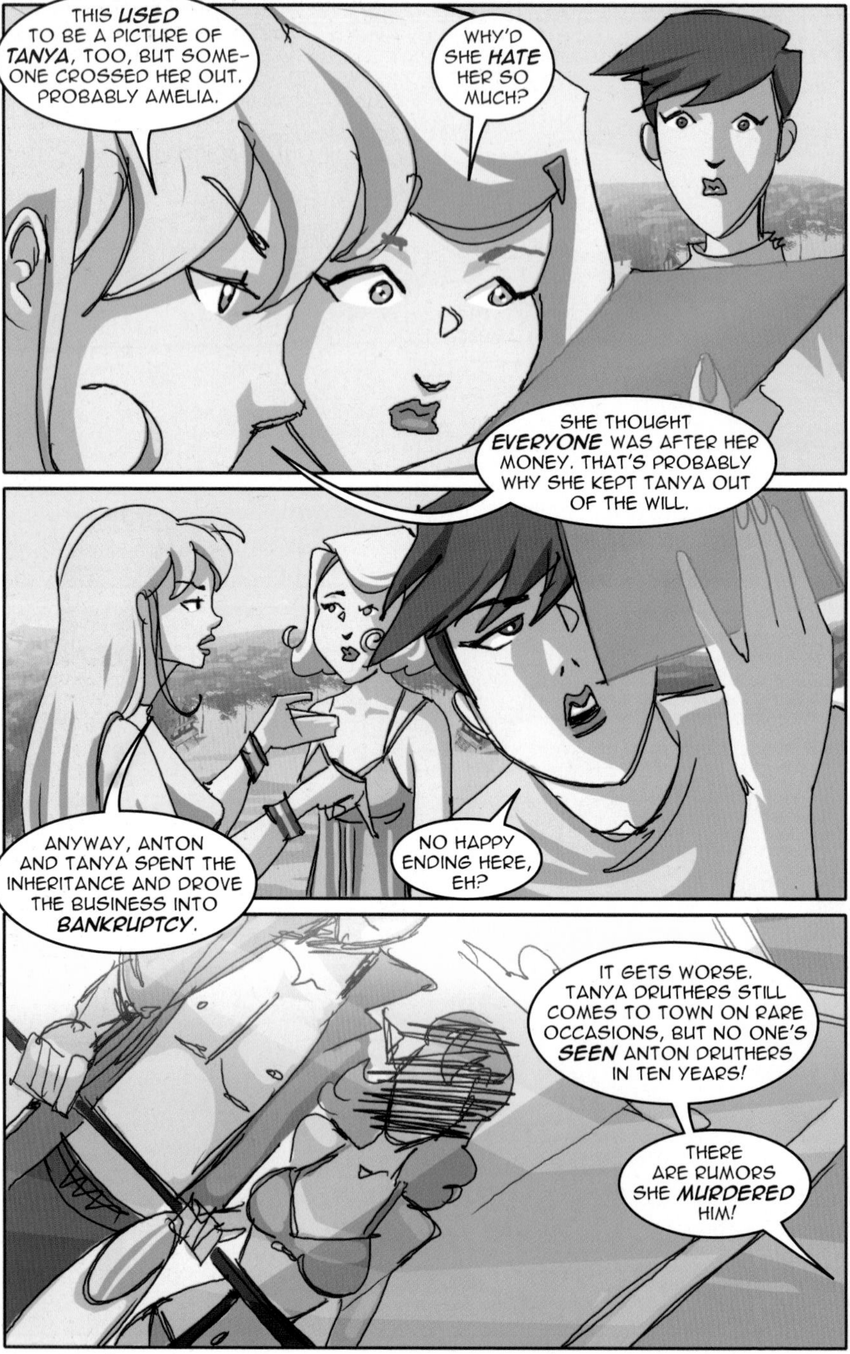
THIS USED TO BE A PICTURE OF TANYA, TOO, BUT SOME-ONE CROSSED HER OUT. PROBABLY AMELIA.
WHY'D SHE HATE HER SO MUCH?
SHE THOUGHT EVERYONE WAS AFTER HER MONEY. THAT'S PROBABLY WHY SHE KEPT TANYA OUT OF THE WILL.
ANYWAY, ANTON AND TANYA SPENT THE INHERITANCE AND DROVE THE BUSINESS INTO BANKRUPTCY.
NO HAPPY ENDING HERE, EH?
IT GETS WORSE. TANYA DRUTHERS STILL COMES TO TOWN ON RARE OCCASIONS, BUT NO ONE'S SEEN ANTON DRUTHERS IN TEN YEARS!
THERE ARE RUMORS SHE MURDERED HIM!

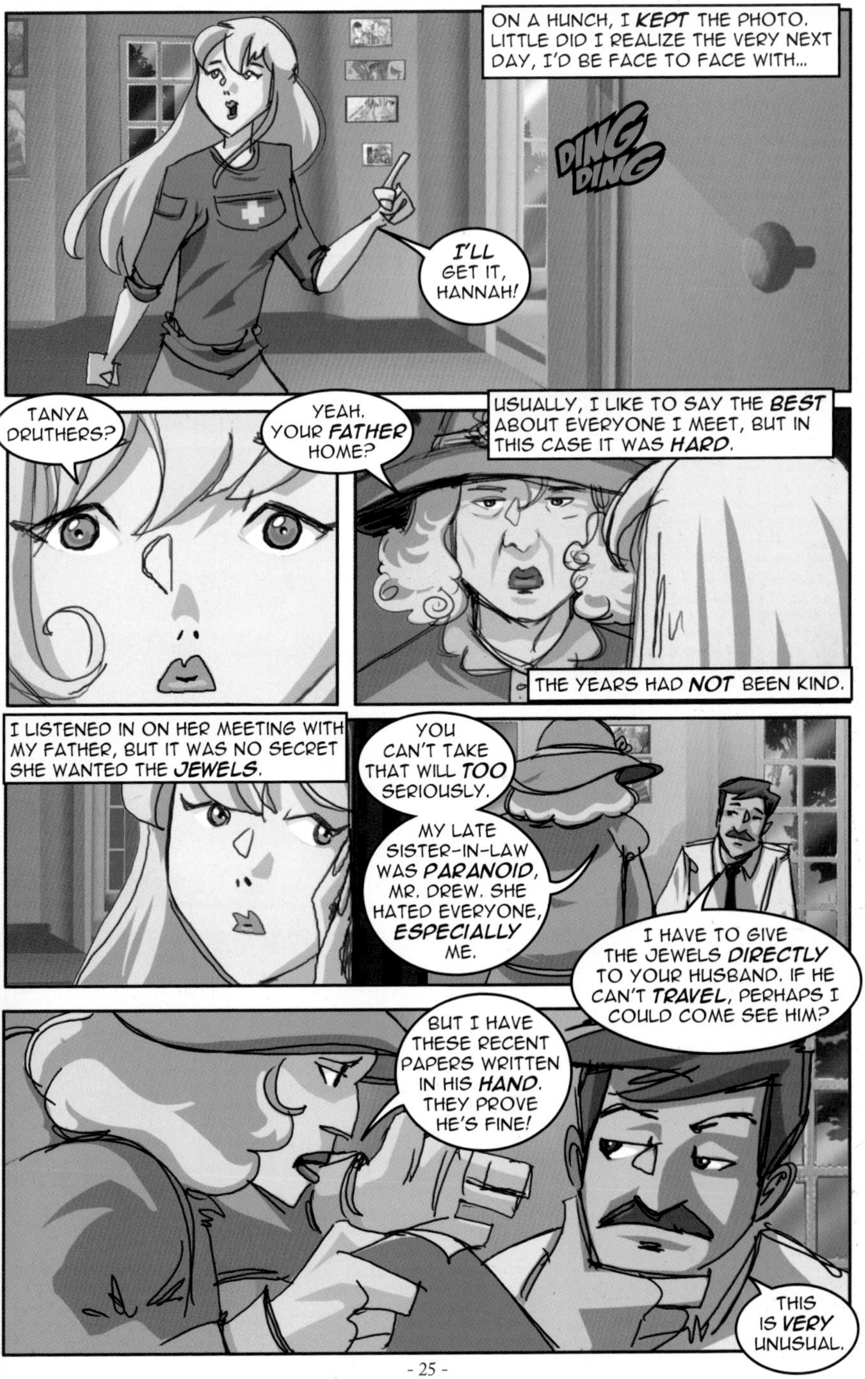
ON A HUNCH, I KEPT THE PHOTO. LITTLE DID I REALIZE THE VERY NEXT DAY, I'D BE FACE TO FACE WITH...
DING DING
I'LL GET IT, HANNAH!
TANYA DRUTHERS?
YEAH. YOUR FATHER HOME?
USUALLY, I LIKE TO SAY THE BEST ABOUT EVERYONE I MEET, BUT IN THIS CASE IT WAS HARD.
THE YEARS HAD NOT BEEN KIND.
I LISTENED IN ON HER MEETING WITH MY FATHER, BUT IT WAS NO SECRET SHE WANTED THE JEWELS.
YOU CAN'T TAKE THAT WILL TOO SERIOUSLY.
MY LATE SISTER-IN-LAW WAS PARANOID, MR. DREW. SHE HATED EVERYONE, ESPECIALLY ME.
I HAVE TO GIVE THE JEWELS DIRECTLY TO YOUR HUSBAND. IF HE CAN'T TRAVEL, PERHAPS I COULD COME SEE HIM?
BUT I HAVE THESE RECENT PAPERS WRITTEN IN HIS HAND. THEY PROVE HE'S FINE!
THIS IS VERY UNUSUAL.

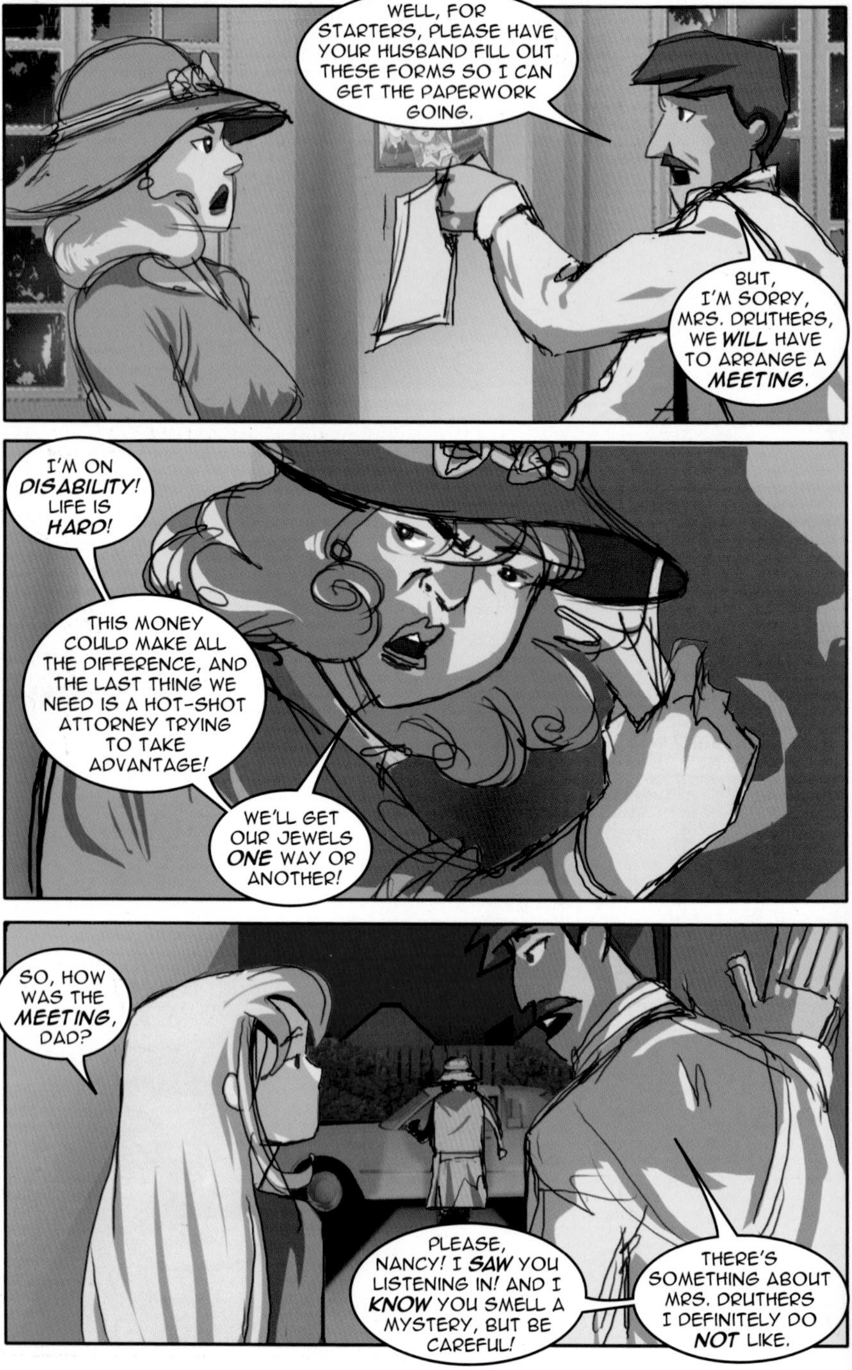
WELL, FOR STARTERS, PLEASE HAVE YOUR HUSBAND FILL OUT THESE FORMS SO I CAN GET THE PAPERWORK GOING.
BUT, I'M SORRY, MRS. DRUTHERS, WE WILL HAVE TO ARRANGE A MEETING.
I'M ON DISABILITY! LIFE IS HARD!
THIS MONEY COULD MAKE ALL THE DIFFERENCE, AND THE LAST THING WE NEED IS A HOT-SHOT ATTORNEY TRYING TO TAKE ADVANTAGE!
WE'LL GET OUR JEWELS ONE WAY OR ANOTHER!
SO, HOW WAS THE MEETING, DAD?
THERE'S SOMETHING ABOUT MRS. DRUTHERS I DEFINITELY DO NOT LIKE.
PLEASE, NANCY! I SAW YOU LISTENING IN! AND I KNOW YOU SMELL A MYSTERY, BUT BE CAREFUL!

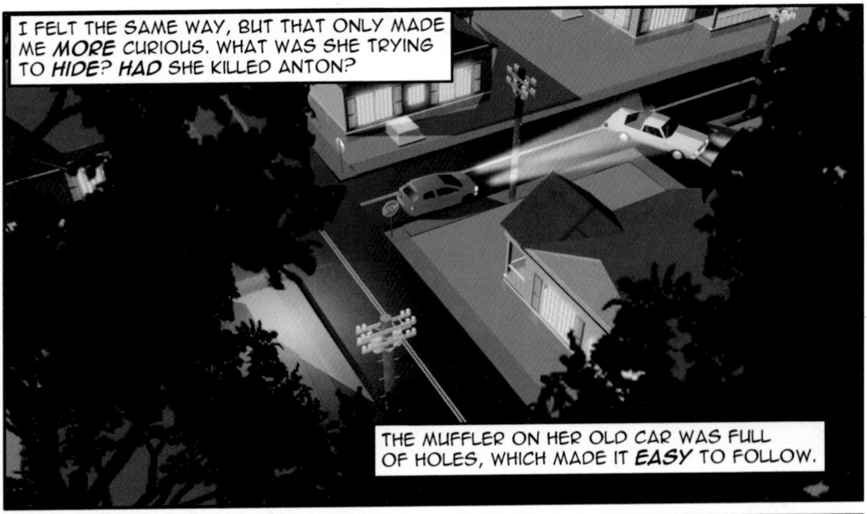
I FELT THE SAME WAY, BUT THAT ONLY MADE ME MORE CURIOUS. WHAT WAS SHE TRYING TO HIDE? HAD SHE KILLED ANTON?
THE MUFFLER ON HER OLD CAR WAS FULL OF HOLES, WHICH MADE IT EASY TO FOLLOW.

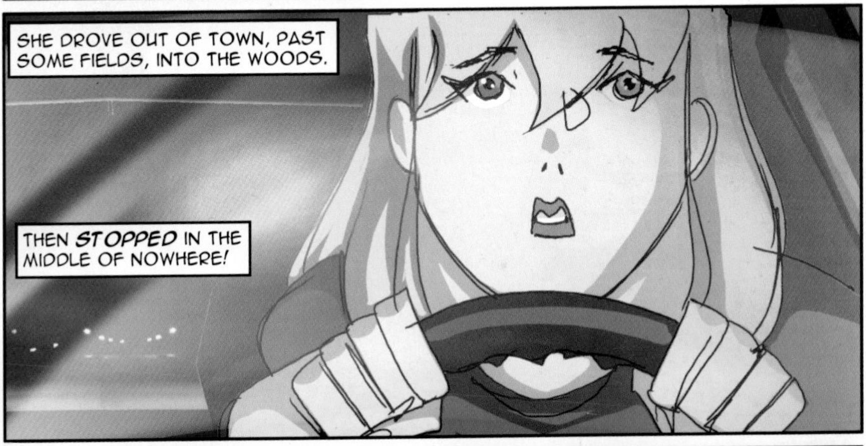
SHE DROVE OUT OF TOWN, PAST SOME FIELDS, INTO THE WOODS.
THEN STOPPED IN THE MIDDLE OF NOWHERE!

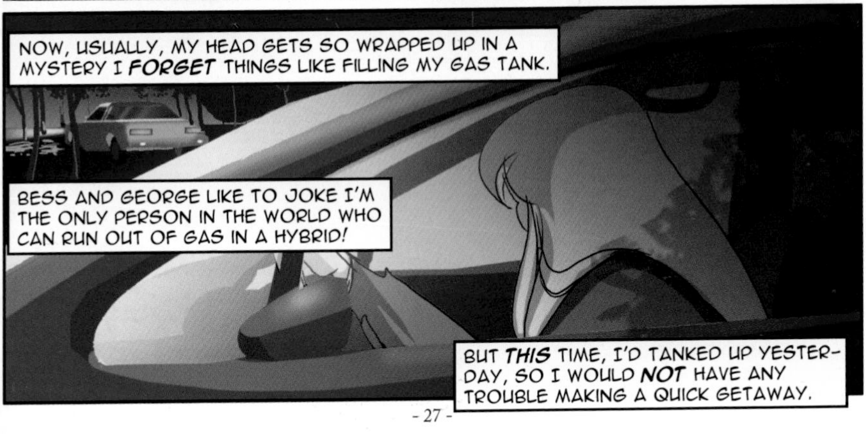
NOW, USUALLY, MY HEAD GETS SO WRAPPED UP IN A MYSTERY I FORGET THINGS LIKE FILLING MY GAS TANK.
BESS AND GEORGE LIKE TO JOKE I'M THE ONLY PERSON IN THE WORLD WHO CAN RUN OUT OF GAS IN A HYBRID!
BUT THIS TIME, I'D TANKED UP YESTERDAY, SO I WOULD NOT HAVE ANY TROUBLE MAKING A QUICK GETAWAY.

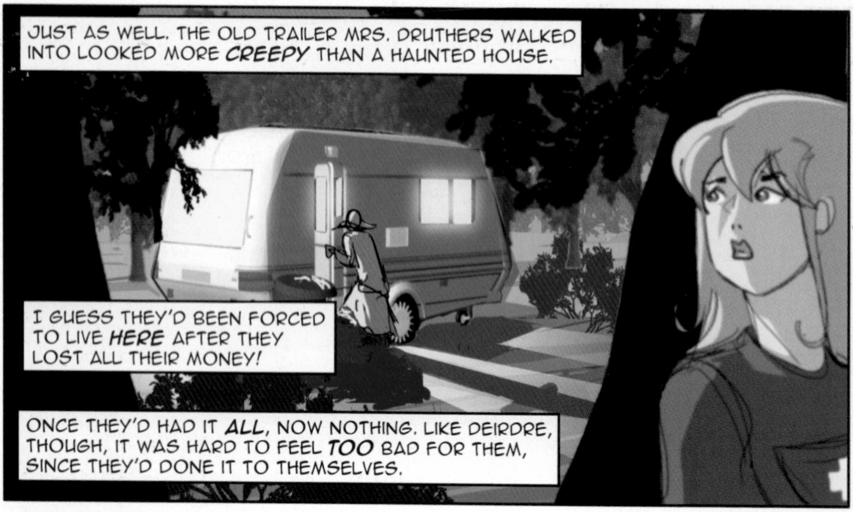
JUST AS WELL. THE OLD TRAILER MRS. DRUTHERS WALKED INTO LOOKED MORE CREEPY THAN A HAUNTED HOUSE.
I GUESS THEY'D BEEN FORCED TO LIVE HERE AFTER THEY LOST ALL THEIR MONEY!
ONCE THEY'D HAD IT ALL, NOW NOTHING. LIKE DEIRDRE, THOUGH, IT WAS HARD TO FEEL TOO BAD FOR THEM, SINCE THEY'D DONE IT TO THEMSELVES.

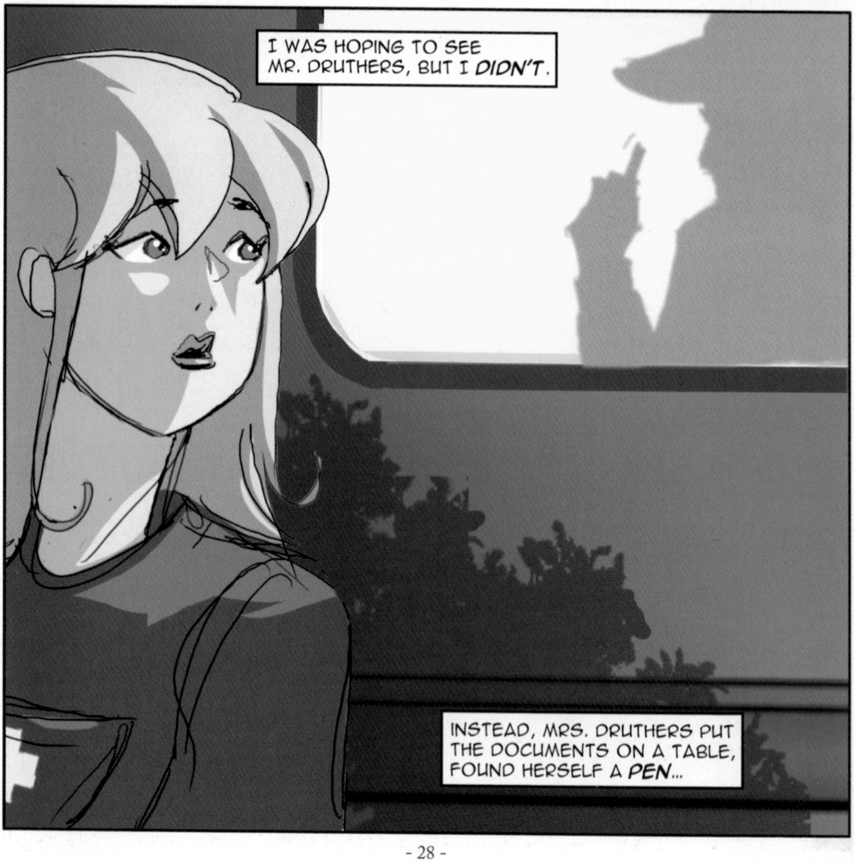
I WAS HOPING TO SEE MR. DRUTHERS, BUT I DIDN'T.
INSTEAD, MRS. DRUTHERS PUT THE DOCUMENTS ON A TABLE, FOUND HERSELF A PEN...

AND STARTED **FORGING** HER HUSBAND'S HAND-WRITING ON THE FORMS MY FATHER GAVE HER!

NOW WHY WOULD SHE DO **THAT**, UNLESS HER HUSBAND WAS **DEAD**?

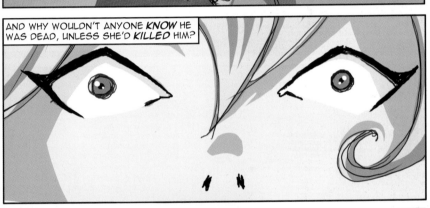

AND WHY WOULDN'T ANYONE **KNOW** HE WAS DEAD, UNLESS SHE'D **KILLED** HIM?

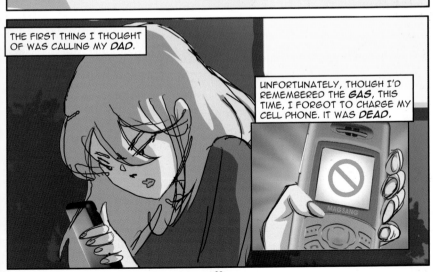

THE FIRST THING I THOUGHT OF WAS CALLING MY **DAD**.

UNFORTUNATELY, THOUGH I'D REMEMBERED THE **GAS**, THIS TIME, I FORGOT TO CHARGE MY CELL PHONE. IT WAS **DEAD**.

NOT SO MY DIGITAL *CAMERA*. IT'S IMPORTANT TO HAVE THAT SORT OF THING AROUND IF YOU WANT TO DO DETECTIVE WORK.

YOU NEVER KNOW WHEN YOU'LL NEED TO COLLECT *EVIDENCE*.

WHORRRR

IT MADE A LITTLE WHIRRING SOUND AS IT POWERED UP, BUT I DON'T THINK MRS. DRUTHERS HEARD IT.

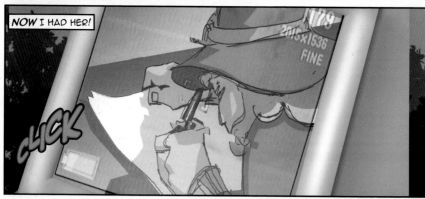

NOW I HAD HER!

CLICK

UH-OH.

UNFORTUNATELY, SHE *ALSO* HAD ME!

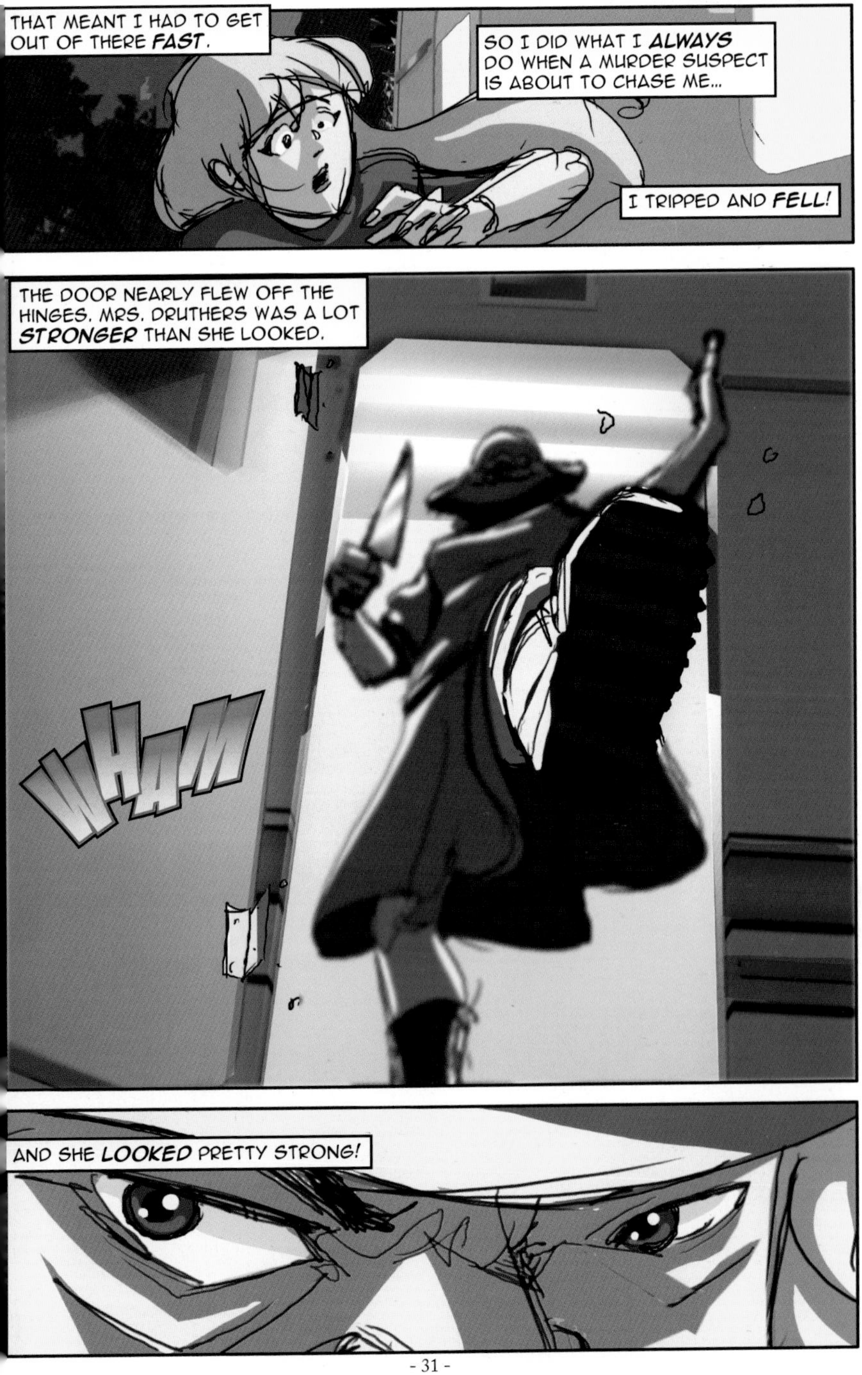
THAT MEANT I HAD TO GET OUT OF THERE FAST.
SO I DID WHAT I ALWAYS DO WHEN A MURDER SUSPECT IS ABOUT TO CHASE ME...
I TRIPPED AND FELL!
THE DOOR NEARLY FLEW OFF THE HINGES. MRS. DRUTHERS WAS A LOT STRONGER THAN SHE LOOKED.
WHAM
AND SHE LOOKED PRETTY STRONG!

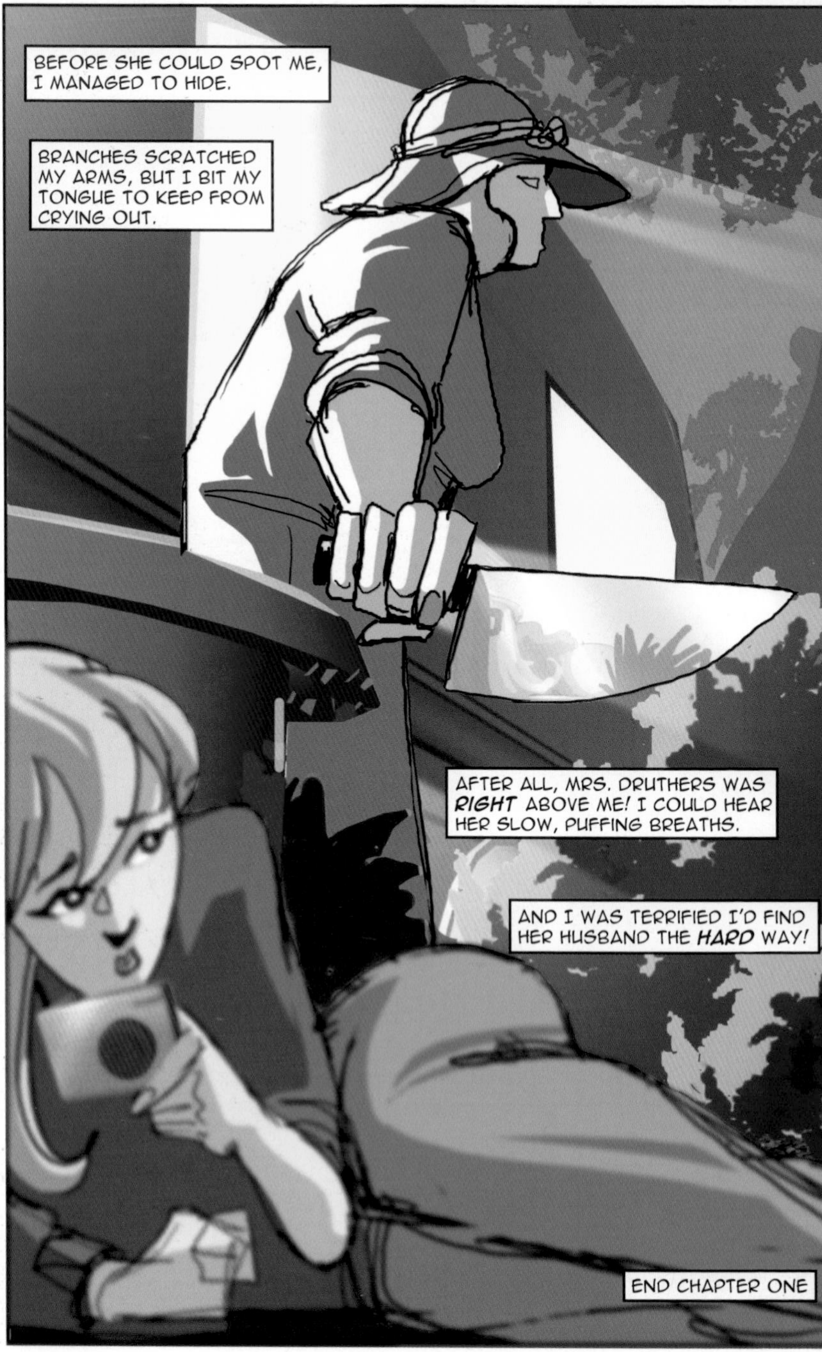
BEFORE SHE COULD SPOT ME, I MANAGED TO HIDE.
BRANCHES SCRATCHED MY ARMS, BUT I BIT MY TONGUE TO KEEP FROM CRYING OUT.
AFTER ALL, MRS. DRUTHERS WAS RIGHT ABOVE ME! I COULD HEAR HER SLOW, PUFFING BREATHS.
AND I WAS TERRIFIED I'D FIND HER HUSBAND THE HARD WAY!
END CHAPTER ONE

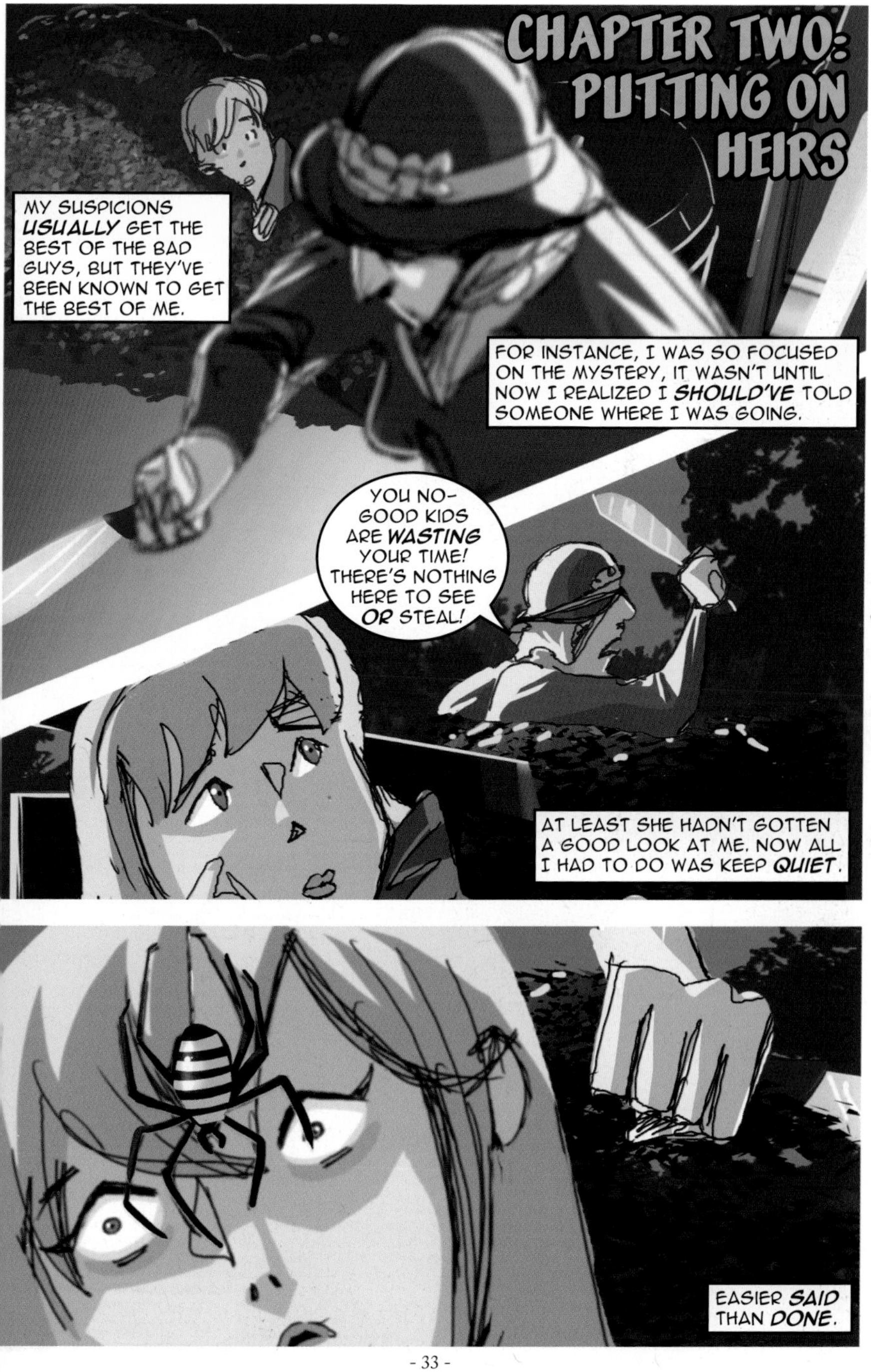
CHAPTER TWO: PUTTING ON HEIRS
MY SUSPICIONS USUALLY GET THE BEST OF THE BAD GUYS, BUT THEY'VE BEEN KNOWN TO GET THE BEST OF ME.
FOR INSTANCE, I WAS SO FOCUSED ON THE MYSTERY, IT WASN'T UNTIL NOW I REALIZED I SHOULD'VE TOLD SOMEONE WHERE I WAS GOING.
YOU NO-GOOD KIDS ARE WASTING YOUR TIME! THERE'S NOTHING HERE TO SEE OR STEAL!
AT LEAST SHE HADN'T GOTTEN A GOOD LOOK AT ME. NOW ALL I HAD TO DO WAS KEEP QUIET.
EASIER SAID THAN DONE.

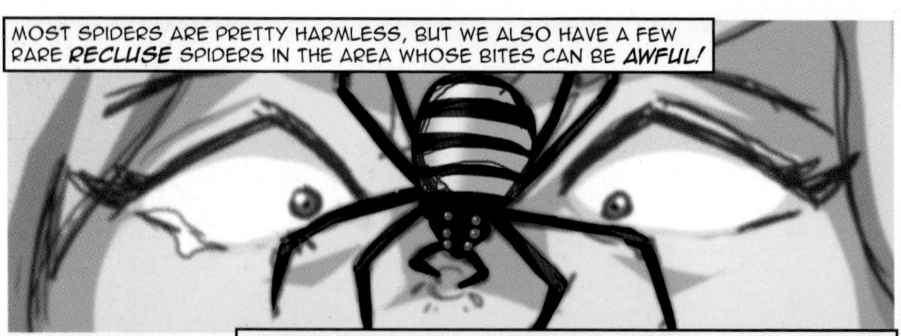
MOST SPIDERS ARE PRETTY HARMLESS, BUT WE ALSO HAVE A FEW RARE **RECLUSE** SPIDERS IN THE AREA WHOSE BITES CAN BE **AWFUL!**
UNFORTUNATELY, I DIDN'T KNOW **WHICH** SPECIES THIS ONE WAS.

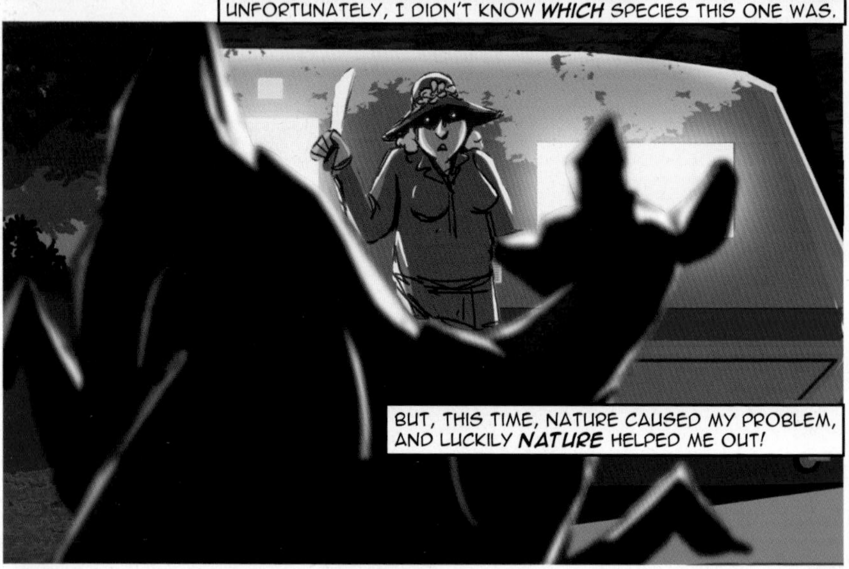
BUT, THIS TIME, NATURE CAUSED MY PROBLEM, AND LUCKILY **NATURE** HELPED ME OUT!

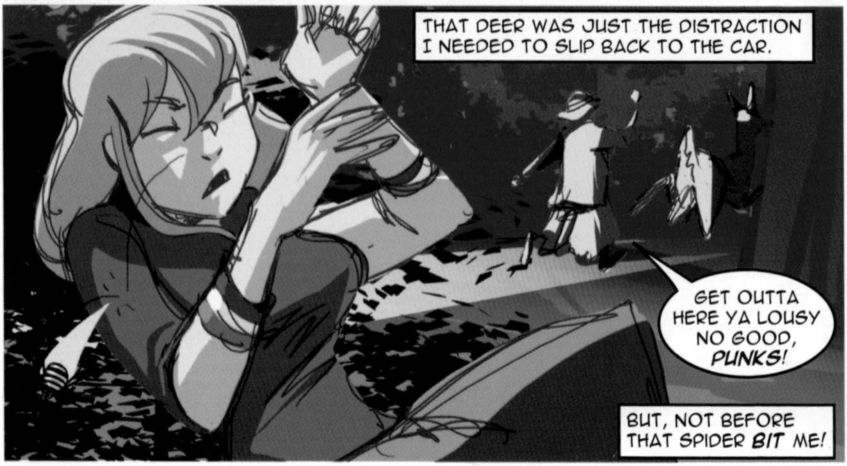
THAT DEER WAS JUST THE DISTRACTION I NEEDED TO SLIP BACK TO THE CAR.
GET OUTTA HERE YA LOUSY NO GOOD, **PUNKS!**
BUT, NOT BEFORE THAT SPIDER **BIT** ME!

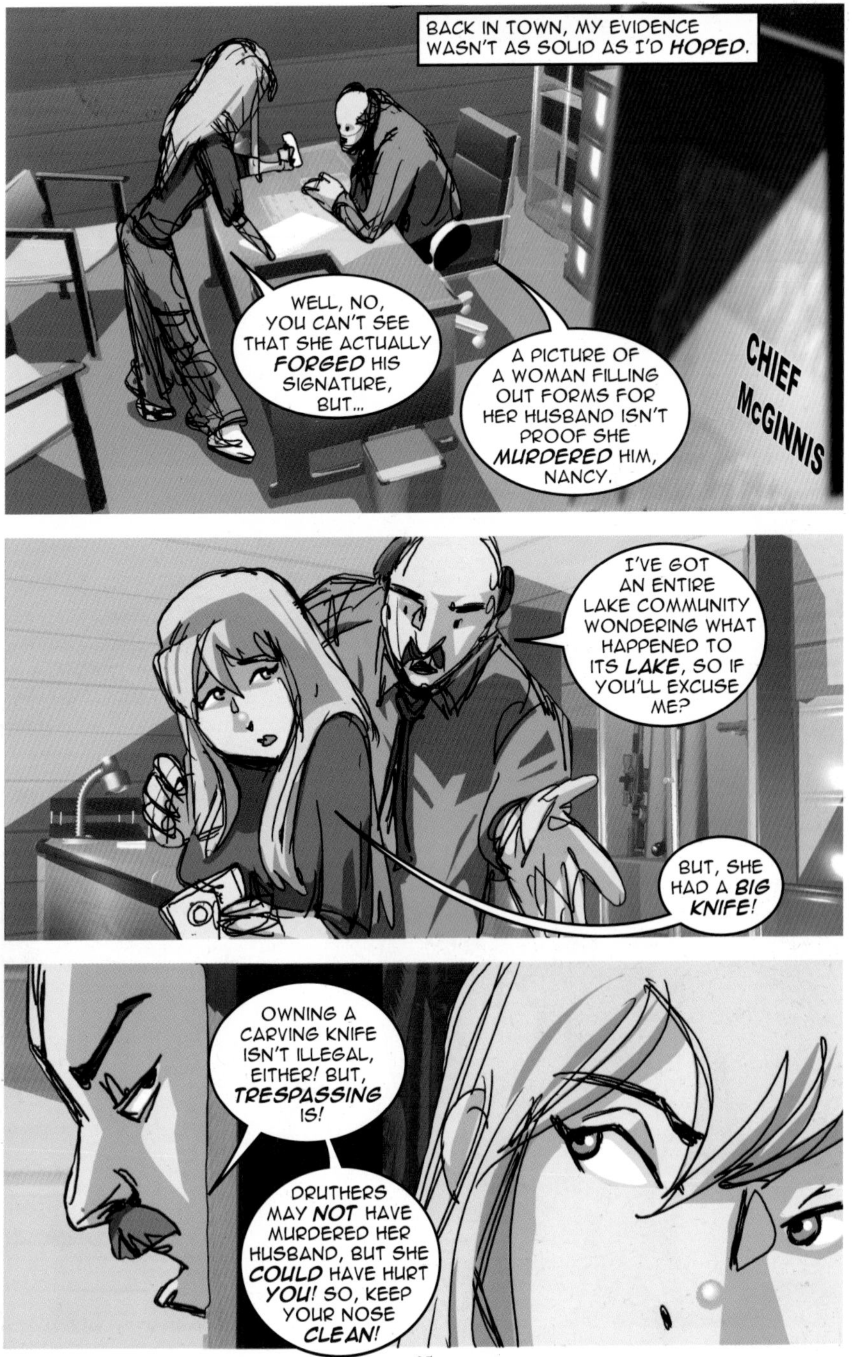
BACK IN TOWN, MY EVIDENCE WASN'T AS SOLID AS I'D *HOPED*.
WELL, NO, YOU CAN'T SEE THAT SHE ACTUALLY *FORGED* HIS SIGNATURE, BUT...
A PICTURE OF A WOMAN FILLING OUT FORMS FOR HER HUSBAND ISN'T PROOF SHE *MURDERED* HIM, NANCY.
CHIEF McGINNIS
I'VE GOT AN ENTIRE LAKE COMMUNITY WONDERING WHAT HAPPENED TO ITS *LAKE*, SO IF YOU'LL EXCUSE ME?
BUT, SHE HAD A *BIG KNIFE*!
OWNING A CARVING KNIFE ISN'T ILLEGAL, EITHER! BUT, *TRESPASSING* IS!
DRUTHERS MAY *NOT* HAVE MURDERED HER HUSBAND, BUT SHE *COULD* HAVE HURT *YOU*! SO, KEEP YOUR NOSE *CLEAN*!

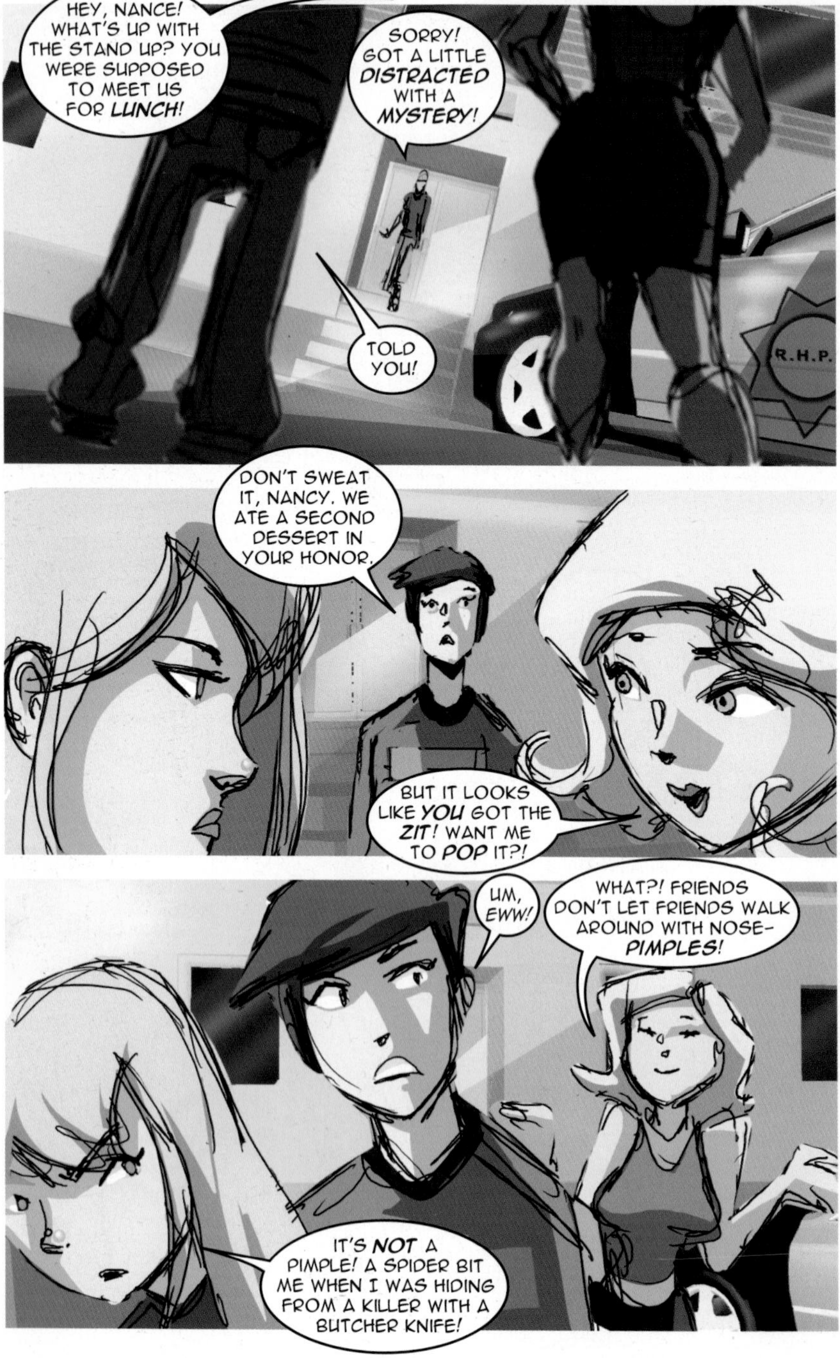
HEY, NANCE! WHAT'S UP WITH THE STAND UP? YOU WERE SUPPOSED TO MEET US FOR LUNCH!
SORRY! GOT A LITTLE DISTRACTED WITH A MYSTERY!
TOLD YOU!
R.H.P.
DON'T SWEAT IT, NANCY. WE ATE A SECOND DESSERT IN YOUR HONOR.
BUT IT LOOKS LIKE YOU GOT THE ZIT! WANT ME TO POP IT?!
UM, EWW!
WHAT?! FRIENDS DON'T LET FRIENDS WALK AROUND WITH NOSE-PIMPLES!
IT'S NOT A PIMPLE! A SPIDER BIT ME WHEN I WAS HIDING FROM A KILLER WITH A BUTCHER KNIFE!

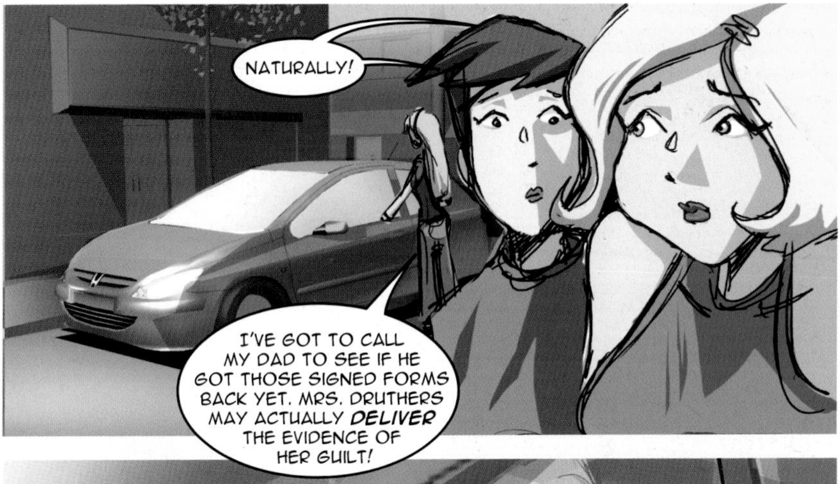
NATURALLY!
I'VE GOT TO CALL MY DAD TO SEE IF HE GOT THOSE SIGNED FORMS BACK YET. MRS. DRUTHERS MAY ACTUALLY DELIVER THE EVIDENCE OF HER GUILT!

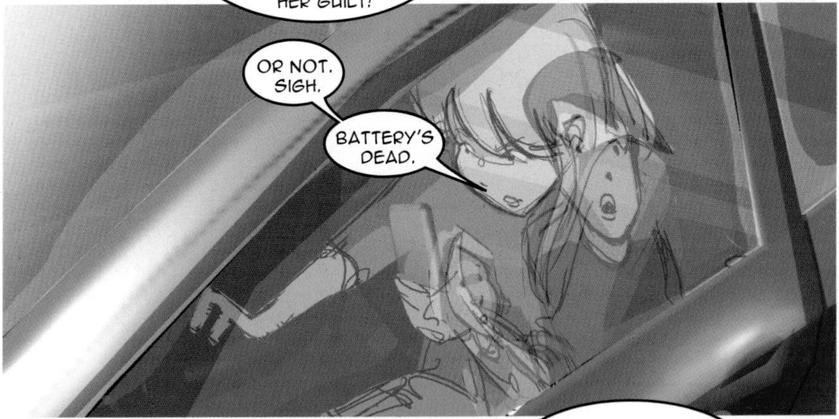
OR NOT. SIGH.
BATTERY'S DEAD.

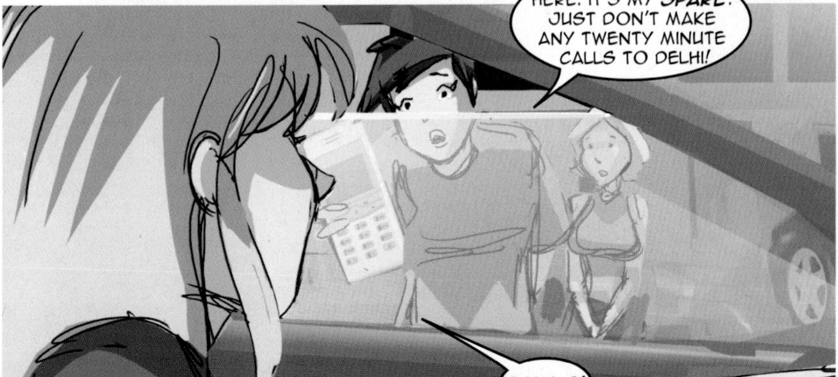
HERE. IT'S MY SPARE. JUST DON'T MAKE ANY TWENTY MINUTE CALLS TO DELHI!
THANKS!

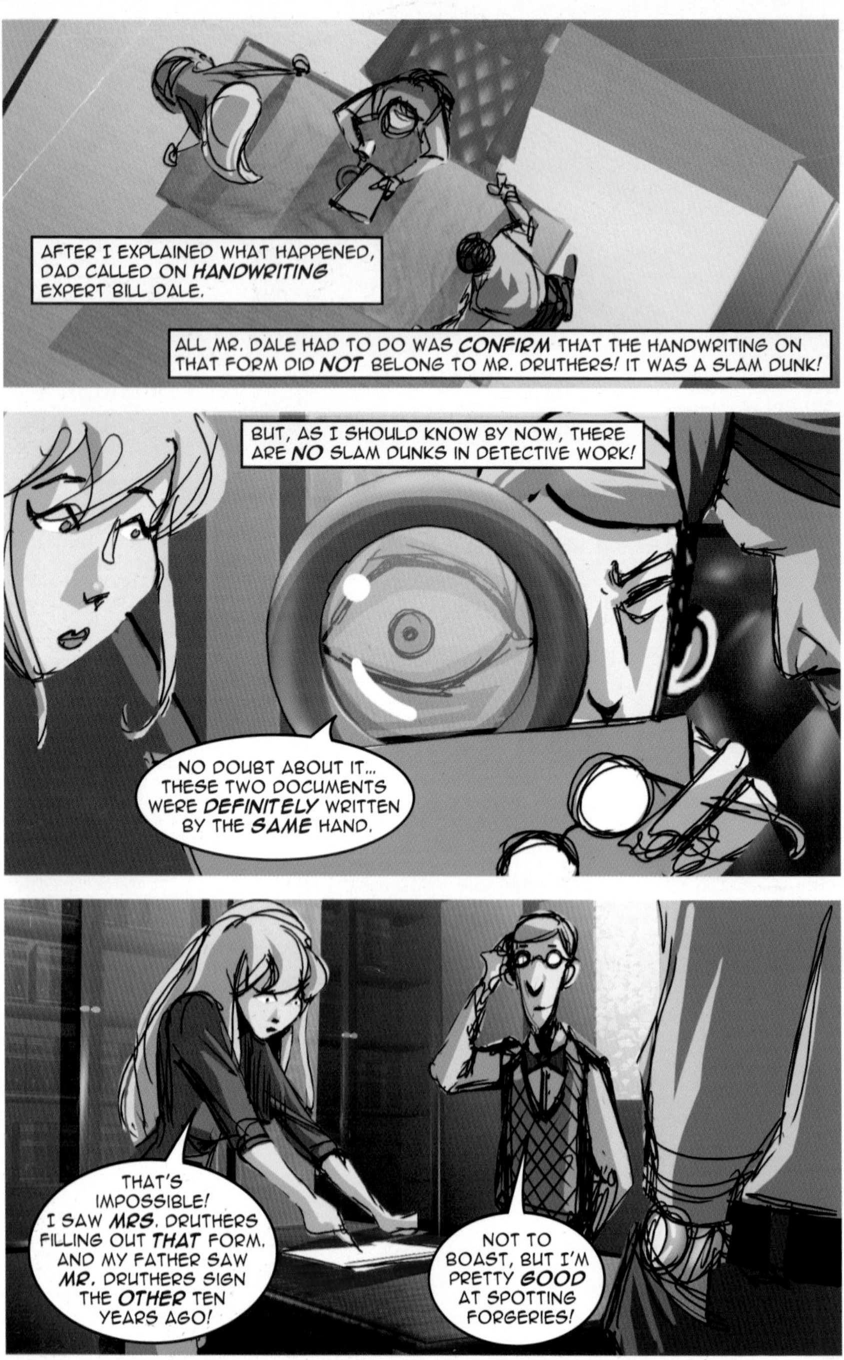
AFTER I EXPLAINED WHAT HAPPENED, DAD CALLED ON HANDWRITING EXPERT BILL DALE.
ALL MR. DALE HAD TO DO WAS CONFIRM THAT THE HANDWRITING ON THAT FORM DID NOT BELONG TO MR. DRUTHERS! IT WAS A SLAM DUNK!
BUT, AS I SHOULD KNOW BY NOW, THERE ARE NO SLAM DUNKS IN DETECTIVE WORK!
NO DOUBT ABOUT IT... THESE TWO DOCUMENTS WERE DEFINITELY WRITTEN BY THE SAME HAND.
THAT'S IMPOSSIBLE! I SAW MRS. DRUTHERS FILLING OUT THAT FORM. AND MY FATHER SAW MR. DRUTHERS SIGN THE OTHER TEN YEARS AGO!
NOT TO BOAST, BUT I'M PRETTY GOOD AT SPOTTING FORGERIES!

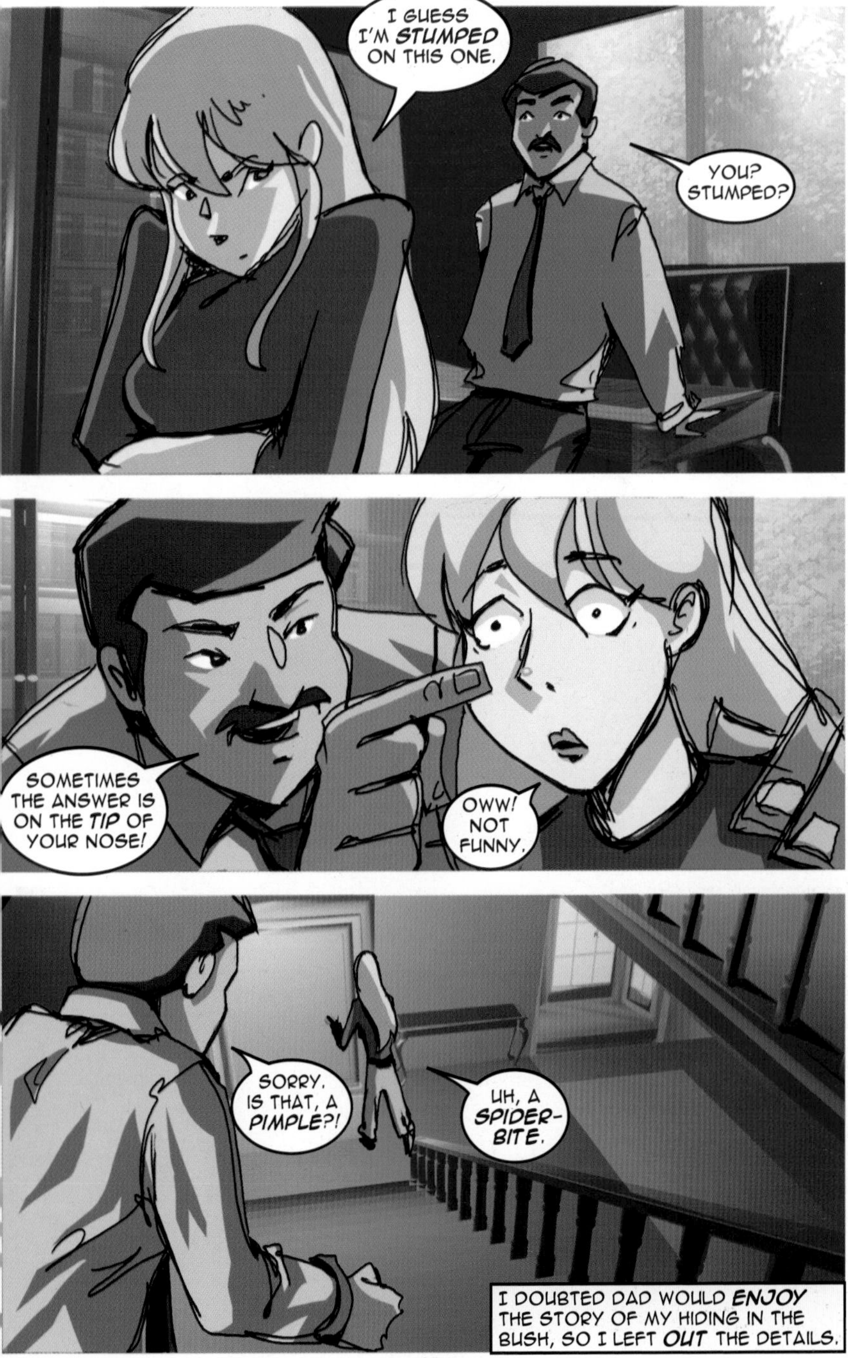
I GUESS I'M STUMPED ON THIS ONE.
YOU? STUMPED?
SOMETIMES THE ANSWER IS ON THE TIP OF YOUR NOSE!
OWW! NOT FUNNY.
SORRY. IS THAT, A PIMPLE?!
UH, A SPIDER-BITE.
I DOUBTED DAD WOULD ENJOY THE STORY OF MY HIDING IN THE BUSH, SO I LEFT OUT THE DETAILS.

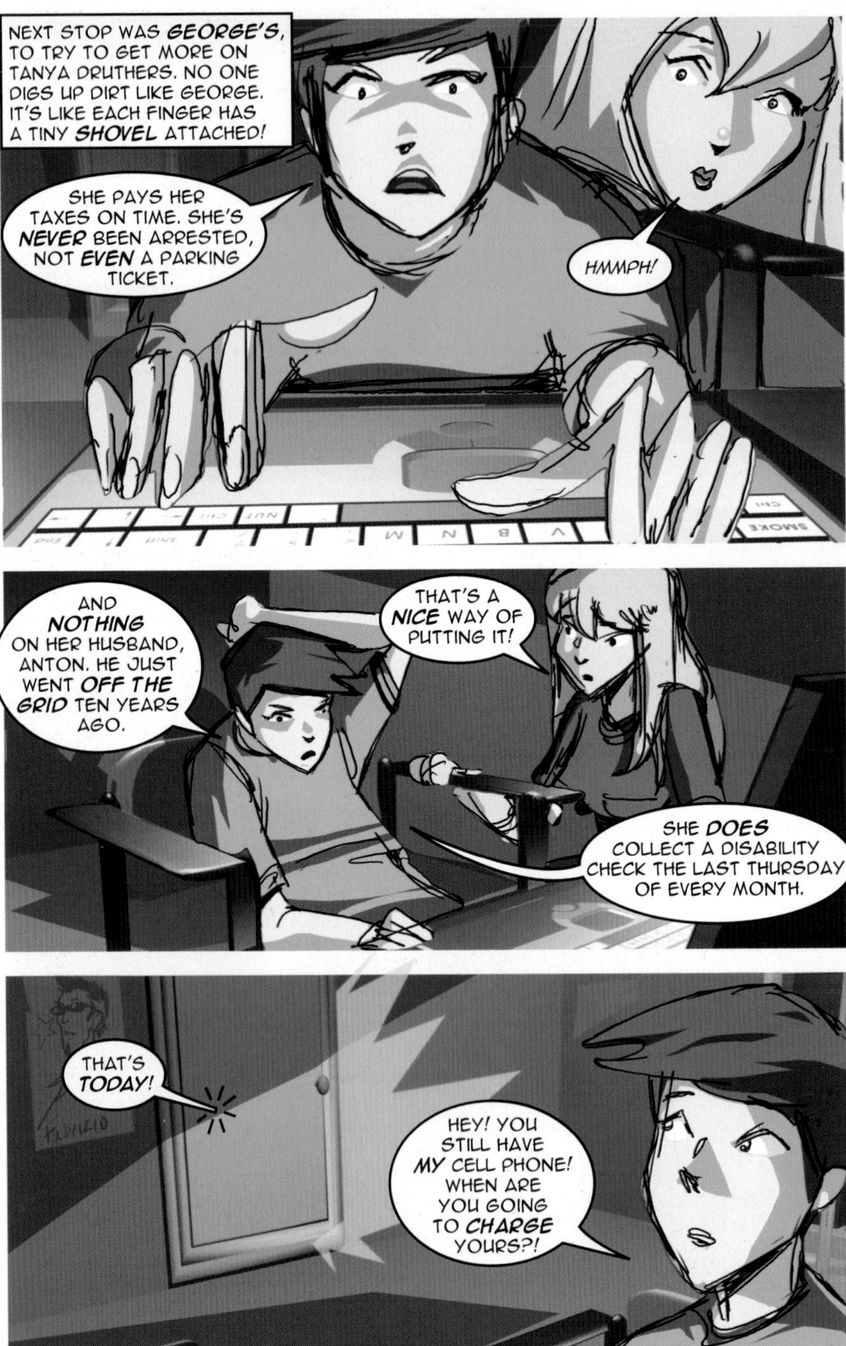
NEXT STOP WAS GEORGE'S, TO TRY TO GET MORE ON TANYA DRUTHERS. NO ONE DIGS UP DIRT LIKE GEORGE. IT'S LIKE EACH FINGER HAS A TINY SHOVEL ATTACHED!
SHE PAYS HER TAXES ON TIME. SHE'S NEVER BEEN ARRESTED, NOT EVEN A PARKING TICKET.
HMMPH!
SMOKE
AND NOTHING ON HER HUSBAND, ANTON. HE JUST WENT OFF THE GRID TEN YEARS AGO.
THAT'S A NICE WAY OF PUTTING IT!
SHE DOES COLLECT A DISABILITY CHECK THE LAST THURSDAY OF EVERY MONTH.
THAT'S TODAY!
HEY! YOU STILL HAVE MY CELL PHONE! WHEN ARE YOU GOING TO CHARGE YOURS?!

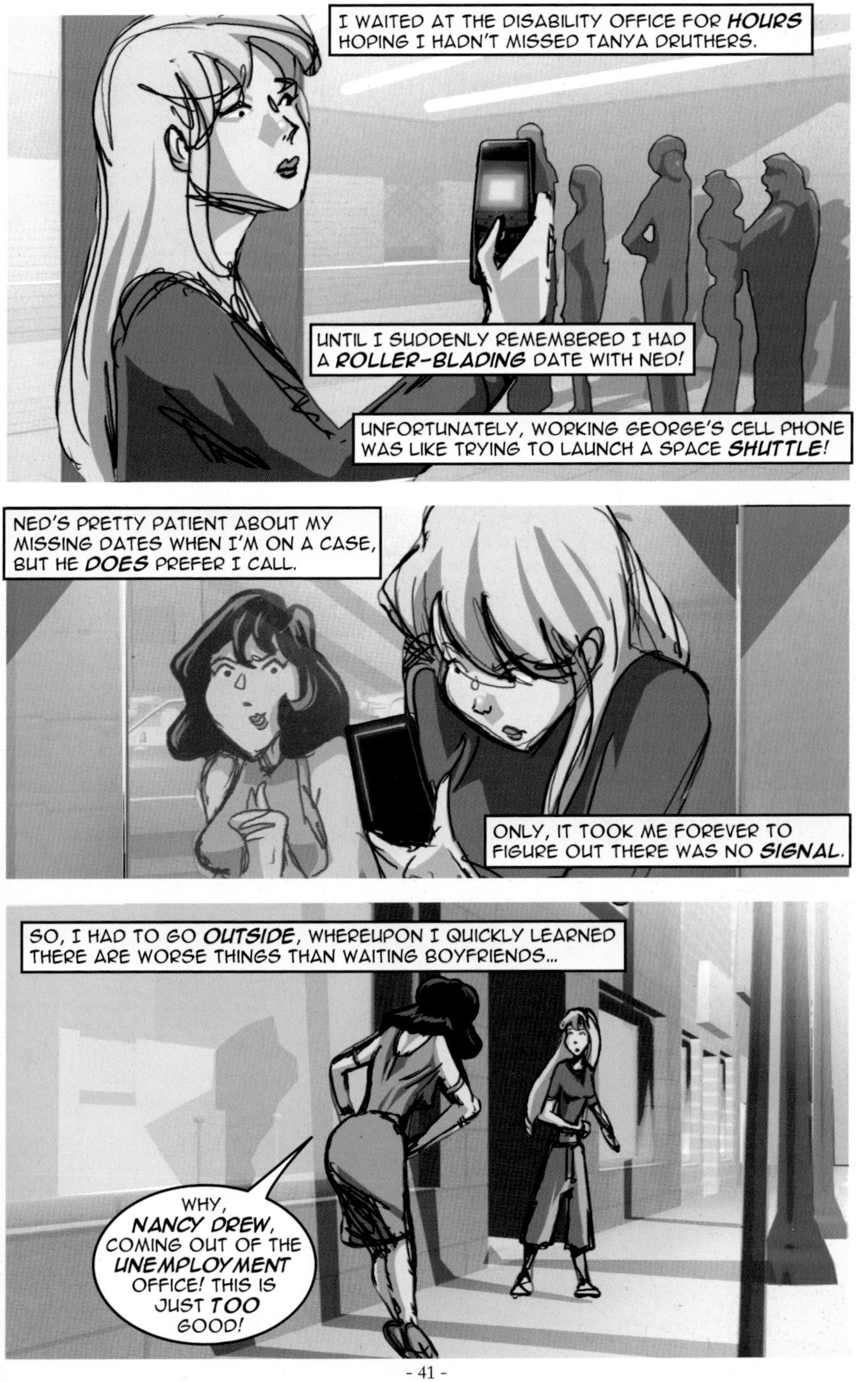
I WAITED AT THE DISABILITY OFFICE FOR HOURS HOPING I HADN'T MISSED TANYA DRUTHERS.
UNTIL I SUDDENLY REMEMBERED I HAD A ROLLER-BLADING DATE WITH NED!
UNFORTUNATELY, WORKING GEORGE'S CELL PHONE WAS LIKE TRYING TO LAUNCH A SPACE SHUTTLE!
NED'S PRETTY PATIENT ABOUT MY MISSING DATES WHEN I'M ON A CASE, BUT HE DOES PREFER I CALL.
ONLY, IT TOOK ME FOREVER TO FIGURE OUT THERE WAS NO SIGNAL.
SO, I HAD TO GO OUTSIDE, WHEREUPON I QUICKLY LEARNED THERE ARE WORSE THINGS THAN WAITING BOYFRIENDS...
WHY, NANCY DREW, COMING OUT OF THE UNEMPLOYMENT OFFICE! THIS IS JUST TOO GOOD!

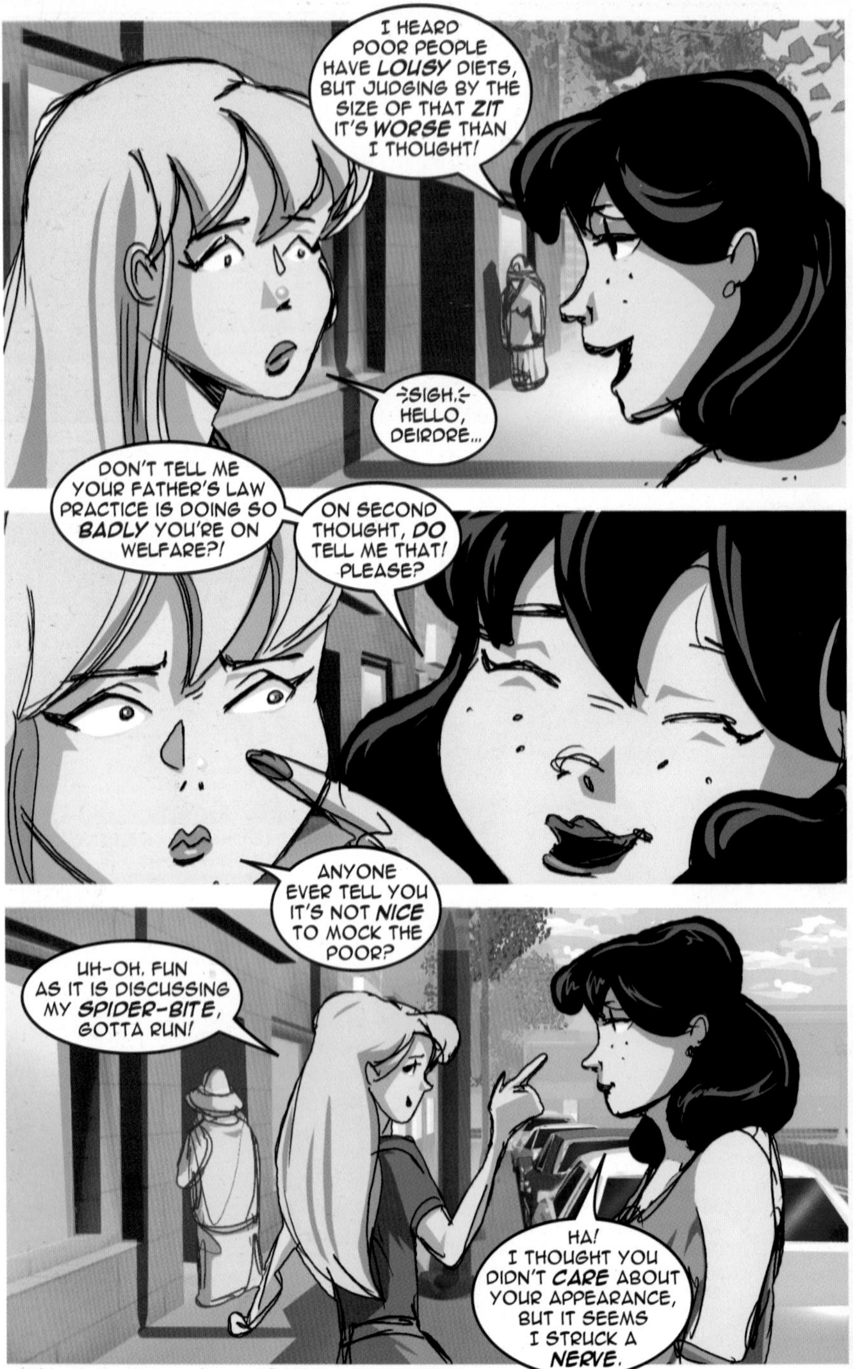
I HEARD POOR PEOPLE HAVE LOUSY DIETS, BUT JUDGING BY THE SIZE OF THAT ZIT IT'S WORSE THAN I THOUGHT!
SIGH. HELLO, DEIRDRE...
DON'T TELL ME YOUR FATHER'S LAW PRACTICE IS DOING SO BADLY YOU'RE ON WELFARE?!
ON SECOND THOUGHT, DO TELL ME THAT! PLEASE?
ANYONE EVER TELL YOU IT'S NOT NICE TO MOCK THE POOR?
UH-OH. FUN AS IT IS DISCUSSING MY SPIDER-BITE, GOTTA RUN!
HA! I THOUGHT YOU DIDN'T CARE ABOUT YOUR APPEARANCE, BUT IT SEEMS I STRUCK A NERVE.

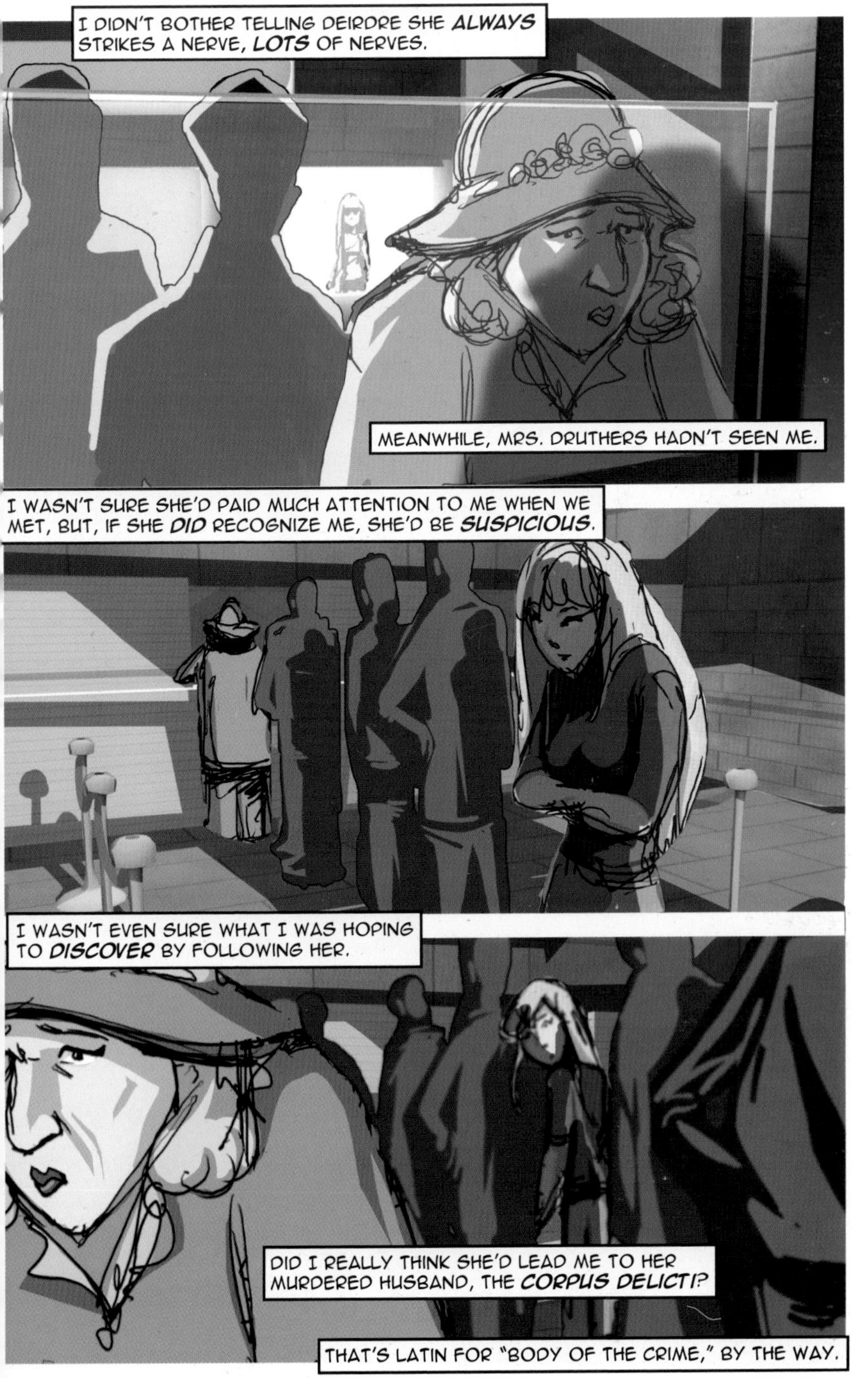
I DIDN'T BOTHER TELLING DEIRDRE SHE ALWAYS STRIKES A NERVE, LOTS OF NERVES.
MEANWHILE, MRS. DRUTHERS HADN'T SEEN ME.
I WASN'T SURE SHE'D PAID MUCH ATTENTION TO ME WHEN WE MET, BUT, IF SHE DID RECOGNIZE ME, SHE'D BE SUSPICIOUS.
I WASN'T EVEN SURE WHAT I WAS HOPING TO DISCOVER BY FOLLOWING HER.
DID I REALLY THINK SHE'D LEAD ME TO HER MURDERED HUSBAND, THE CORPUS DELICTI?
THAT'S LATIN FOR "BODY OF THE CRIME," BY THE WAY.

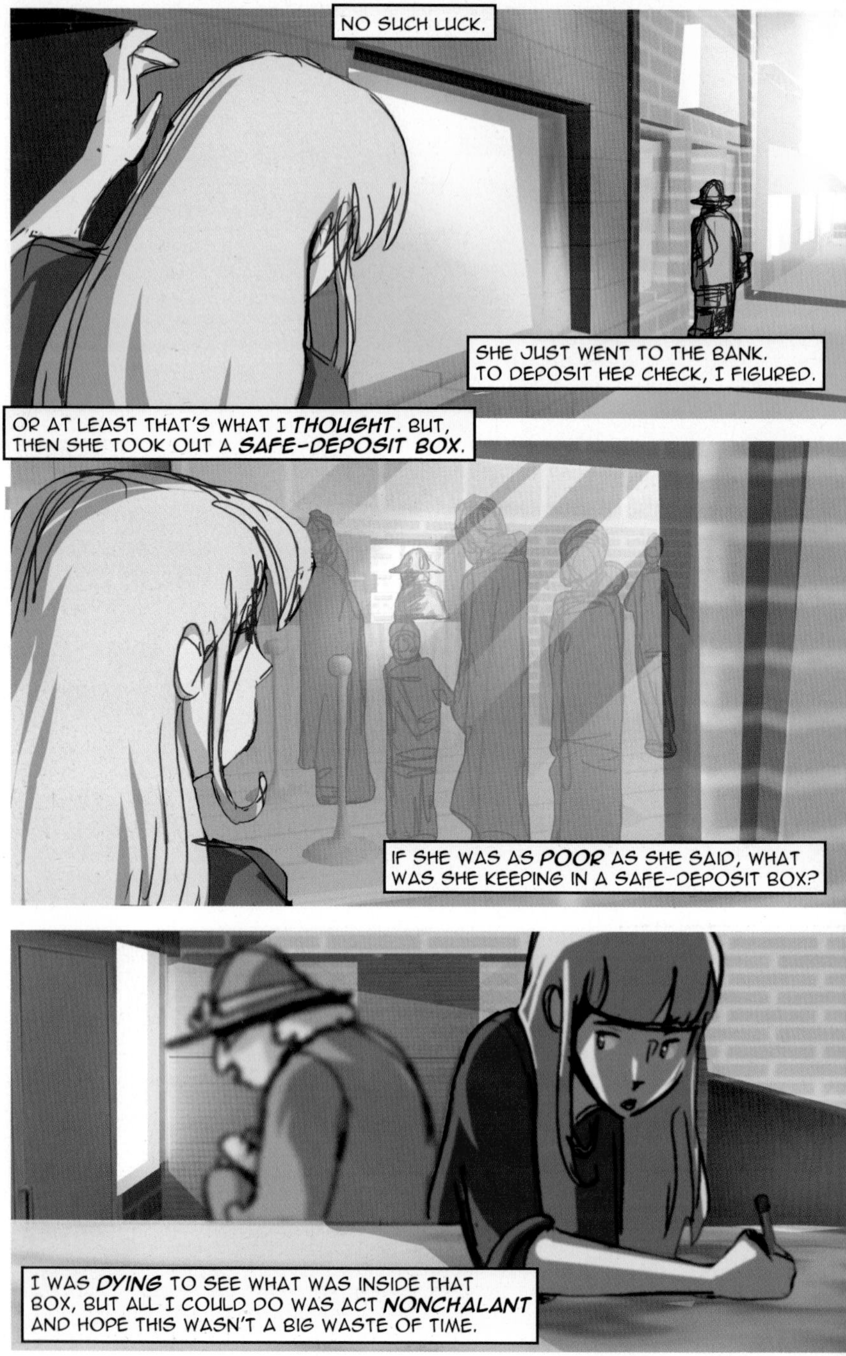
NO SUCH LUCK.
SHE JUST WENT TO THE BANK. TO DEPOSIT HER CHECK, I FIGURED.
OR AT LEAST THAT'S WHAT I THOUGHT. BUT, THEN SHE TOOK OUT A SAFE-DEPOSIT BOX.
IF SHE WAS AS POOR AS SHE SAID, WHAT WAS SHE KEEPING IN A SAFE-DEPOSIT BOX?
I WAS DYING TO SEE WHAT WAS INSIDE THAT BOX, BUT ALL I COULD DO WAS ACT NONCHALANT AND HOPE THIS WASN'T A BIG WASTE OF TIME.

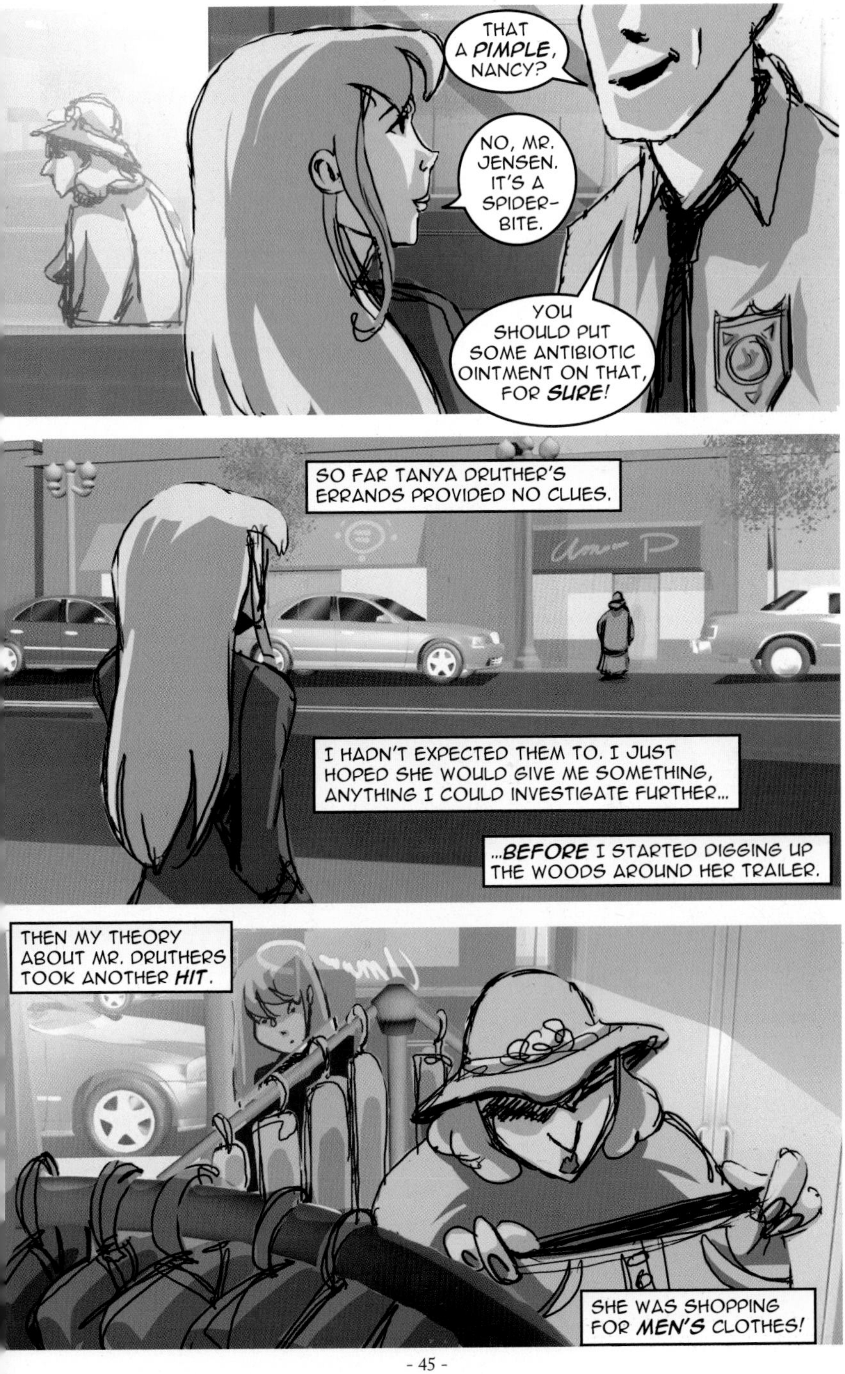
THAT A PIMPLE, NANCY?
NO, MR. JENSEN. IT'S A SPIDER-BITE.
YOU SHOULD PUT SOME ANTIBIOTIC OINTMENT ON THAT, FOR SURE!
SO FAR TANYA DRUTHER'S ERRANDS PROVIDED NO CLUES.
I HADN'T EXPECTED THEM TO. I JUST HOPED SHE WOULD GIVE ME SOMETHING, ANYTHING I COULD INVESTIGATE FURTHER...
...BEFORE I STARTED DIGGING UP THE WOODS AROUND HER TRAILER.
THEN MY THEORY ABOUT MR. DRUTHERS TOOK ANOTHER HIT.
SHE WAS SHOPPING FOR MEN'S CLOTHES!

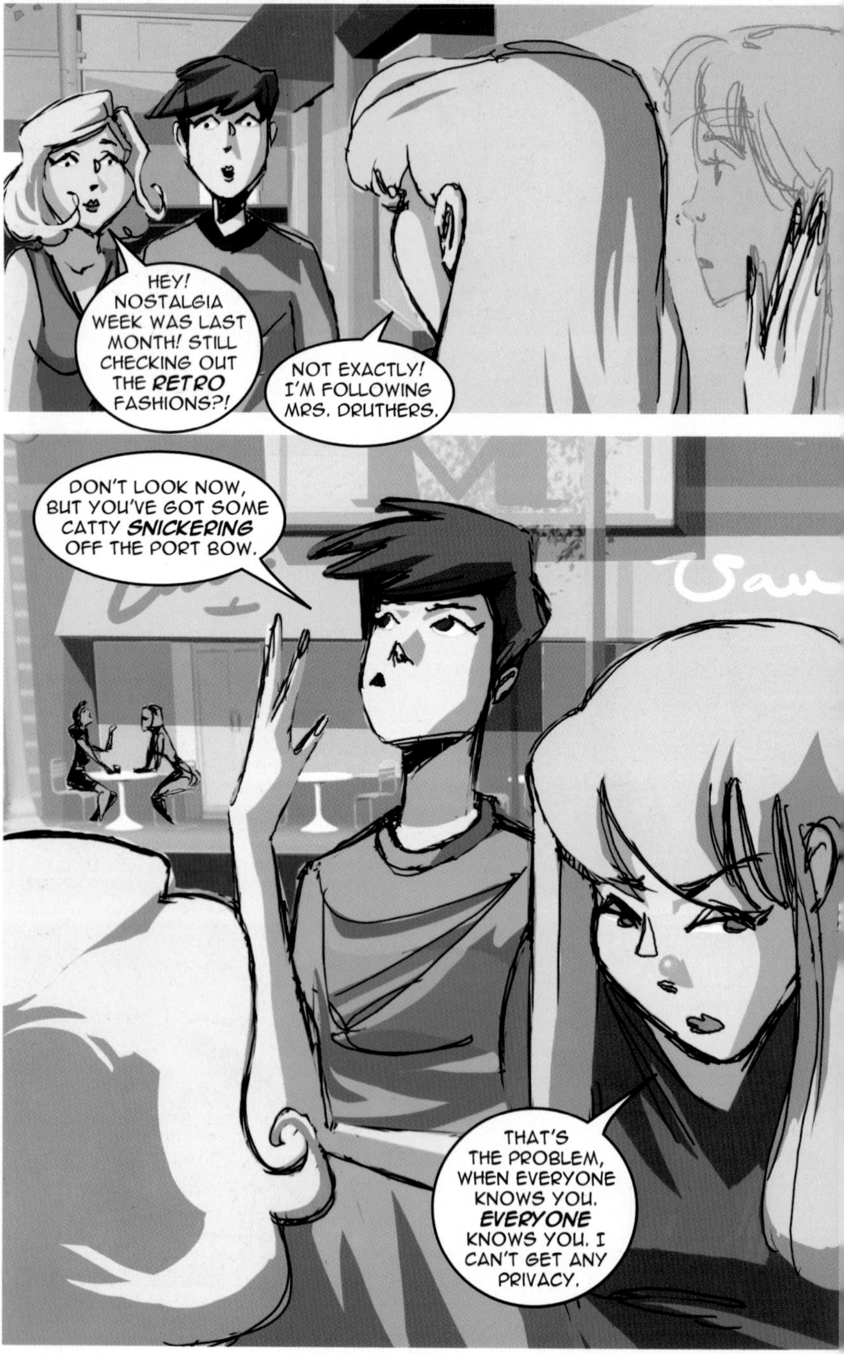
HEY! NOSTALGIA WEEK WAS LAST MONTH! STILL CHECKING OUT THE *RETRO* FASHIONS?!
NOT EXACTLY! I'M FOLLOWING MRS. DRUTHERS.
DON'T LOOK NOW, BUT YOU'VE GOT SOME CATTY *SNICKERING* OFF THE PORT BOW.
THAT'S THE PROBLEM, WHEN EVERYONE KNOWS YOU. *EVERYONE* KNOWS YOU. I CAN'T GET ANY PRIVACY.

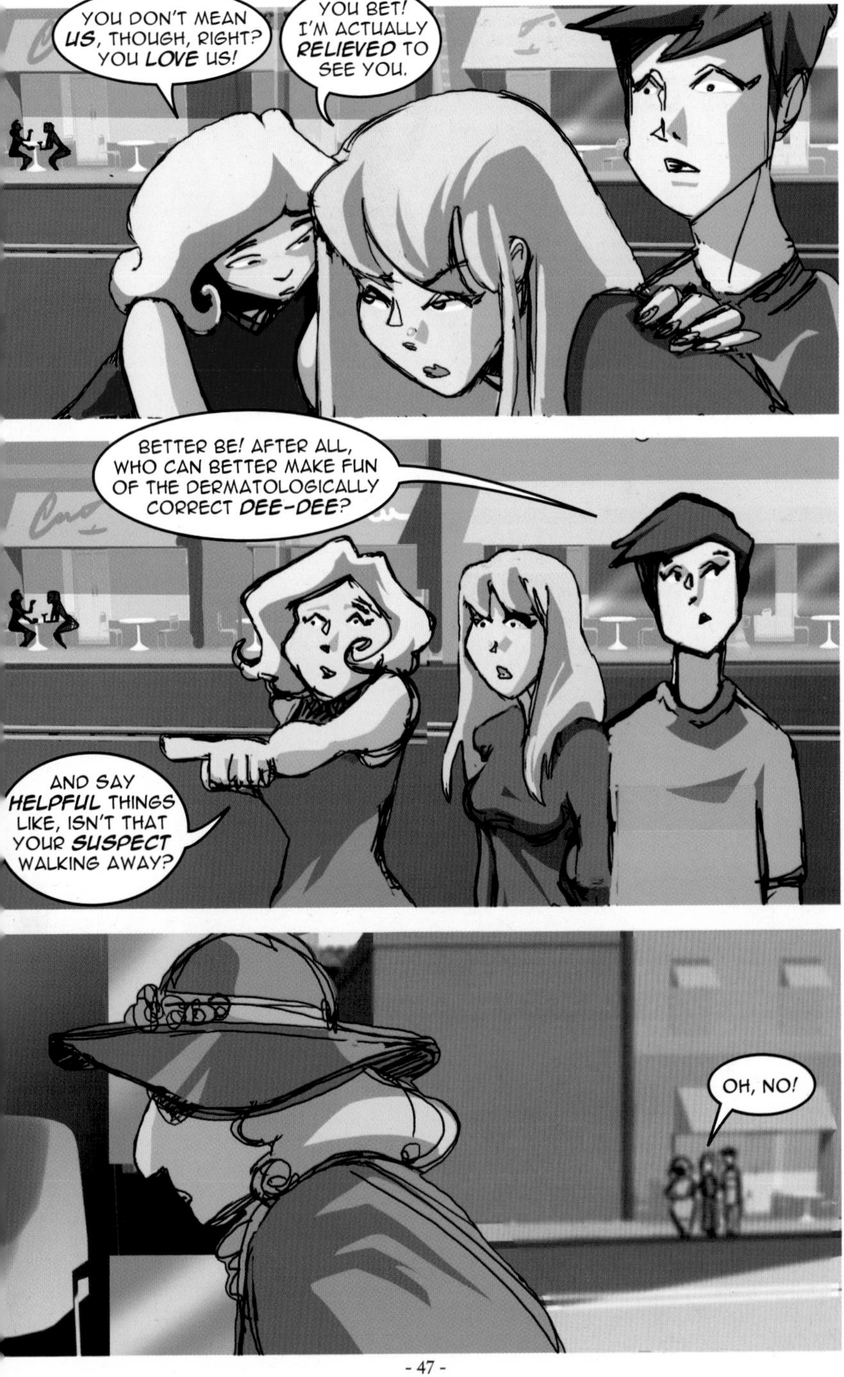
YOU DON'T MEAN US, THOUGH, RIGHT? YOU LOVE US!
YOU BET! I'M ACTUALLY RELIEVED TO SEE YOU.
BETTER BE! AFTER ALL, WHO CAN BETTER MAKE FUN OF THE DERMATOLOGICALLY CORRECT DEE-DEE?
AND SAY HELPFUL THINGS LIKE, ISN'T THAT YOUR SUSPECT WALKING AWAY?
OH, NO!

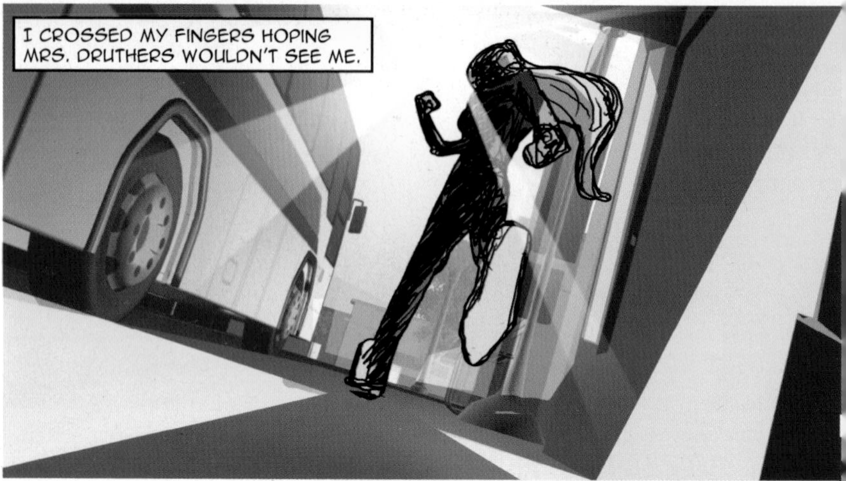
I CROSSED MY FINGERS HOPING MRS. DRUTHERS WOULDN'T SEE ME.

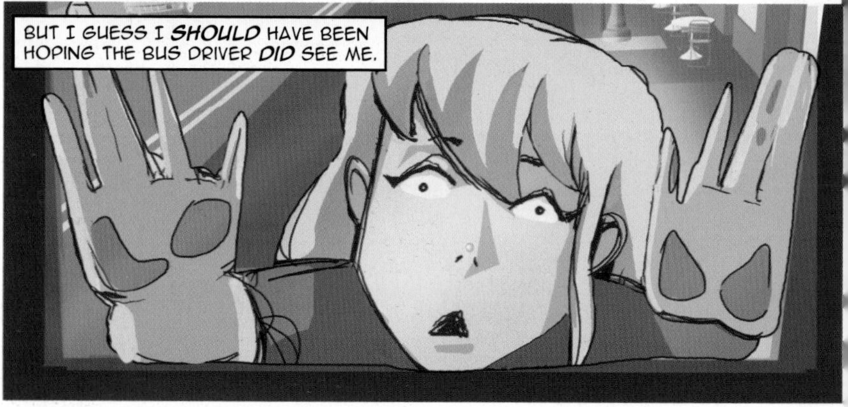
BUT I GUESS I SHOULD HAVE BEEN HOPING THE BUS DRIVER DID SEE ME.

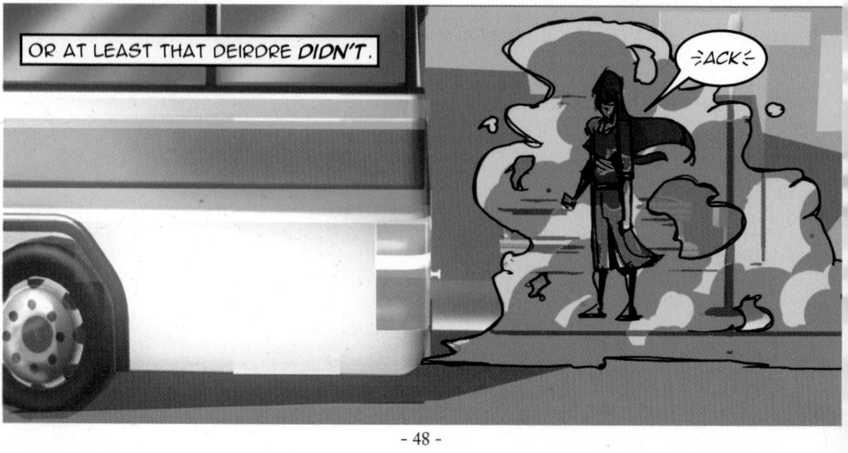
OR AT LEAST THAT DEIRDRE DIDN'T.
ACK

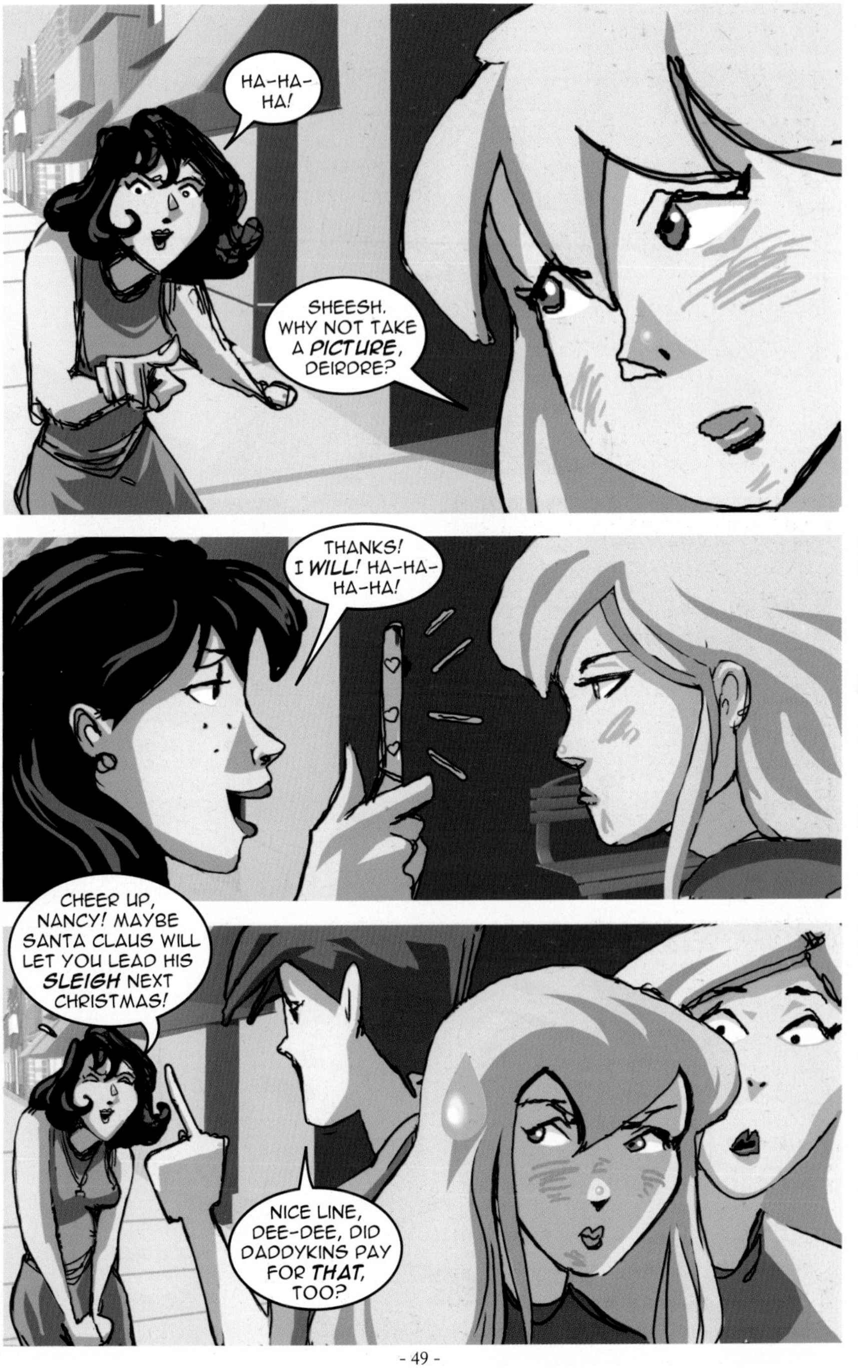
HA-HA-HA!
SHEESH. WHY NOT TAKE A *PICTURE*, DEIRDRE?
THANKS! I *WILL!* HA-HA-HA-HA!
CHEER UP, NANCY! MAYBE SANTA CLAUS WILL LET YOU LEAD HIS *SLEIGH* NEXT CHRISTMAS!
NICE LINE, DEE-DEE, DID DADDYKINS PAY FOR *THAT*, TOO?

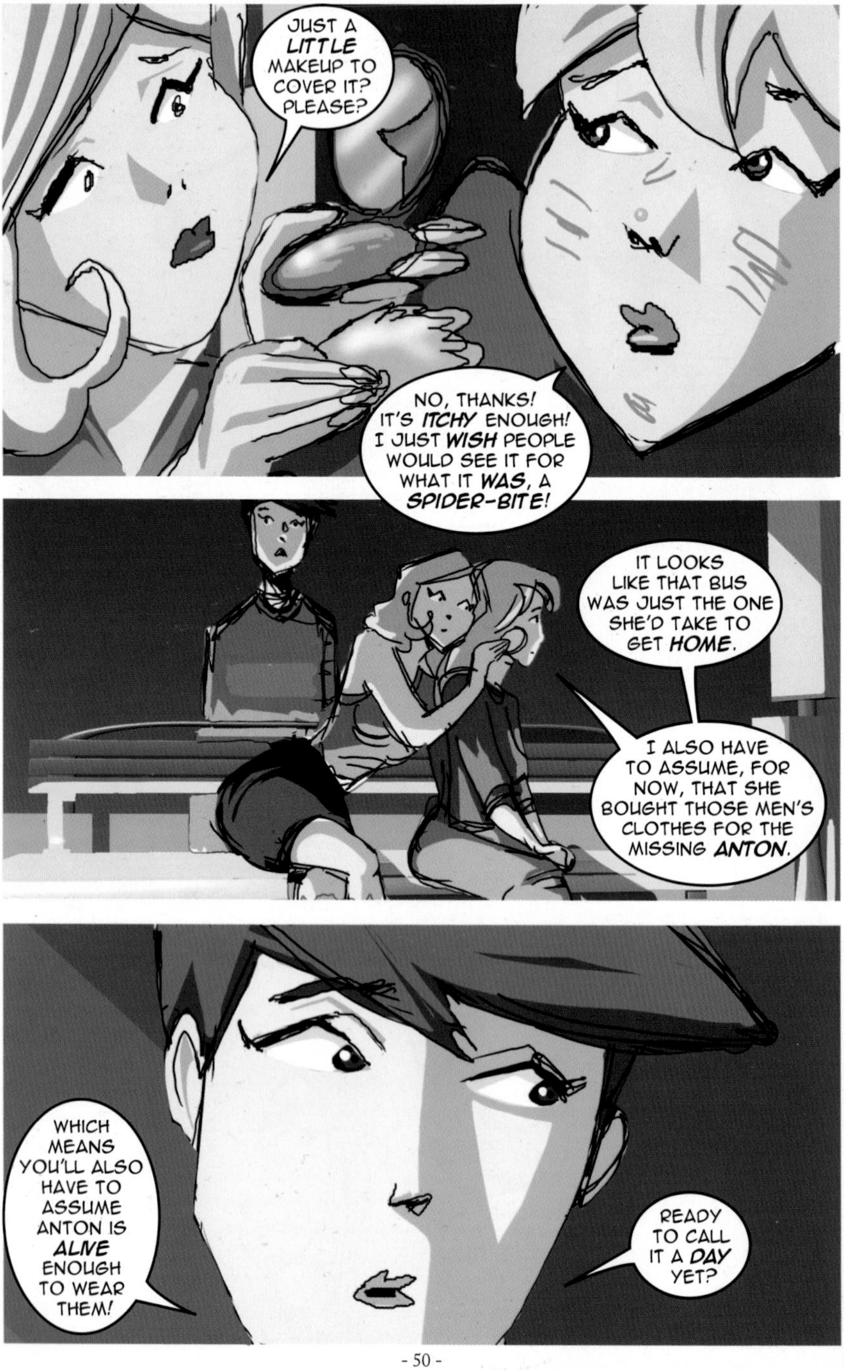
JUST A LITTLE MAKEUP TO COVER IT? PLEASE?
NO, THANKS! IT'S ITCHY ENOUGH! I JUST WISH PEOPLE WOULD SEE IT FOR WHAT IT WAS, A SPIDER-BITE!
IT LOOKS LIKE THAT BUS WAS JUST THE ONE SHE'D TAKE TO GET HOME.
I ALSO HAVE TO ASSUME, FOR NOW, THAT SHE BOUGHT THOSE MEN'S CLOTHES FOR THE MISSING ANTON.
WHICH MEANS YOU'LL ALSO HAVE TO ASSUME ANTON IS ALIVE ENOUGH TO WEAR THEM!
READY TO CALL IT A DAY YET?

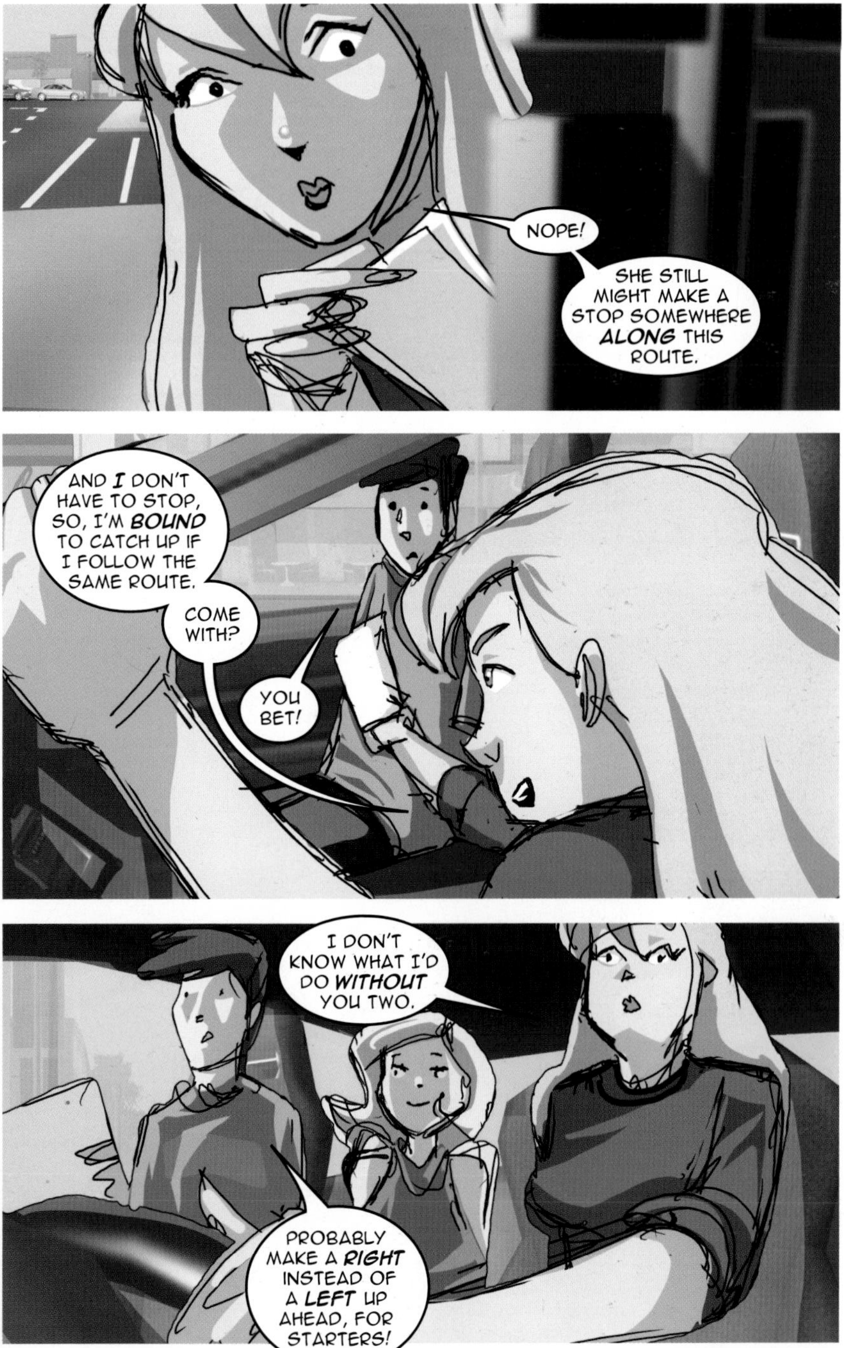
NOPE!
SHE STILL MIGHT MAKE A STOP SOMEWHERE ALONG THIS ROUTE.
AND I DON'T HAVE TO STOP, SO, I'M BOUND TO CATCH UP IF I FOLLOW THE SAME ROUTE.
COME WITH?
YOU BET!
I DON'T KNOW WHAT I'D DO WITHOUT YOU TWO.
PROBABLY MAKE A RIGHT INSTEAD OF A LEFT UP AHEAD, FOR STARTERS!

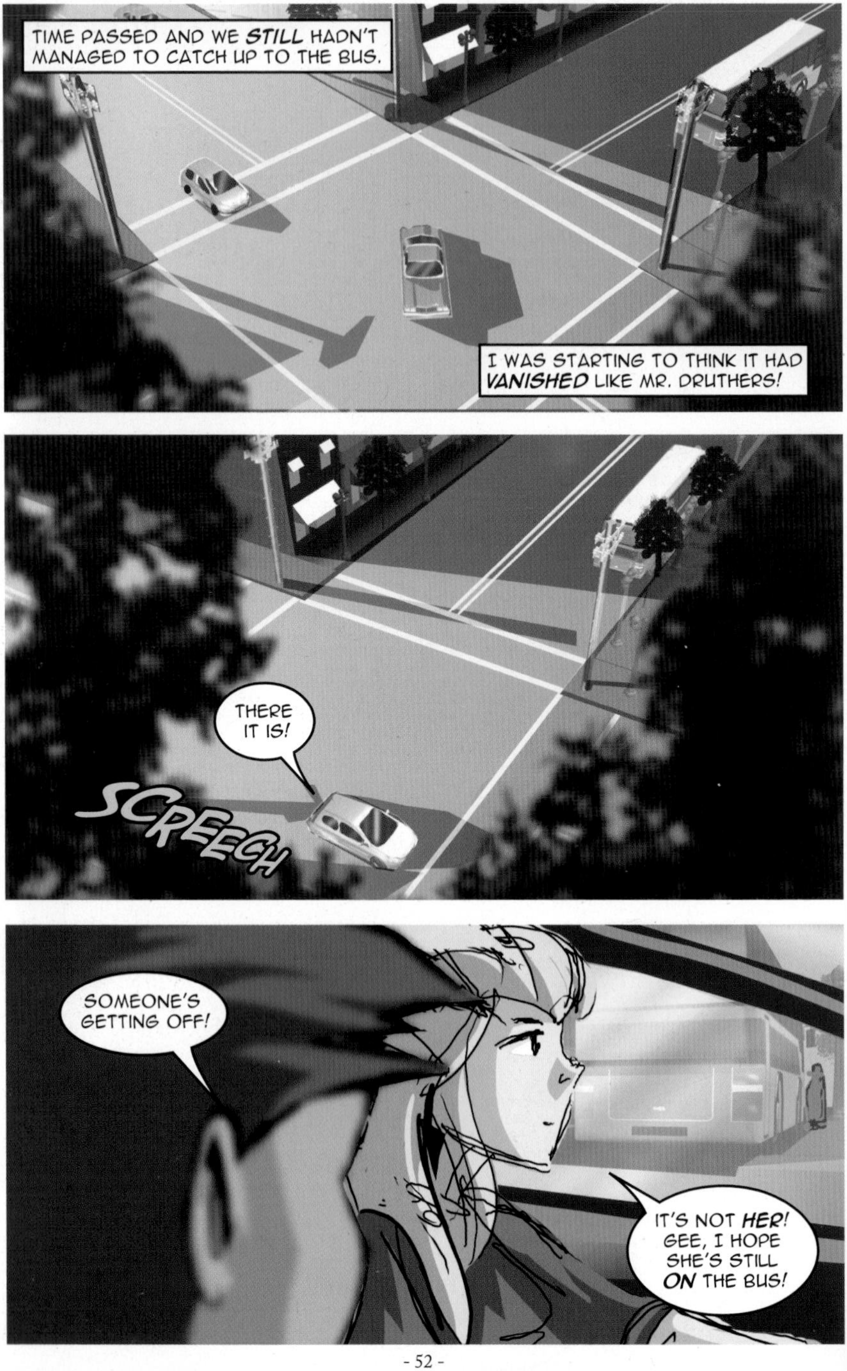
TIME PASSED AND WE STILL HADN'T MANAGED TO CATCH UP TO THE BUS.
I WAS STARTING TO THINK IT HAD VANISHED LIKE MR. DRUTHERS!
THERE IT IS!
SCREECH
SOMEONE'S GETTING OFF!
IT'S NOT HER! GEE, I HOPE SHE'S STILL ON THE BUS!

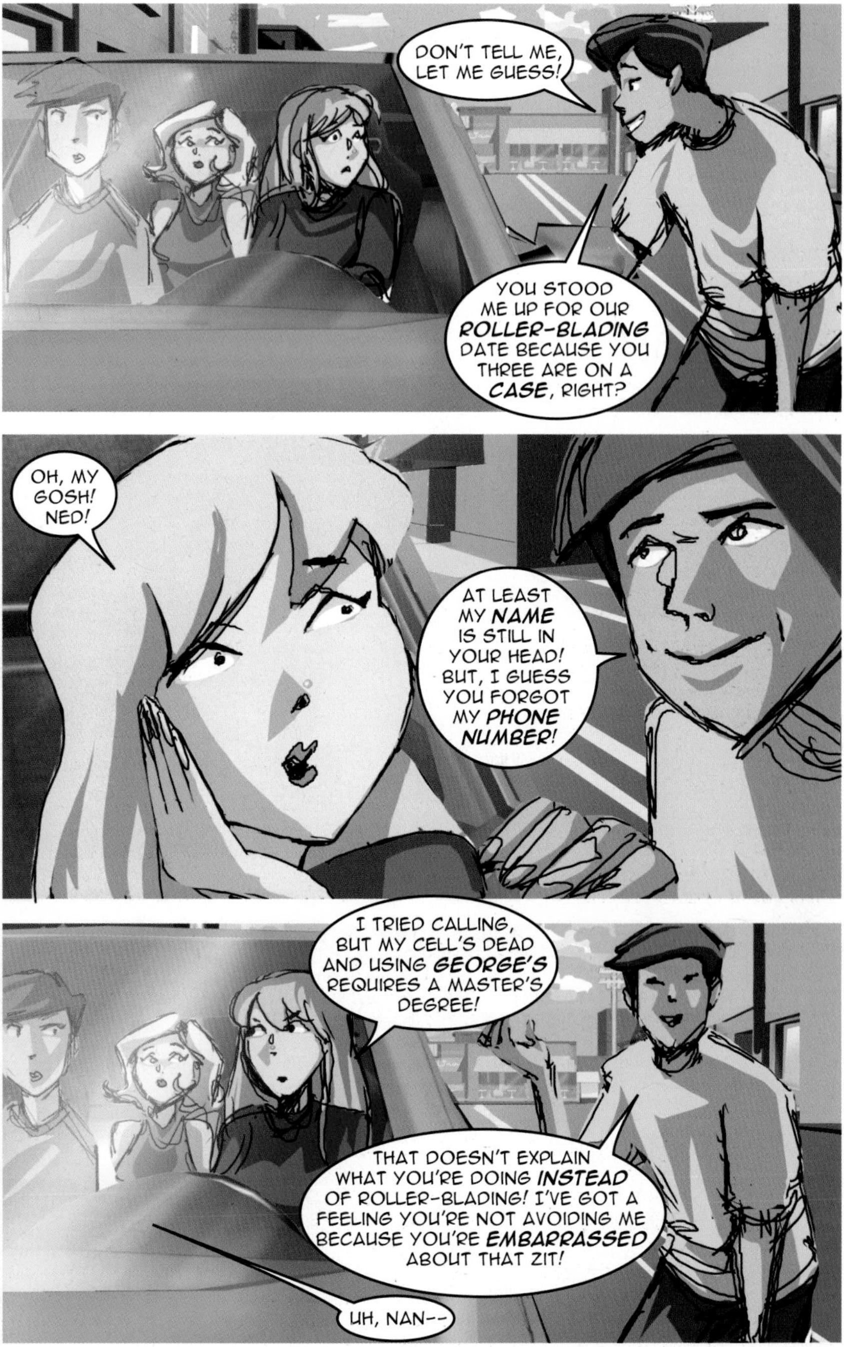
DON'T TELL ME, LET ME GUESS!
YOU STOOD ME UP FOR OUR ROLLER-BLADING DATE BECAUSE YOU THREE ARE ON A CASE, RIGHT?
OH, MY GOSH! NED!
AT LEAST MY NAME IS STILL IN YOUR HEAD! BUT, I GUESS YOU FORGOT MY PHONE NUMBER!
I TRIED CALLING, BUT MY CELL'S DEAD AND USING GEORGE'S REQUIRES A MASTER'S DEGREE!
THAT DOESN'T EXPLAIN WHAT YOU'RE DOING INSTEAD OF ROLLER-BLADING! I'VE GOT A FEELING YOU'RE NOT AVOIDING ME BECAUSE YOU'RE EMBARRASSED ABOUT THAT ZIT!
UH, NAN--

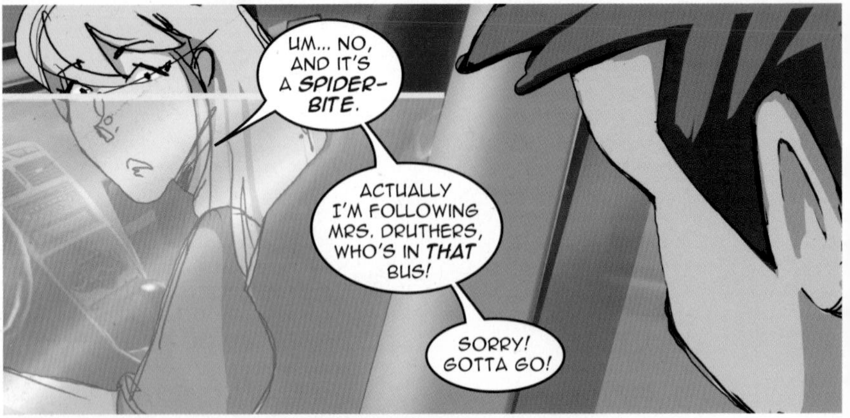
UM... NO, AND IT'S A SPIDER-BITE.
ACTUALLY I'M FOLLOWING MRS. DRUTHERS, WHO'S IN THAT BUS!
SORRY! GOTTA GO!

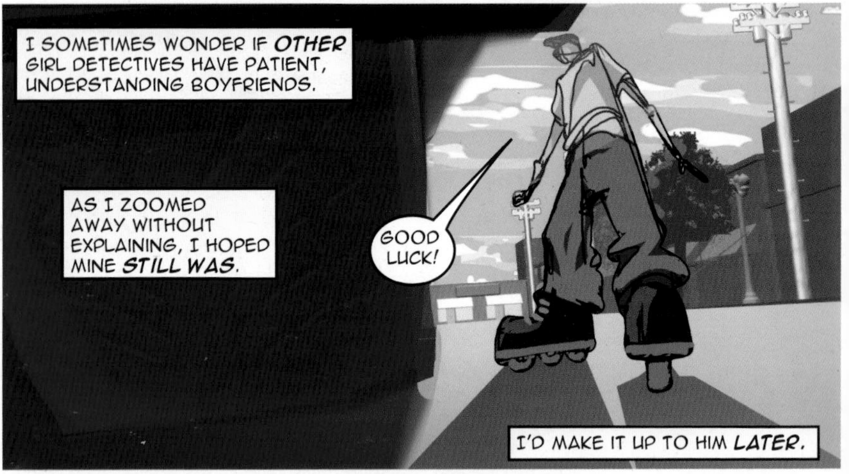
I SOMETIMES WONDER IF OTHER GIRL DETECTIVES HAVE PATIENT, UNDERSTANDING BOYFRIENDS.
AS I ZOOMED AWAY WITHOUT EXPLAINING, I HOPED MINE STILL WAS.
GOOD LUCK!
I'D MAKE IT UP TO HIM LATER.

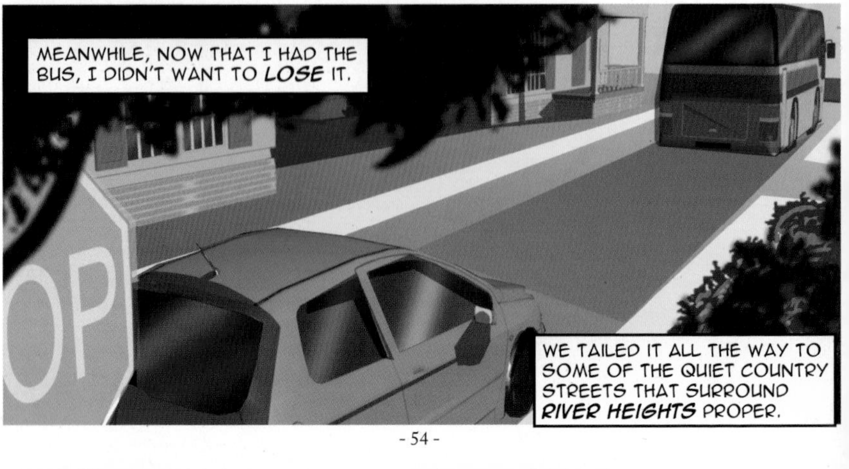
MEANWHILE, NOW THAT I HAD THE BUS, I DIDN'T WANT TO LOSE IT.
OP
WE TAILED IT ALL THE WAY TO SOME OF THE QUIET COUNTRY STREETS THAT SURROUND RIVER HEIGHTS PROPER.

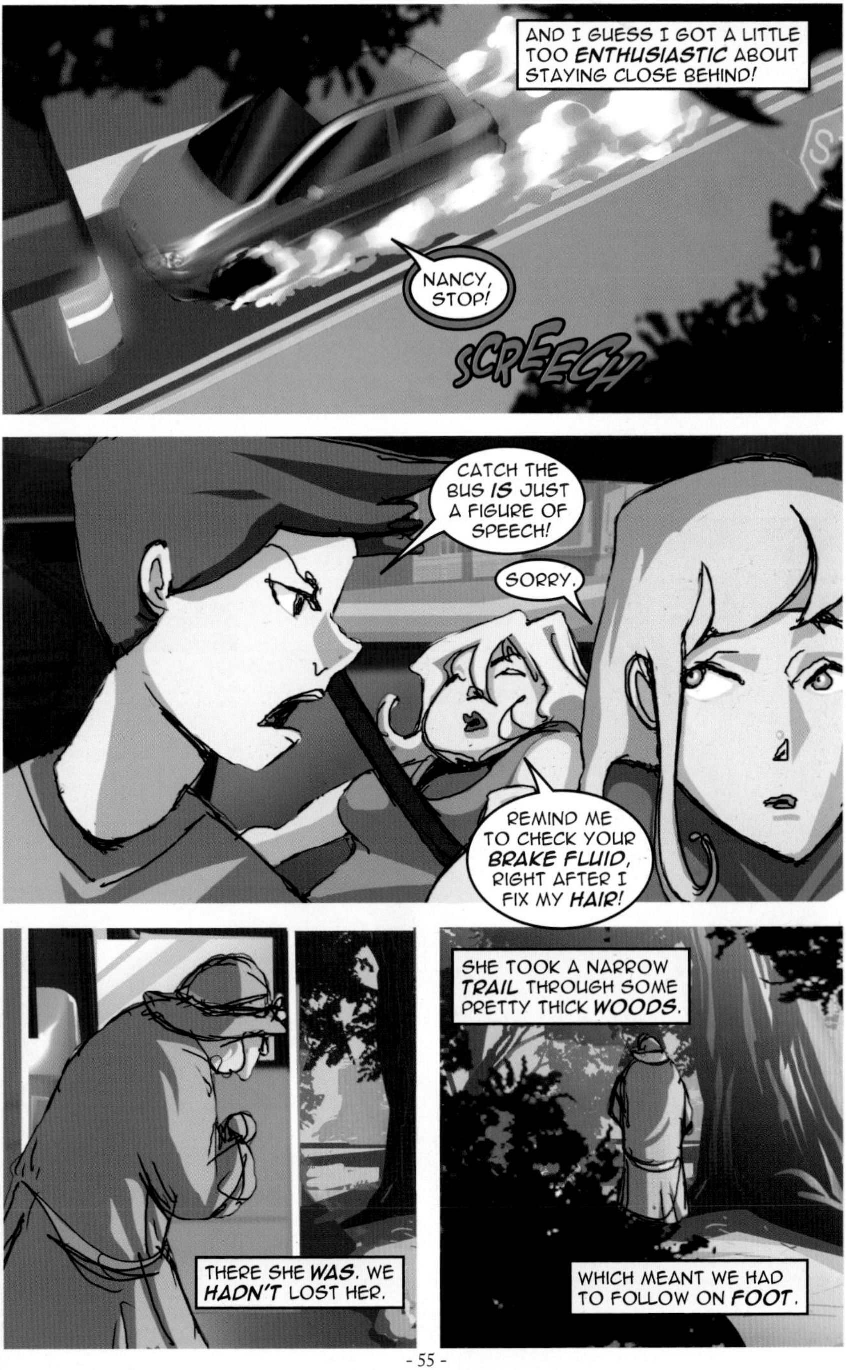
AND I GUESS I GOT A LITTLE TOO ENTHUSIASTIC ABOUT STAYING CLOSE BEHIND!
NANCY, STOP!
SCREECH
CATCH THE BUS IS JUST A FIGURE OF SPEECH!
SORRY.
REMIND ME TO CHECK YOUR BRAKE FLUID, RIGHT AFTER I FIX MY HAIR!
THERE SHE WAS. WE HADN'T LOST HER.
SHE TOOK A NARROW TRAIL THROUGH SOME PRETTY THICK WOODS.
WHICH MEANT WE HAD TO FOLLOW ON FOOT.

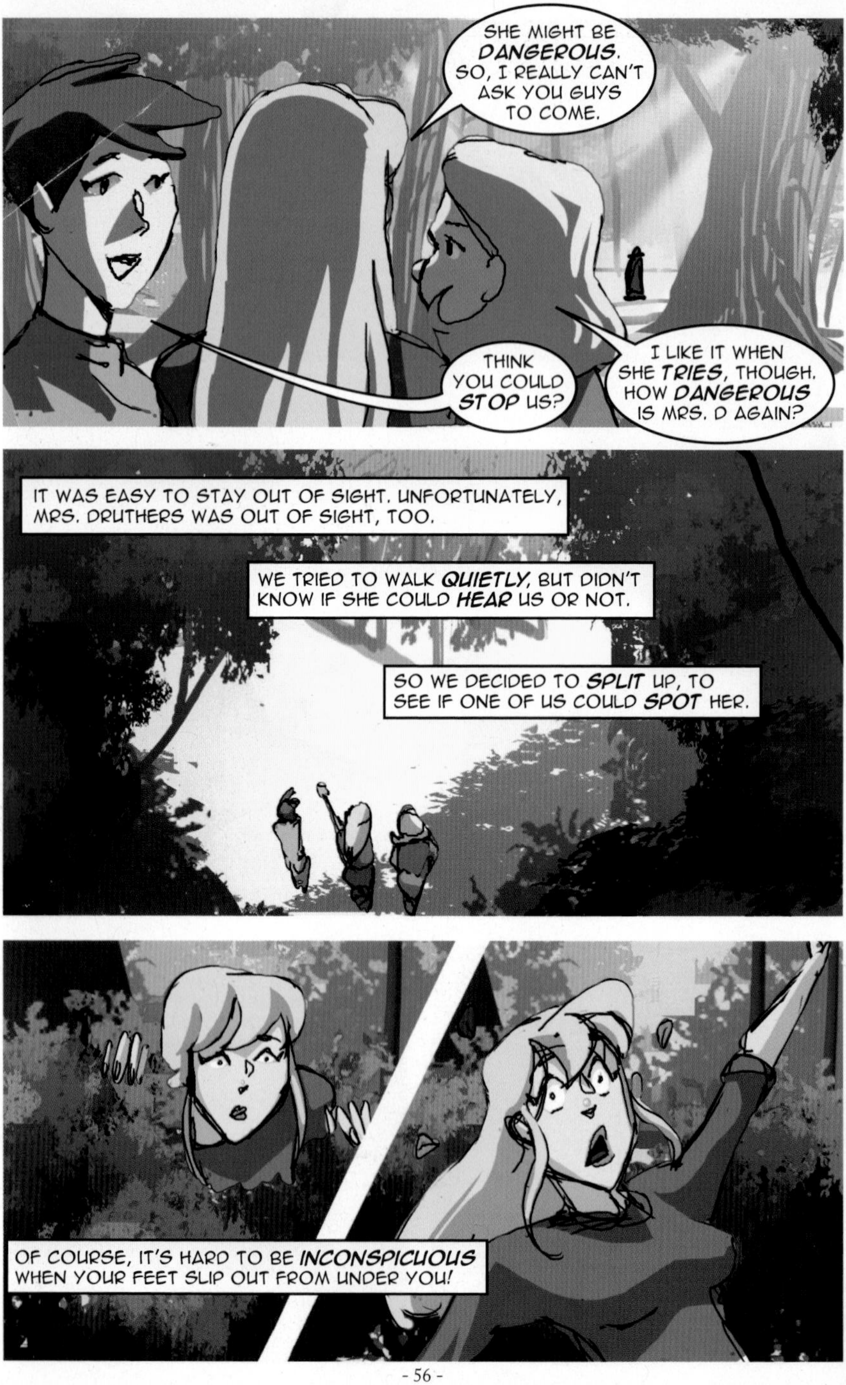
SHE MIGHT BE DANGEROUS. SO, I REALLY CAN'T ASK YOU GUYS TO COME.
THINK YOU COULD STOP US?
I LIKE IT WHEN SHE TRIES, THOUGH. HOW DANGEROUS IS MRS. D AGAIN?
IT WAS EASY TO STAY OUT OF SIGHT. UNFORTUNATELY, MRS. DRUTHERS WAS OUT OF SIGHT, TOO.
WE TRIED TO WALK QUIETLY, BUT DIDN'T KNOW IF SHE COULD HEAR US OR NOT.
SO WE DECIDED TO SPLIT UP, TO SEE IF ONE OF US COULD SPOT HER.
OF COURSE, IT'S HARD TO BE INCONSPICUOUS WHEN YOUR FEET SLIP OUT FROM UNDER YOU!

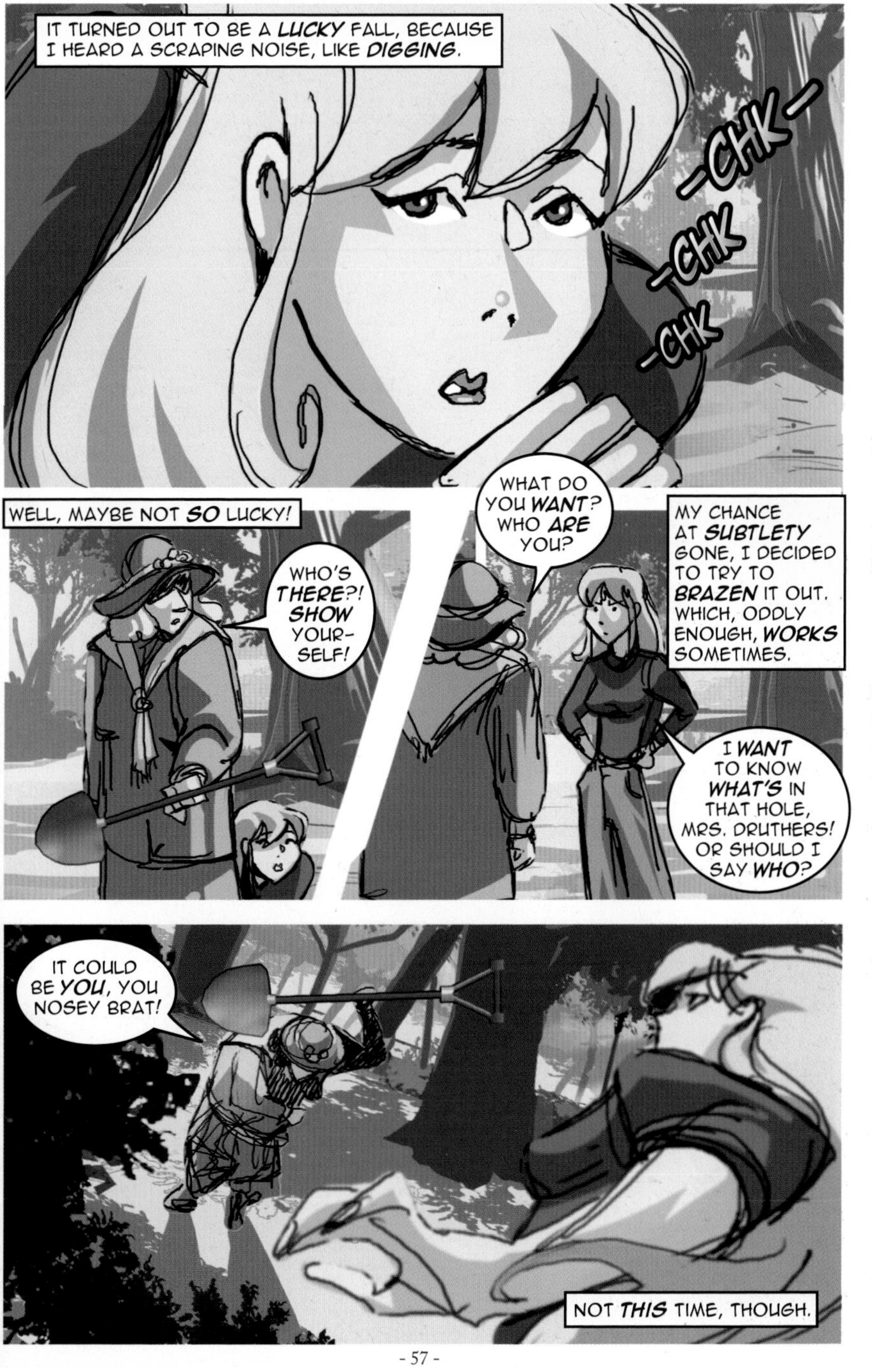
IT TURNED OUT TO BE A LUCKY FALL, BECAUSE I HEARD A SCRAPING NOISE, LIKE DIGGING.
-CHK-
-CHK
-CHK
WELL, MAYBE NOT SO LUCKY!
WHO'S THERE?! SHOW YOURSELF!
WHAT DO YOU WANT? WHO ARE YOU?
MY CHANCE AT SUBTLETY GONE, I DECIDED TO TRY TO BRAZEN IT OUT. WHICH, ODDLY ENOUGH, WORKS SOMETIMES.
I WANT TO KNOW WHAT'S IN THAT HOLE, MRS. DRUTHERS! OR SHOULD I SAY WHO?
IT COULD BE YOU, YOU NOSEY BRAT!
NOT THIS TIME, THOUGH.

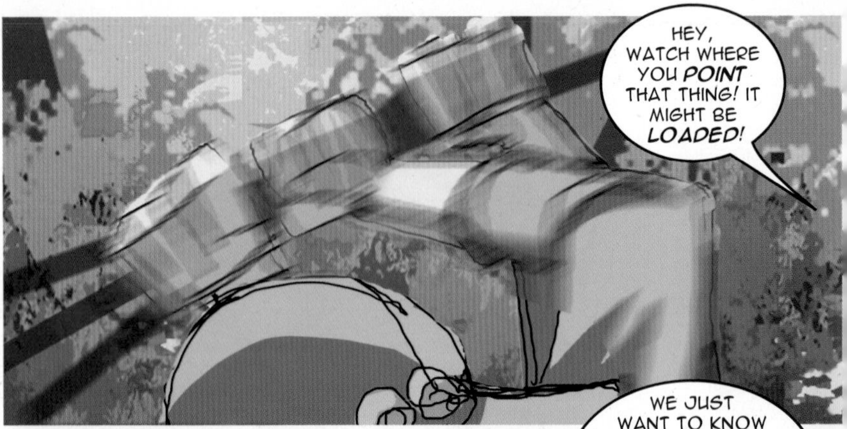
HEY, WATCH WHERE YOU POINT THAT THING! IT MIGHT BE LOADED!

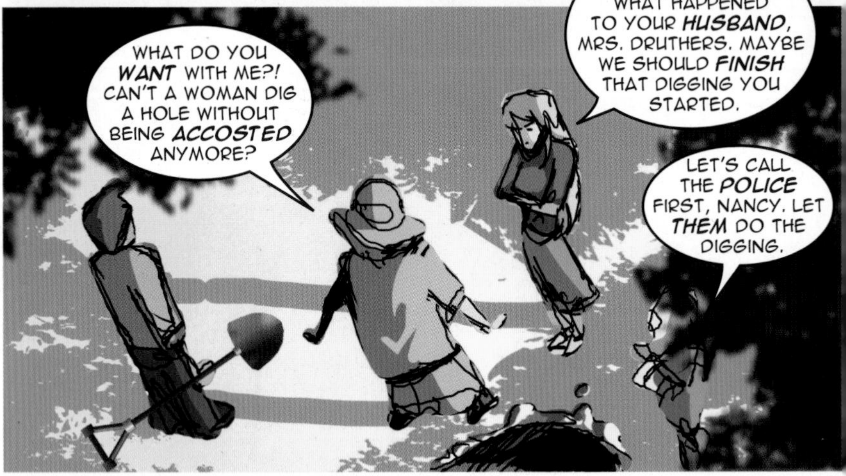
WHAT DO YOU WANT WITH ME?! CAN'T A WOMAN DIG A HOLE WITHOUT BEING ACCOSTED ANYMORE?
WE JUST WANT TO KNOW WHAT HAPPENED TO YOUR HUSBAND, MRS. DRUTHERS. MAYBE WE SHOULD FINISH THAT DIGGING YOU STARTED.
LET'S CALL THE POLICE FIRST, NANCY. LET THEM DO THE DIGGING.

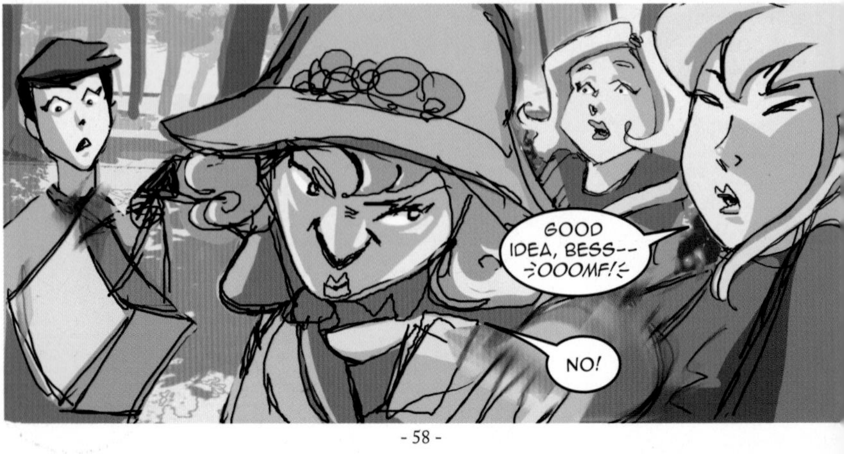
GOOD IDEA, BESS-- OOOMF!
NO!

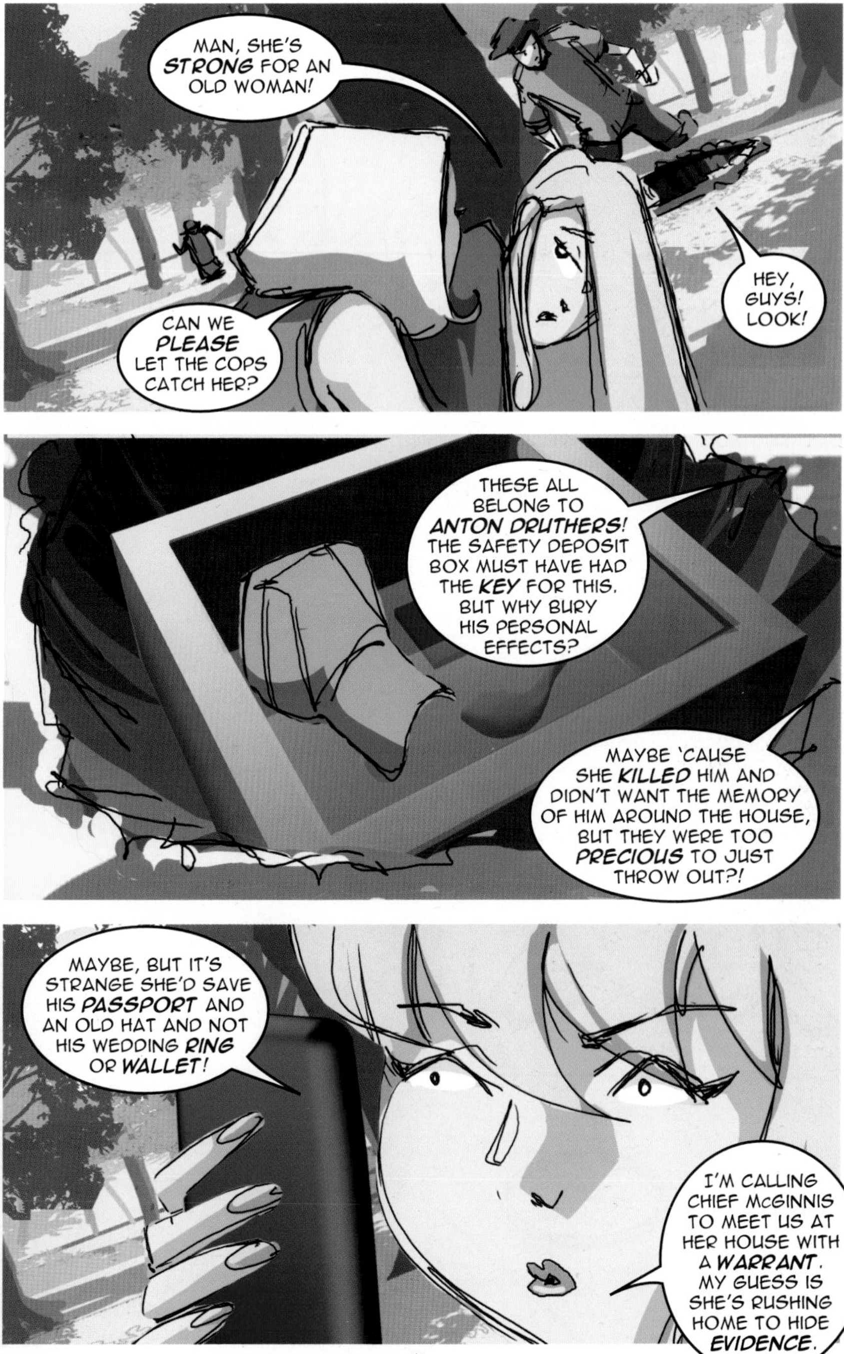
MAN, SHE'S STRONG FOR AN OLD WOMAN!
CAN WE PLEASE LET THE COPS CATCH HER?
HEY, GUYS! LOOK!
THESE ALL BELONG TO ANTON DRUTHERS! THE SAFETY DEPOSIT BOX MUST HAVE HAD THE KEY FOR THIS. BUT WHY BURY HIS PERSONAL EFFECTS?
MAYBE 'CAUSE SHE KILLED HIM AND DIDN'T WANT THE MEMORY OF HIM AROUND THE HOUSE, BUT THEY WERE TOO PRECIOUS TO JUST THROW OUT?!
MAYBE, BUT IT'S STRANGE SHE'D SAVE HIS PASSPORT AND AN OLD HAT AND NOT HIS WEDDING RING OR WALLET!
I'M CALLING CHIEF McGINNIS TO MEET US AT HER HOUSE WITH A WARRANT. MY GUESS IS SHE'S RUSHING HOME TO HIDE EVIDENCE.

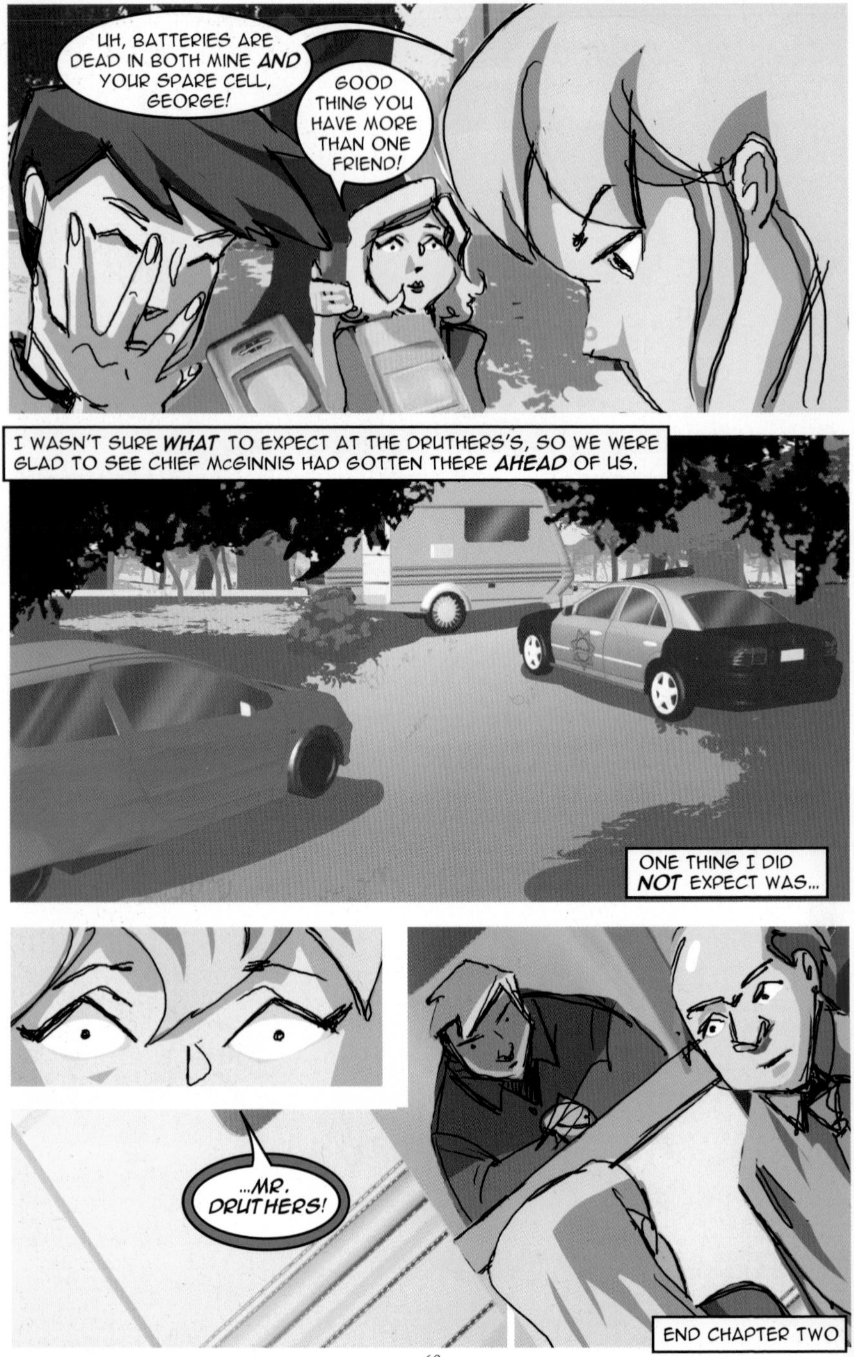
UH, BATTERIES ARE DEAD IN BOTH MINE AND YOUR SPARE CELL, GEORGE!
GOOD THING YOU HAVE MORE THAN ONE FRIEND!
I WASN'T SURE WHAT TO EXPECT AT THE DRUTHERS'S, SO WE WERE GLAD TO SEE CHIEF McGINNIS HAD GOTTEN THERE AHEAD OF US.
ONE THING I DID NOT EXPECT WAS...
...MR. DRUTHERS!
END CHAPTER TWO

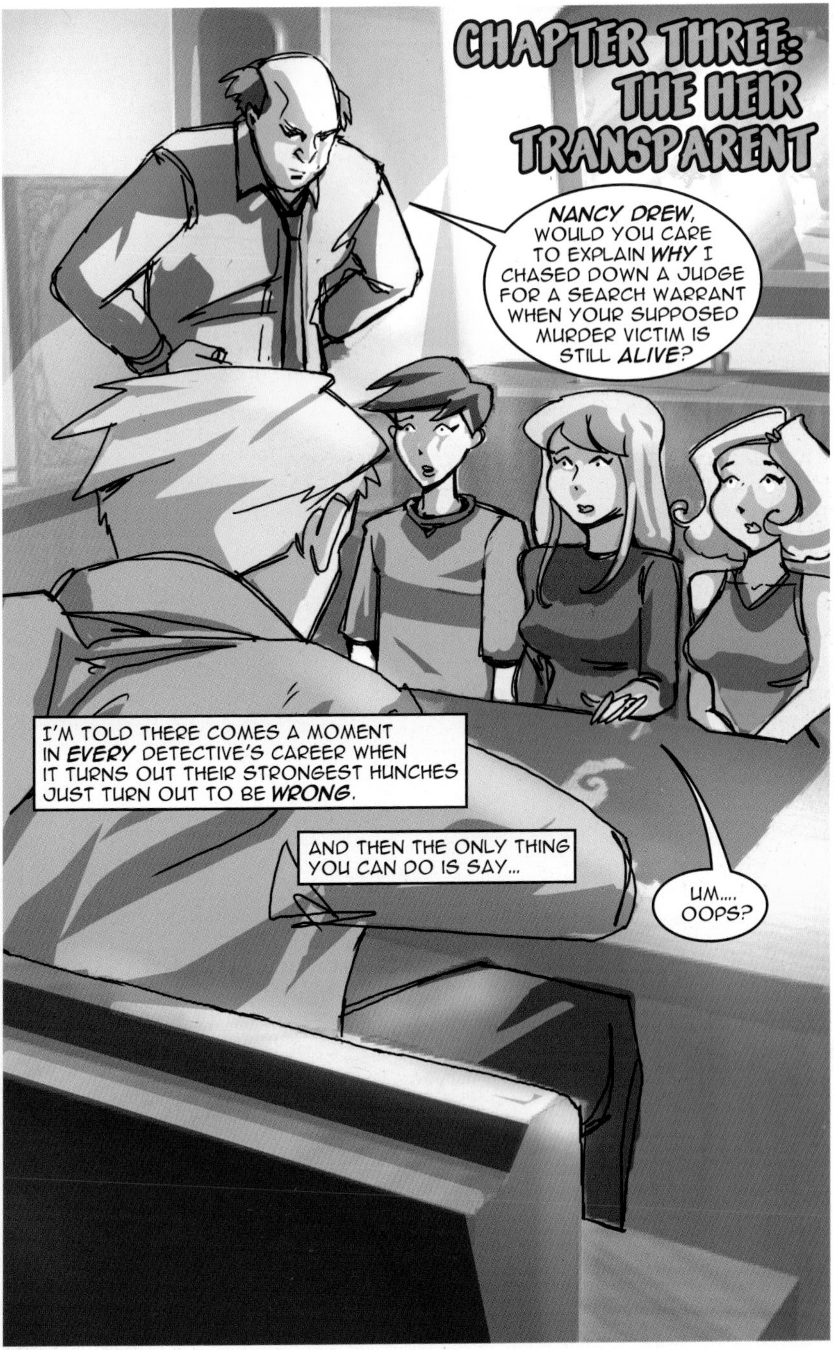
CHAPTER THREE: THE HEIR TRANSPARENT
NANCY DREW, WOULD YOU CARE TO EXPLAIN WHY I CHASED DOWN A JUDGE FOR A SEARCH WARRANT WHEN YOUR SUPPOSED MURDER VICTIM IS STILL ALIVE?
I'M TOLD THERE COMES A MOMENT IN EVERY DETECTIVE'S CAREER WHEN IT TURNS OUT THEIR STRONGEST HUNCHES JUST TURN OUT TO BE WRONG.
AND THEN THE ONLY THING YOU CAN DO IS SAY...
UM.... OOPS?

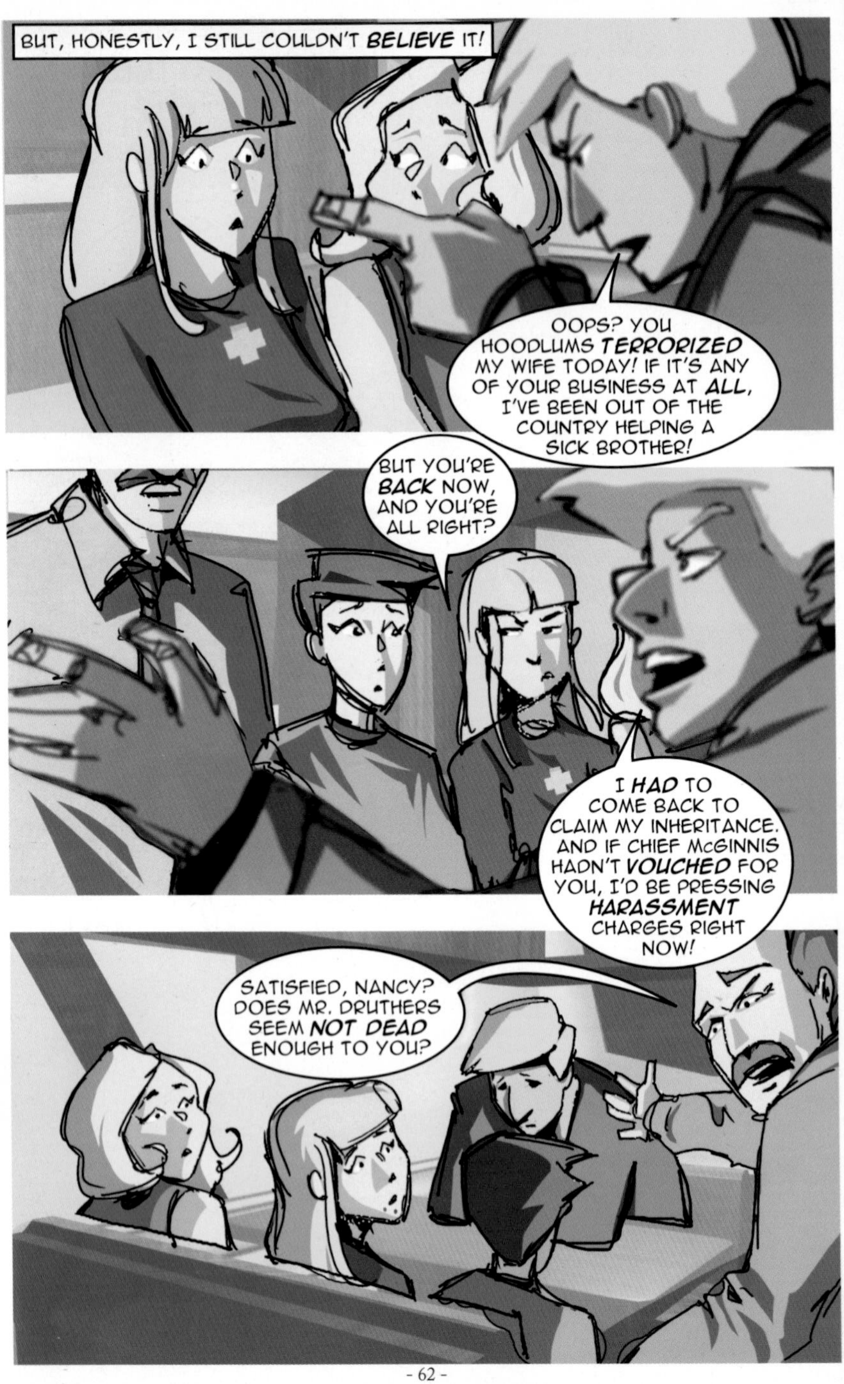
BUT, HONESTLY, I STILL COULDN'T BELIEVE IT!
OOPS? YOU HOODLUMS TERRORIZED MY WIFE TODAY! IF IT'S ANY OF YOUR BUSINESS AT ALL, I'VE BEEN OUT OF THE COUNTRY HELPING A SICK BROTHER!
BUT YOU'RE BACK NOW, AND YOU'RE ALL RIGHT?
I HAD TO COME BACK TO CLAIM MY INHERITANCE. AND IF CHIEF McGINNIS HADN'T VOUCHED FOR YOU, I'D BE PRESSING HARASSMENT CHARGES RIGHT NOW!
SATISFIED, NANCY? DOES MR. DRUTHERS SEEM NOT DEAD ENOUGH TO YOU?

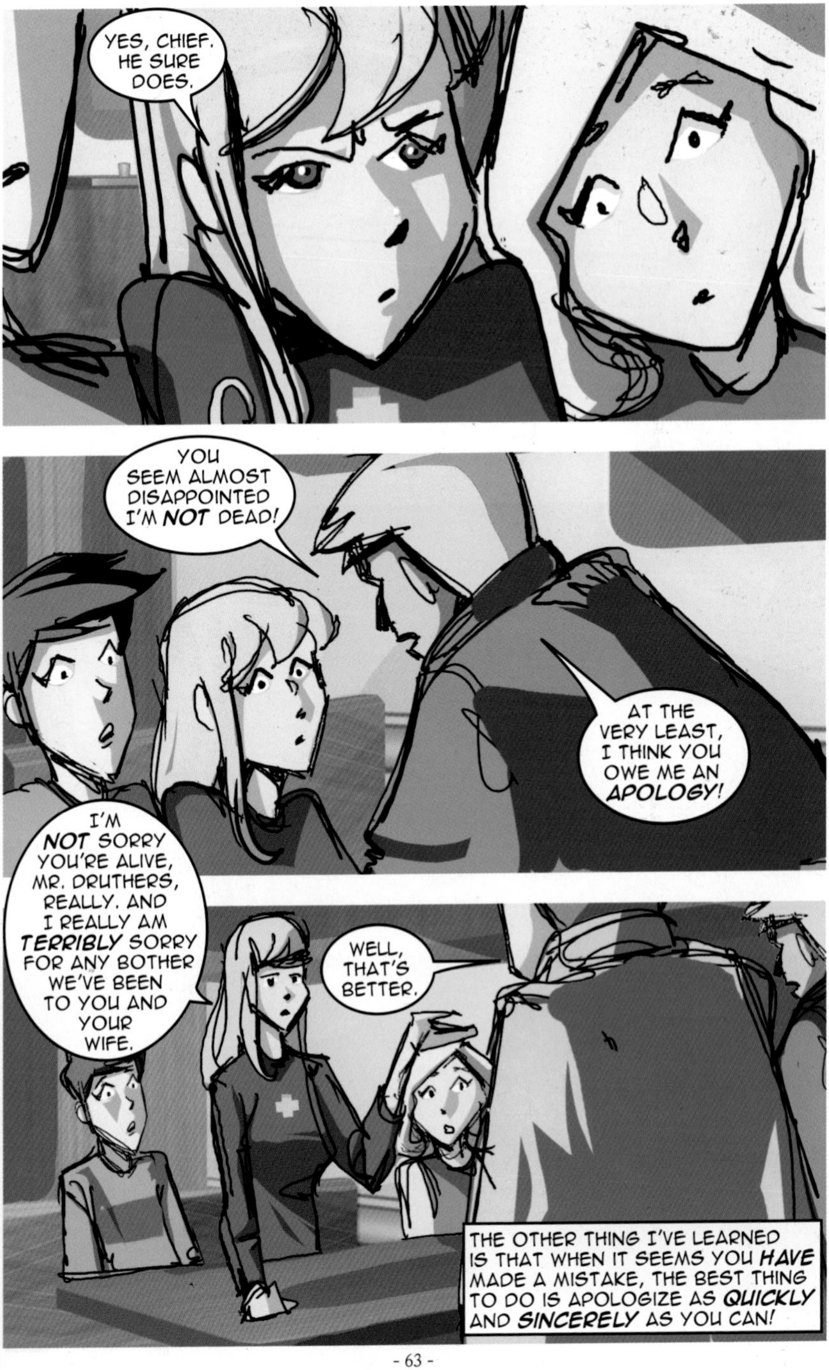
YES, CHIEF. HE SURE DOES.
YOU SEEM ALMOST DISAPPOINTED I'M **NOT** DEAD!
AT THE VERY LEAST, I THINK YOU OWE ME AN ***APOLOGY***!
I'M ***NOT*** SORRY YOU'RE ALIVE, MR. DRUTHERS, REALLY. AND I REALLY AM ***TERRIBLY*** SORRY FOR ANY BOTHER WE'VE BEEN TO YOU AND YOUR WIFE.
WELL, THAT'S BETTER.
THE OTHER THING I'VE LEARNED IS THAT WHEN IT SEEMS YOU ***HAVE*** MADE A MISTAKE, THE BEST THING TO DO IS APOLOGIZE AS ***QUICKLY*** AND ***SINCERELY*** AS YOU CAN!

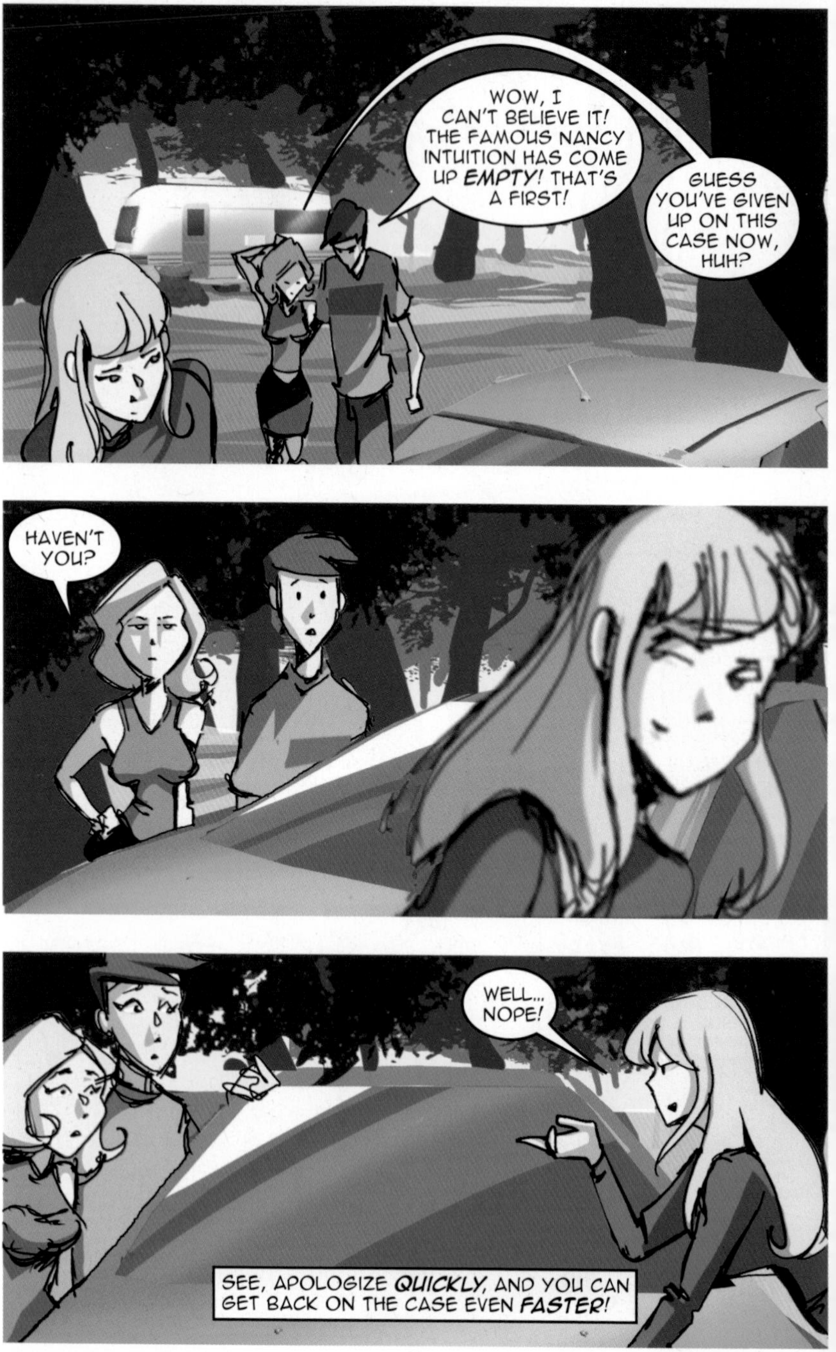
WOW, I CAN'T BELIEVE IT! THE FAMOUS NANCY INTUITION HAS COME UP *EMPTY*! THAT'S A FIRST!
GUESS YOU'VE GIVEN UP ON THIS CASE NOW, HUH?
HAVEN'T YOU?
WELL... NOPE!
SEE, APOLOGIZE *QUICKLY*, AND YOU CAN GET BACK ON THE CASE EVEN *FASTER*!

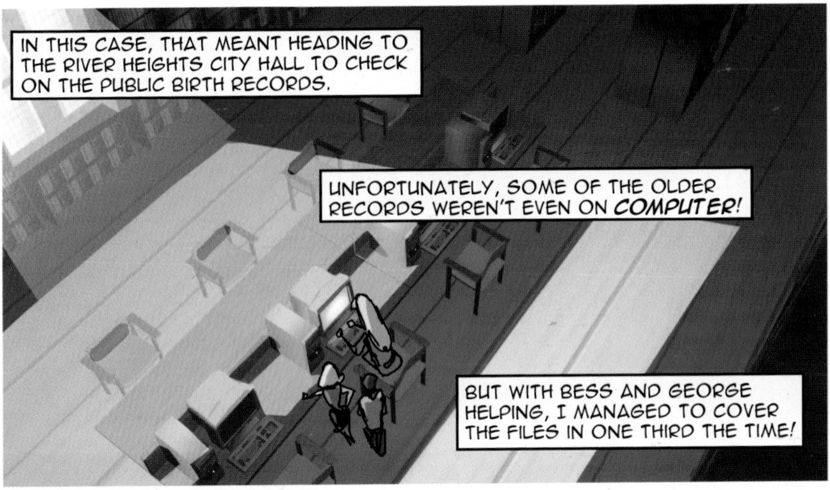
IN THIS CASE, THAT MEANT HEADING TO THE RIVER HEIGHTS CITY HALL TO CHECK ON THE PUBLIC BIRTH RECORDS.
UNFORTUNATELY, SOME OF THE OLDER RECORDS WEREN'T EVEN ON *COMPUTER*!
BUT WITH BESS AND GEORGE HELPING, I MANAGED TO COVER THE FILES IN ONE THIRD THE TIME!

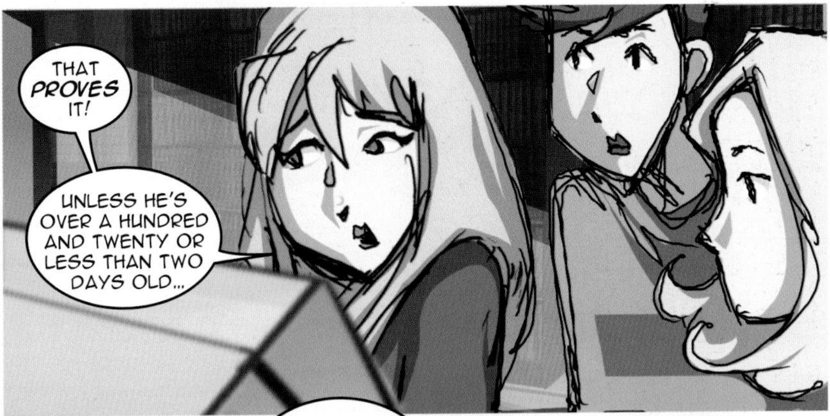
THAT *PROVES* IT!
UNLESS HE'S OVER A HUNDRED AND TWENTY OR LESS THAN TWO DAYS OLD...

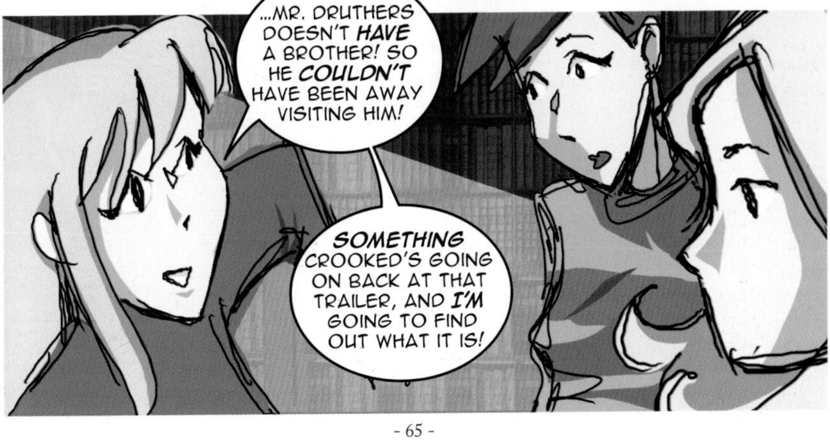
...MR. DRUTHERS DOESN'T *HAVE* A BROTHER! SO HE *COULDN'T* HAVE BEEN AWAY VISITING HIM!
SOMETHING CROOKED'S GOING ON BACK AT THAT TRAILER, AND *I'M* GOING TO FIND OUT WHAT IT IS!

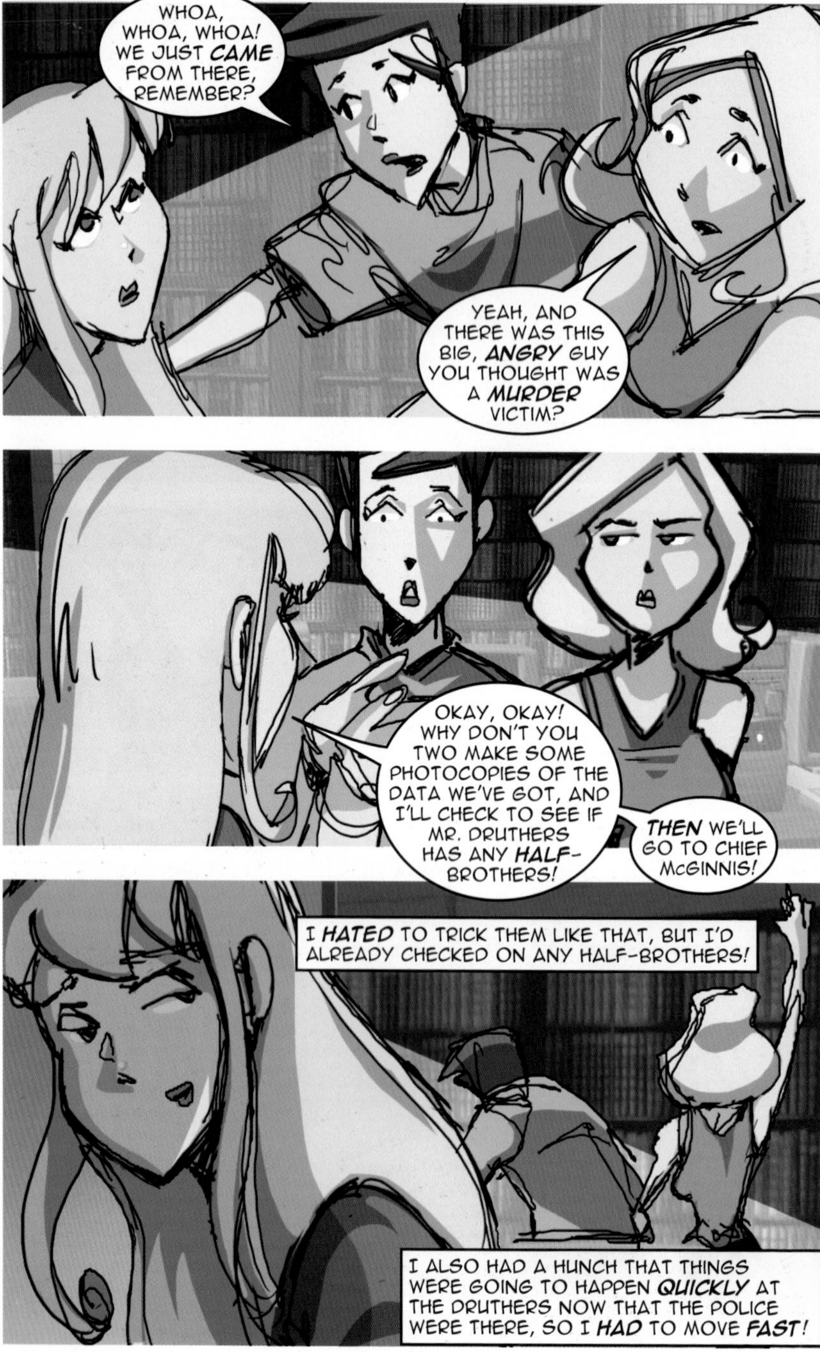
WHOA, WHOA, WHOA! WE JUST CAME FROM THERE, REMEMBER?
YEAH, AND THERE WAS THIS BIG, ANGRY GUY YOU THOUGHT WAS A MURDER VICTIM?
OKAY, OKAY! WHY DON'T YOU TWO MAKE SOME PHOTOCOPIES OF THE DATA WE'VE GOT, AND I'LL CHECK TO SEE IF MR. DRUTHERS HAS ANY HALF-BROTHERS!
THEN WE'LL GO TO CHIEF McGINNIS!
I HATED TO TRICK THEM LIKE THAT, BUT I'D ALREADY CHECKED ON ANY HALF-BROTHERS!
I ALSO HAD A HUNCH THAT THINGS WERE GOING TO HAPPEN QUICKLY AT THE DRUTHERS NOW THAT THE POLICE WERE THERE, SO I HAD TO MOVE FAST!

I PARKED MY CAR A HALF MILE AWAY, AND *HID* IT UNDER SOME BRUSH.

THE PLACE SEEMED EMPTY WHEN I ARRIVED, SO IT WAS A *PERFECT* CHANCE TO SEARCH FOR CLUES.

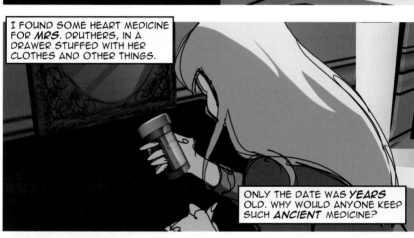

I FOUND SOME HEART MEDICINE FOR *MRS.* DRUTHERS, IN A DRAWER STUFFED WITH HER CLOTHES AND OTHER THINGS.

ONLY THE DATE WAS *YEARS* OLD. WHY WOULD ANYONE KEEP SUCH *ANCIENT* MEDICINE?

THEN, WHEN I SAW MY SPIDER-BITTEN NOSE IN A MIRROR, THE ONE THAT LOOKED JUST LIKE A *PIMPLE*, I REALIZED *EXACTLY* WHAT HAD BEEN GOING ON.

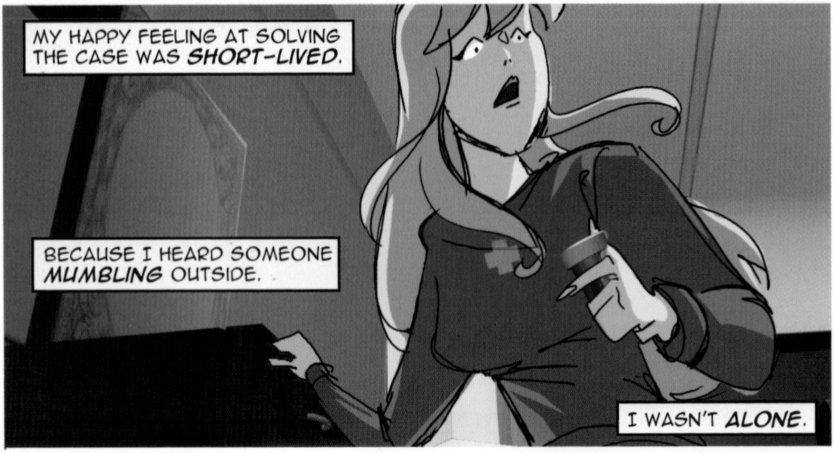
MY HAPPY FEELING AT SOLVING THE CASE WAS SHORT-LIVED.
BECAUSE I HEARD SOMEONE MUMBLING OUTSIDE.
I WASN'T ALONE.

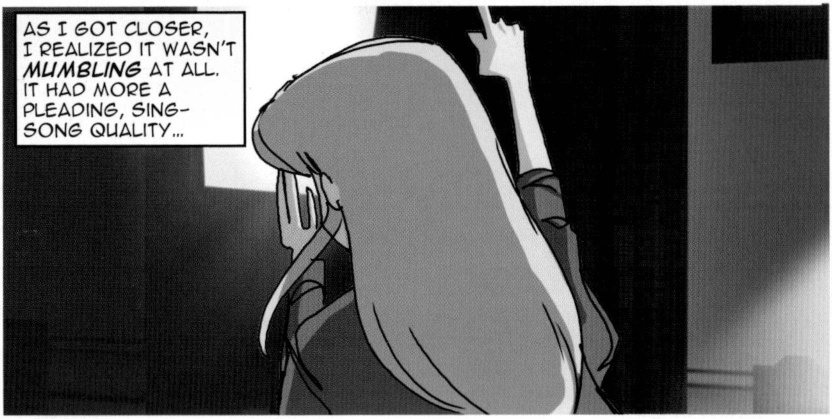
AS I GOT CLOSER, I REALIZED IT WASN'T MUMBLING AT ALL. IT HAD MORE A PLEADING, SING-SONG QUALITY...

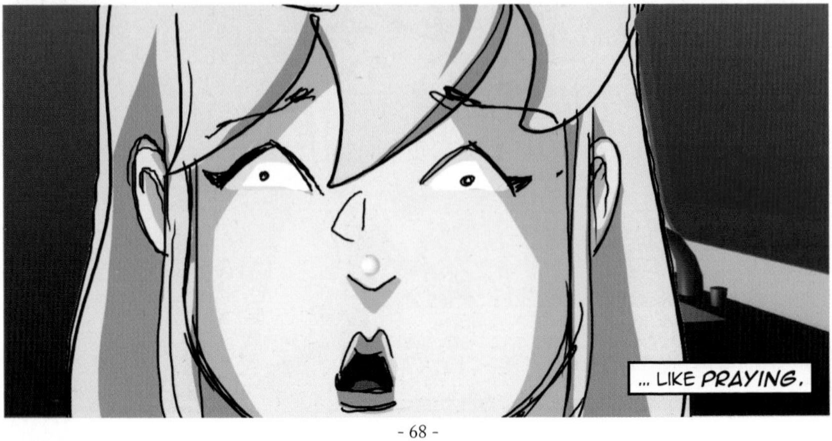
... LIKE PRAYING.

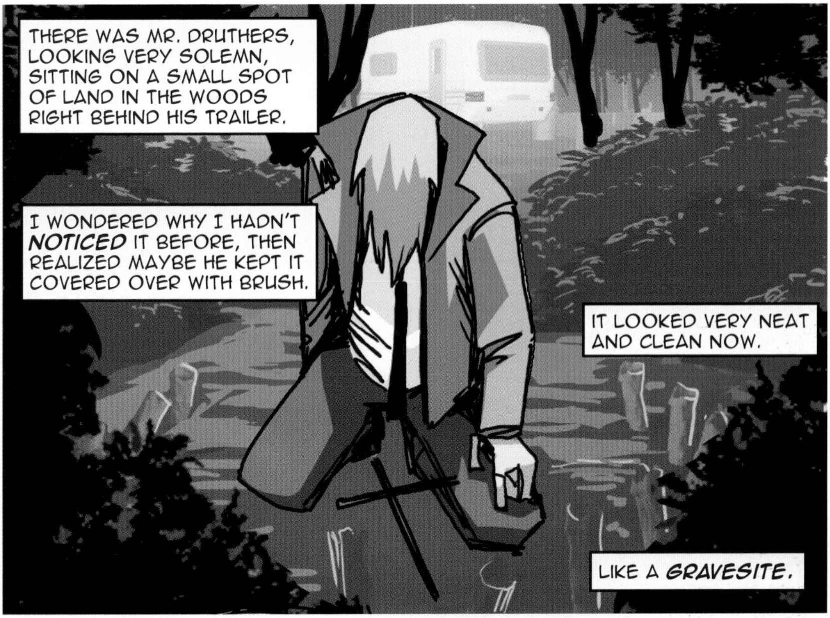
THERE WAS MR. DRUTHERS, LOOKING VERY SOLEMN, SITTING ON A SMALL SPOT OF LAND IN THE WOODS RIGHT BEHIND HIS TRAILER.
I WONDERED WHY I HADN'T NOTICED IT BEFORE, THEN REALIZED MAYBE HE KEPT IT COVERED OVER WITH BRUSH.
IT LOOKED VERY NEAT AND CLEAN NOW.
LIKE A GRAVESITE.

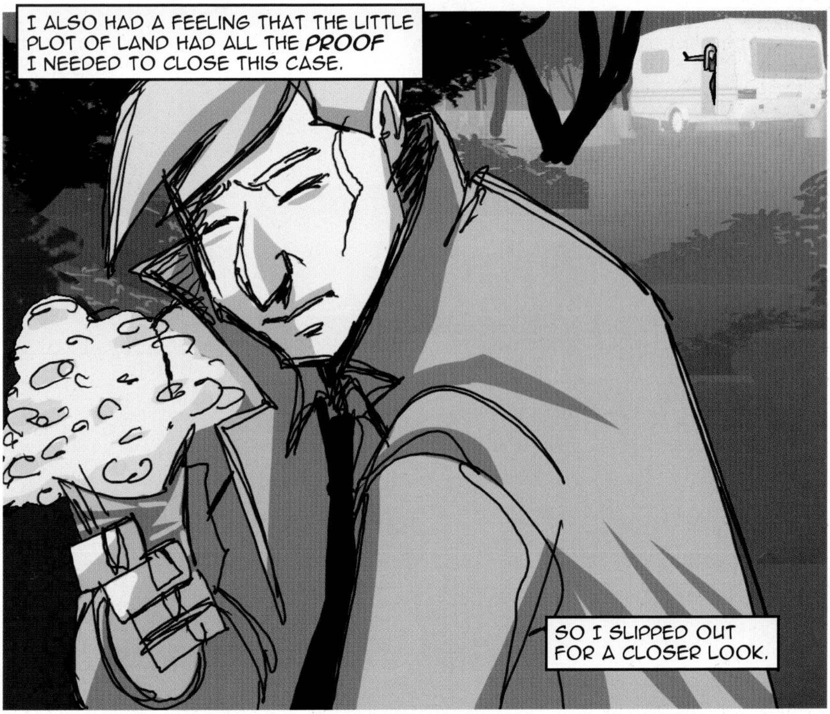
I ALSO HAD A FEELING THAT THE LITTLE PLOT OF LAND HAD ALL THE PROOF I NEEDED TO CLOSE THIS CASE.
SO I SLIPPED OUT FOR A CLOSER LOOK.

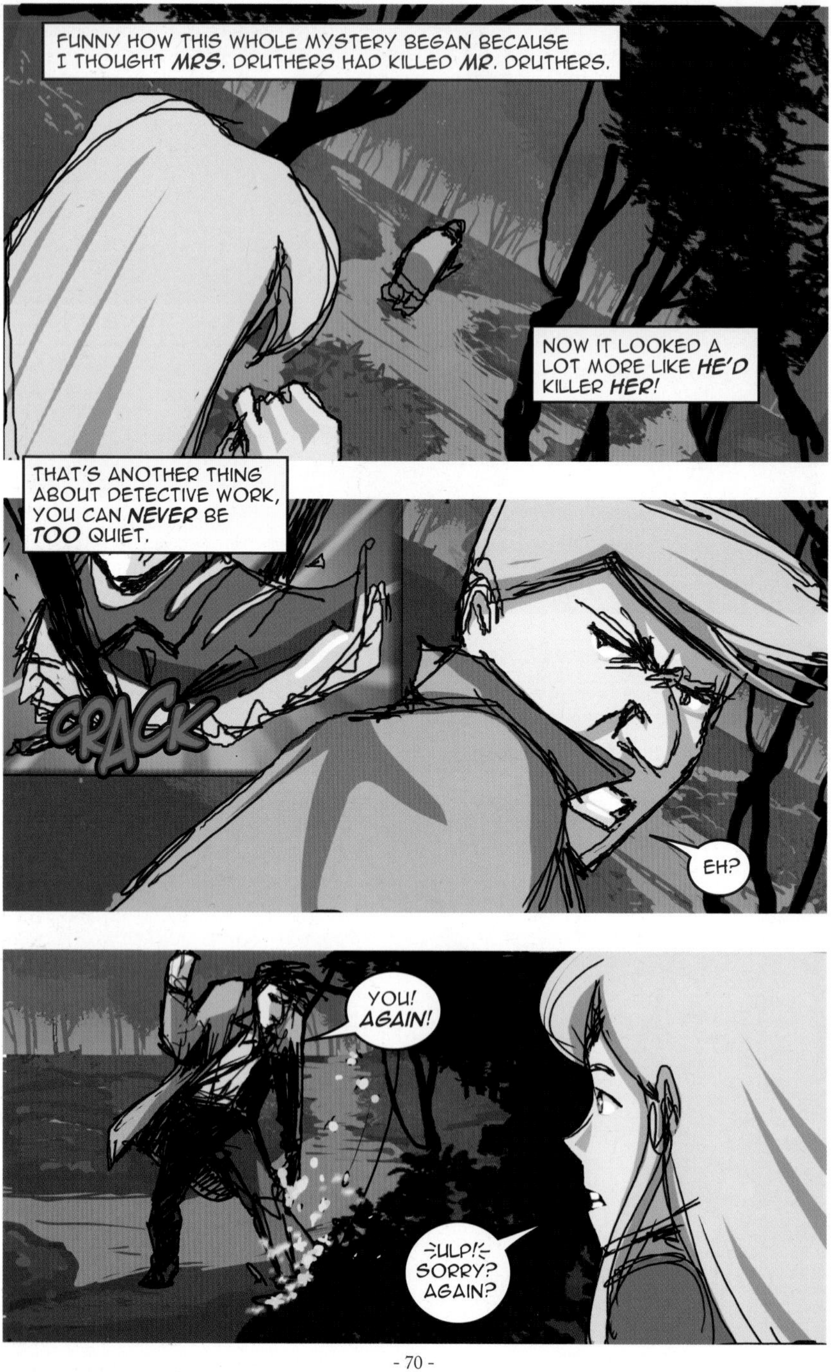
FUNNY HOW THIS WHOLE MYSTERY BEGAN BECAUSE I THOUGHT *MRS.* DRUTHERS HAD KILLED *MR.* DRUTHERS.
NOW IT LOOKED A LOT MORE LIKE *HE'D* KILLER *HER!*
THAT'S ANOTHER THING ABOUT DETECTIVE WORK, YOU CAN *NEVER* BE *TOO* QUIET.
CRACK
EH?
YOU! *AGAIN!*
ULP! SORRY? AGAIN?

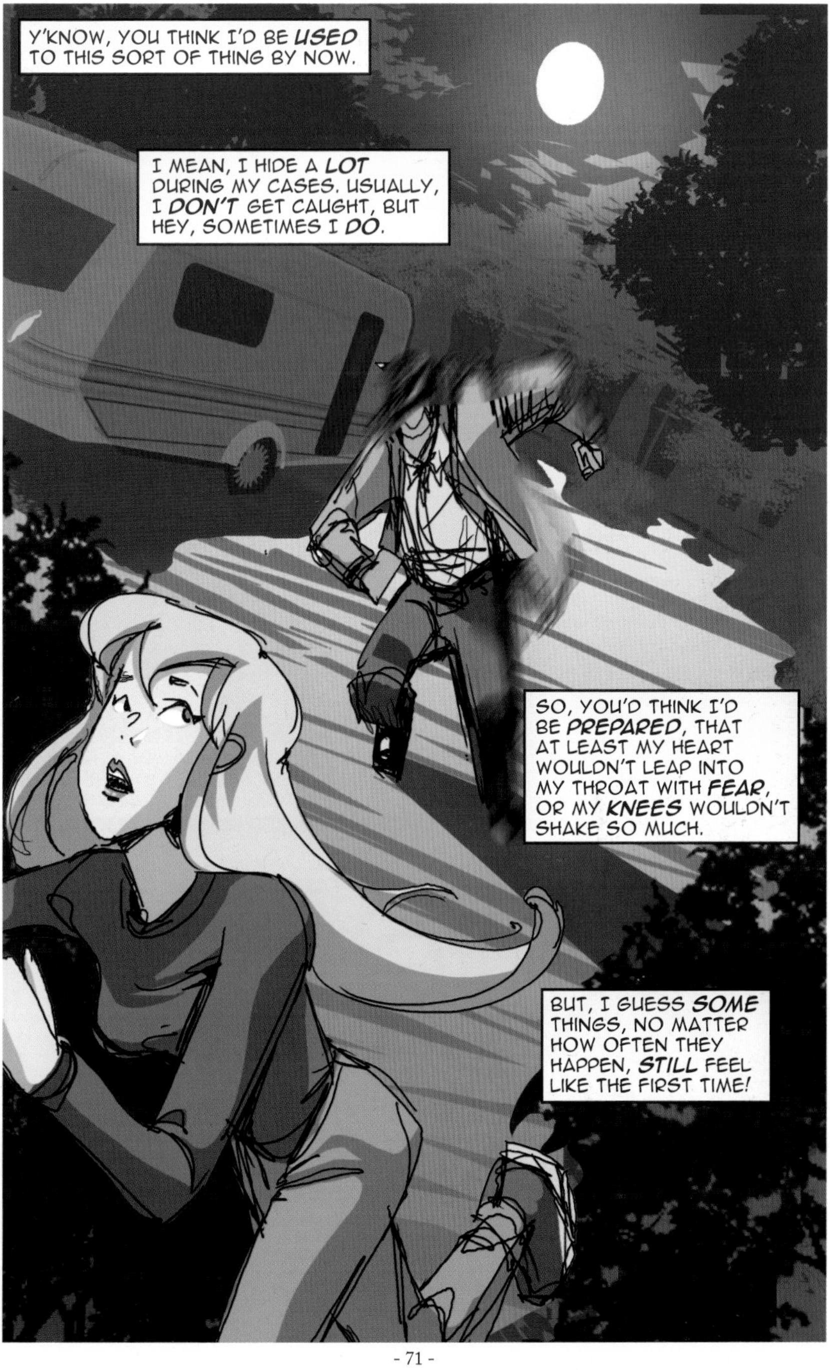
Y'KNOW, YOU THINK I'D BE USED TO THIS SORT OF THING BY NOW.
I MEAN, I HIDE A LOT DURING MY CASES. USUALLY, I DON'T GET CAUGHT, BUT HEY, SOMETIMES I DO.
SO, YOU'D THINK I'D BE PREPARED, THAT AT LEAST MY HEART WOULDN'T LEAP INTO MY THROAT WITH FEAR, OR MY KNEES WOULDN'T SHAKE SO MUCH.
BUT, I GUESS SOME THINGS, NO MATTER HOW OFTEN THEY HAPPEN, STILL FEEL LIKE THE FIRST TIME!

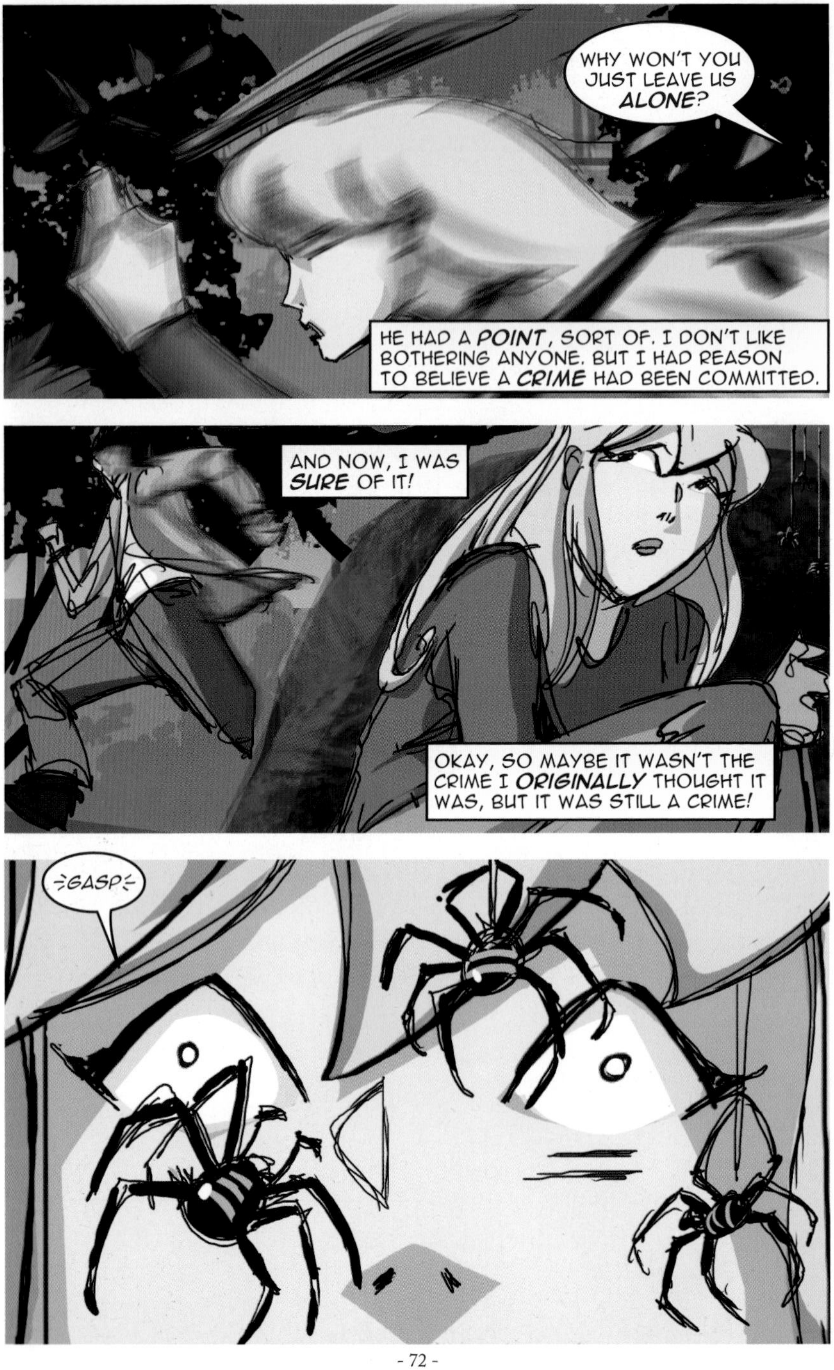
WHY WON'T YOU JUST LEAVE US ALONE?
HE HAD A POINT, SORT OF. I DON'T LIKE BOTHERING ANYONE. BUT I HAD REASON TO BELIEVE A CRIME HAD BEEN COMMITTED.
AND NOW, I WAS SURE OF IT!
OKAY, SO MAYBE IT WASN'T THE CRIME I ORIGINALLY THOUGHT IT WAS, BUT IT WAS STILL A CRIME!
GASP

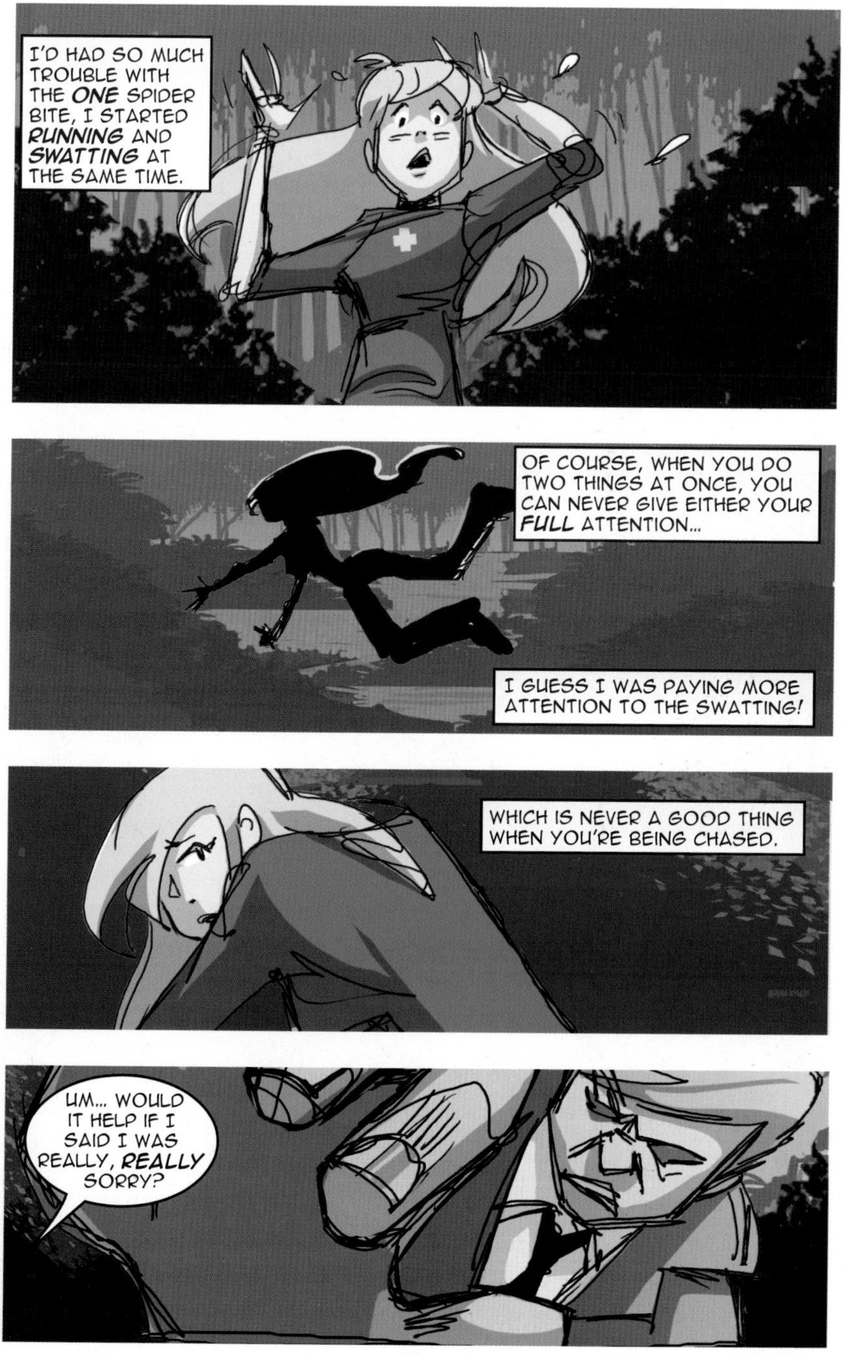
I'D HAD SO MUCH TROUBLE WITH THE ONE SPIDER BITE, I STARTED RUNNING AND SWATTING AT THE SAME TIME.
OF COURSE, WHEN YOU DO TWO THINGS AT ONCE, YOU CAN NEVER GIVE EITHER YOUR FULL ATTENTION...
I GUESS I WAS PAYING MORE ATTENTION TO THE SWATTING!
WHICH IS NEVER A GOOD THING WHEN YOU'RE BEING CHASED.
UM... WOULD IT HELP IF I SAID I WAS REALLY, REALLY SORRY?

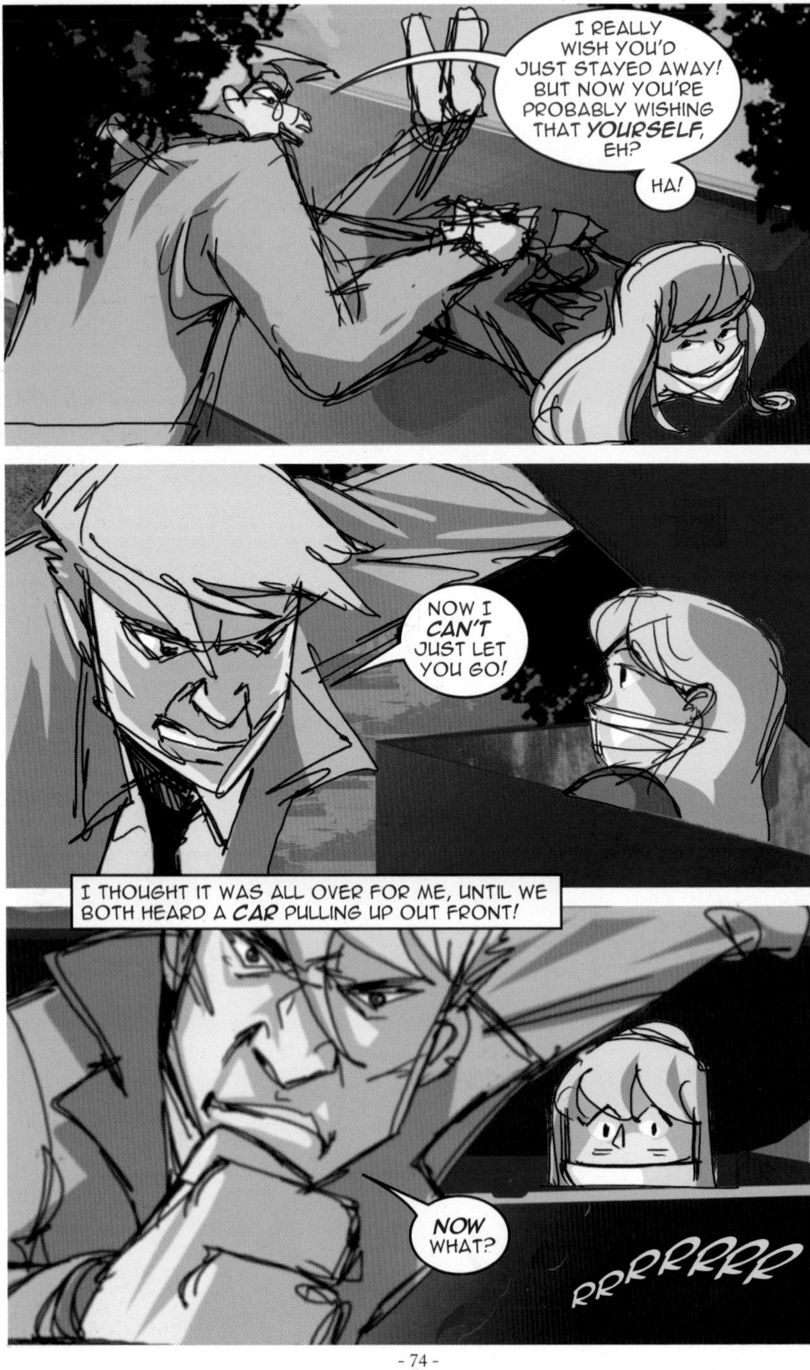
I REALLY WISH YOU'D JUST STAYED AWAY! BUT NOW YOU'RE PROBABLY WISHING THAT YOURSELF, EH?
HA!
NOW I CAN'T JUST LET YOU GO!
I THOUGHT IT WAS ALL OVER FOR ME, UNTIL WE BOTH HEARD A CAR PULLING UP OUT FRONT!
NOW WHAT?
RRRRRRRR

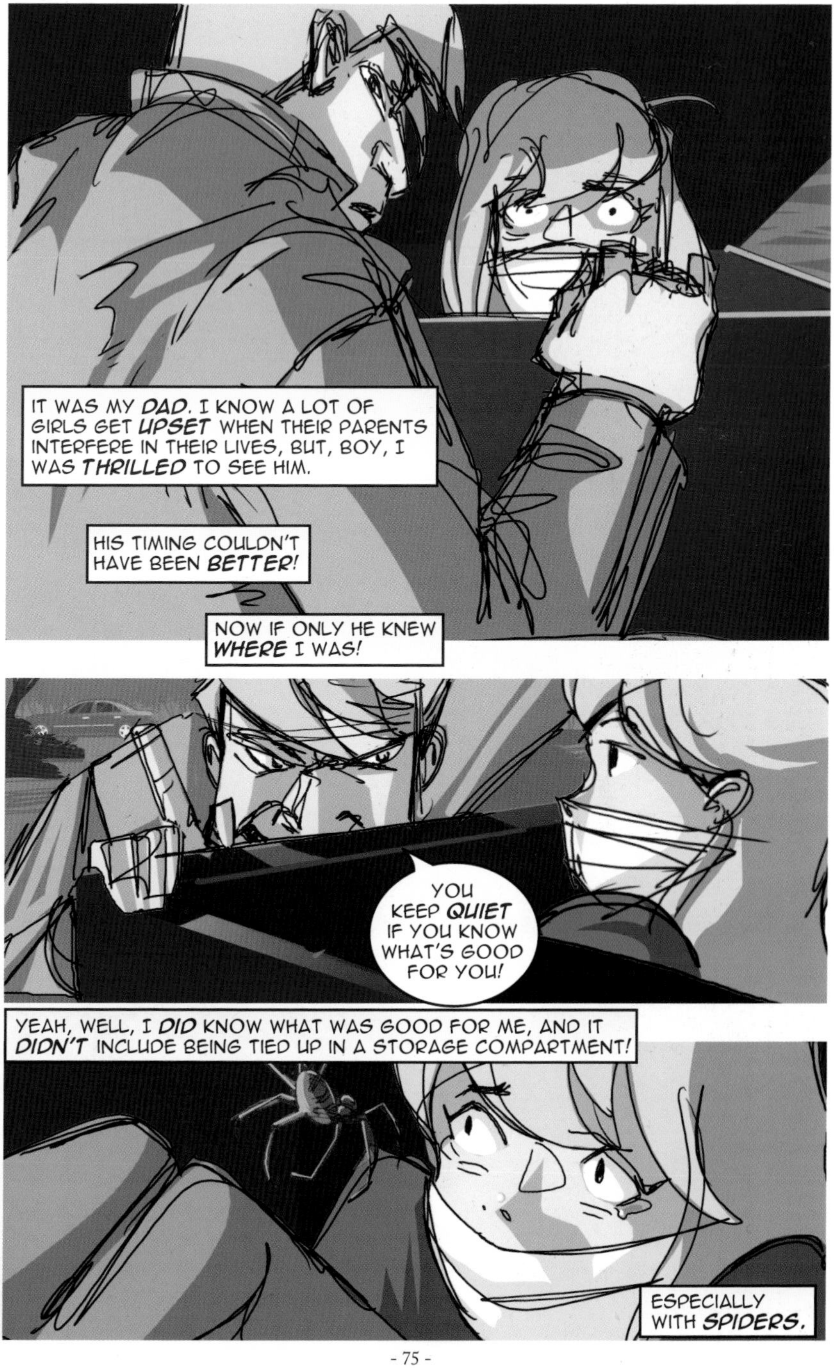
IT WAS MY DAD. I KNOW A LOT OF GIRLS GET UPSET WHEN THEIR PARENTS INTERFERE IN THEIR LIVES, BUT, BOY, I WAS THRILLED TO SEE HIM.
HIS TIMING COULDN'T HAVE BEEN BETTER!
NOW IF ONLY HE KNEW WHERE I WAS!
YOU KEEP QUIET IF YOU KNOW WHAT'S GOOD FOR YOU!
YEAH, WELL, I DID KNOW WHAT WAS GOOD FOR ME, AND IT DIDN'T INCLUDE BEING TIED UP IN A STORAGE COMPARTMENT!
ESPECIALLY WITH SPIDERS.

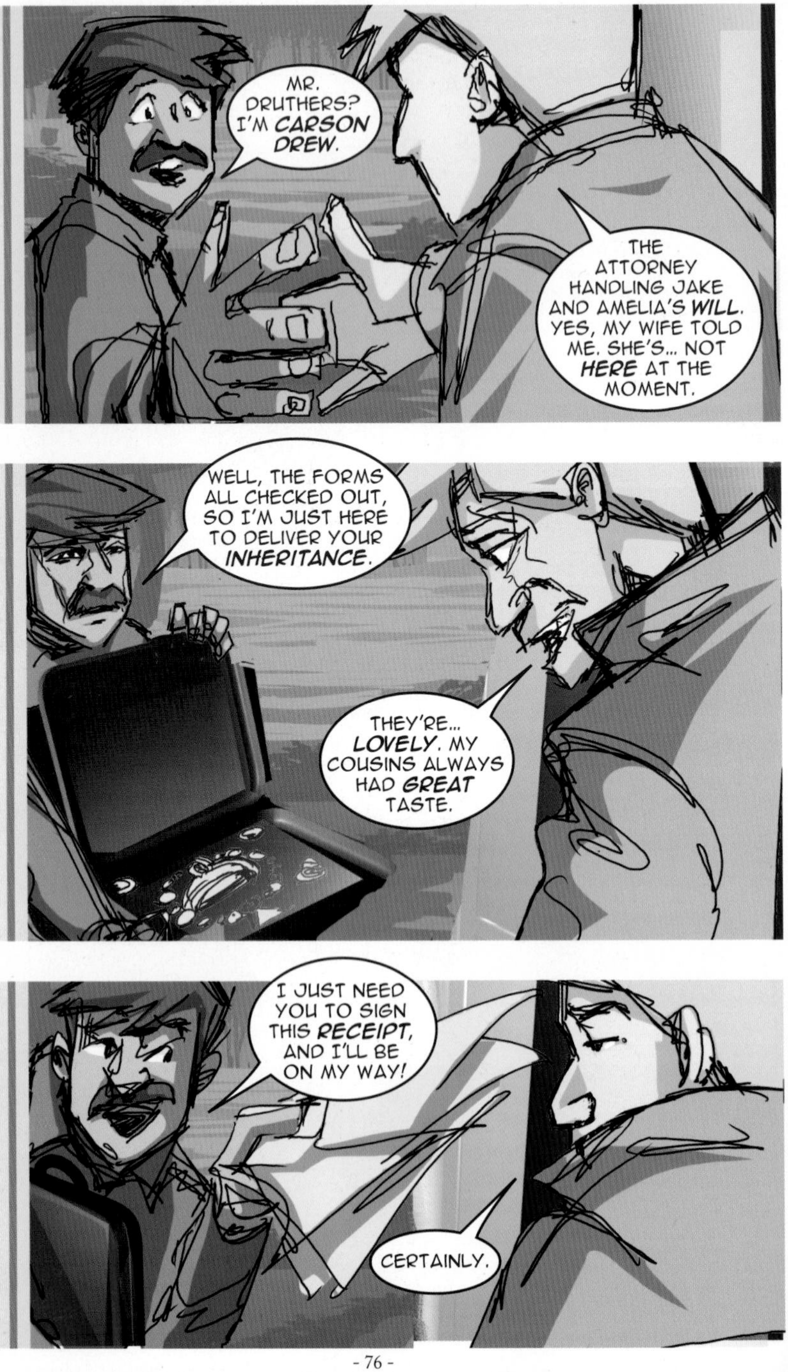
MR. DRUTHERS? I'M CARSON DREW.
THE ATTORNEY HANDLING JAKE AND AMELIA'S WILL. YES, MY WIFE TOLD ME. SHE'S... NOT HERE AT THE MOMENT.
WELL, THE FORMS ALL CHECKED OUT, SO I'M JUST HERE TO DELIVER YOUR INHERITANCE.
THEY'RE... LOVELY. MY COUSINS ALWAYS HAD GREAT TASTE.
I JUST NEED YOU TO SIGN THIS RECEIPT, AND I'LL BE ON MY WAY!
CERTAINLY.

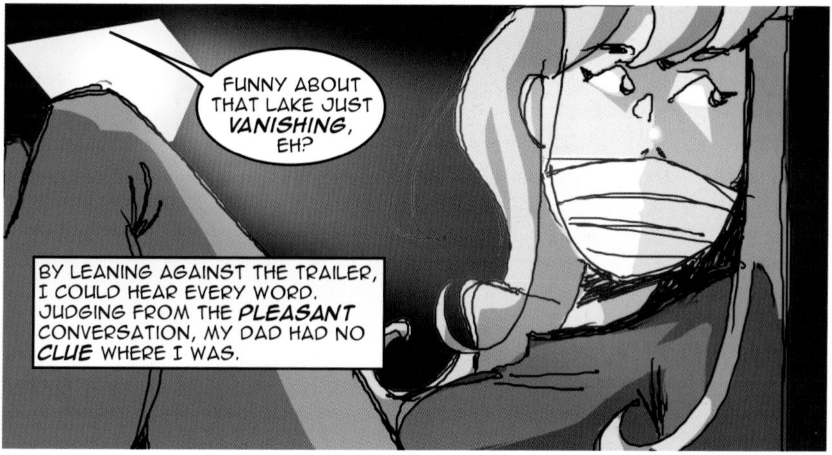
FUNNY ABOUT THAT LAKE JUST VANISHING, EH?
BY LEANING AGAINST THE TRAILER, I COULD HEAR EVERY WORD. JUDGING FROM THE PLEASANT CONVERSATION, MY DAD HAD NO CLUE WHERE I WAS.

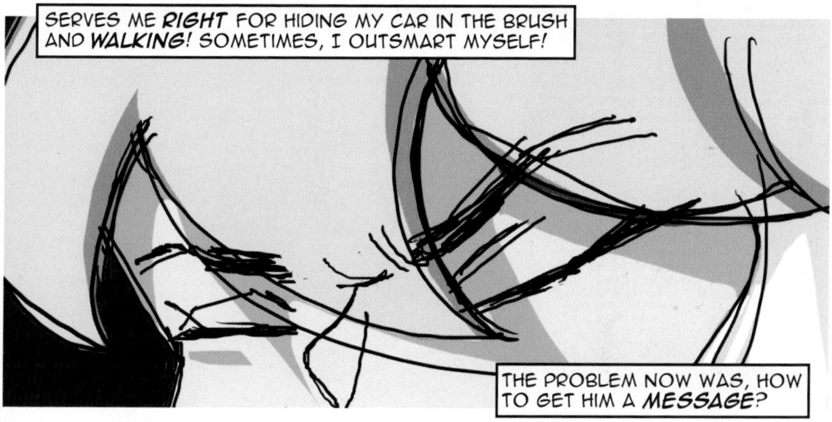
SERVES ME RIGHT FOR HIDING MY CAR IN THE BRUSH AND WALKING! SOMETIMES, I OUTSMART MYSELF!
THE PROBLEM NOW WAS, HOW TO GET HIM A MESSAGE?

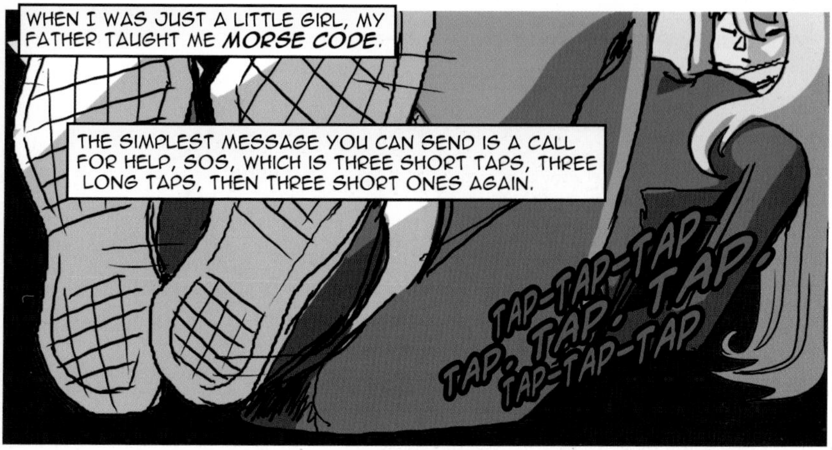
WHEN I WAS JUST A LITTLE GIRL, MY FATHER TAUGHT ME MORSE CODE.
THE SIMPLEST MESSAGE YOU CAN SEND IS A CALL FOR HELP, SOS, WHICH IS THREE SHORT TAPS, THREE LONG TAPS, THEN THREE SHORT ONES AGAIN.
TAP-TAP-TAP
TAP. TAP. TAP.
TAP-TAP-TAP

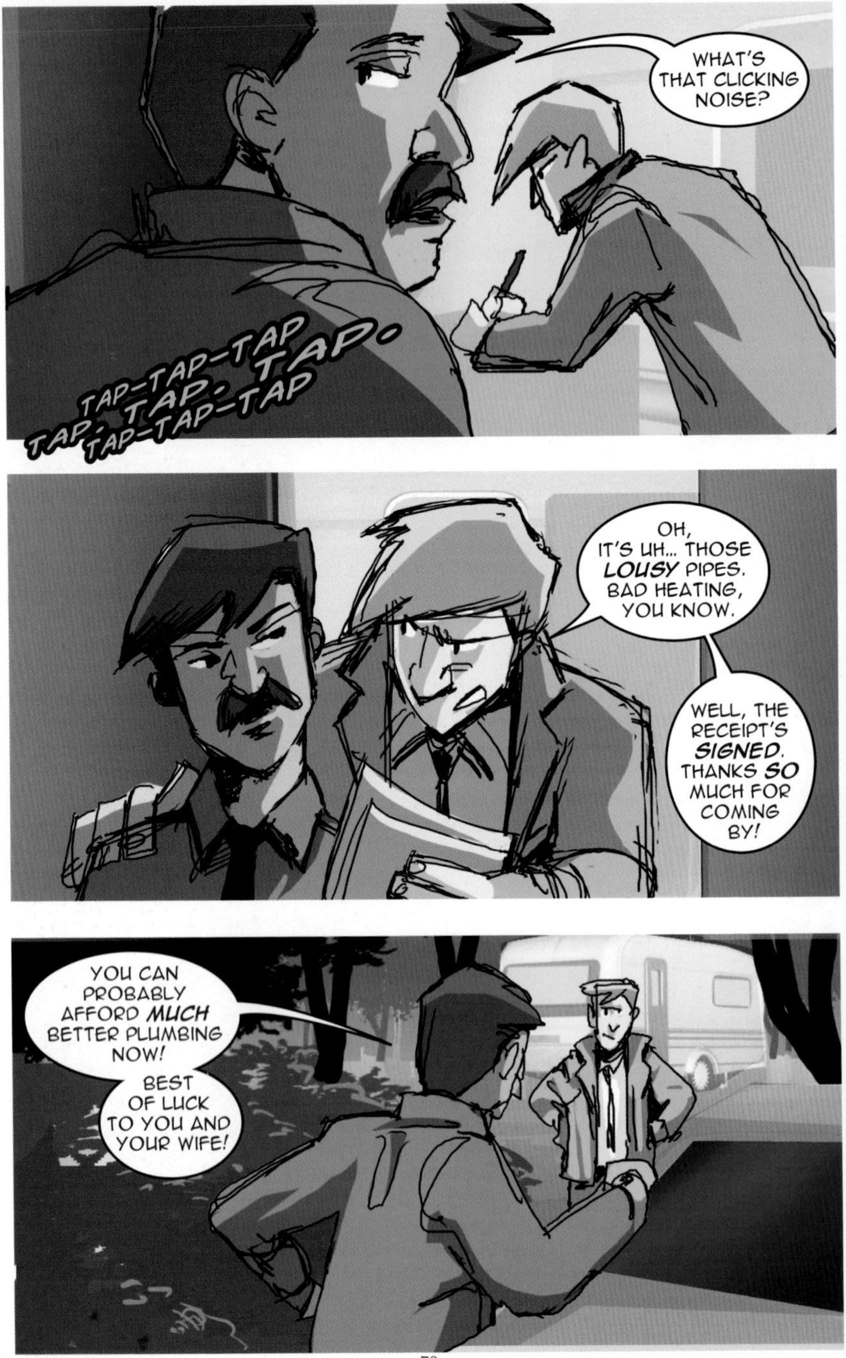
WHAT'S THAT CLICKING NOISE?
TAP-TAP-TAP TAP- TAP- TAP- TAP-TAP-TAP
OH, IT'S UH... THOSE LOUSY PIPES. BAD HEATING, YOU KNOW.
WELL, THE RECEIPT'S SIGNED. THANKS SO MUCH FOR COMING BY!
YOU CAN PROBABLY AFFORD MUCH BETTER PLUMBING NOW!
BEST OF LUCK TO YOU AND YOUR WIFE!

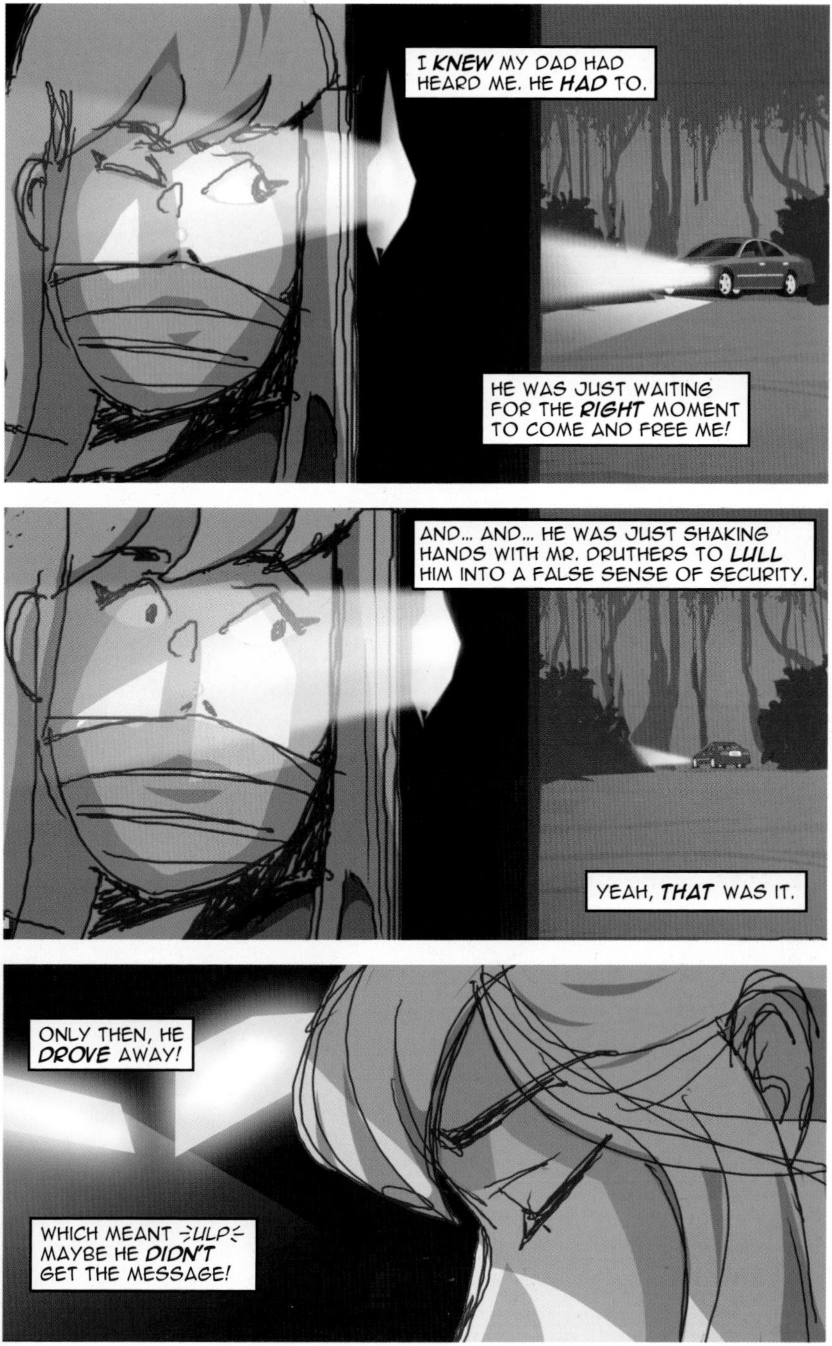
I KNEW MY DAD HAD HEARD ME. HE HAD TO.
HE WAS JUST WAITING FOR THE RIGHT MOMENT TO COME AND FREE ME!
AND... AND... HE WAS JUST SHAKING HANDS WITH MR. DRUTHERS TO LULL HIM INTO A FALSE SENSE OF SECURITY.
YEAH, THAT WAS IT.
ONLY THEN, HE DROVE AWAY!
WHICH MEANT ⋞ULP⋟ MAYBE HE DIDN'T GET THE MESSAGE!

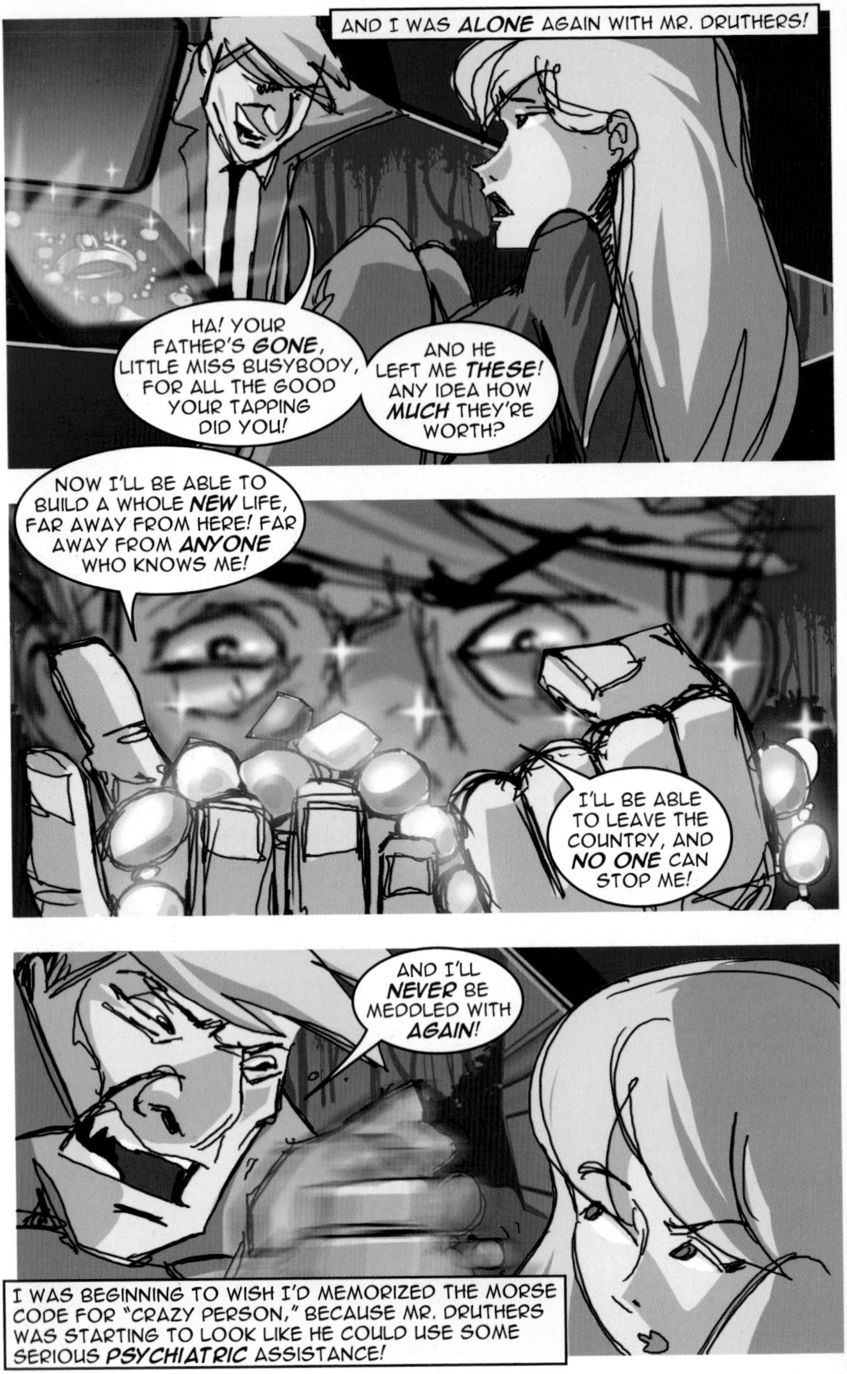
AND I WAS ALONE AGAIN WITH MR. DRUTHERS!
HA! YOUR FATHER'S GONE, LITTLE MISS BUSYBODY, FOR ALL THE GOOD YOUR TAPPING DID YOU!
AND HE LEFT ME THESE! ANY IDEA HOW MUCH THEY'RE WORTH?
NOW I'LL BE ABLE TO BUILD A WHOLE NEW LIFE, FAR AWAY FROM HERE! FAR AWAY FROM ANYONE WHO KNOWS ME!
I'LL BE ABLE TO LEAVE THE COUNTRY, AND NO ONE CAN STOP ME!
AND I'LL NEVER BE MEDDLED WITH AGAIN!
I WAS BEGINNING TO WISH I'D MEMORIZED THE MORSE CODE FOR "CRAZY PERSON," BECAUSE MR. DRUTHERS WAS STARTING TO LOOK LIKE HE COULD USE SOME SERIOUS PSYCHIATRIC ASSISTANCE!

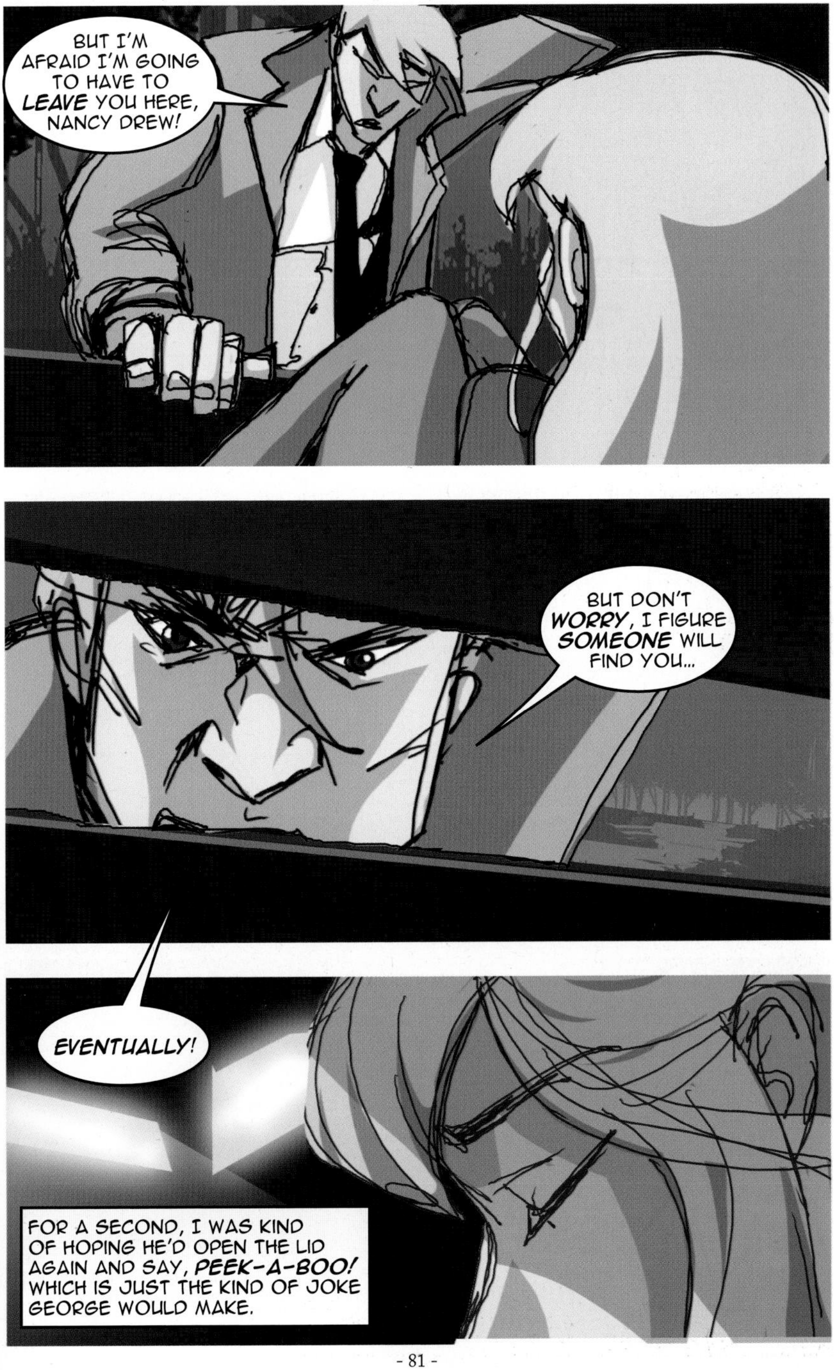
BUT I'M AFRAID I'M GOING TO HAVE TO LEAVE YOU HERE, NANCY DREW!
BUT DON'T WORRY, I FIGURE SOMEONE WILL FIND YOU...
EVENTUALLY!
FOR A SECOND, I WAS KIND OF HOPING HE'D OPEN THE LID AGAIN AND SAY, PEEK-A-BOO! WHICH IS JUST THE KIND OF JOKE GEORGE WOULD MAKE.

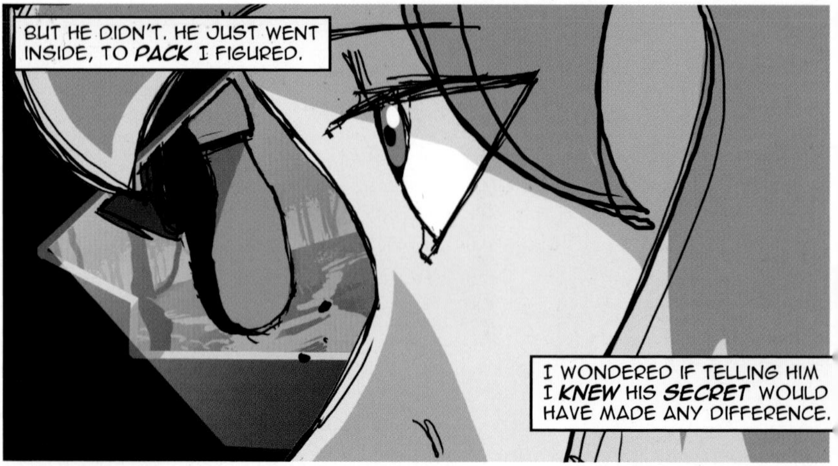
BUT HE DIDN'T. HE JUST WENT INSIDE, TO PACK I FIGURED.
I WONDERED IF TELLING HIM I KNEW HIS SECRET WOULD HAVE MADE ANY DIFFERENCE.

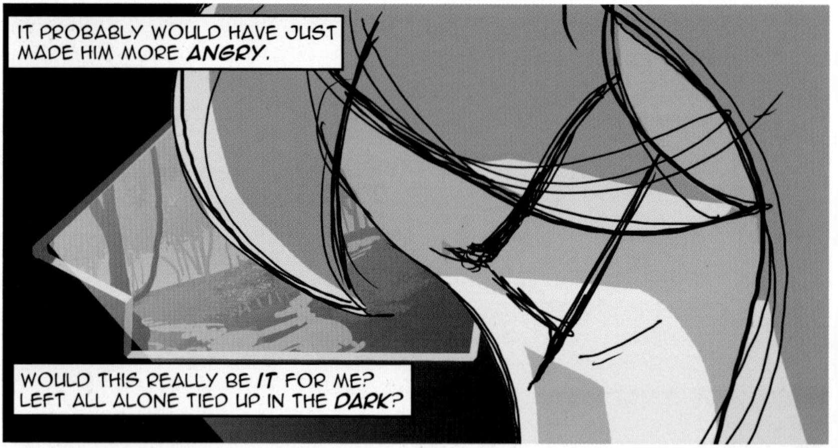
IT PROBABLY WOULD HAVE JUST MADE HIM MORE ANGRY.
WOULD THIS REALLY BE IT FOR ME? LEFT ALL ALONE TIED UP IN THE DARK?

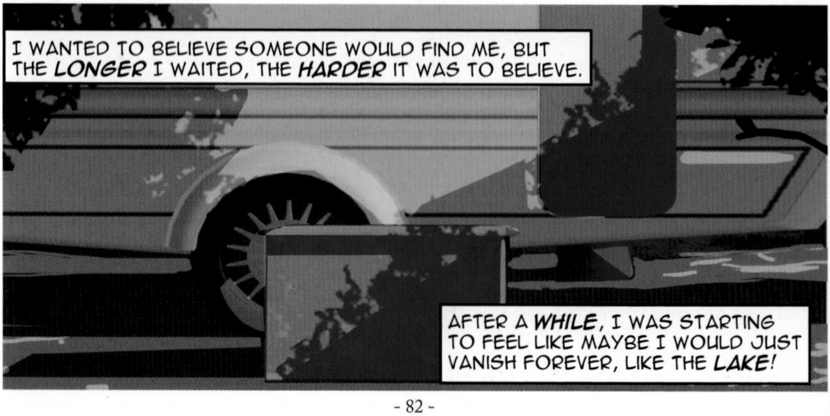
I WANTED TO BELIEVE SOMEONE WOULD FIND ME, BUT THE LONGER I WAITED, THE HARDER IT WAS TO BELIEVE.
AFTER A WHILE, I WAS STARTING TO FEEL LIKE MAYBE I WOULD JUST VANISH FOREVER, LIKE THE LAKE!

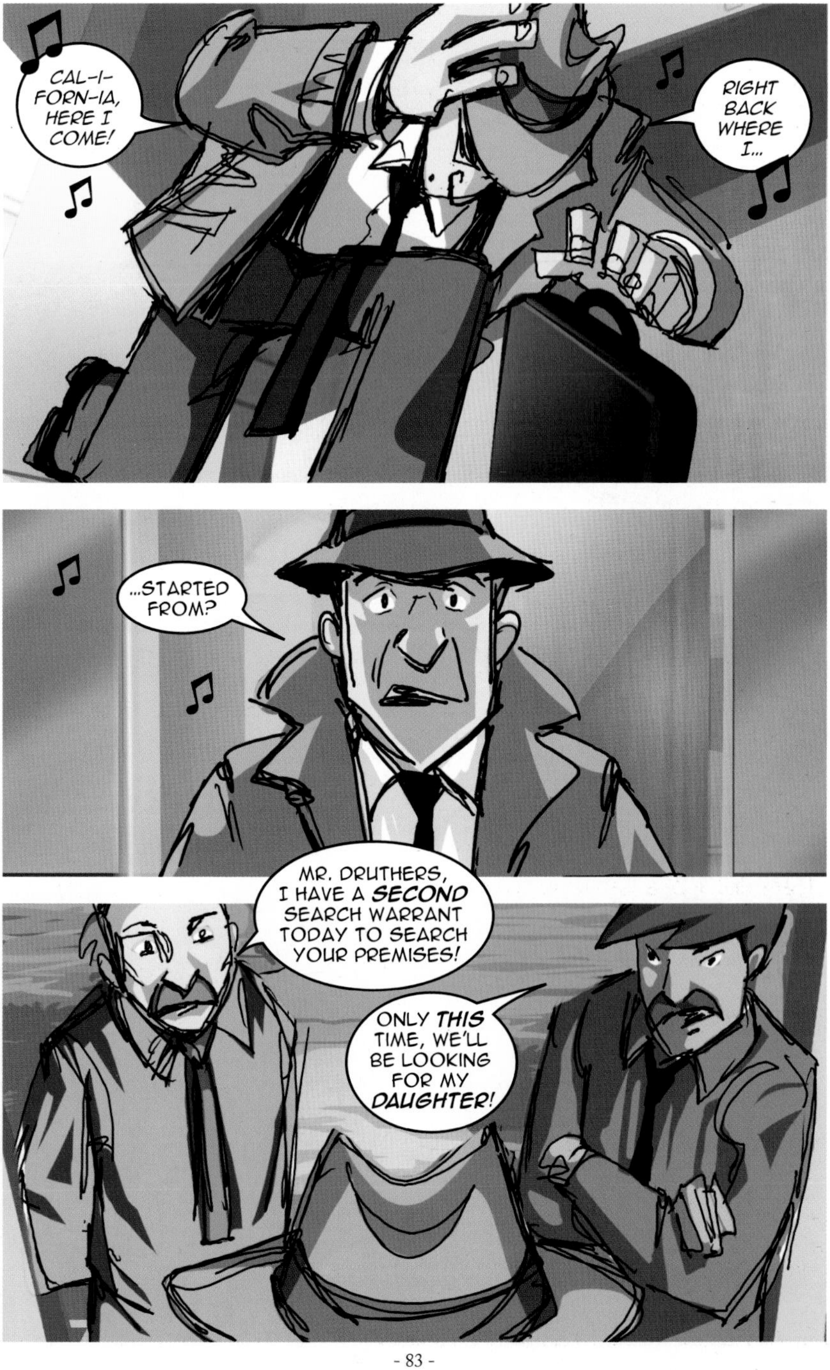
CAL-I-FORN-IA, HERE I COME!
RIGHT BACK WHERE I...
...STARTED FROM?
MR. DRUTHERS, I HAVE A SECOND SEARCH WARRANT TODAY TO SEARCH YOUR PREMISES!
ONLY THIS TIME, WE'LL BE LOOKING FOR MY DAUGHTER!

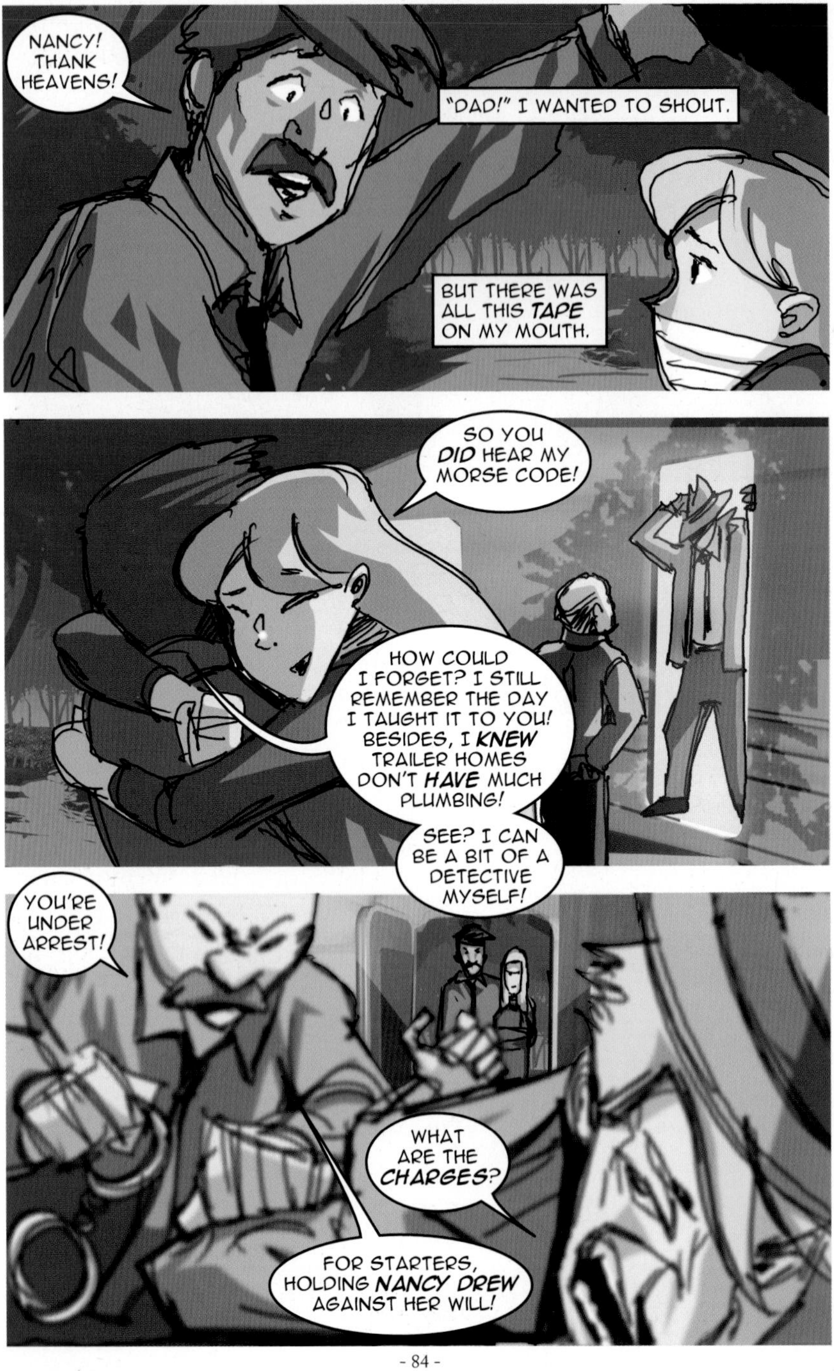
NANCY! THANK HEAVENS!
"DAD!" I WANTED TO SHOUT.
BUT THERE WAS ALL THIS TAPE ON MY MOUTH.
SO YOU DID HEAR MY MORSE CODE!
HOW COULD I FORGET? I STILL REMEMBER THE DAY I TAUGHT IT TO YOU! BESIDES, I KNEW TRAILER HOMES DON'T HAVE MUCH PLUMBING!
SEE? I CAN BE A BIT OF A DETECTIVE MYSELF!
YOU'RE UNDER ARREST!
WHAT ARE THE CHARGES?
FOR STARTERS, HOLDING NANCY DREW AGAINST HER WILL!

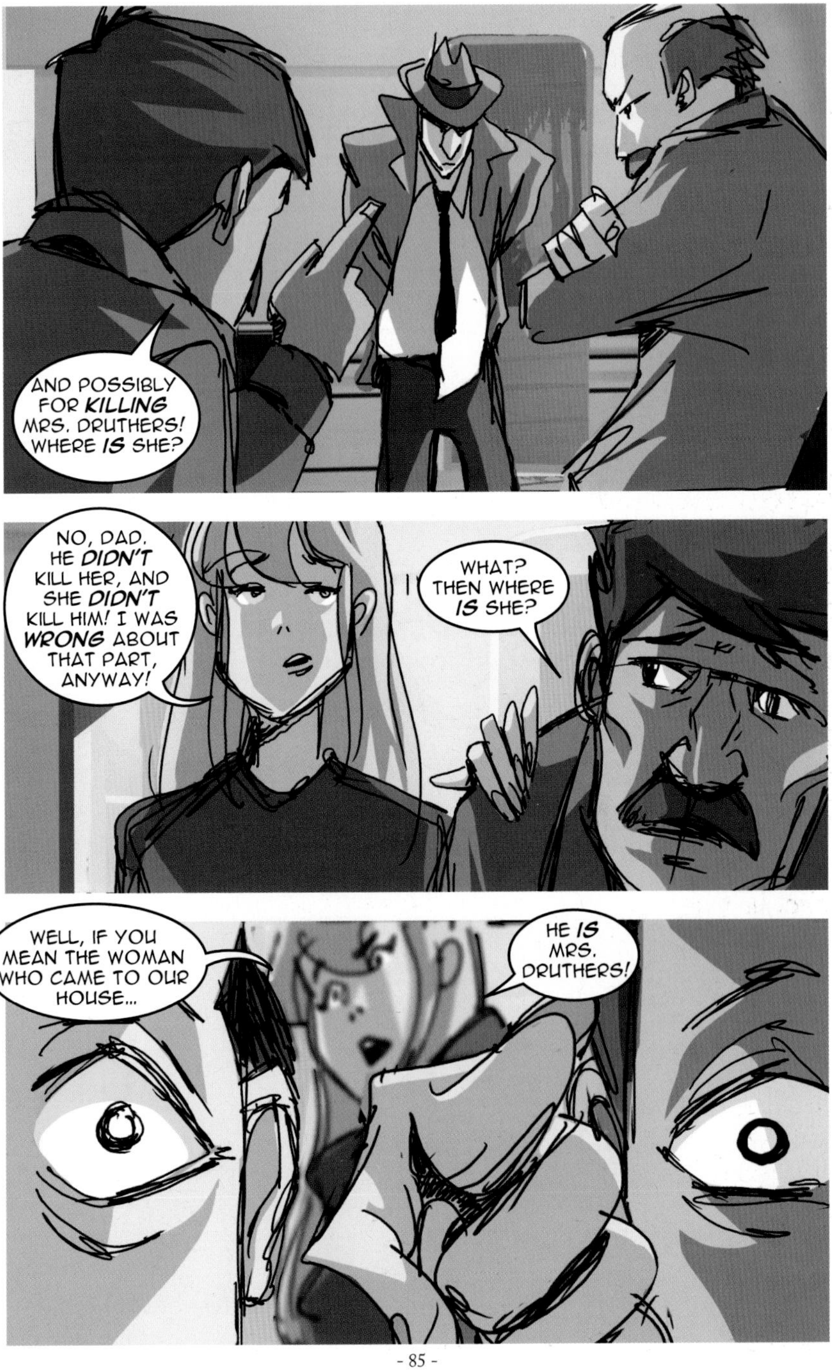
AND POSSIBLY FOR KILLING MRS. DRUTHERS! WHERE IS SHE?
NO, DAD. HE DIDN'T KILL HER, AND SHE DIDN'T KILL HIM! I WAS WRONG ABOUT THAT PART, ANYWAY!
WHAT? THEN WHERE IS SHE?
WELL, IF YOU MEAN THE WOMAN WHO CAME TO OUR HOUSE...
HE IS MRS. DRUTHERS!

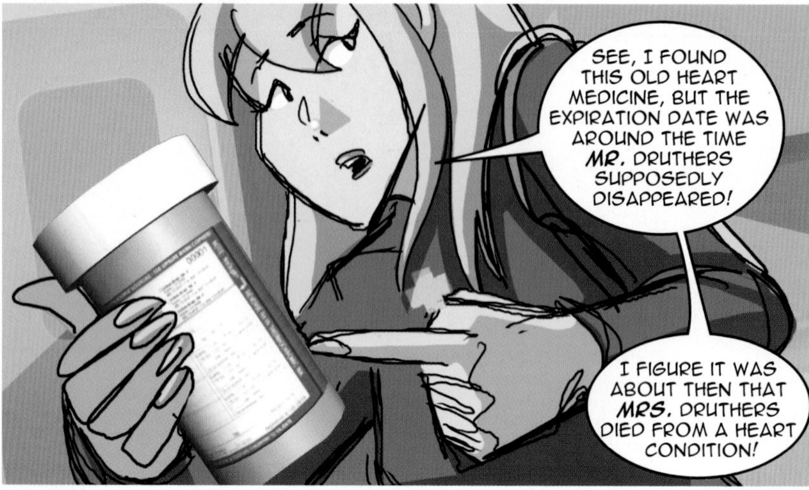
SEE, I FOUND THIS OLD HEART MEDICINE, BUT THE EXPIRATION DATE WAS AROUND THE TIME *MR.* DRUTHERS SUPPOSEDLY DISAPPEARED!
I FIGURE IT WAS ABOUT THEN THAT *MRS.* DRUTHERS DIED FROM A HEART CONDITION!

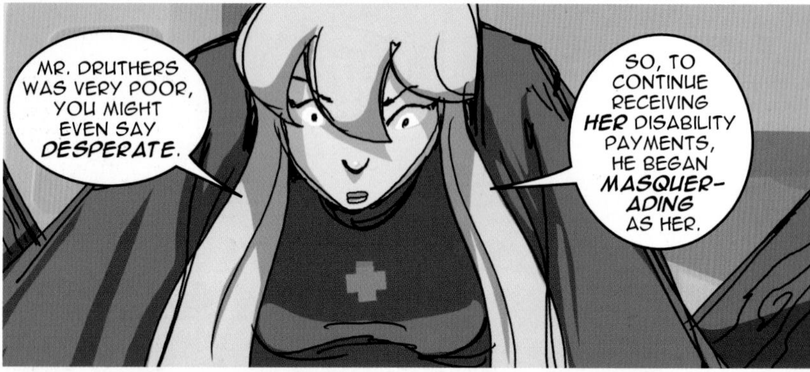
MR. DRUTHERS WAS VERY POOR, YOU MIGHT EVEN SAY *DESPERATE*.
SO, TO CONTINUE RECEIVING *HER* DISABILITY PAYMENTS, HE BEGAN *MASQUER-ADING* AS HER.

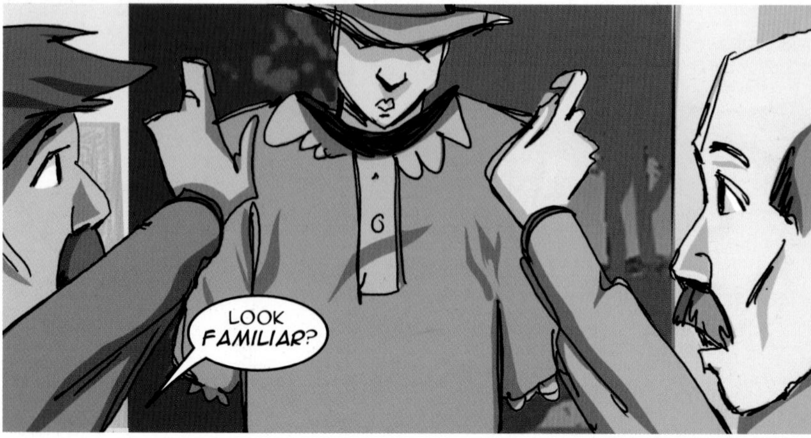
LOOK *FAMILIAR?*

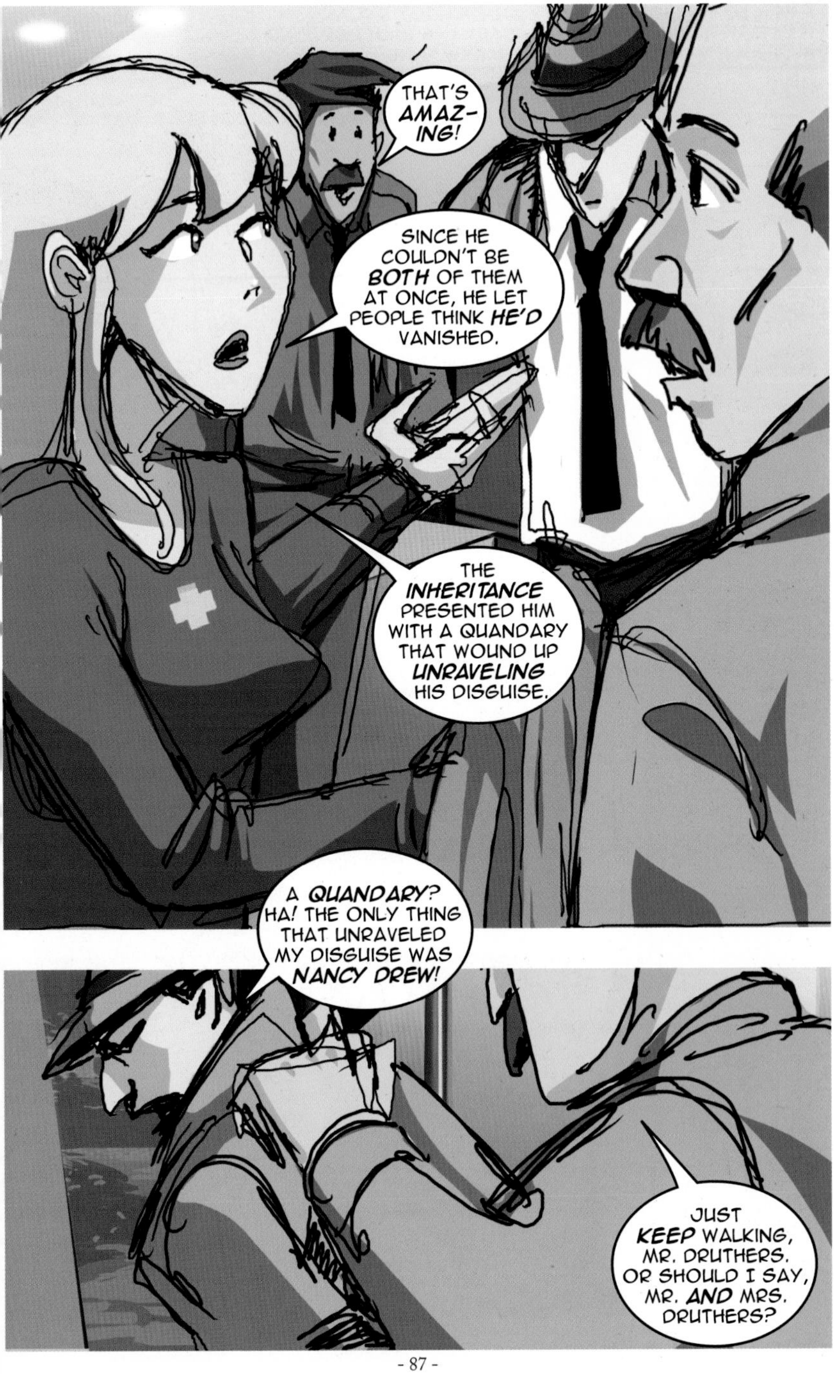
THAT'S AMAZ- ING!
SINCE HE COULDN'T BE BOTH OF THEM AT ONCE, HE LET PEOPLE THINK HE'D VANISHED.
THE INHERITANCE PRESENTED HIM WITH A QUANDARY THAT WOUND UP UNRAVELING HIS DISGUISE.
A QUANDARY? HA! THE ONLY THING THAT UNRAVELED MY DISGUISE WAS NANCY DREW!
JUST KEEP WALKING, MR. DRUTHERS. OR SHOULD I SAY, MR. AND MRS. DRUTHERS?

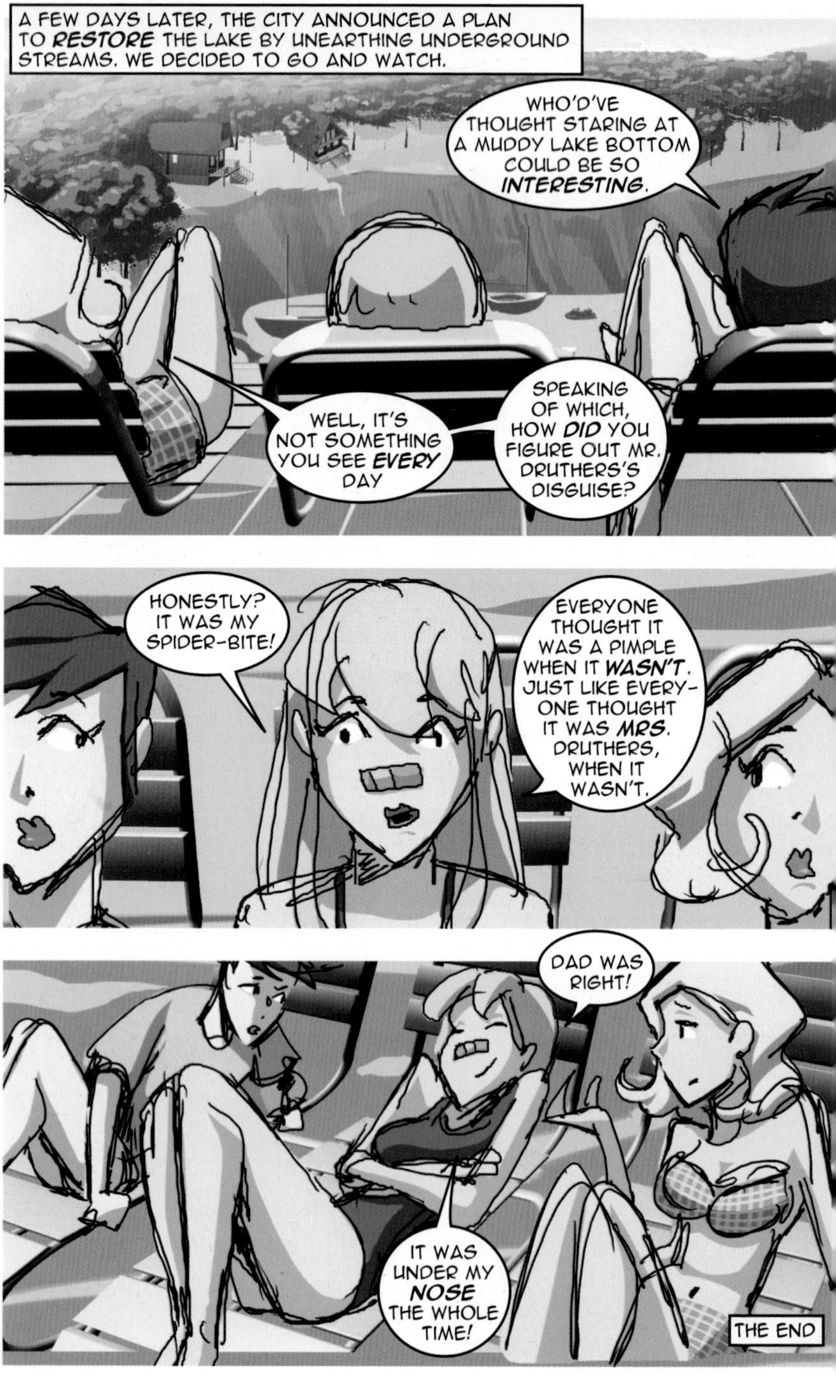
A FEW DAYS LATER, THE CITY ANNOUNCED A PLAN TO RESTORE THE LAKE BY UNEARTHING UNDERGROUND STREAMS. WE DECIDED TO GO AND WATCH.
WHO'D'VE THOUGHT STARING AT A MUDDY LAKE BOTTOM COULD BE SO INTERESTING.
WELL, IT'S NOT SOMETHING YOU SEE EVERY DAY
SPEAKING OF WHICH, HOW DID YOU FIGURE OUT MR. DRUTHERS'S DISGUISE?
HONESTLY? IT WAS MY SPIDER-BITE!
EVERYONE THOUGHT IT WAS A PIMPLE WHEN IT WASN'T. JUST LIKE EVERY-ONE THOUGHT IT WAS MRS. DRUTHERS, WHEN IT WASN'T.
DAD WAS RIGHT!
IT WAS UNDER MY NOSE THE WHOLE TIME!
THE END

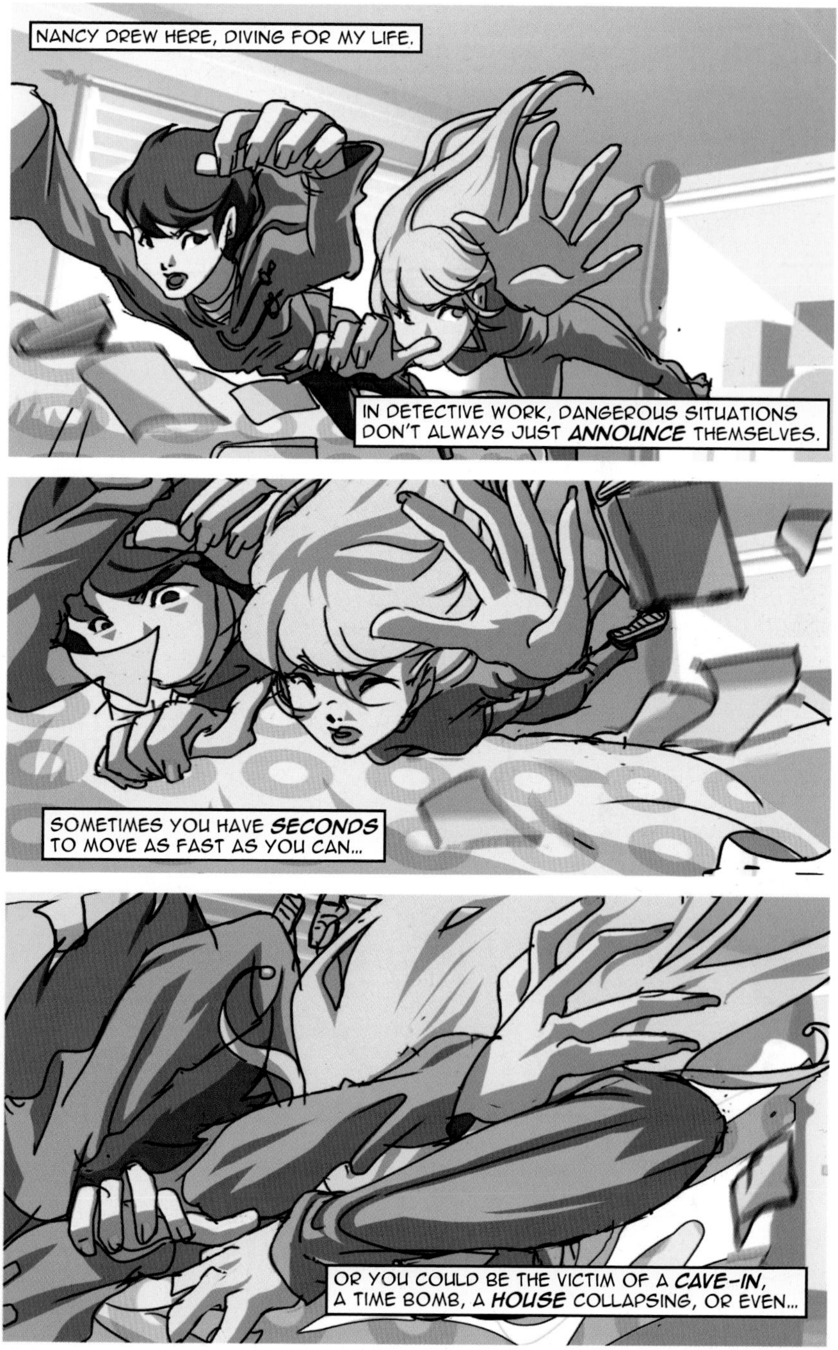
NANCY DREW HERE, DIVING FOR MY LIFE.
IN DETECTIVE WORK, DANGEROUS SITUATIONS DON'T ALWAYS JUST ANNOUNCE THEMSELVES.
SOMETIMES YOU HAVE SECONDS TO MOVE AS FAST AS YOU CAN...
OR YOU COULD BE THE VICTIM OF A CAVE-IN, A TIME BOMB, A HOUSE COLLAPSING, OR EVEN...

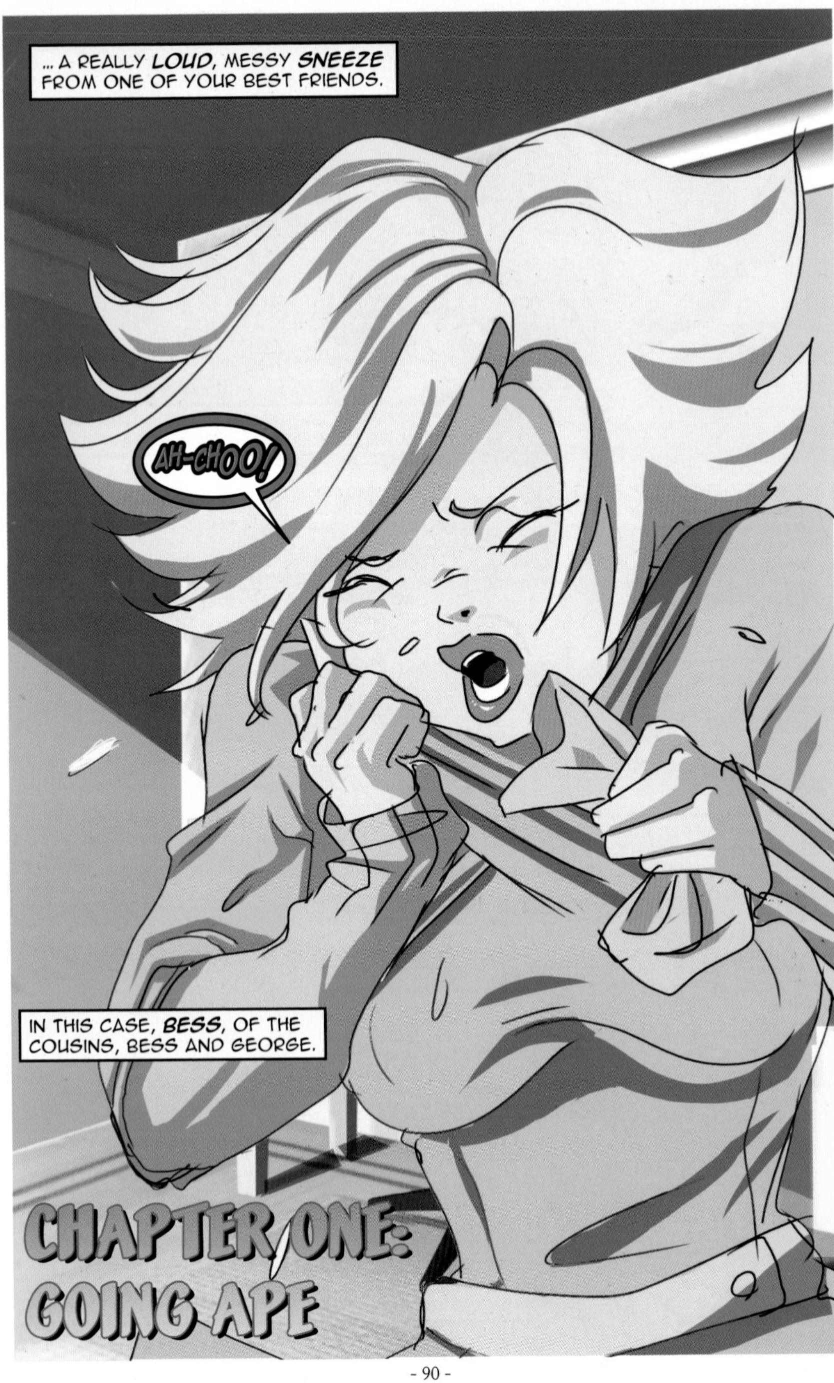
... A REALLY LOUD, MESSY SNEEZE FROM ONE OF YOUR BEST FRIENDS.
AH-CHOO!
IN THIS CASE, BESS, OF THE COUSINS, BESS AND GEORGE.
CHAPTER ONE: GOING APE

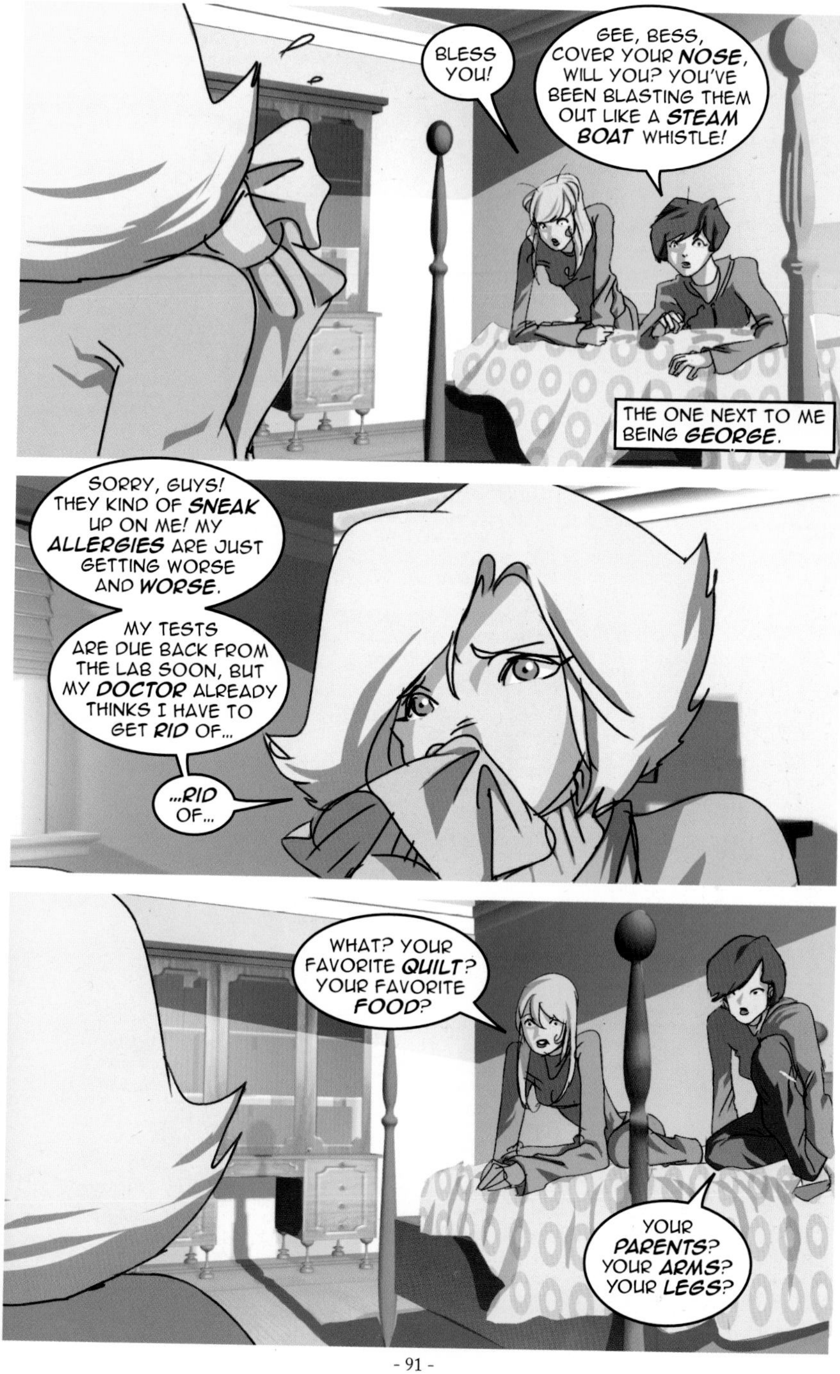

BLESS YOU!
GEE, BESS, COVER YOUR NOSE, WILL YOU? YOU'VE BEEN BLASTING THEM OUT LIKE A STEAM BOAT WHISTLE!
THE ONE NEXT TO ME BEING GEORGE.
SORRY, GUYS! THEY KIND OF SNEAK UP ON ME! MY ALLERGIES ARE JUST GETTING WORSE AND WORSE.
MY TESTS ARE DUE BACK FROM THE LAB SOON, BUT MY DOCTOR ALREADY THINKS I HAVE TO GET RID OF...
...RID OF...
WHAT? YOUR FAVORITE QUILT? YOUR FAVORITE FOOD?
YOUR PARENTS? YOUR ARMS? YOUR LEGS?

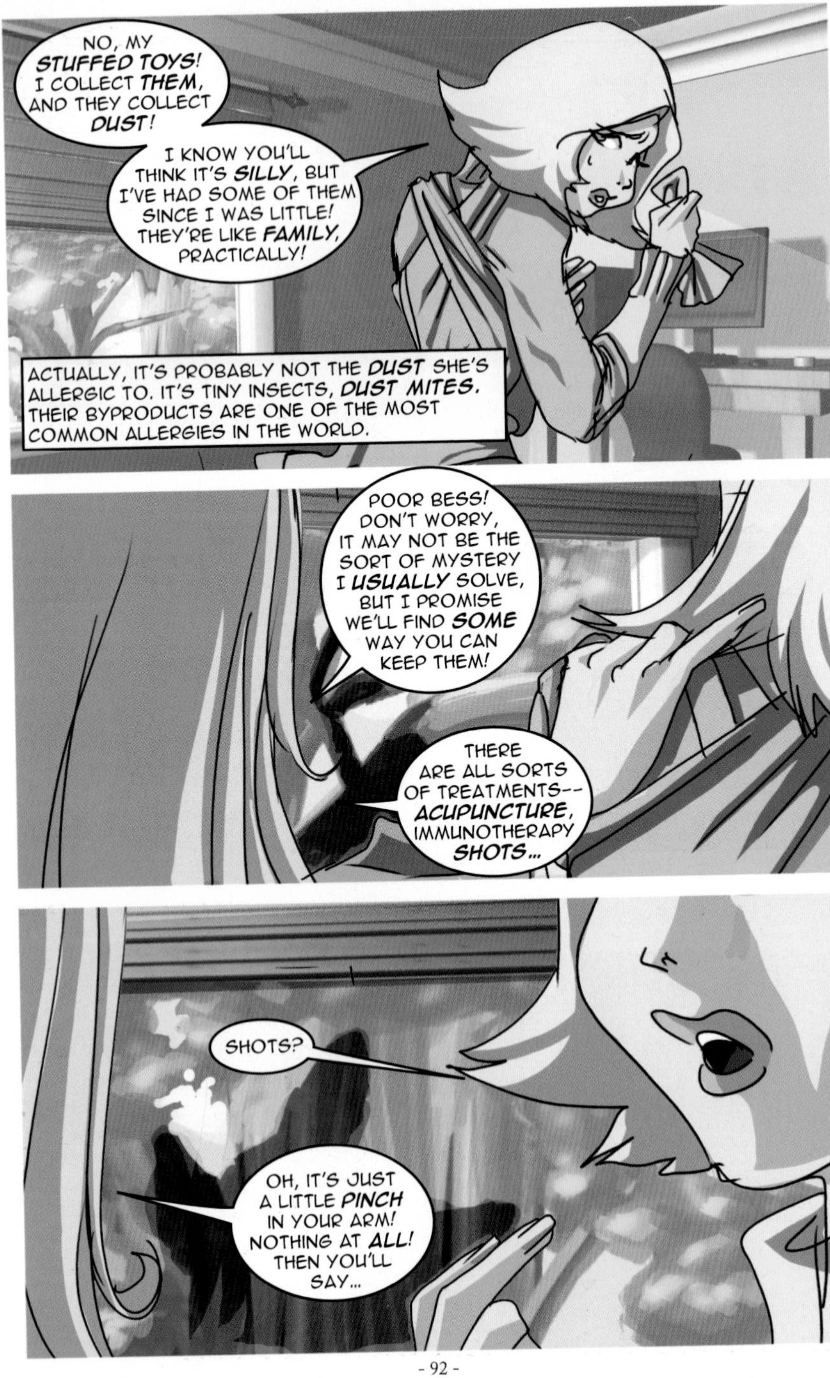
NO, MY STUFFED TOYS! I COLLECT THEM, AND THEY COLLECT DUST!
I KNOW YOU'LL THINK IT'S SILLY, BUT I'VE HAD SOME OF THEM SINCE I WAS LITTLE! THEY'RE LIKE FAMILY, PRACTICALLY!
ACTUALLY, IT'S PROBABLY NOT THE DUST SHE'S ALLERGIC TO. IT'S TINY INSECTS, DUST MITES. THEIR BYPRODUCTS ARE ONE OF THE MOST COMMON ALLERGIES IN THE WORLD.
POOR BESS! DON'T WORRY, IT MAY NOT BE THE SORT OF MYSTERY I USUALLY SOLVE, BUT I PROMISE WE'LL FIND SOME WAY YOU CAN KEEP THEM!
THERE ARE ALL SORTS OF TREATMENTS--ACUPUNCTURE, IMMUNOTHERAPY SHOTS...
SHOTS?
OH, IT'S JUST A LITTLE PINCH IN YOUR ARM! NOTHING AT ALL! THEN YOU'LL SAY...

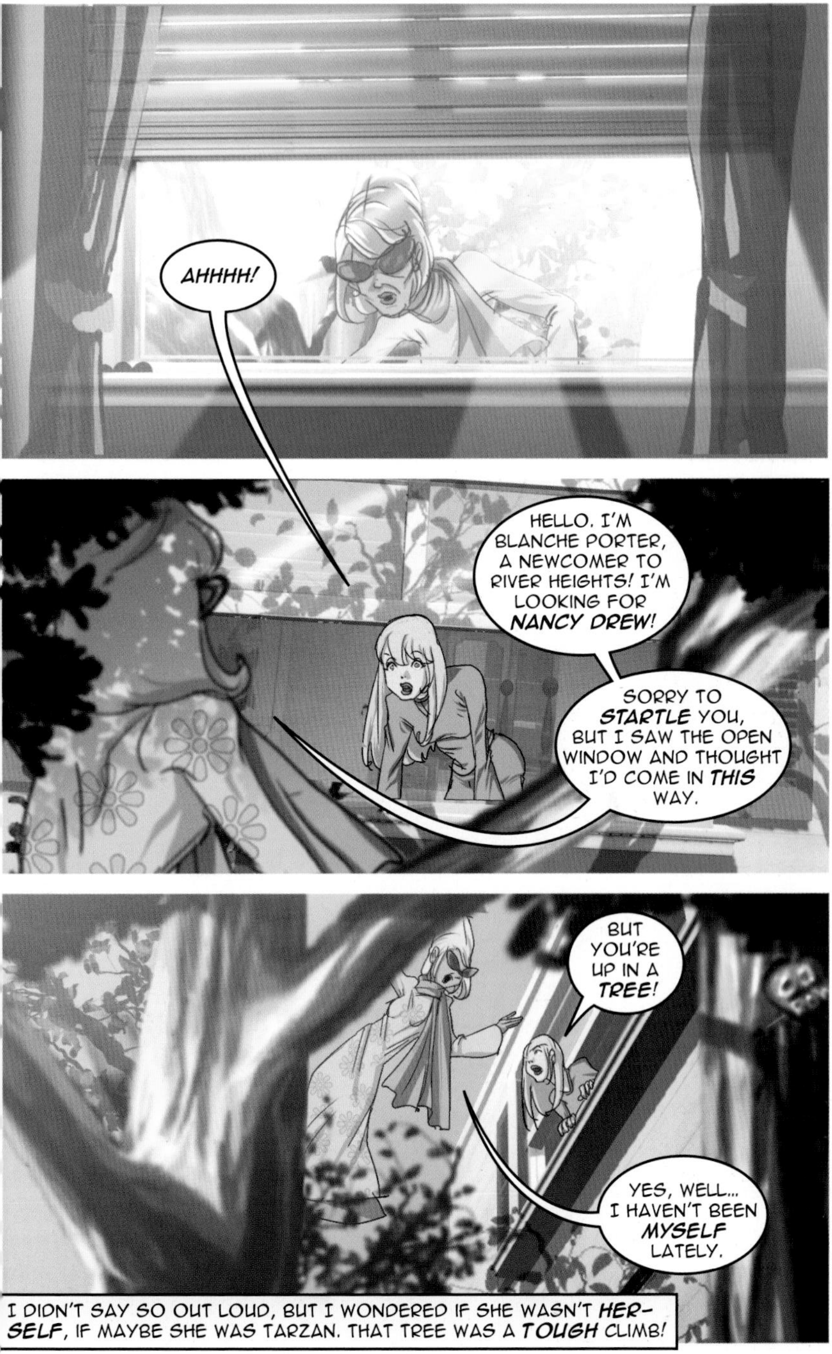
AHHHH!
HELLO. I'M BLANCHE PORTER, A NEWCOMER TO RIVER HEIGHTS! I'M LOOKING FOR NANCY DREW!
SORRY TO STARTLE YOU, BUT I SAW THE OPEN WINDOW AND THOUGHT I'D COME IN THIS WAY.
BUT YOU'RE UP IN A TREE!
YES, WELL... I HAVEN'T BEEN MYSELF LATELY.
I DIDN'T SAY SO OUT LOUD, BUT I WONDERED IF SHE WASN'T HER-SELF, IF MAYBE SHE WAS TARZAN. THAT TREE WAS A TOUGH CLIMB!

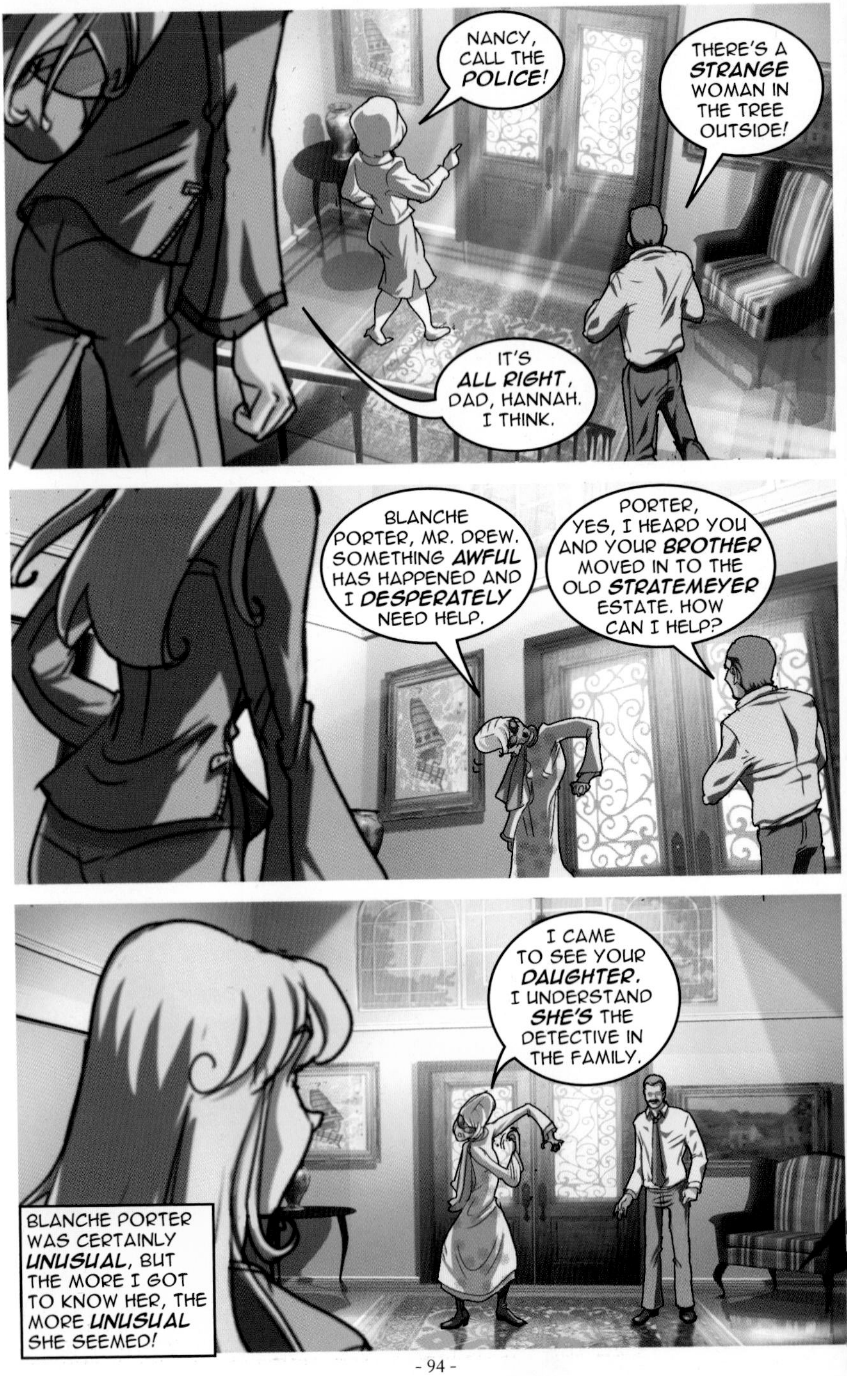
NANCY, CALL THE POLICE!
THERE'S A STRANGE WOMAN IN THE TREE OUTSIDE!
IT'S ALL RIGHT, DAD, HANNAH. I THINK.
BLANCHE PORTER, MR. DREW. SOMETHING AWFUL HAS HAPPENED AND I DESPERATELY NEED HELP.
PORTER, YES, I HEARD YOU AND YOUR BROTHER MOVED IN TO THE OLD STRATEMEYER ESTATE. HOW CAN I HELP?
I CAME TO SEE YOUR DAUGHTER. I UNDERSTAND SHE'S THE DETECTIVE IN THE FAMILY.
BLANCHE PORTER WAS CERTAINLY UNUSUAL, BUT THE MORE I GOT TO KNOW HER, THE MORE UNUSUAL SHE SEEMED!

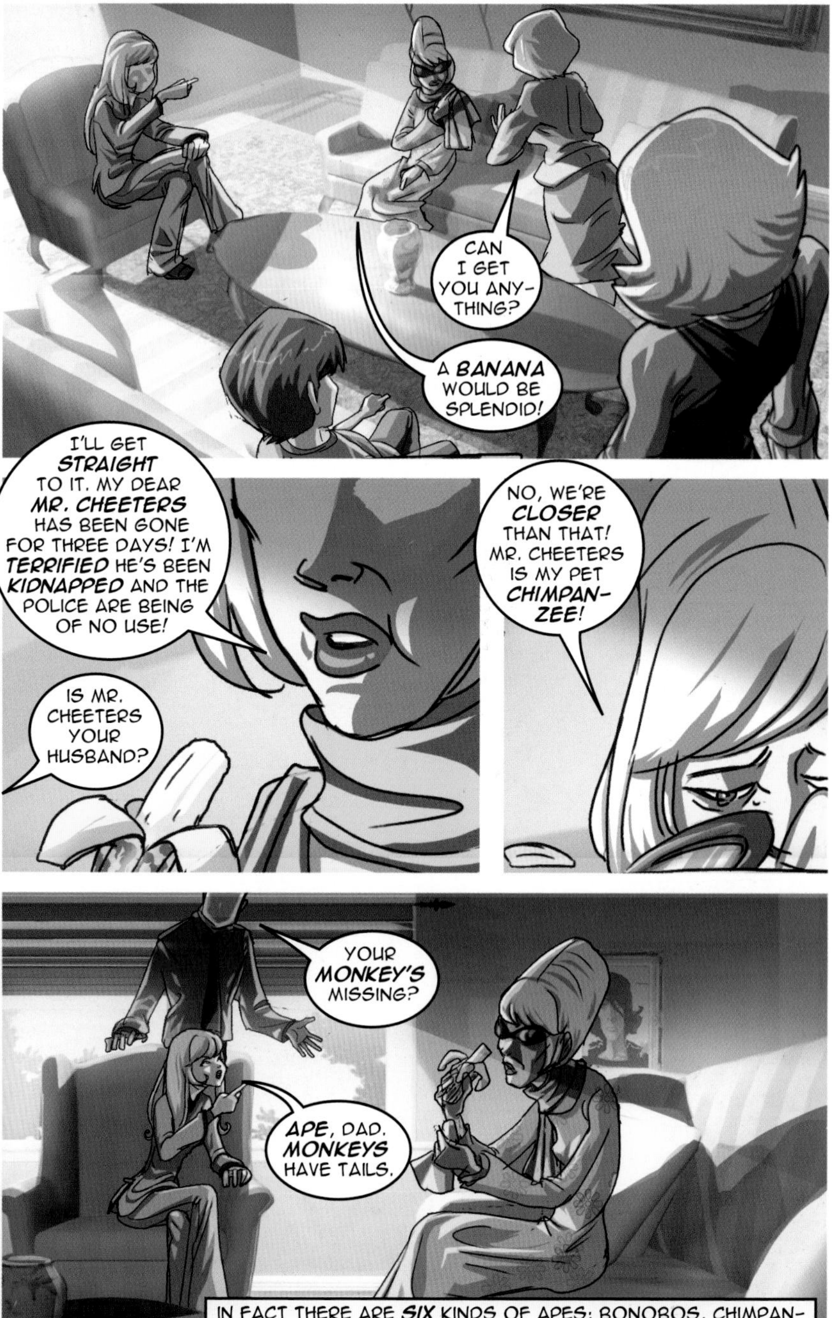
CAN I GET YOU ANYTHING?
A BANANA WOULD BE SPLENDID!
I'LL GET STRAIGHT TO IT. MY DEAR MR. CHEETERS HAS BEEN GONE FOR THREE DAYS! I'M TERRIFIED HE'S BEEN KIDNAPPED AND THE POLICE ARE BEING OF NO USE!
IS MR. CHEETERS YOUR HUSBAND?
NO, WE'RE CLOSER THAN THAT! MR. CHEETERS IS MY PET CHIMPANZEE!
YOUR MONKEY'S MISSING?
APE, DAD. MONKEYS HAVE TAILS.
IN FACT THERE ARE SIX KINDS OF APES; BONOBOS, CHIMPANZEES, GORILLAS, ORANGUTANS, GIBBONS, AND SIAMANGS!

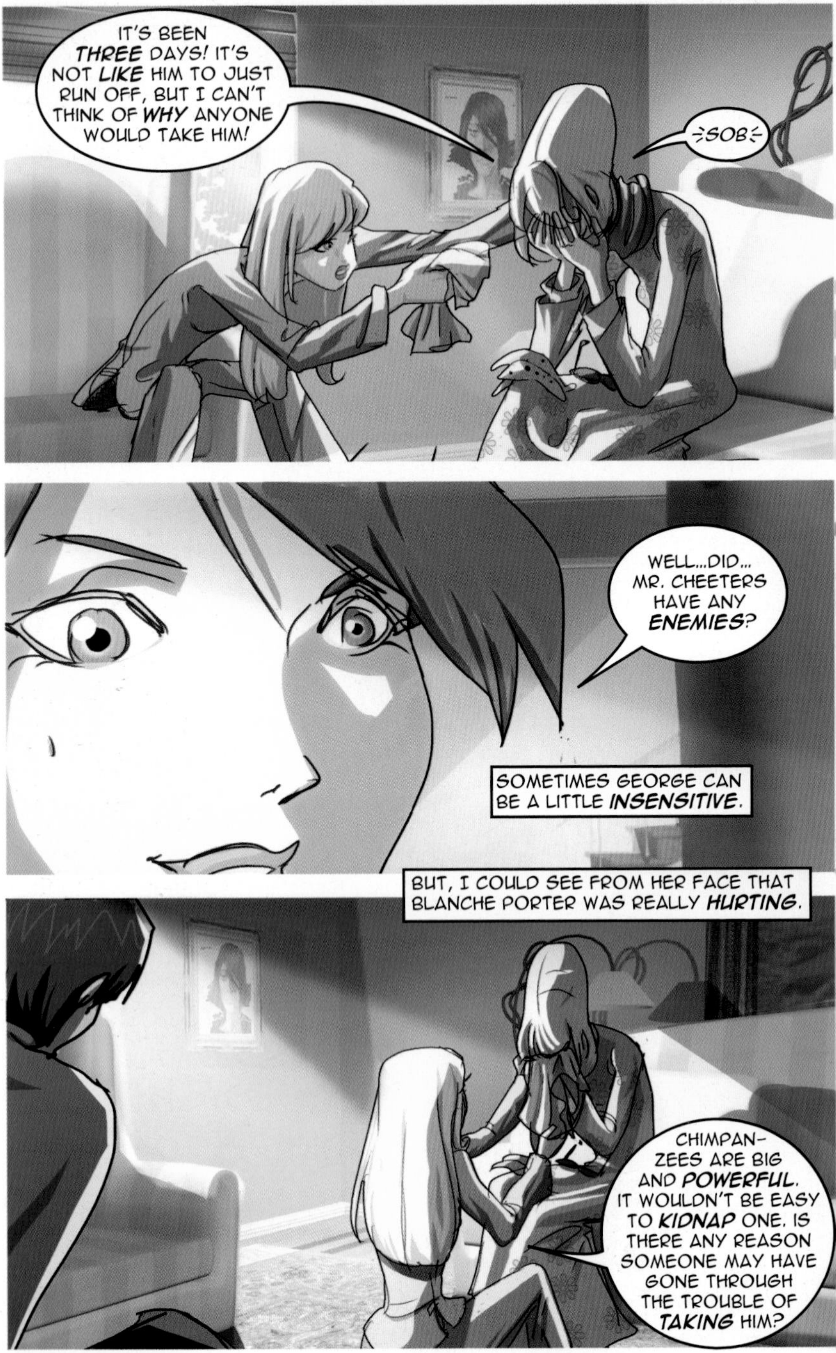
IT'S BEEN THREE DAYS! IT'S NOT LIKE HIM TO JUST RUN OFF, BUT I CAN'T THINK OF WHY ANYONE WOULD TAKE HIM!
SOB
WELL...DID... MR. CHEETERS HAVE ANY ENEMIES?
SOMETIMES GEORGE CAN BE A LITTLE INSENSITIVE.
BUT, I COULD SEE FROM HER FACE THAT BLANCHE PORTER WAS REALLY HURTING.
CHIMPAN-ZEES ARE BIG AND POWERFUL. IT WOULDN'T BE EASY TO KIDNAP ONE. IS THERE ANY REASON SOMEONE MAY HAVE GONE THROUGH THE TROUBLE OF TAKING HIM?

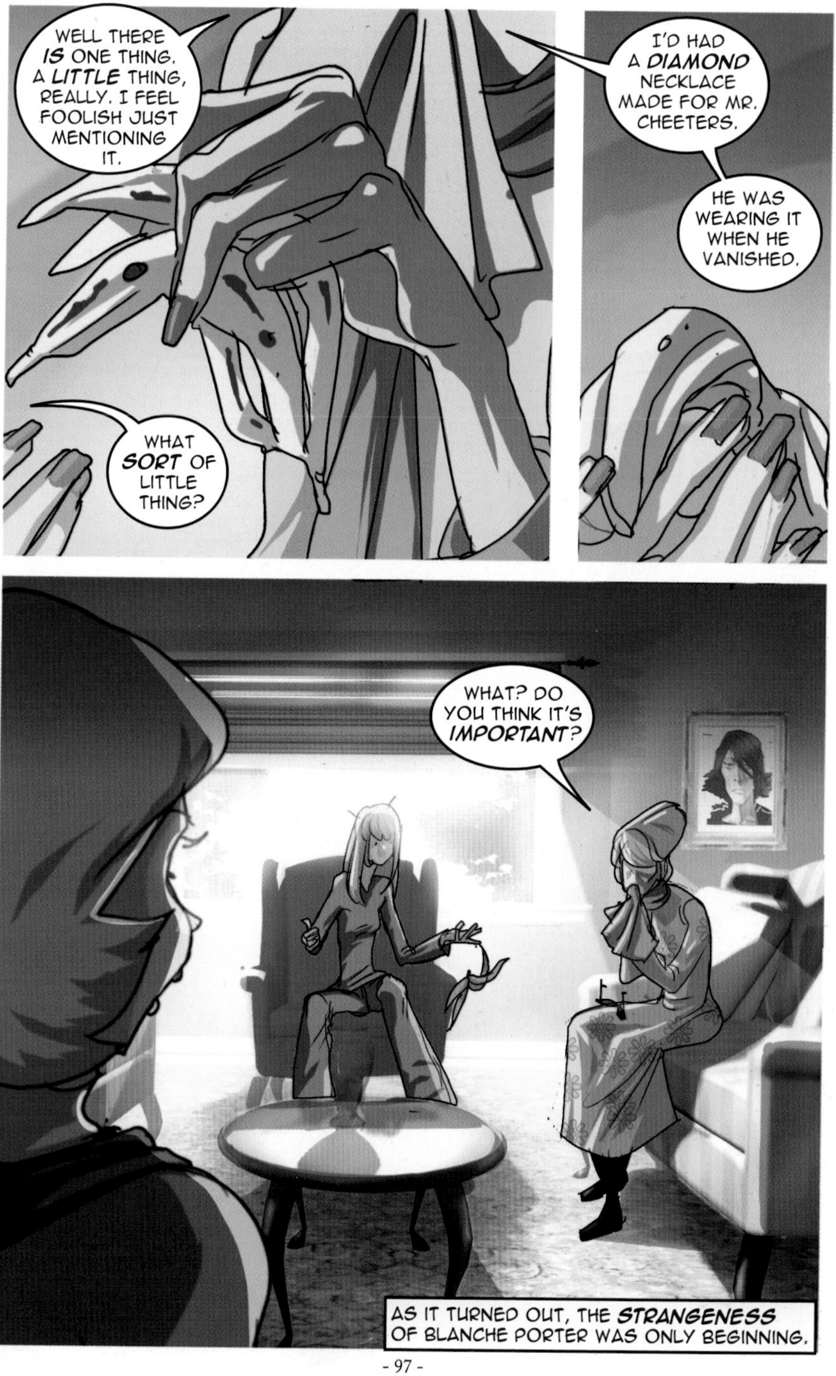
WELL THERE IS ONE THING. A LITTLE THING, REALLY. I FEEL FOOLISH JUST MENTIONING IT.
WHAT SORT OF LITTLE THING?
I'D HAD A DIAMOND NECKLACE MADE FOR MR. CHEETERS.
HE WAS WEARING IT WHEN HE VANISHED.
WHAT? DO YOU THINK IT'S IMPORTANT?
AS IT TURNED OUT, THE STRANGENESS OF BLANCHE PORTER WAS ONLY BEGINNING.

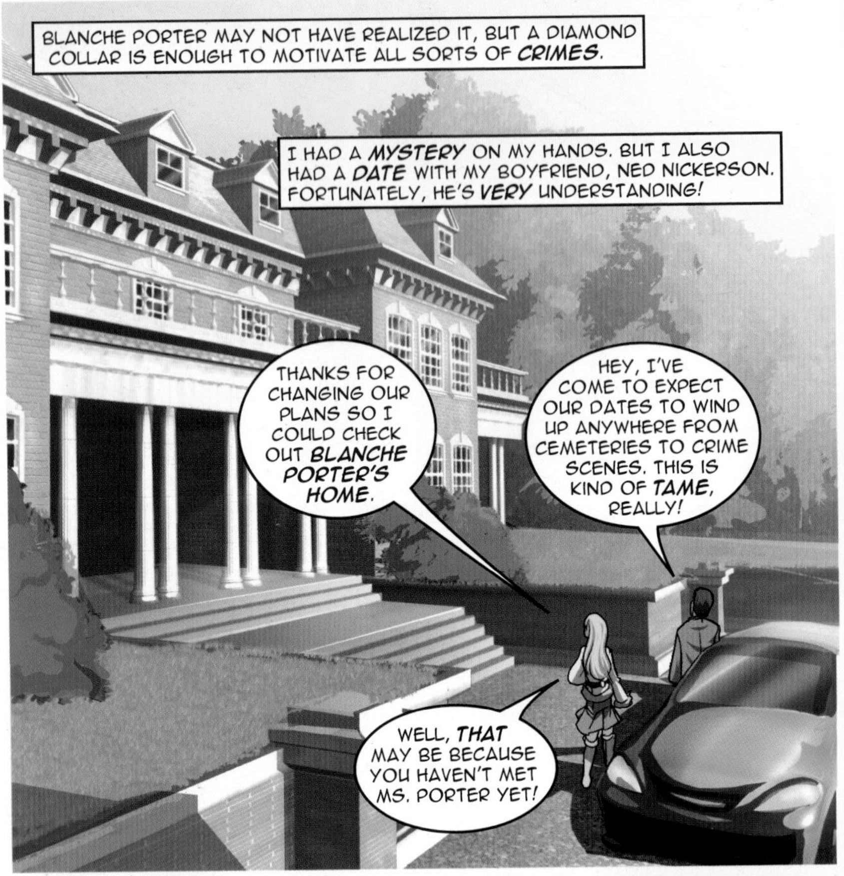
BLANCHE PORTER MAY NOT HAVE REALIZED IT, BUT A DIAMOND COLLAR IS ENOUGH TO MOTIVATE ALL SORTS OF CRIMES.
I HAD A MYSTERY ON MY HANDS. BUT I ALSO HAD A DATE WITH MY BOYFRIEND, NED NICKERSON. FORTUNATELY, HE'S VERY UNDERSTANDING!
THANKS FOR CHANGING OUR PLANS SO I COULD CHECK OUT BLANCHE PORTER'S HOME.
HEY, I'VE COME TO EXPECT OUR DATES TO WIND UP ANYWHERE FROM CEMETERIES TO CRIME SCENES. THIS IS KIND OF TAME, REALLY!
WELL, THAT MAY BE BECAUSE YOU HAVEN'T MET MS. PORTER YET!

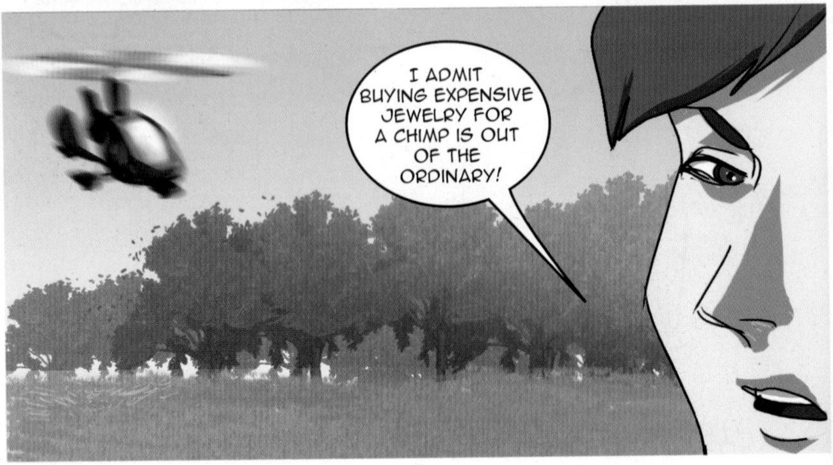
I ADMIT BUYING EXPENSIVE JEWELRY FOR A CHIMP IS OUT OF THE ORDINARY!

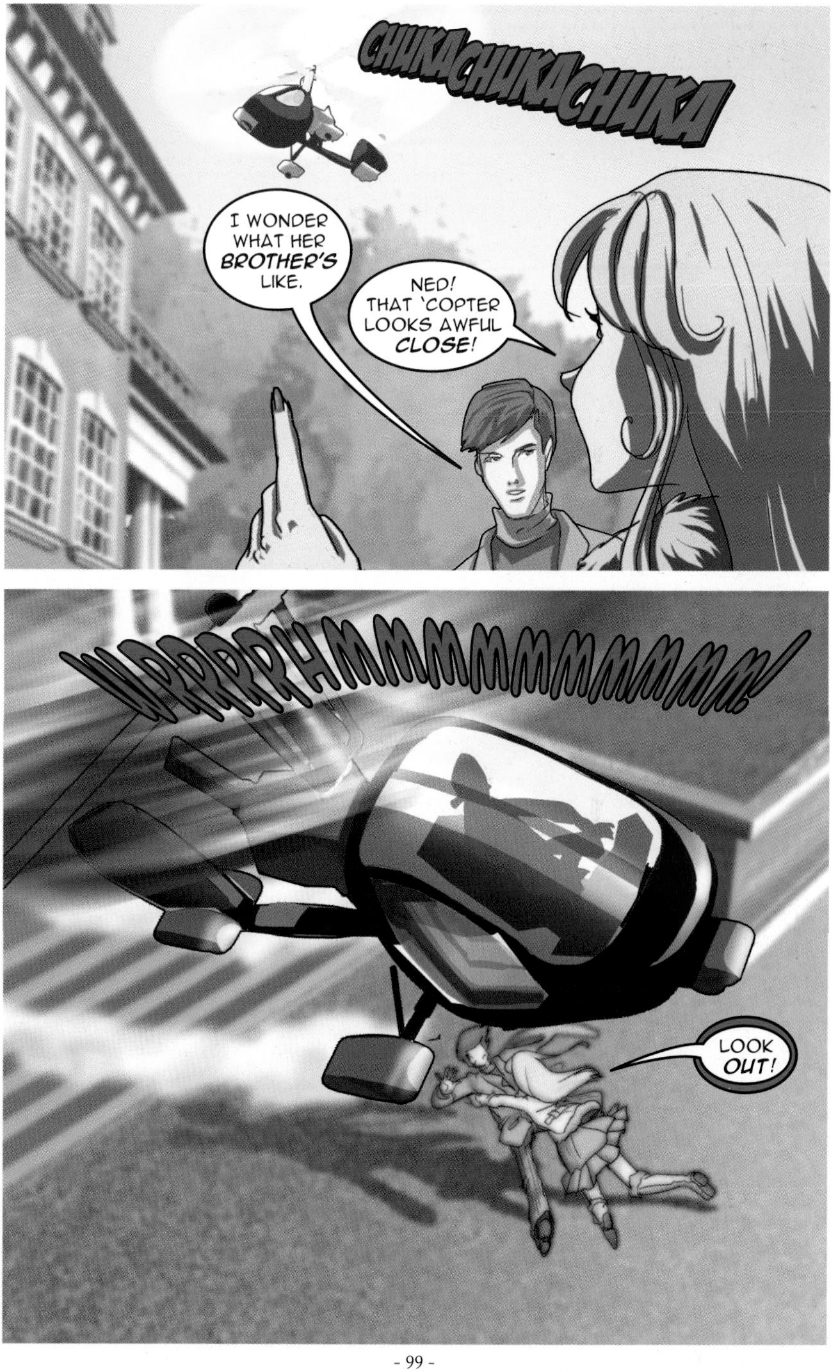
CHUKACHUKACHUKA
I WONDER WHAT HER **BROTHER'S** LIKE.
NED! THAT 'COPTER LOOKS AWFUL **CLOSE**!
WRRRRHMMMMMMMMMMMMM!
LOOK **OUT**!

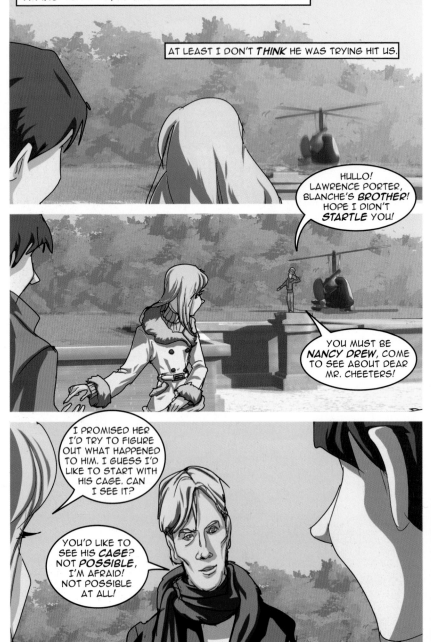

IT WASN'T UNTIL AFTER HE *LANDED* I REALIZED HE WASN'T *TRYING* TO HIT US, HE WAS JUST HEADED FOR A HELIPORT.

AT LEAST I DON'T *THINK* HE WAS TRYING HIT US.

HULLO! LAWRENCE PORTER, BLANCHE'S *BROTHER!* HOPE I DIDN'T *STARTLE* YOU!

YOU MUST BE *NANCY DREW,* COME TO SEE ABOUT DEAR MR. CHEETERS!

I PROMISED HER I'D TRY TO FIGURE OUT WHAT HAPPENED TO HIM. I GUESS I'D LIKE TO START WITH HIS CAGE. CAN I SEE IT?

YOU'D LIKE TO SEE HIS *CAGE?* NOT *POSSIBLE,* I'M AFRAID! NOT POSSIBLE AT ALL!

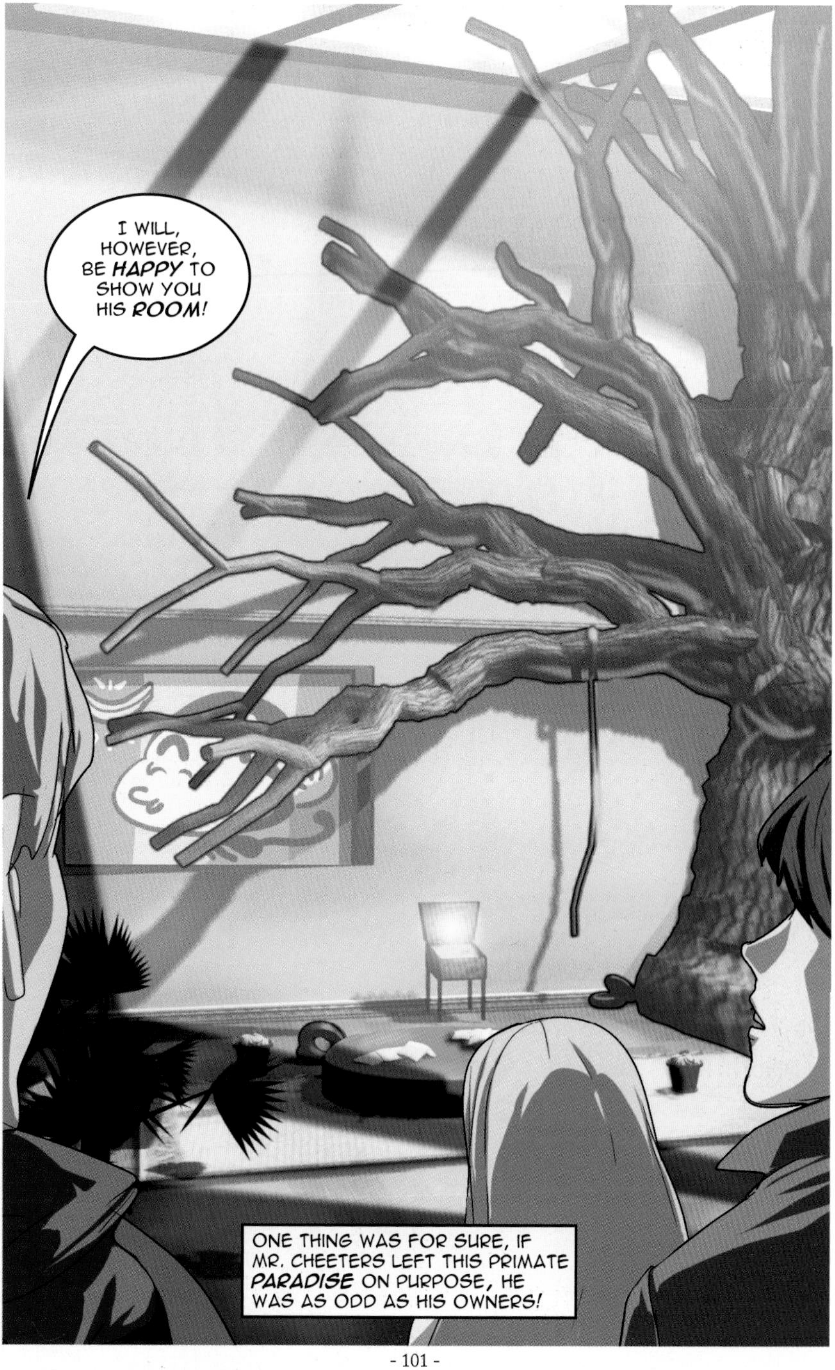
I WILL, HOWEVER, BE HAPPY TO SHOW YOU HIS ROOM!
ONE THING WAS FOR SURE, IF MR. CHEETERS LEFT THIS PRIMATE PARADISE ON PURPOSE, HE WAS AS ODD AS HIS OWNERS!

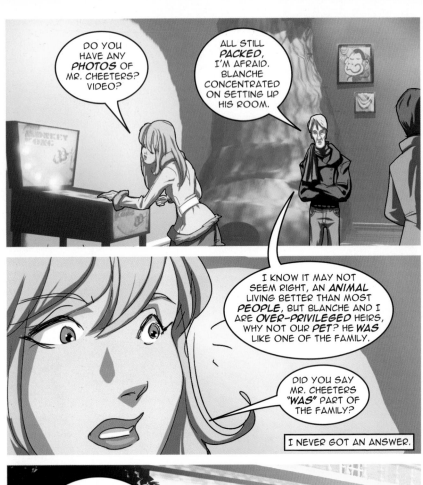

DO YOU HAVE ANY *PHOTOS* OF MR. CHEETERS? VIDEO?

ALL STILL *PACKED*, I'M AFRAID. BLANCHE CONCENTRATED ON SETTING UP HIS ROOM.

I KNOW IT MAY NOT SEEM RIGHT, AN *ANIMAL* LIVING BETTER THAN MOST *PEOPLE*, BUT BLANCHE AND I ARE *OVER-PRIVILEGED* HEIRS, WHY NOT OUR *PET*? HE *WAS* LIKE ONE OF THE FAMILY.

DID YOU SAY MR. CHEETERS *"WAS"* PART OF THE FAMILY?

I NEVER GOT AN ANSWER.

BLANCHE IS TOO *UPSET* TO COME DOWN. I KNOW SHE MAY SEEM *ECCENTRIC*, AND YOU MAY HEAR *STORIES*, BUT I ASSURE YOU SHE'S AS *SANE* AS YOU OR I.

I REALLY WISHED HE HADN'T INCLUDED *ME* ON THAT LIST!

I ALSO WISHED HE HADN'T *RUSHED* US OUT SO *QUICKLY*!

- 102 -

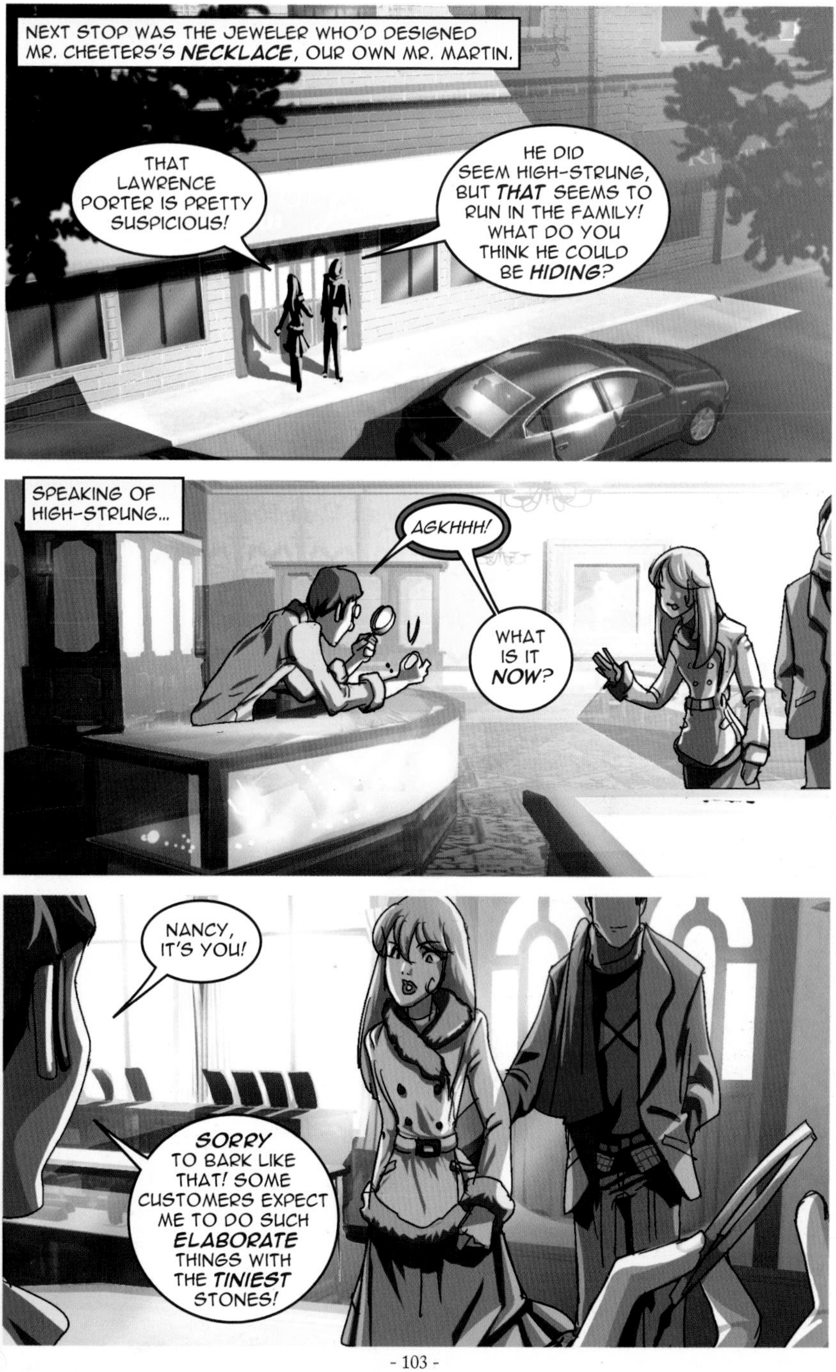
NEXT STOP WAS THE JEWELER WHO'D DESIGNED MR. CHEETERS'S NECKLACE, OUR OWN MR. MARTIN.
THAT LAWRENCE PORTER IS PRETTY SUSPICIOUS!
HE DID SEEM HIGH-STRUNG, BUT THAT SEEMS TO RUN IN THE FAMILY! WHAT DO YOU THINK HE COULD BE HIDING?
SPEAKING OF HIGH-STRUNG...
AGKHHH!
WHAT IS IT NOW?
NANCY, IT'S YOU!
SORRY TO BARK LIKE THAT! SOME CUSTOMERS EXPECT ME TO DO SUCH ELABORATE THINGS WITH THE TINIEST STONES!

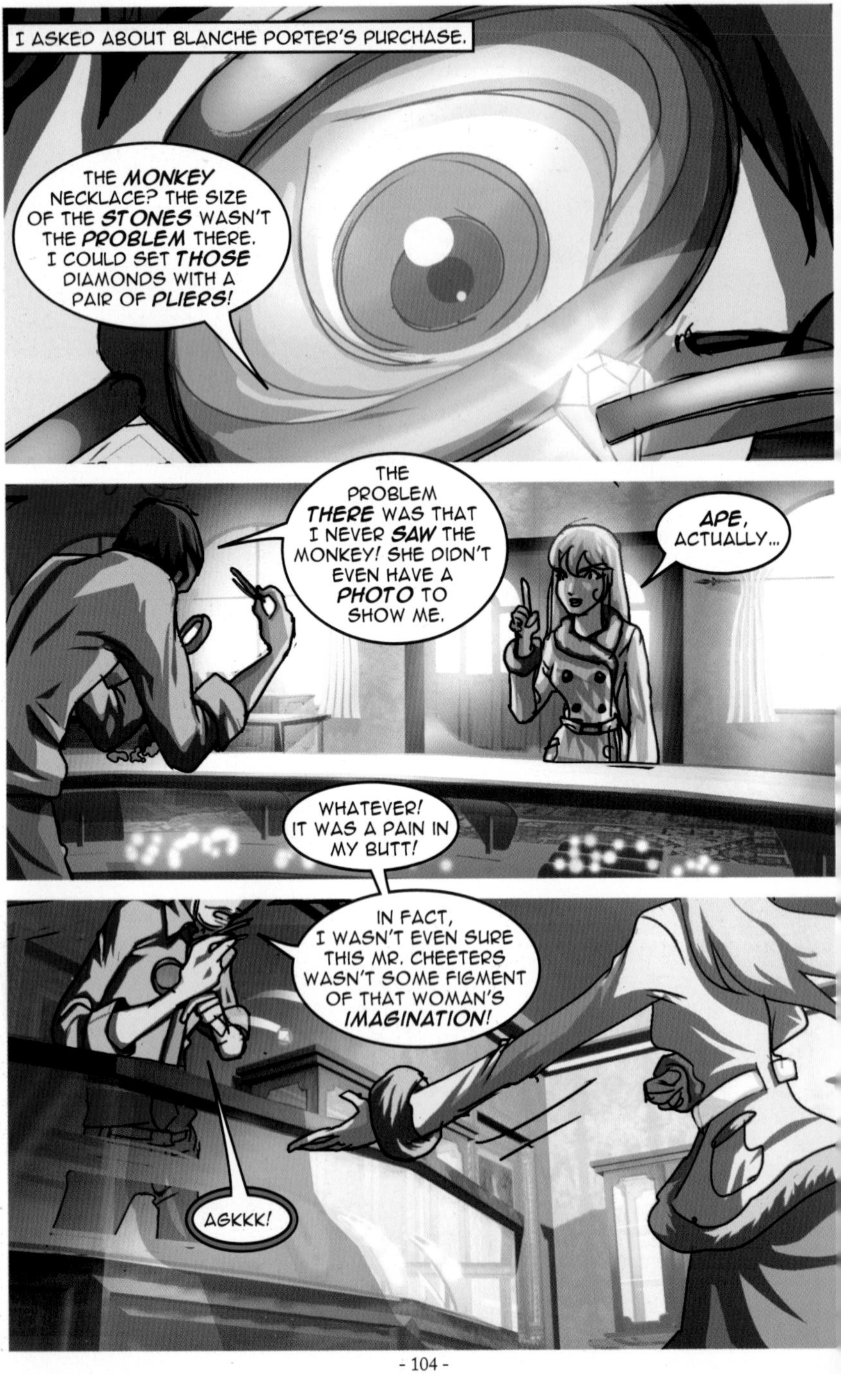
I ASKED ABOUT BLANCHE PORTER'S PURCHASE.
THE MONKEY NECKLACE? THE SIZE OF THE STONES WASN'T THE PROBLEM THERE. I COULD SET THOSE DIAMONDS WITH A PAIR OF PLIERS!
THE PROBLEM THERE WAS THAT I NEVER SAW THE MONKEY! SHE DIDN'T EVEN HAVE A PHOTO TO SHOW ME.
APE, ACTUALLY...
WHATEVER! IT WAS A PAIN IN MY BUTT!
IN FACT, I WASN'T EVEN SURE THIS MR. CHEETERS WASN'T SOME FIGMENT OF THAT WOMAN'S IMAGINATION!
AGKKK!

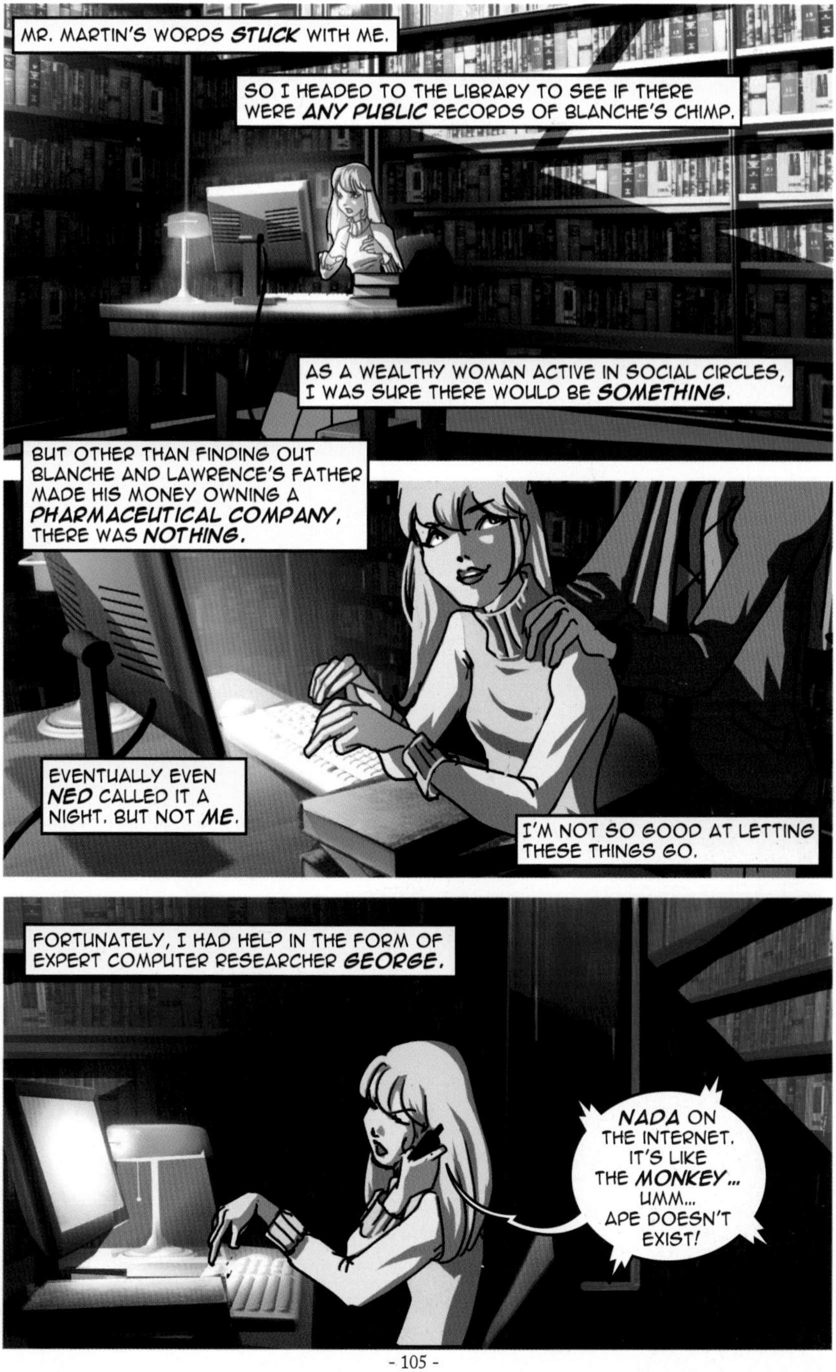
MR. MARTIN'S WORDS STUCK WITH ME.
SO I HEADED TO THE LIBRARY TO SEE IF THERE WERE ANY PUBLIC RECORDS OF BLANCHE'S CHIMP.
AS A WEALTHY WOMAN ACTIVE IN SOCIAL CIRCLES, I WAS SURE THERE WOULD BE SOMETHING.
BUT OTHER THAN FINDING OUT BLANCHE AND LAWRENCE'S FATHER MADE HIS MONEY OWNING A PHARMACEUTICAL COMPANY, THERE WAS NOTHING.
EVENTUALLY EVEN NED CALLED IT A NIGHT. BUT NOT ME.
I'M NOT SO GOOD AT LETTING THESE THINGS GO.
FORTUNATELY, I HAD HELP IN THE FORM OF EXPERT COMPUTER RESEARCHER GEORGE.
NADA ON THE INTERNET. IT'S LIKE THE MONKEY... UMM... APE DOESN'T EXIST!

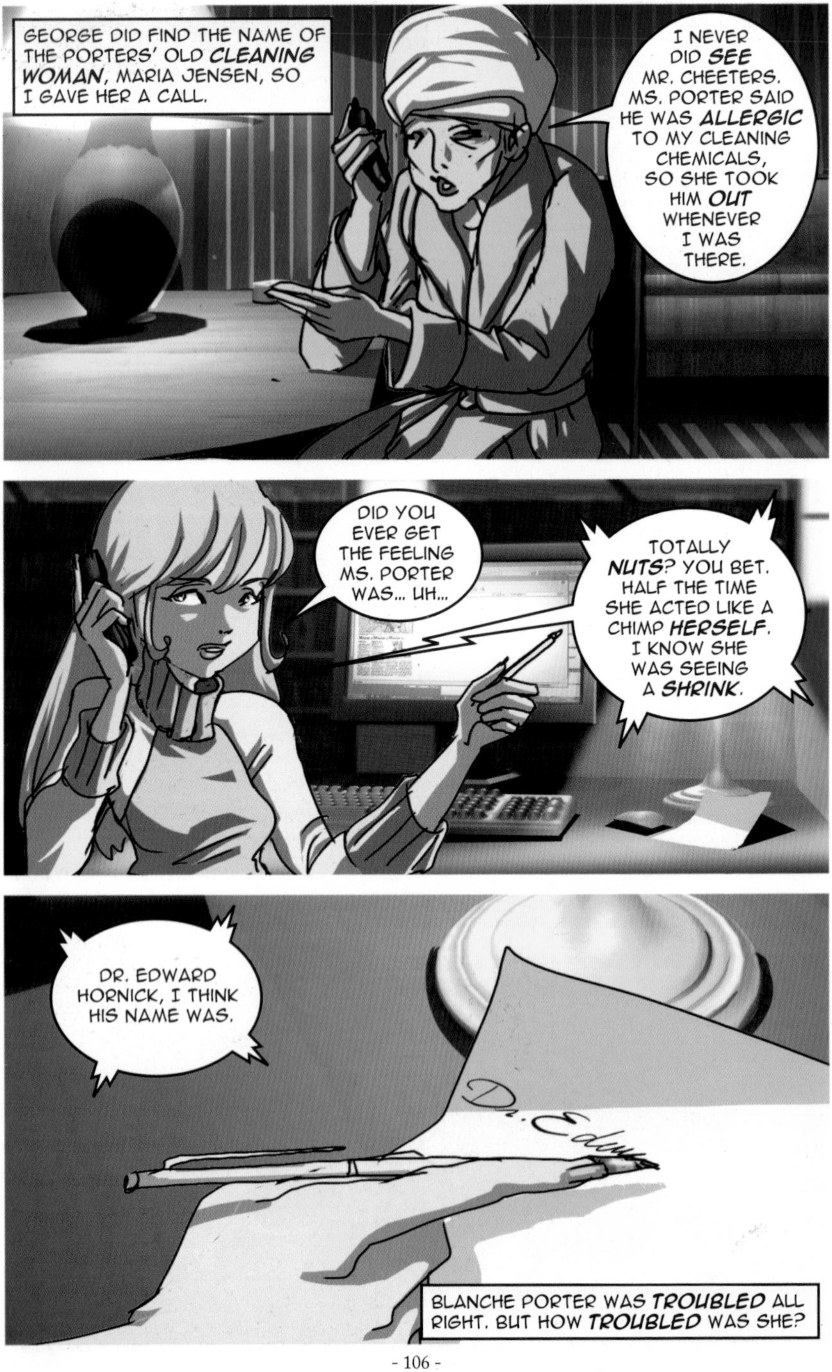
GEORGE DID FIND THE NAME OF THE PORTERS' OLD *CLEANING WOMAN*, MARIA JENSEN, SO I GAVE HER A CALL.
I NEVER DID *SEE* MR. CHEETERS. MS. PORTER SAID HE WAS *ALLERGIC* TO MY CLEANING CHEMICALS, SO SHE TOOK HIM *OUT* WHENEVER I WAS THERE.
DID YOU EVER GET THE FEELING MS. PORTER WAS... UH...
TOTALLY *NUTS*? YOU BET. HALF THE TIME SHE ACTED LIKE A CHIMP *HERSELF*. I KNOW SHE WAS SEEING A *SHRINK*.
DR. EDWARD HORNICK, I THINK HIS NAME WAS.
BLANCHE PORTER WAS *TROUBLED* ALL RIGHT. BUT HOW *TROUBLED* WAS SHE?

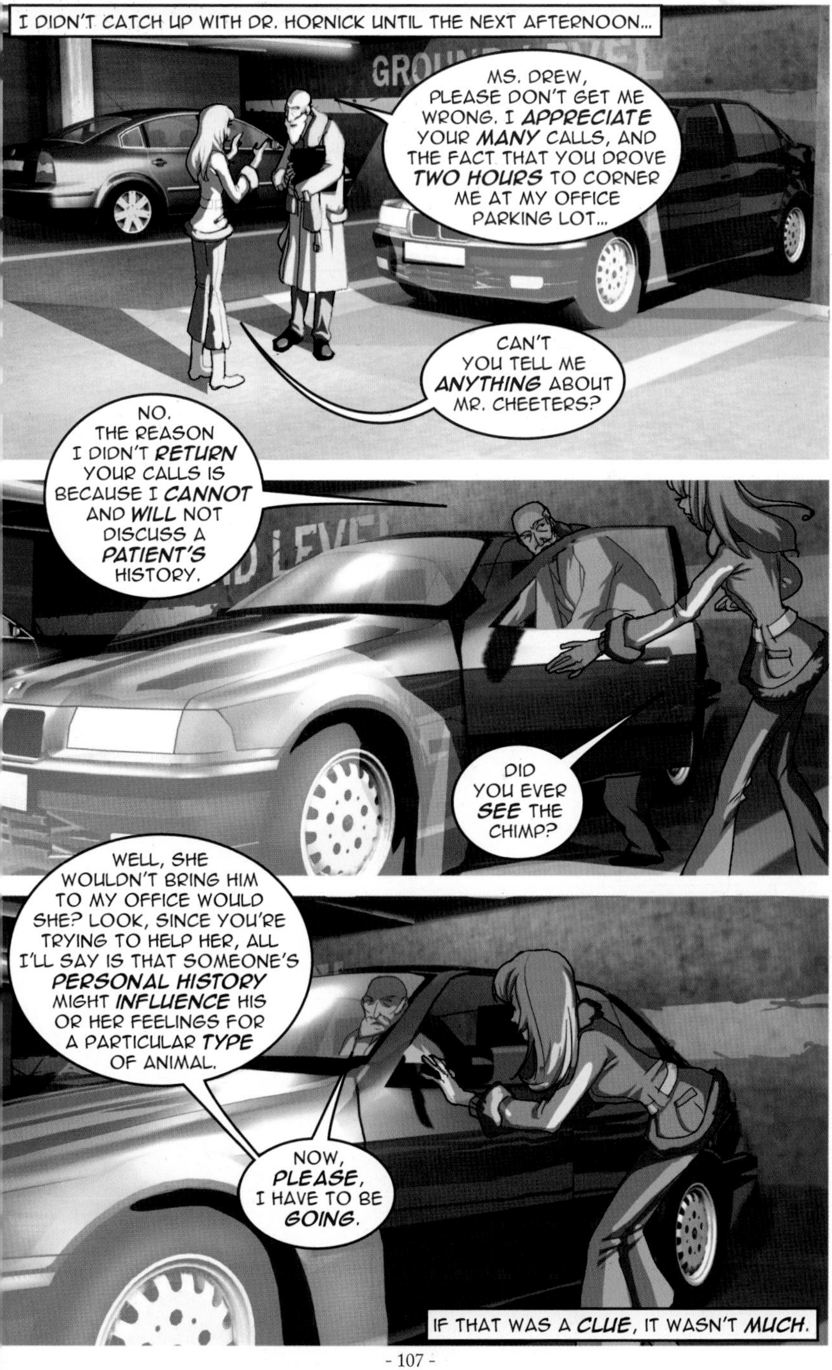
I DIDN'T CATCH UP WITH DR. HORNICK UNTIL THE NEXT AFTERNOON...
MS. DREW, PLEASE DON'T GET ME WRONG. I APPRECIATE YOUR MANY CALLS, AND THE FACT THAT YOU DROVE TWO HOURS TO CORNER ME AT MY OFFICE PARKING LOT...
CAN'T YOU TELL ME ANYTHING ABOUT MR. CHEETERS?
NO. THE REASON I DIDN'T RETURN YOUR CALLS IS BECAUSE I CANNOT AND WILL NOT DISCUSS A PATIENT'S HISTORY.
DID YOU EVER SEE THE CHIMP?
WELL, SHE WOULDN'T BRING HIM TO MY OFFICE WOULD SHE? LOOK, SINCE YOU'RE TRYING TO HELP HER, ALL I'LL SAY IS THAT SOMEONE'S PERSONAL HISTORY MIGHT INFLUENCE HIS OR HER FEELINGS FOR A PARTICULAR TYPE OF ANIMAL.
NOW, PLEASE, I HAVE TO BE GOING.
IF THAT WAS A CLUE, IT WASN'T MUCH.

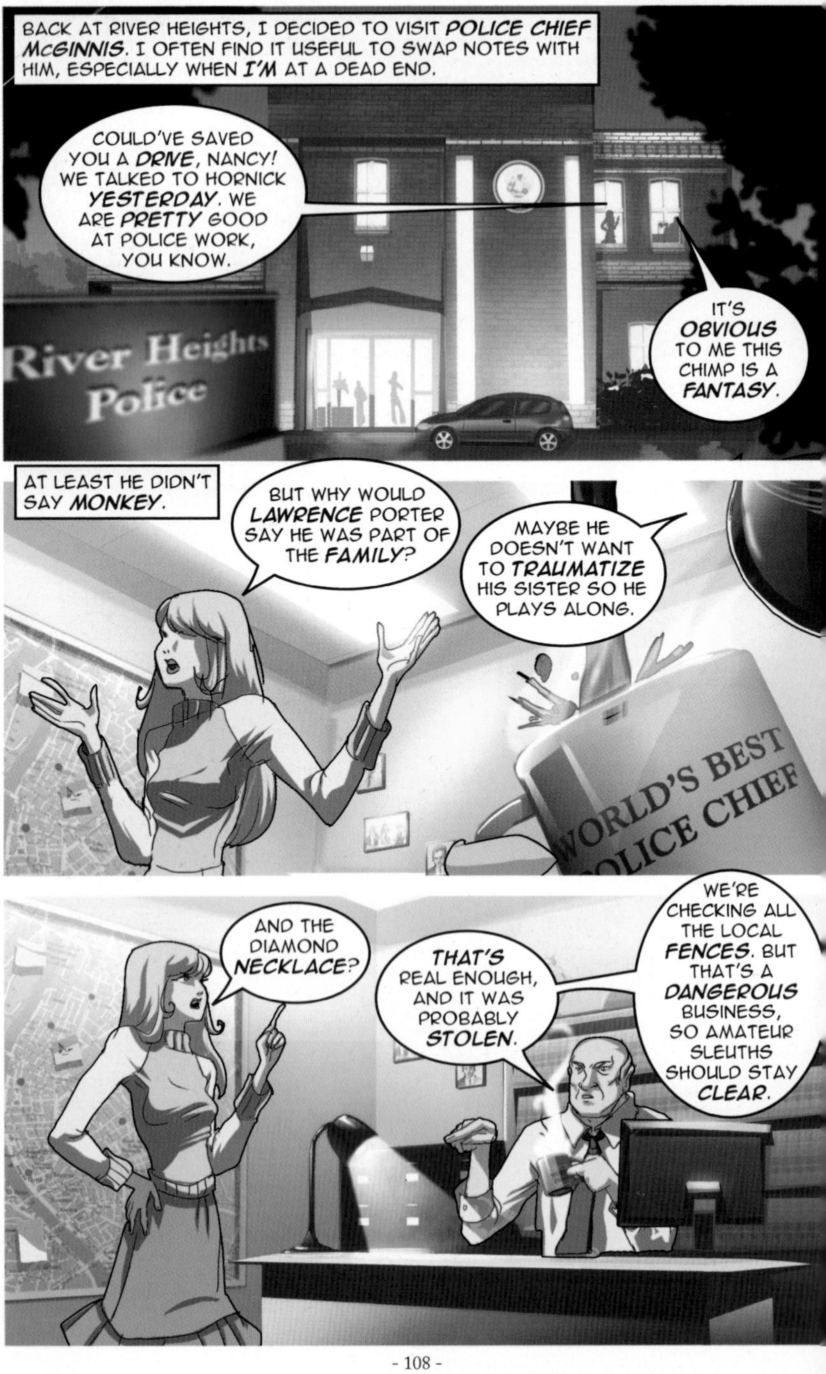

BACK AT RIVER HEIGHTS, I DECIDED TO VISIT POLICE CHIEF McGINNIS. I OFTEN FIND IT USEFUL TO SWAP NOTES WITH HIM, ESPECIALLY WHEN I'M AT A DEAD END.
COULD'VE SAVED YOU A DRIVE, NANCY! WE TALKED TO HORNICK YESTERDAY. WE ARE PRETTY GOOD AT POLICE WORK, YOU KNOW.
IT'S OBVIOUS TO ME THIS CHIMP IS A FANTASY.
River Heights Police
AT LEAST HE DIDN'T SAY MONKEY.
BUT WHY WOULD LAWRENCE PORTER SAY HE WAS PART OF THE FAMILY?
MAYBE HE DOESN'T WANT TO TRAUMATIZE HIS SISTER SO HE PLAYS ALONG.
WORLD'S BEST POLICE CHIEF
AND THE DIAMOND NECKLACE?
THAT'S REAL ENOUGH, AND IT WAS PROBABLY STOLEN.
WE'RE CHECKING ALL THE LOCAL FENCES. BUT THAT'S A DANGEROUS BUSINESS, SO AMATEUR SLEUTHS SHOULD STAY CLEAR.

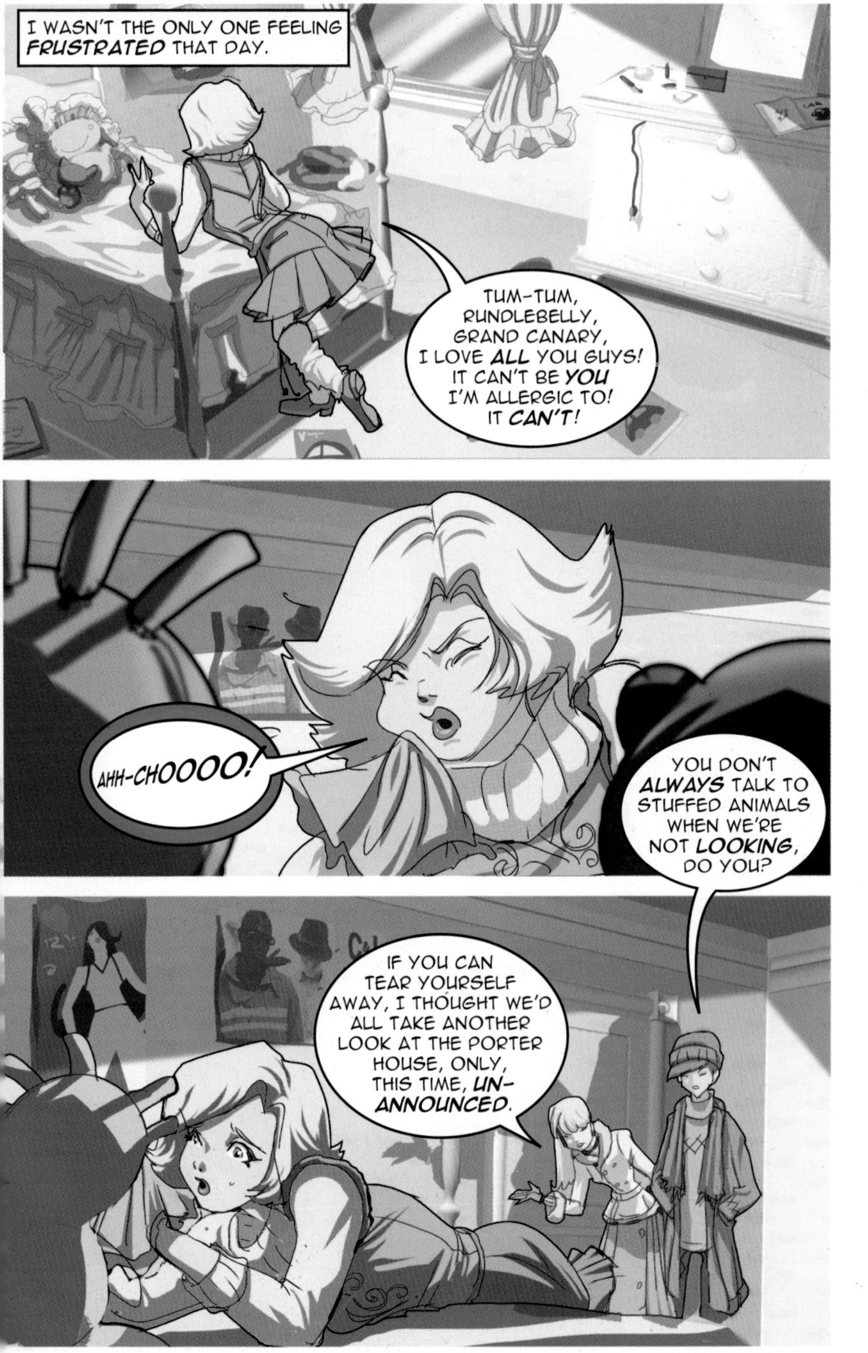
I WASN'T THE ONLY ONE FEELING **FRUSTRATED** THAT DAY.
TUM-TUM, RUNDLEBELLY, GRAND CANARY, I LOVE **ALL** YOU GUYS! IT CAN'T BE ***YOU*** I'M ALLERGIC TO! IT ***CAN'T***!
AHH-CHOOOO!
YOU DON'T **ALWAYS** TALK TO STUFFED ANIMALS WHEN WE'RE NOT **LOOKING**, DO YOU?
IF YOU CAN TEAR YOURSELF AWAY, I THOUGHT WE'D ALL TAKE ANOTHER LOOK AT THE PORTER HOUSE, ONLY, THIS TIME, **UN-ANNOUNCED**.

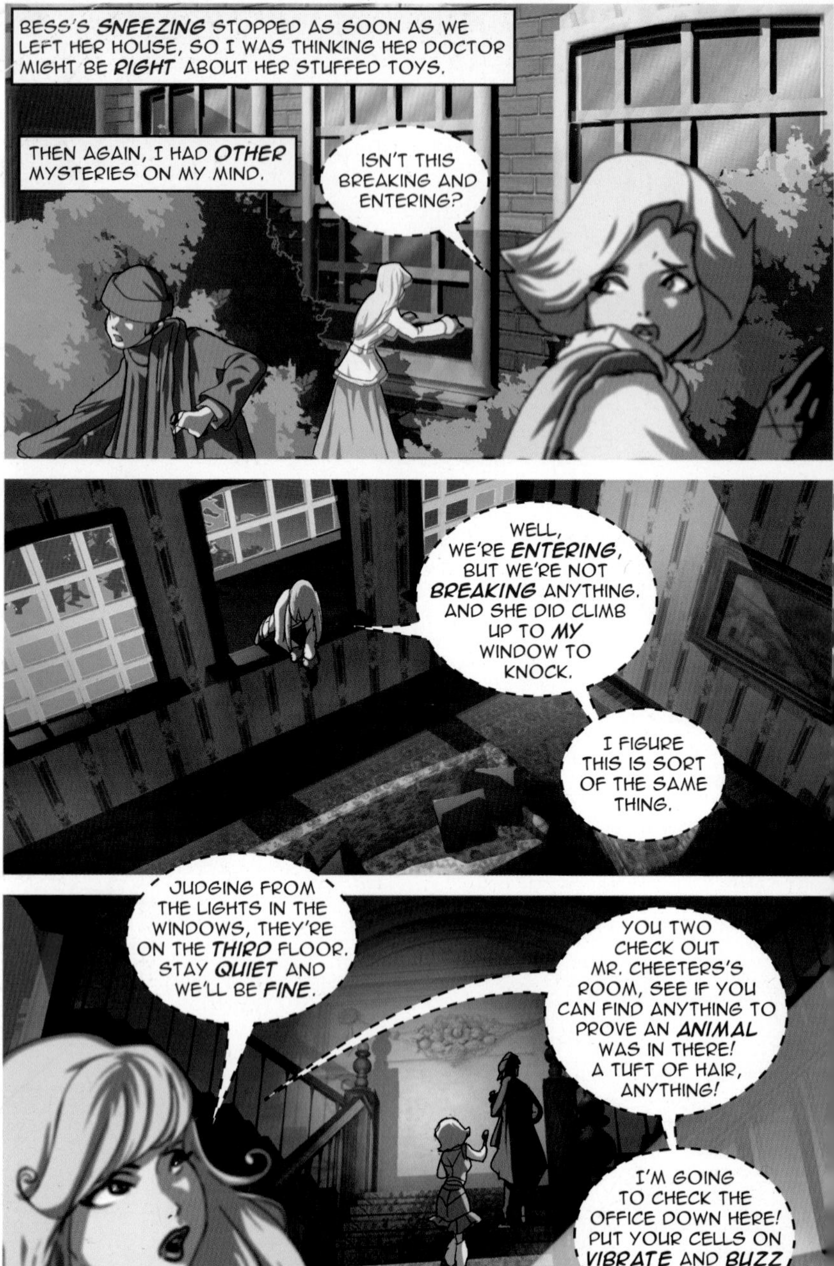
BESS'S SNEEZING STOPPED AS SOON AS WE LEFT HER HOUSE, SO I WAS THINKING HER DOCTOR MIGHT BE RIGHT ABOUT HER STUFFED TOYS.
THEN AGAIN, I HAD OTHER MYSTERIES ON MY MIND.
ISN'T THIS BREAKING AND ENTERING?
WELL, WE'RE ENTERING, BUT WE'RE NOT BREAKING ANYTHING. AND SHE DID CLIMB UP TO MY WINDOW TO KNOCK.
I FIGURE THIS IS SORT OF THE SAME THING.
JUDGING FROM THE LIGHTS IN THE WINDOWS, THEY'RE ON THE THIRD FLOOR. STAY QUIET AND WE'LL BE FINE.
YOU TWO CHECK OUT MR. CHEETERS'S ROOM, SEE IF YOU CAN FIND ANYTHING TO PROVE AN ANIMAL WAS IN THERE! A TUFT OF HAIR, ANYTHING!
I'M GOING TO CHECK THE OFFICE DOWN HERE! PUT YOUR CELLS ON VIBRATE AND BUZZ ME IF YOU FIND ANYTHING!

THE *COMPUTER* WAS WHAT I WAS AFTER. IF MR. CHEETERS WAS REAL, THERE HAD TO BE A DIGITIZED PHOTO OR *SOMETHING* ON THERE.

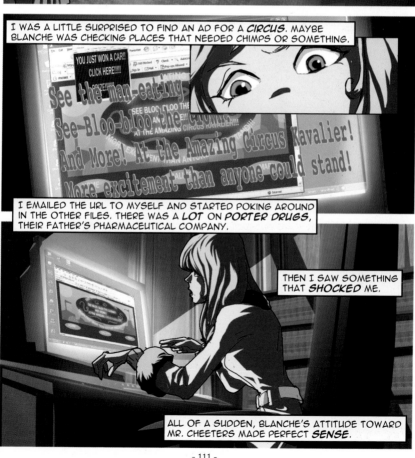

I WAS A LITTLE SURPRISED TO FIND AN AD FOR A *CIRCUS*. MAYBE BLANCHE WAS CHECKING PLACES THAT NEEDED CHIMPS OR SOMETHING.

YOU JUST WON A CAR!! CLICK HERE!!!!!

See the man-eating
See-Bloo-bloo the Clown!!!
And More! At the Amazing Circus Kavalier!
More excitement than anyone could stand!

I EMAILED THE URL TO MYSELF AND STARTED POKING AROUND IN THE OTHER FILES. THERE WAS A *LOT* ON *PORTER DRUGS*, THEIR FATHER'S PHARMACEUTICAL COMPANY.

THEN I SAW SOMETHING THAT *SHOCKED* ME.

ALL OF A SUDDEN, BLANCHE'S ATTITUDE TOWARD MR. CHEETERS MADE PERFECT *SENSE*.

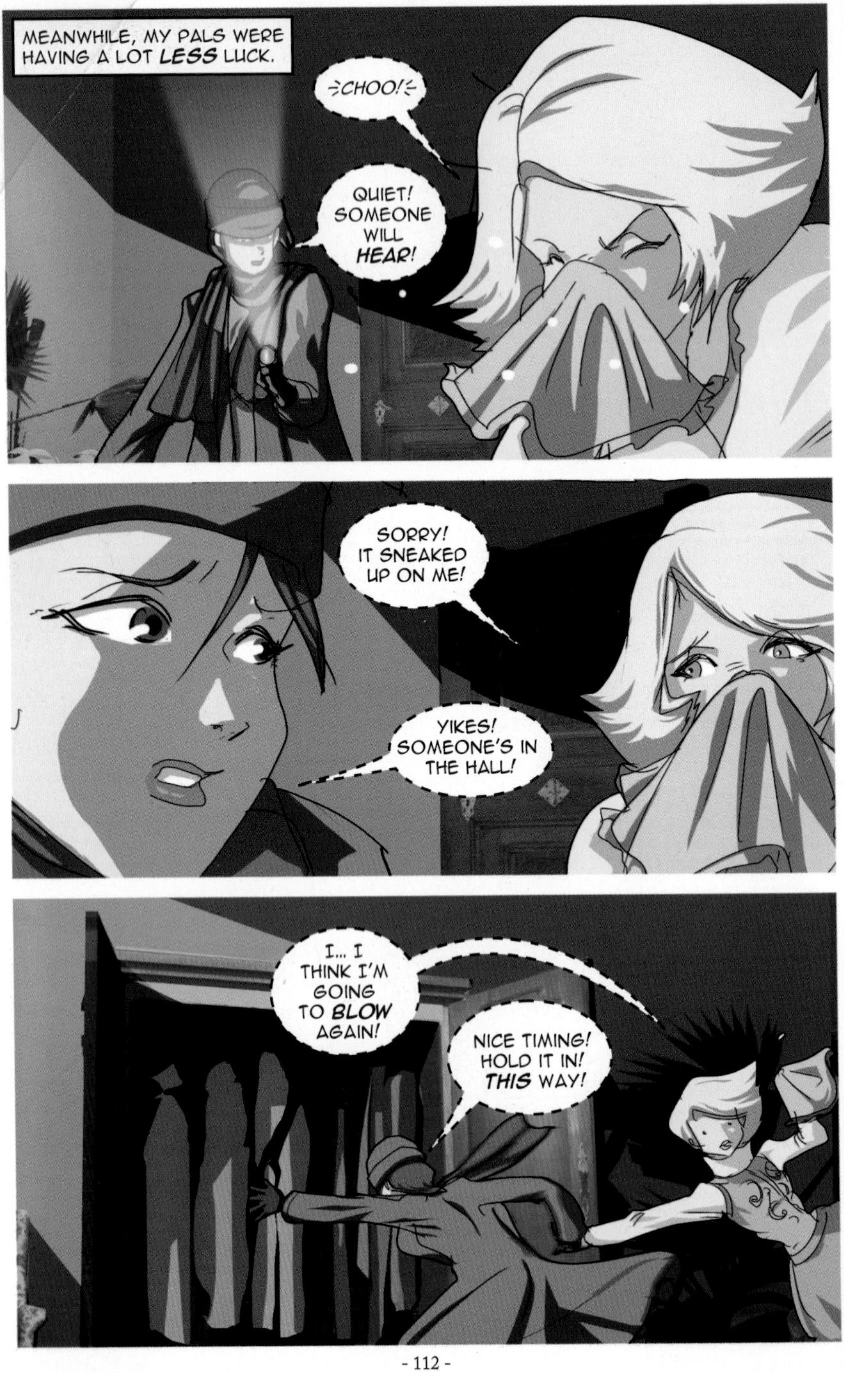
MEANWHILE, MY PALS WERE HAVING A LOT **LESS** LUCK.
CHOO!
QUIET! SOMEONE WILL **HEAR**!
SORRY! IT SNEAKED UP ON ME!
YIKES! SOMEONE'S IN THE HALL!
I... I THINK I'M GOING TO **BLOW** AGAIN!
NICE TIMING! HOLD IT IN! **THIS** WAY!

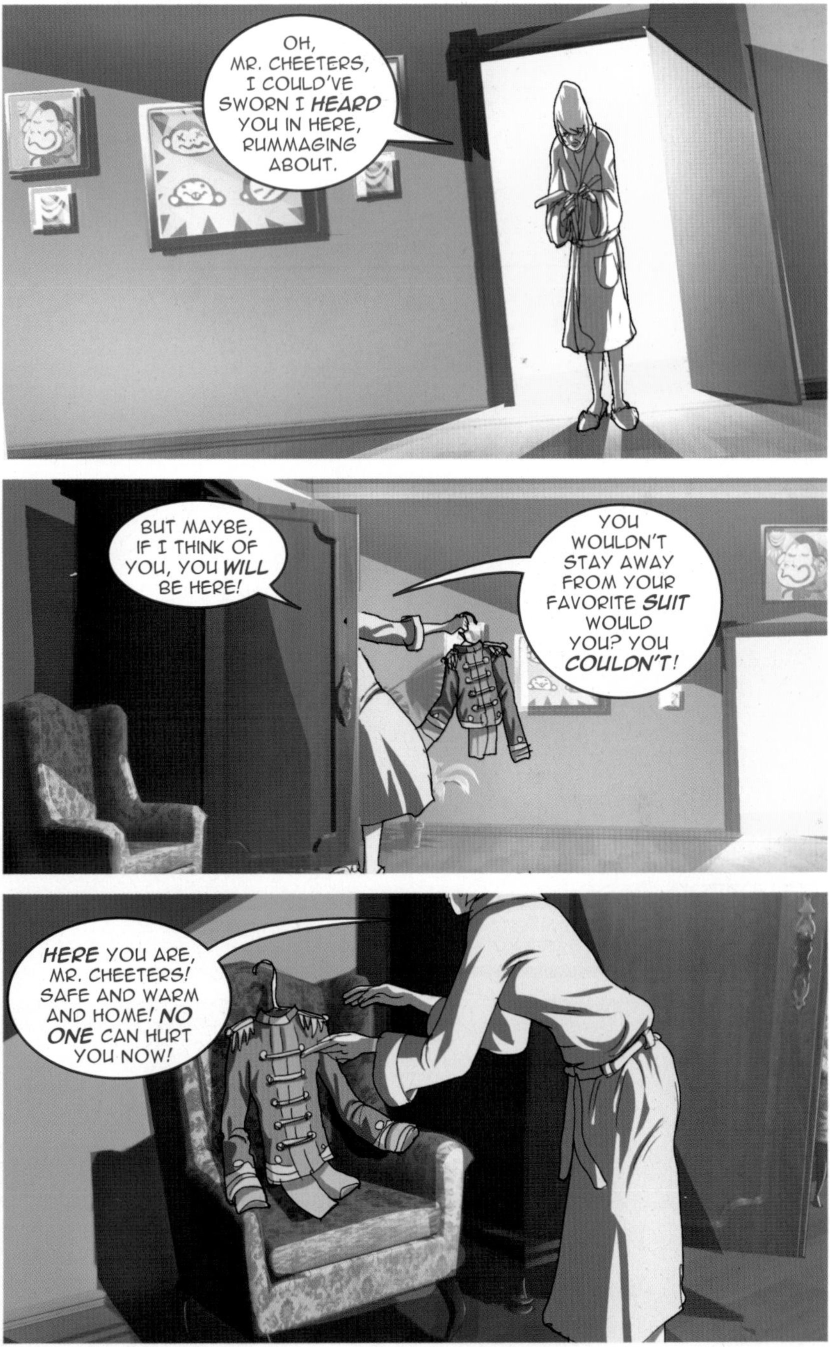
OH, MR. CHEETERS, I COULD'VE SWORN I HEARD YOU IN HERE, RUMMAGING ABOUT.
BUT MAYBE, IF I THINK OF YOU, YOU WILL BE HERE!
YOU WOULDN'T STAY AWAY FROM YOUR FAVORITE SUIT WOULD YOU? YOU COULDN'T!
HERE YOU ARE, MR. CHEETERS! SAFE AND WARM AND HOME! NO ONE CAN HURT YOU NOW!

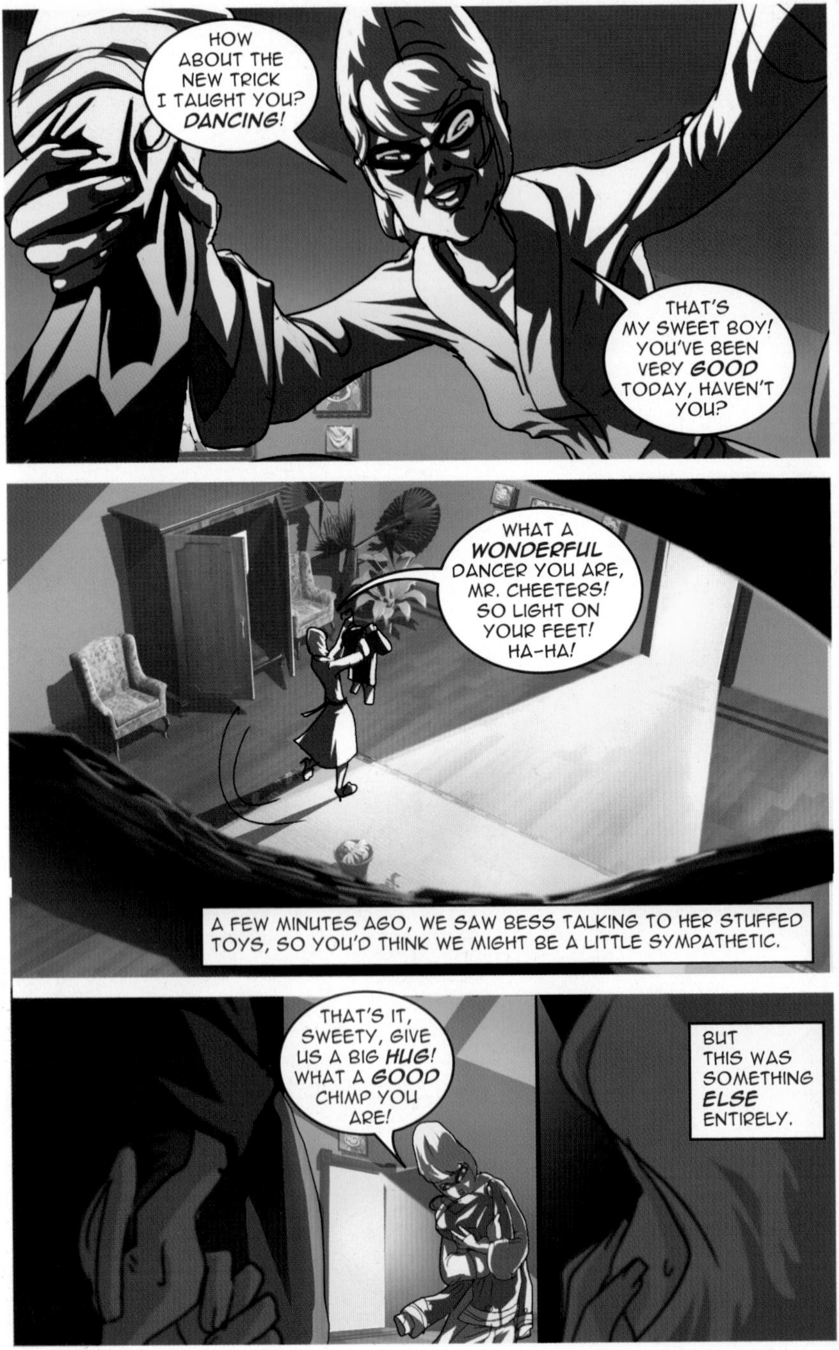
HOW ABOUT THE NEW TRICK I TAUGHT YOU? DANCING!
THAT'S MY SWEET BOY! YOU'VE BEEN VERY GOOD TODAY, HAVEN'T YOU?
WHAT A WONDERFUL DANCER YOU ARE, MR. CHEETERS! SO LIGHT ON YOUR FEET! HA-HA!
A FEW MINUTES AGO, WE SAW BESS TALKING TO HER STUFFED TOYS, SO YOU'D THINK WE MIGHT BE A LITTLE SYMPATHETIC.
THAT'S IT, SWEETY, GIVE US A BIG HUG! WHAT A GOOD CHIMP YOU ARE!
BUT THIS WAS SOMETHING ELSE ENTIRELY.

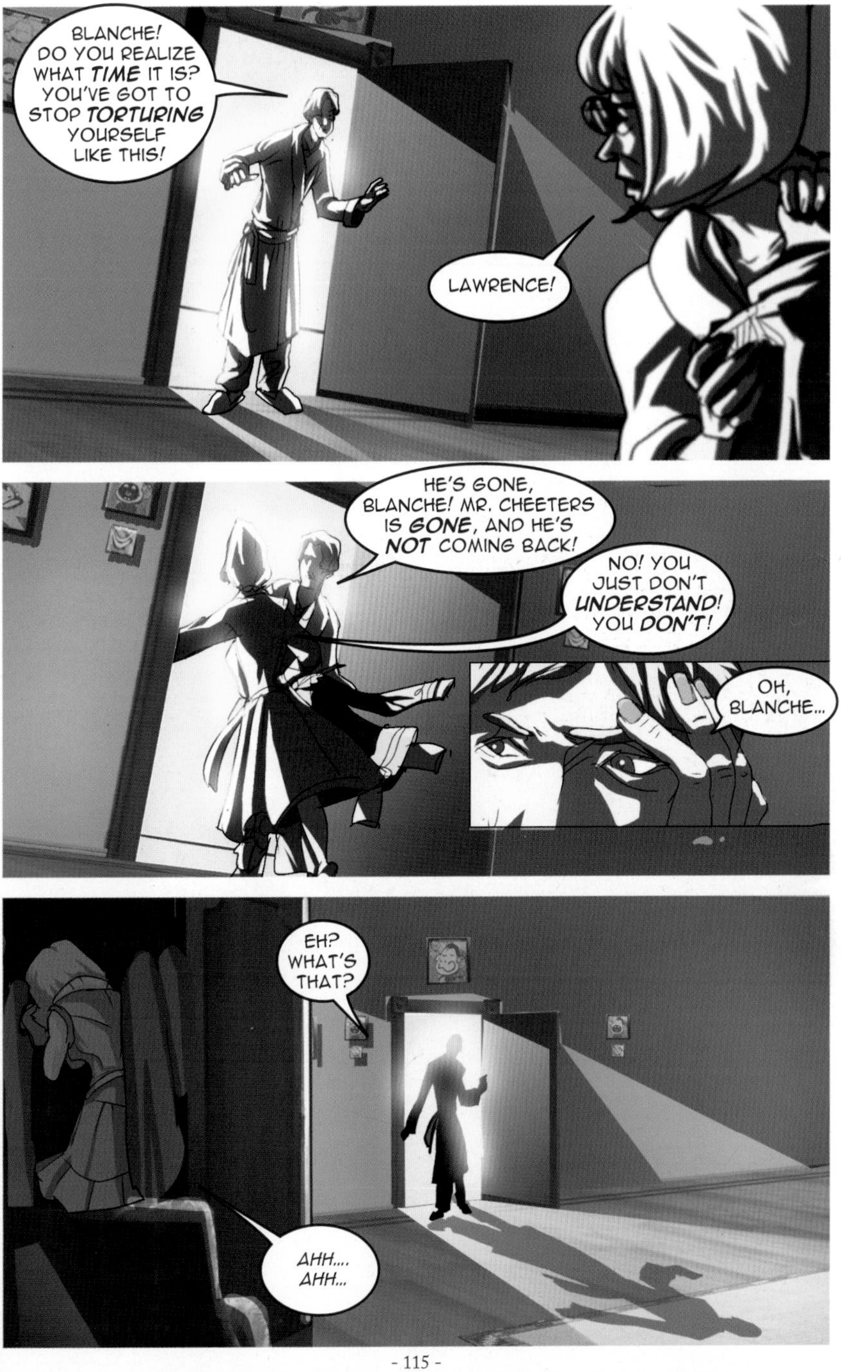
BLANCHE! DO YOU REALIZE WHAT *TIME* IT IS? YOU'VE GOT TO STOP *TORTURING* YOURSELF LIKE THIS!
LAWRENCE!
HE'S GONE, BLANCHE! MR. CHEETERS IS *GONE*, AND HE'S *NOT* COMING BACK!
NO! YOU JUST DON'T *UNDERSTAND*! YOU *DON'T*!
OH, BLANCHE...
EH? WHAT'S THAT?
AHH.... AHH...

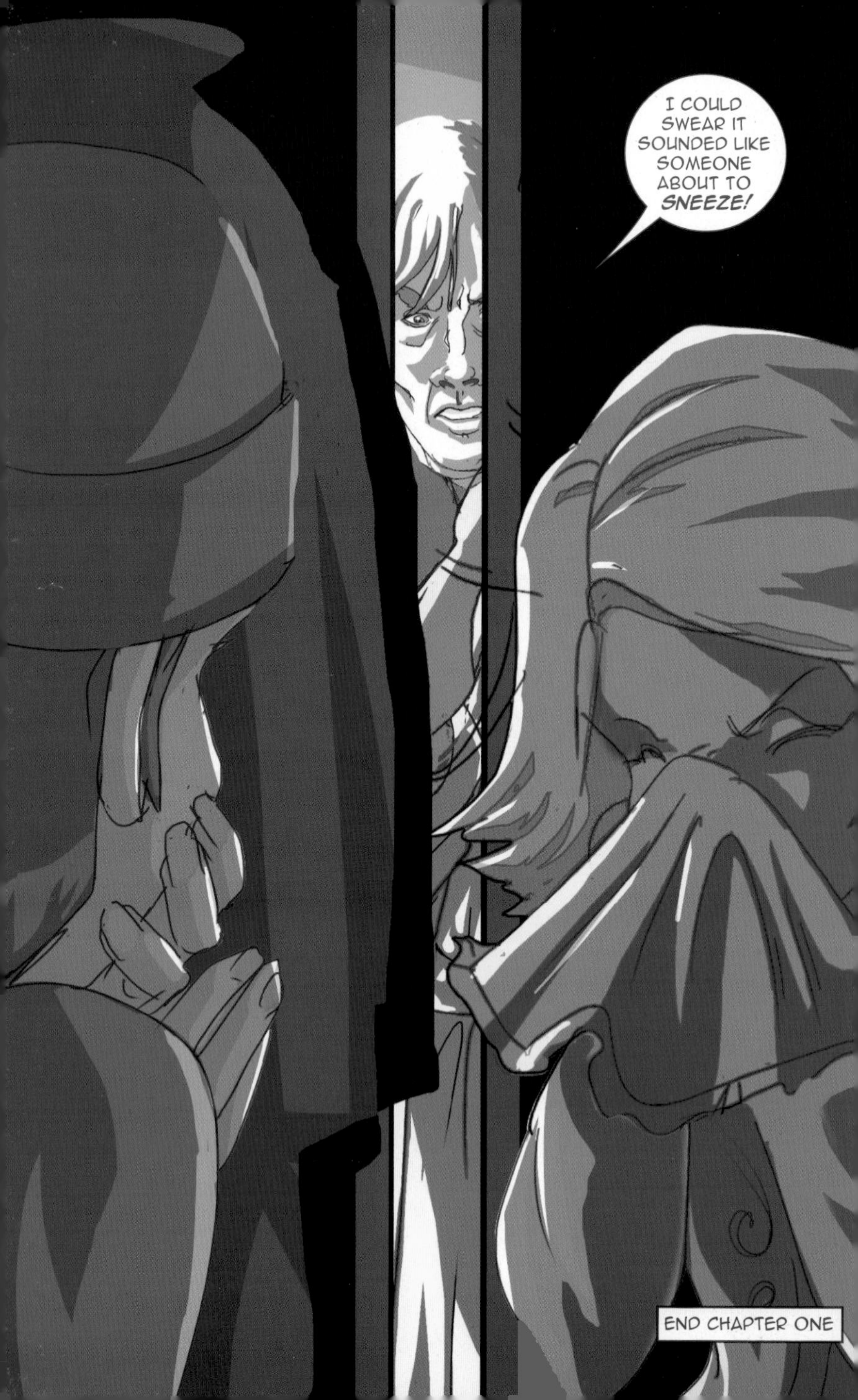
I COULD SWEAR IT SOUNDED LIKE SOMEONE ABOUT TO SNEEZE!
END CHAPTER ONE

CHAPTER TWO: ANATOMY OF A SNEEZE

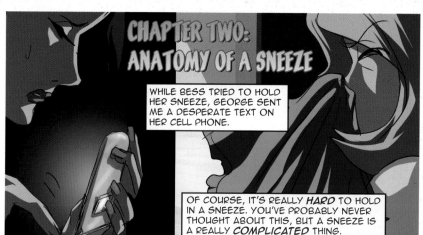

WHILE BESS TRIED TO HOLD HER SNEEZE, GEORGE SENT ME A DESPERATE TEXT ON HER CELL PHONE.

OF COURSE, IT'S REALLY *HARD* TO HOLD IN A SNEEZE. YOU'VE PROBABLY NEVER THOUGHT ABOUT THIS, BUT A SNEEZE IS A REALLY *COMPLICATED* THING.

THERE'S A WHOLE SECTION OF THE BRAIN *DEVOTED* TO SNEEZES, AND YES, IT'S CALLED THE *SNEEZE CENTER*. NOT THE *BEST* NAME, BUT WHAT CAN YOU DO?

ANYWAY, THANKS TO GEORGE'S TEXT MESSAGE I KNEW I HAD TO DO *SOMETHING* FAST!

WHEN THE INSIDE OF A NOSE IS *IRRITATED*, IMPULSES ARE SENT TO ALL THE MUSCLES NEEDED TO MAKE A SNEEZE.

AND THERE'S QUITE A *FEW*.

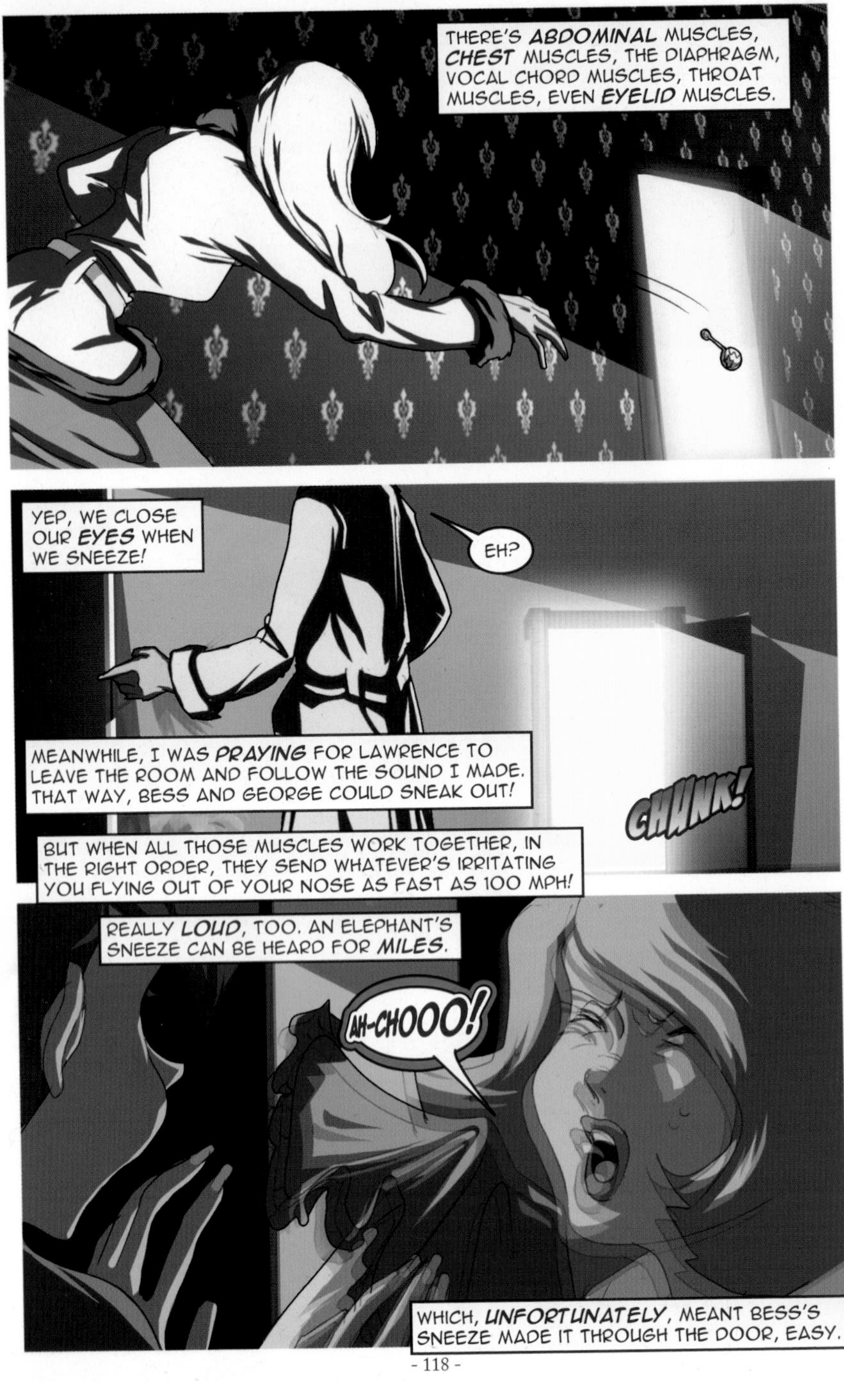
THERE'S ABDOMINAL MUSCLES, CHEST MUSCLES, THE DIAPHRAGM, VOCAL CHORD MUSCLES, THROAT MUSCLES, EVEN EYELID MUSCLES.
YEP, WE CLOSE OUR EYES WHEN WE SNEEZE!
EH?
MEANWHILE, I WAS PRAYING FOR LAWRENCE TO LEAVE THE ROOM AND FOLLOW THE SOUND I MADE. THAT WAY, BESS AND GEORGE COULD SNEAK OUT!
CHUNK!
BUT WHEN ALL THOSE MUSCLES WORK TOGETHER, IN THE RIGHT ORDER, THEY SEND WHATEVER'S IRRITATING YOU FLYING OUT OF YOUR NOSE AS FAST AS 100 MPH!
REALLY LOUD, TOO. AN ELEPHANT'S SNEEZE CAN BE HEARD FOR MILES.
AH-CHOOO!
WHICH, UNFORTUNATELY, MEANT BESS'S SNEEZE MADE IT THROUGH THE DOOR, EASY.

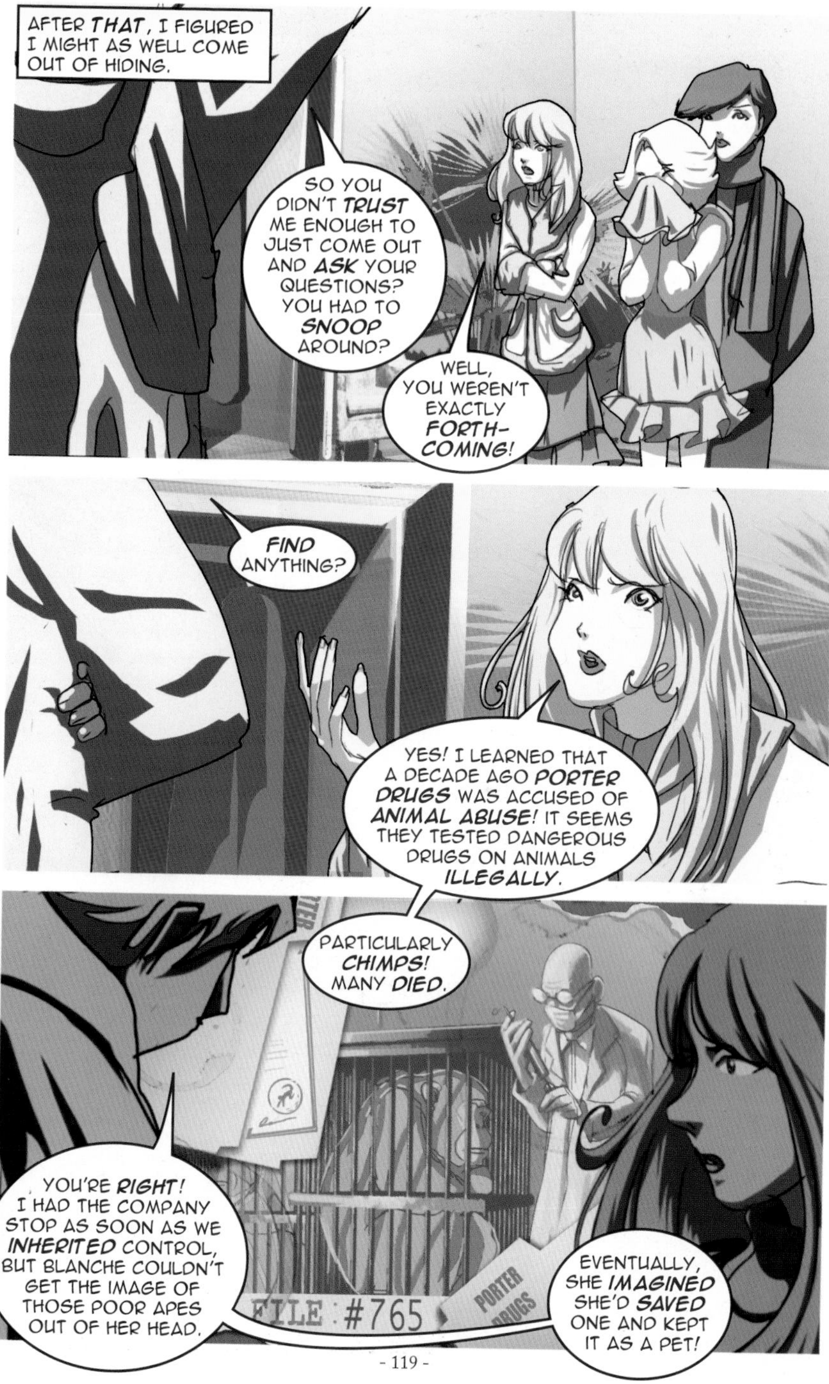

AFTER THAT, I FIGURED I MIGHT AS WELL COME OUT OF HIDING.
SO YOU DIDN'T TRUST ME ENOUGH TO JUST COME OUT AND ASK YOUR QUESTIONS? YOU HAD TO SNOOP AROUND?
WELL, YOU WEREN'T EXACTLY FORTH-COMING!
FIND ANYTHING?
YES! I LEARNED THAT A DECADE AGO PORTER DRUGS WAS ACCUSED OF ANIMAL ABUSE! IT SEEMS THEY TESTED DANGEROUS DRUGS ON ANIMALS ILLEGALLY.
PARTICULARLY CHIMPS! MANY DIED.
YOU'RE RIGHT! I HAD THE COMPANY STOP AS SOON AS WE INHERITED CONTROL, BUT BLANCHE COULDN'T GET THE IMAGE OF THOSE POOR APES OUT OF HER HEAD.
FILE :#765
PORTER DRUGS
EVENTUALLY, SHE IMAGINED SHE'D SAVED ONE AND KEPT IT AS A PET!

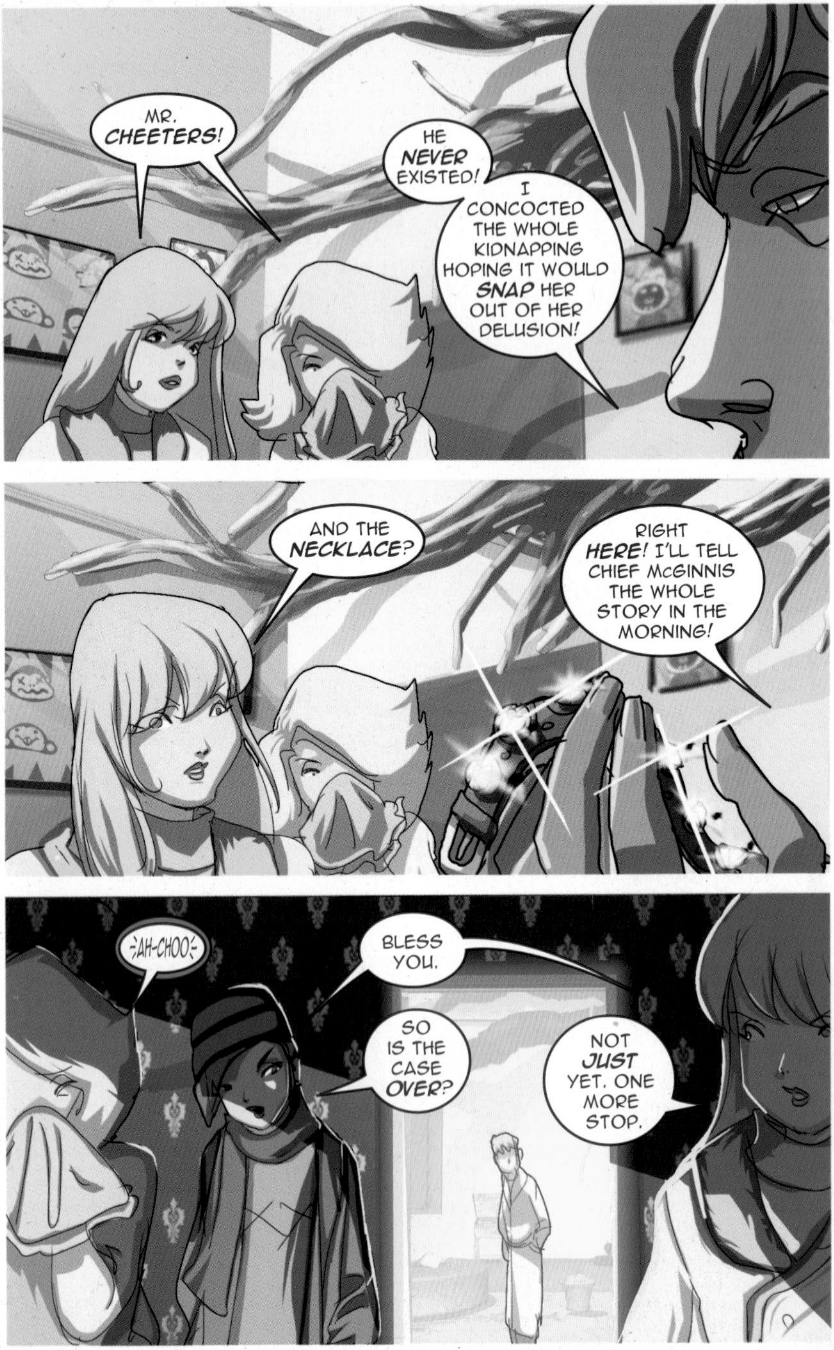
MR. CHEETERS!
HE NEVER EXISTED!
I CONCOCTED THE WHOLE KIDNAPPING HOPING IT WOULD SNAP HER OUT OF HER DELUSION!
AND THE NECKLACE?
RIGHT HERE! I'LL TELL CHIEF McGINNIS THE WHOLE STORY IN THE MORNING!
AH-CHOO
BLESS YOU.
SO IS THE CASE OVER?
NOT JUST YET. ONE MORE STOP.

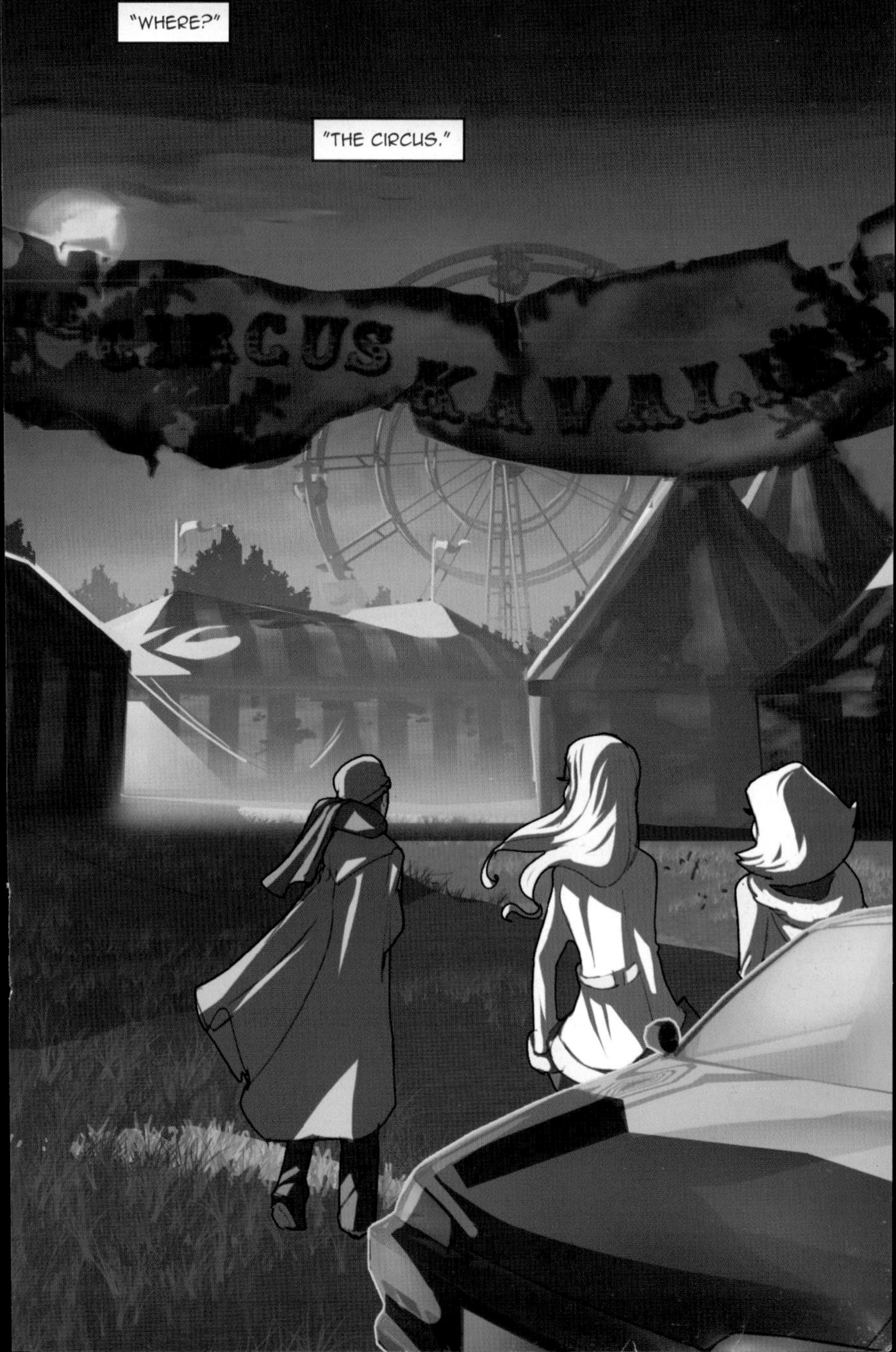
"WHERE?"
"THE CIRCUS."

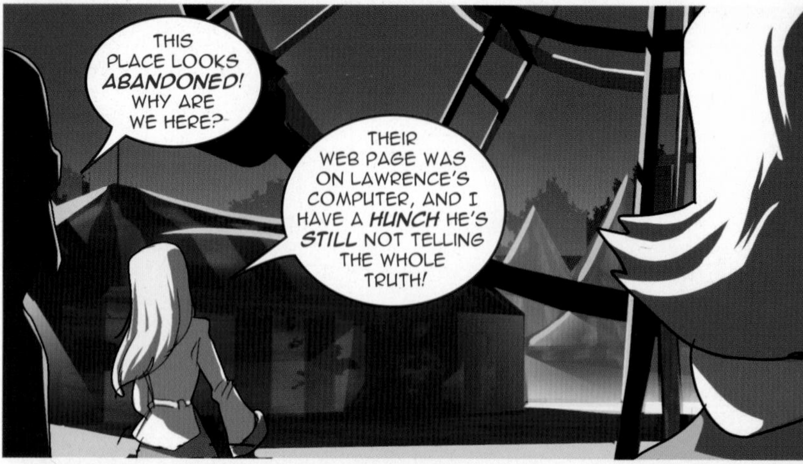
THIS PLACE LOOKS ABANDONED! WHY ARE WE HERE?
THEIR WEB PAGE WAS ON LAWRENCE'S COMPUTER, AND I HAVE A HUNCH HE'S STILL NOT TELLING THE WHOLE TRUTH!

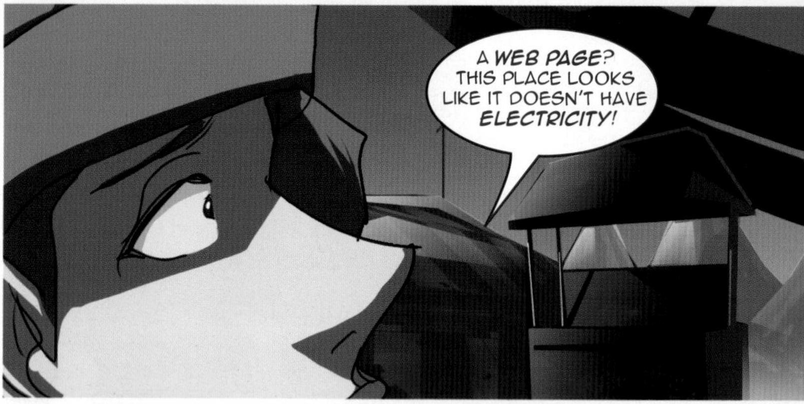
A WEB PAGE? THIS PLACE LOOKS LIKE IT DOESN'T HAVE ELECTRICITY!

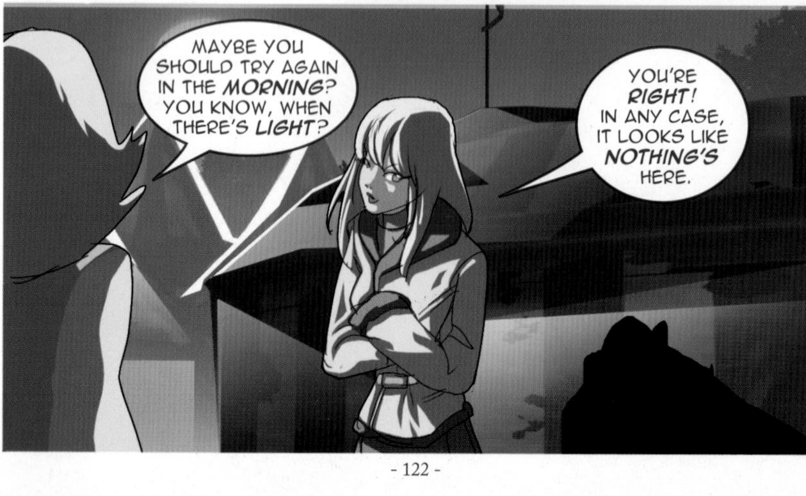
MAYBE YOU SHOULD TRY AGAIN IN THE MORNING? YOU KNOW, WHEN THERE'S LIGHT?
YOU'RE RIGHT! IN ANY CASE, IT LOOKS LIKE NOTHING'S HERE.

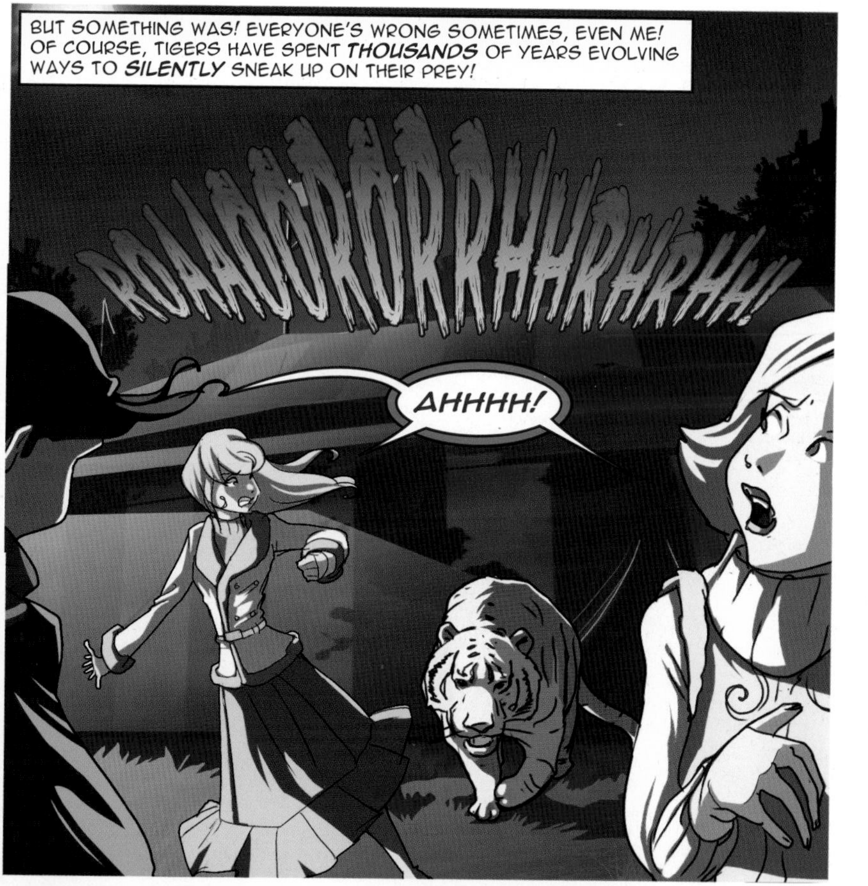
BUT SOMETHING WAS! EVERYONE'S WRONG SOMETIMES, EVEN ME! OF COURSE, TIGERS HAVE SPENT *THOUSANDS* OF YEARS EVOLVING WAYS TO *SILENTLY* SNEAK UP ON THEIR PREY!
ROAAOORORRHHRHRHH!
AHHHH!

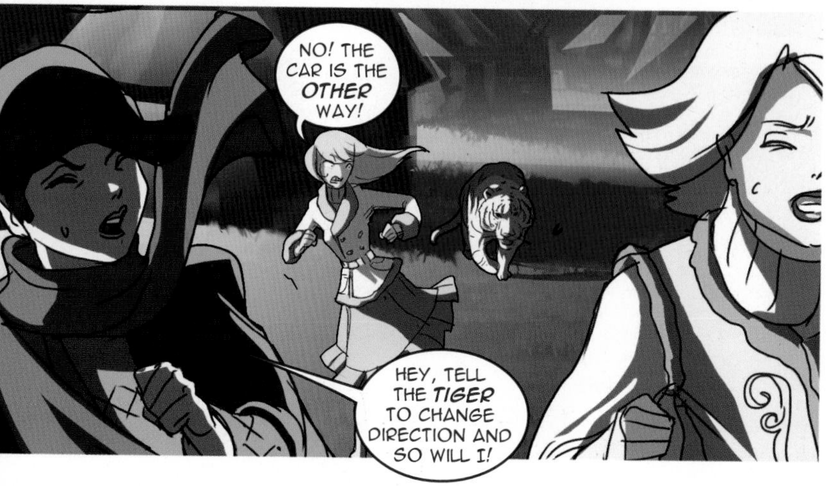
NO! THE CAR IS THE *OTHER* WAY!
HEY, TELL THE *TIGER* TO CHANGE DIRECTION AND SO WILL I!

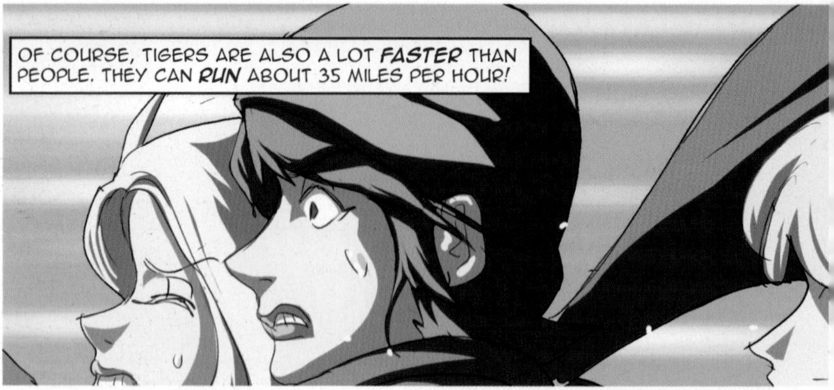
OF COURSE, TIGERS ARE ALSO A LOT FASTER THAN PEOPLE. THEY CAN RUN ABOUT 35 MILES PER HOUR!

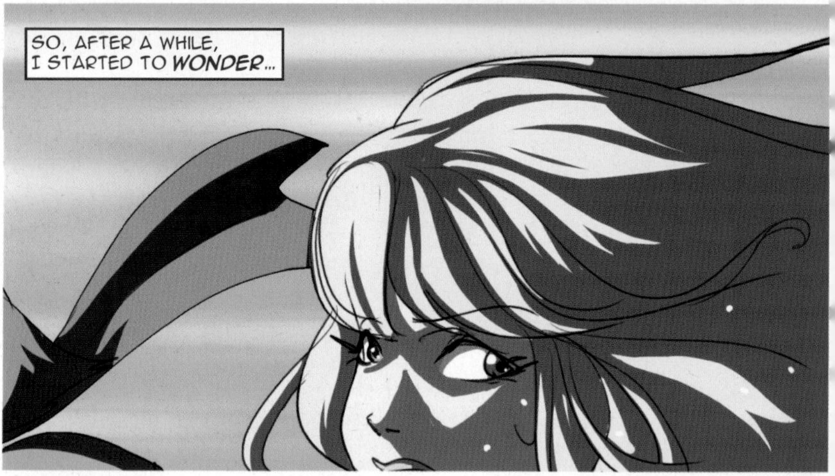
SO, AFTER A WHILE, I STARTED TO WONDER...

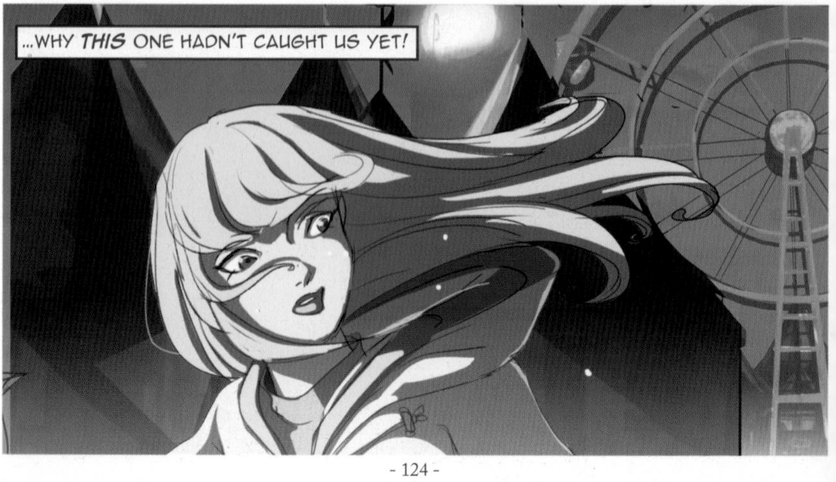
...WHY THIS ONE HADN'T CAUGHT US YET!

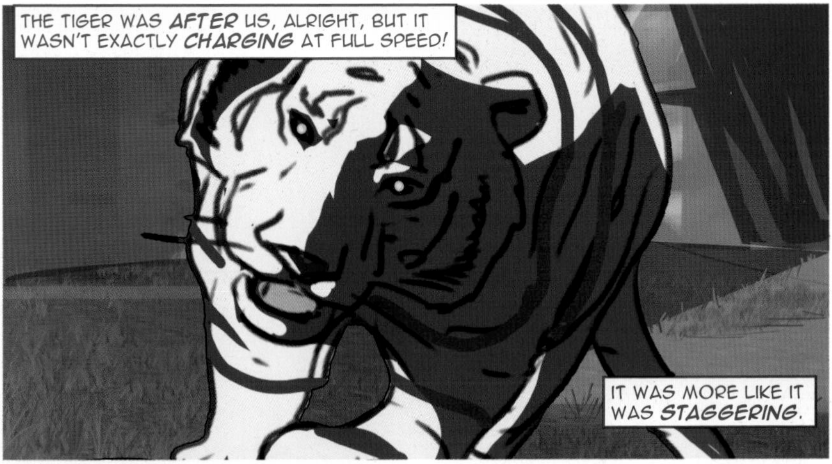
THE TIGER WAS AFTER US, ALRIGHT, BUT IT WASN'T EXACTLY CHARGING AT FULL SPEED!
IT WAS MORE LIKE IT WAS STAGGERING.

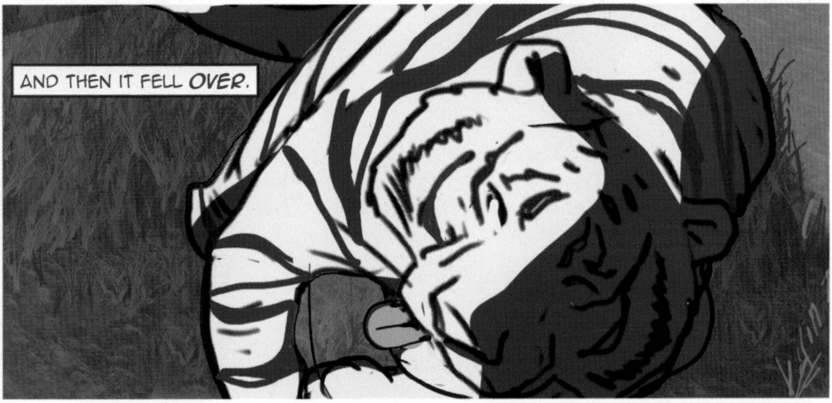
AND THEN IT FELL OVER.

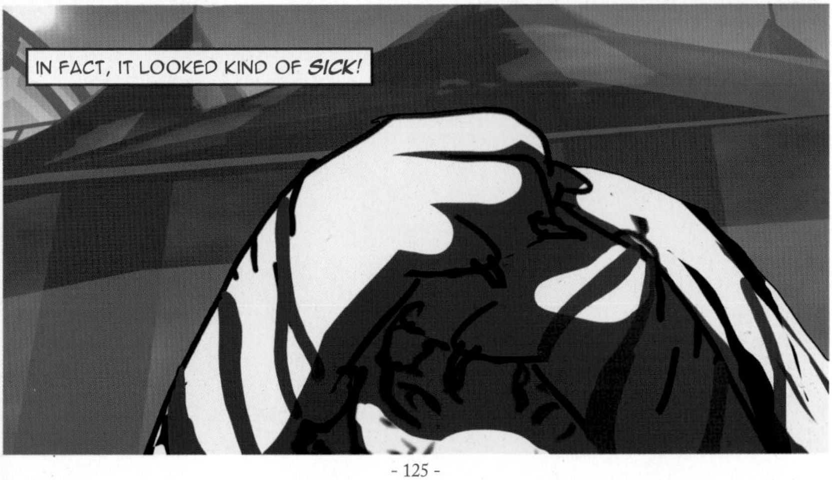
IN FACT, IT LOOKED KIND OF SICK!

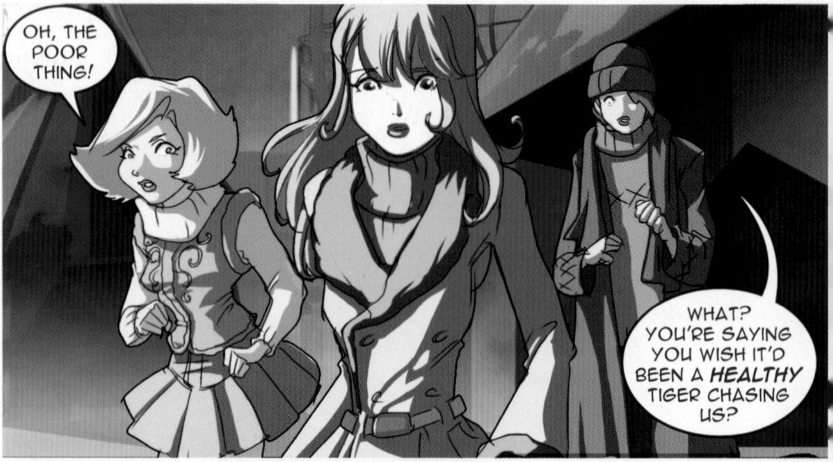
OH, THE POOR THING!
WHAT? YOU'RE SAYING YOU WISH IT'D BEEN A HEALTHY TIGER CHASING US?

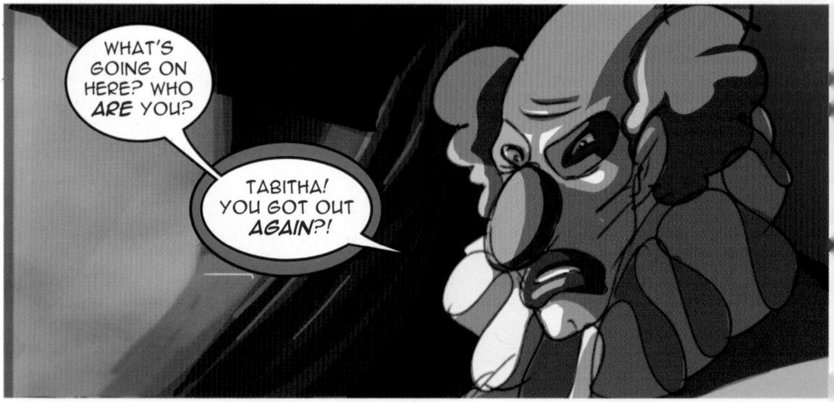
WHAT'S GOING ON HERE? WHO ARE YOU?
TABITHA! YOU GOT OUT AGAIN?!

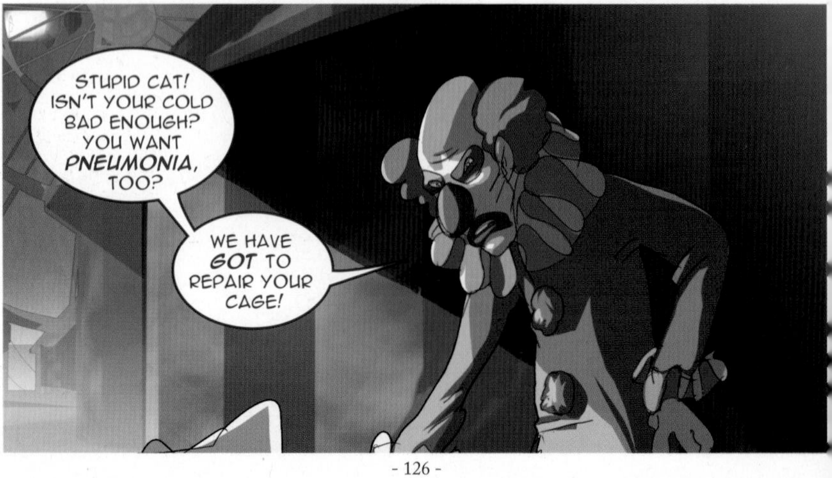
STUPID CAT! ISN'T YOUR COLD BAD ENOUGH? YOU WANT PNEUMONIA, TOO?
WE HAVE GOT TO REPAIR YOUR CAGE!

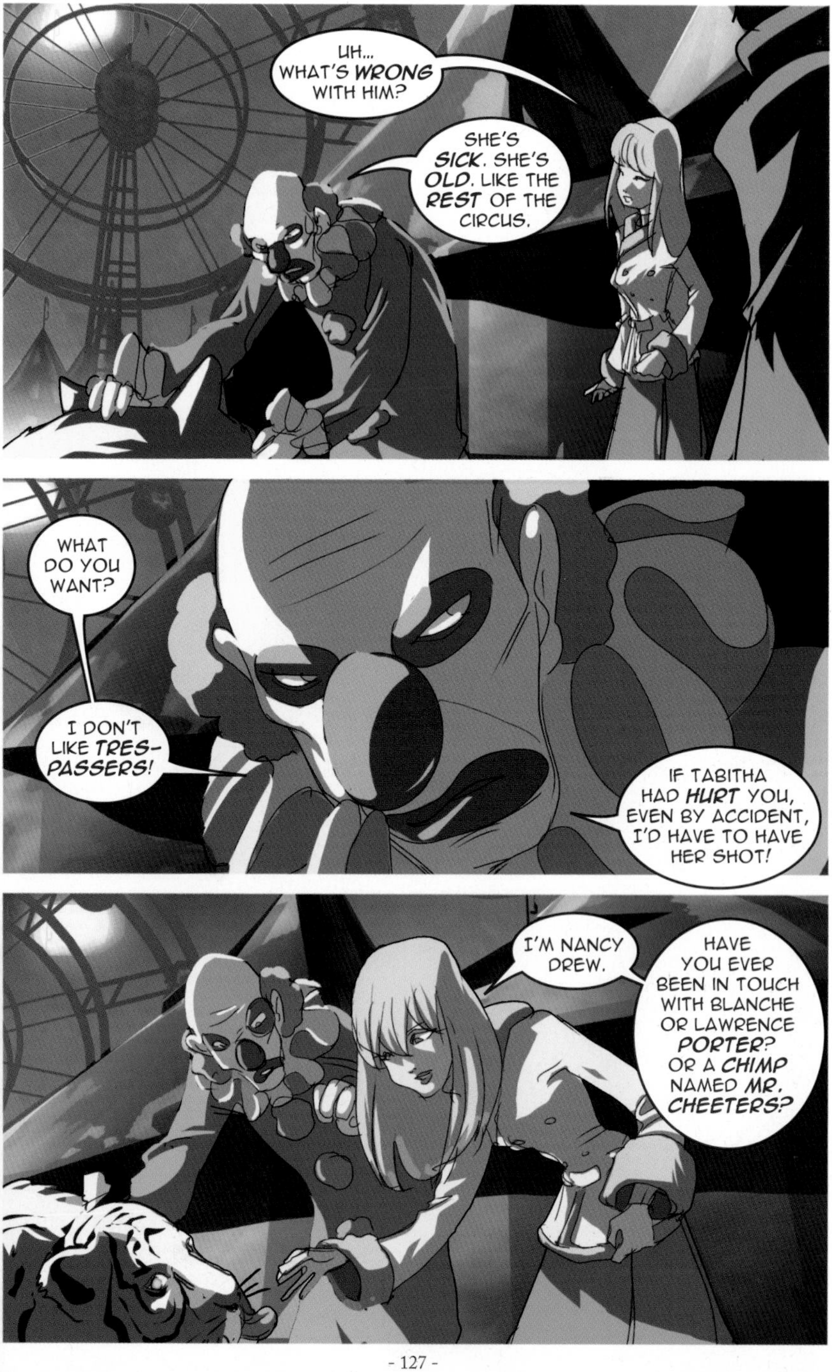
UH... WHAT'S WRONG WITH HIM?
SHE'S SICK. SHE'S OLD. LIKE THE REST OF THE CIRCUS.
WHAT DO YOU WANT?
I DON'T LIKE TRES-PASSERS!
IF TABITHA HAD HURT YOU, EVEN BY ACCIDENT, I'D HAVE TO HAVE HER SHOT!
I'M NANCY DREW.
HAVE YOU EVER BEEN IN TOUCH WITH BLANCHE OR LAWRENCE PORTER? OR A CHIMP NAMED MR. CHEETERS?

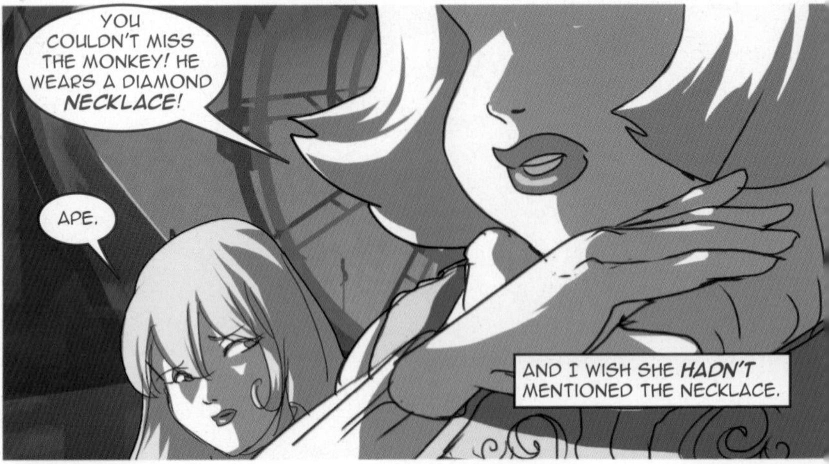
YOU COULDN'T MISS THE MONKEY! HE WEARS A DIAMOND *NECKLACE*!
APE.
AND I WISH SHE *HADN'T* MENTIONED THE NECKLACE.

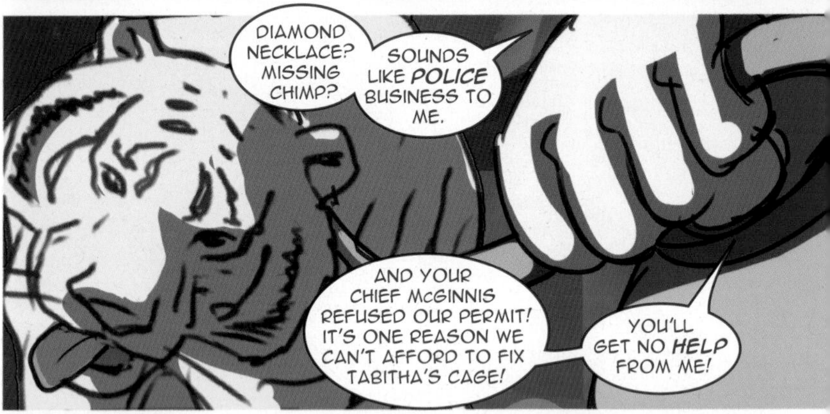
DIAMOND NECKLACE? MISSING CHIMP?
SOUNDS LIKE *POLICE* BUSINESS TO ME.
AND YOUR CHIEF McGINNIS REFUSED OUR PERMIT! IT'S ONE REASON WE CAN'T AFFORD TO FIX TABITHA'S CAGE!
YOU'LL GET NO *HELP* FROM ME!

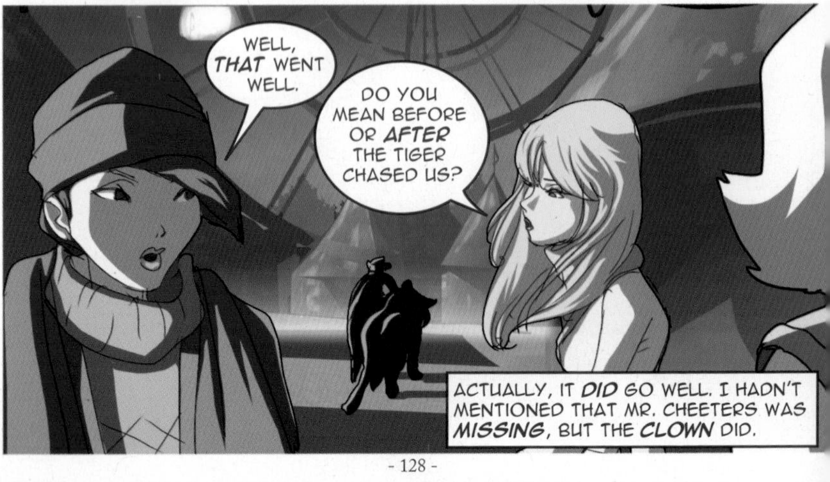
WELL, *THAT* WENT WELL.
DO YOU MEAN BEFORE OR *AFTER* THE TIGER CHASED US?
ACTUALLY, IT *DID* GO WELL. I HADN'T MENTIONED THAT MR. CHEETERS WAS *MISSING*, BUT THE *CLOWN* DID.

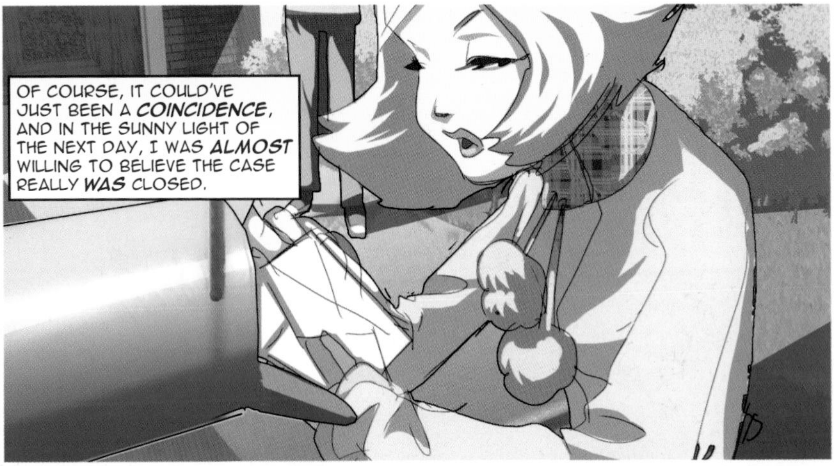
OF COURSE, IT COULD'VE JUST BEEN A *COINCIDENCE*, AND IN THE SUNNY LIGHT OF THE NEXT DAY, I WAS *ALMOST* WILLING TO BELIEVE THE CASE REALLY *WAS* CLOSED.

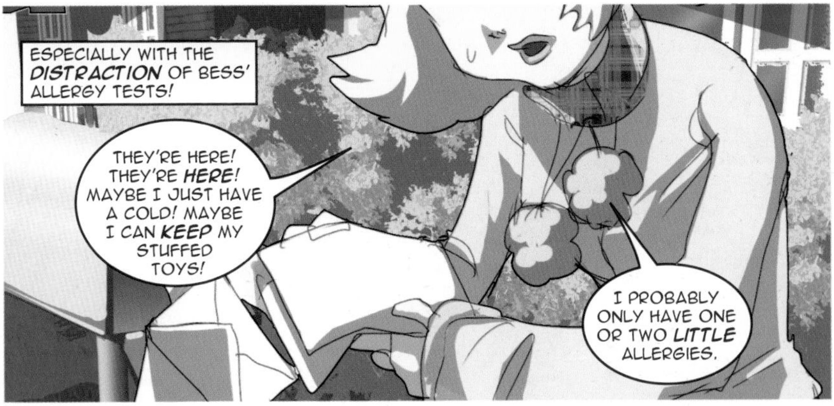
ESPECIALLY WITH THE *DISTRACTION* OF BESS' ALLERGY TESTS!
THEY'RE HERE! THEY'RE *HERE*! MAYBE I JUST HAVE A COLD! MAYBE I CAN *KEEP* MY STUFFED TOYS!
I PROBABLY ONLY HAVE ONE OR TWO *LITTLE* ALLERGIES.

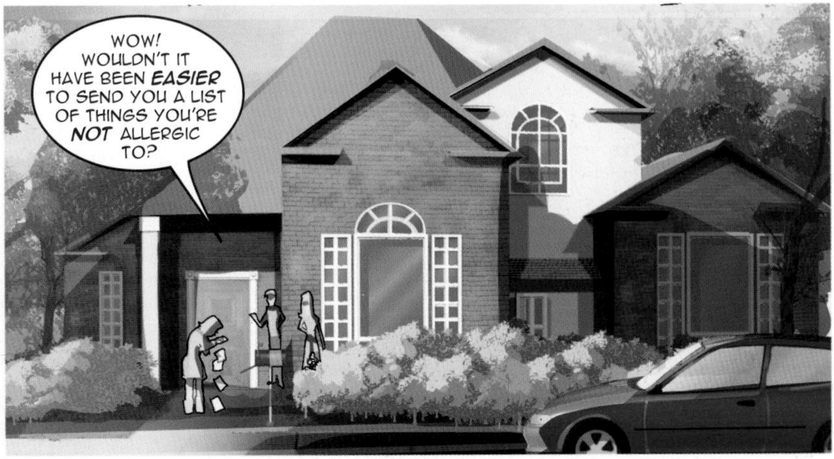
WOW! WOULDN'T IT HAVE BEEN *EASIER* TO SEND YOU A LIST OF THINGS YOU'RE *NOT* ALLERGIC TO?

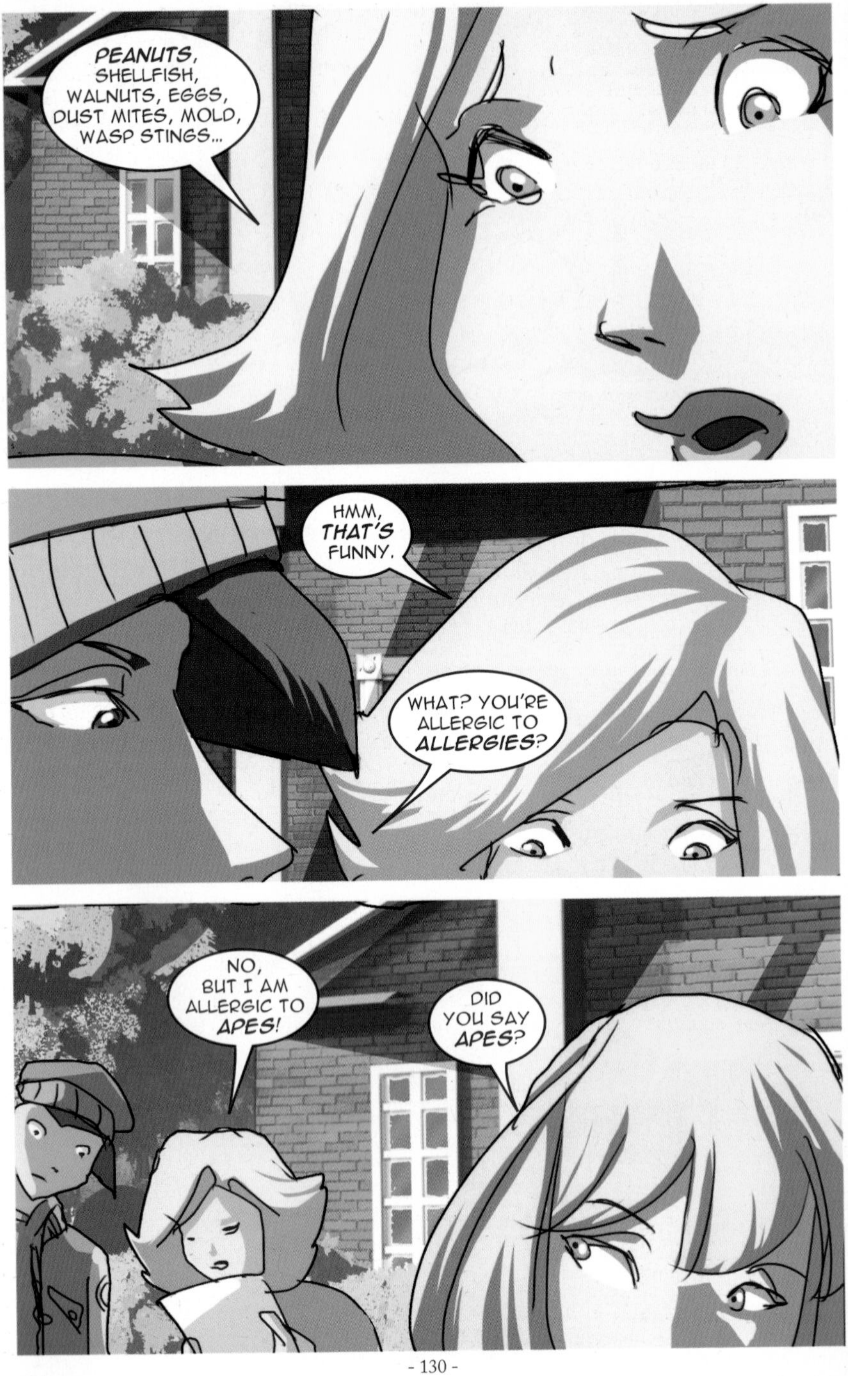
PEANUTS, SHELLFISH, WALNUTS, EGGS, DUST MITES, MOLD, WASP STINGS...
HMM, THAT'S FUNNY.
WHAT? YOU'RE ALLERGIC TO ALLERGIES?
NO, BUT I AM ALLERGIC TO APES!
DID YOU SAY APES?

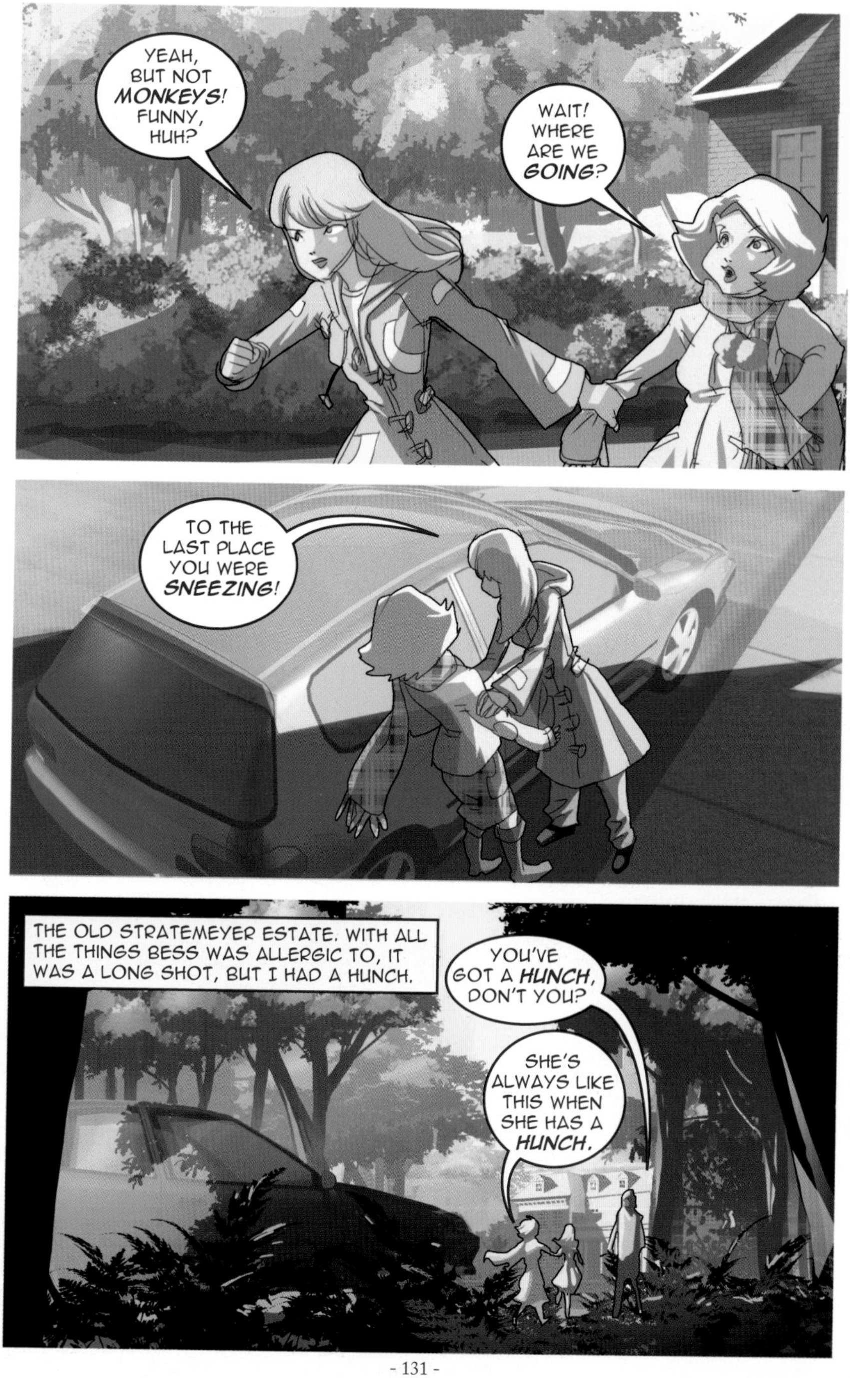
YEAH, BUT NOT MONKEYS! FUNNY, HUH?
WAIT! WHERE ARE WE GOING?
TO THE LAST PLACE YOU WERE SNEEZING!
THE OLD STRATEMEYER ESTATE. WITH ALL THE THINGS BESS WAS ALLERGIC TO, IT WAS A LONG SHOT, BUT I HAD A HUNCH.
YOU'VE GOT A HUNCH, DON'T YOU?
SHE'S ALWAYS LIKE THIS WHEN SHE HAS A HUNCH.

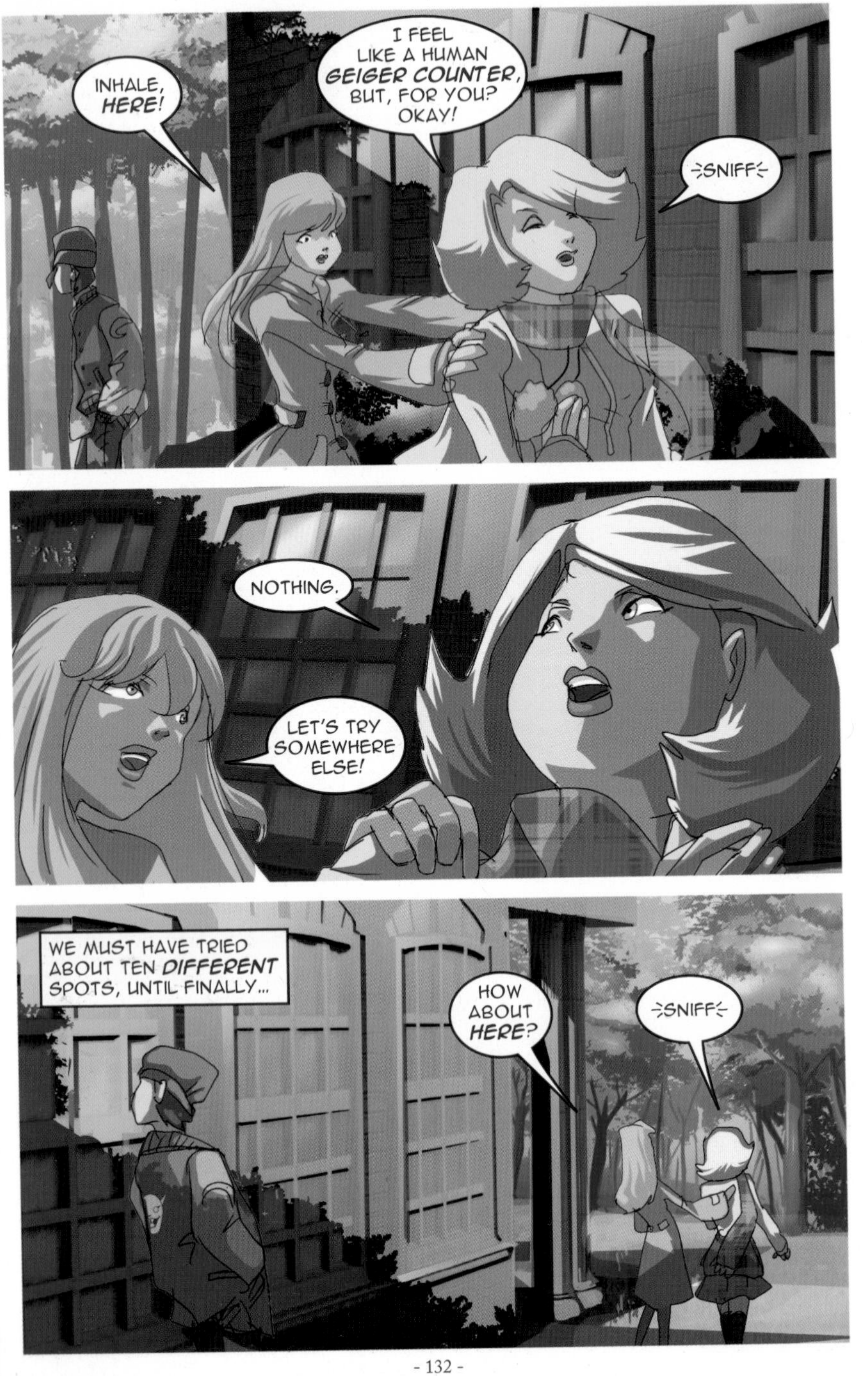

INHALE, **HERE**!
I FEEL LIKE A HUMAN **GEIGER COUNTER**, BUT, FOR YOU? OKAY!
SNIFF
NOTHING.
LET'S TRY SOMEWHERE ELSE!
WE MUST HAVE TRIED ABOUT TEN ***DIFFERENT*** SPOTS, UNTIL FINALLY...
HOW ABOUT **HERE**?
SNIFF

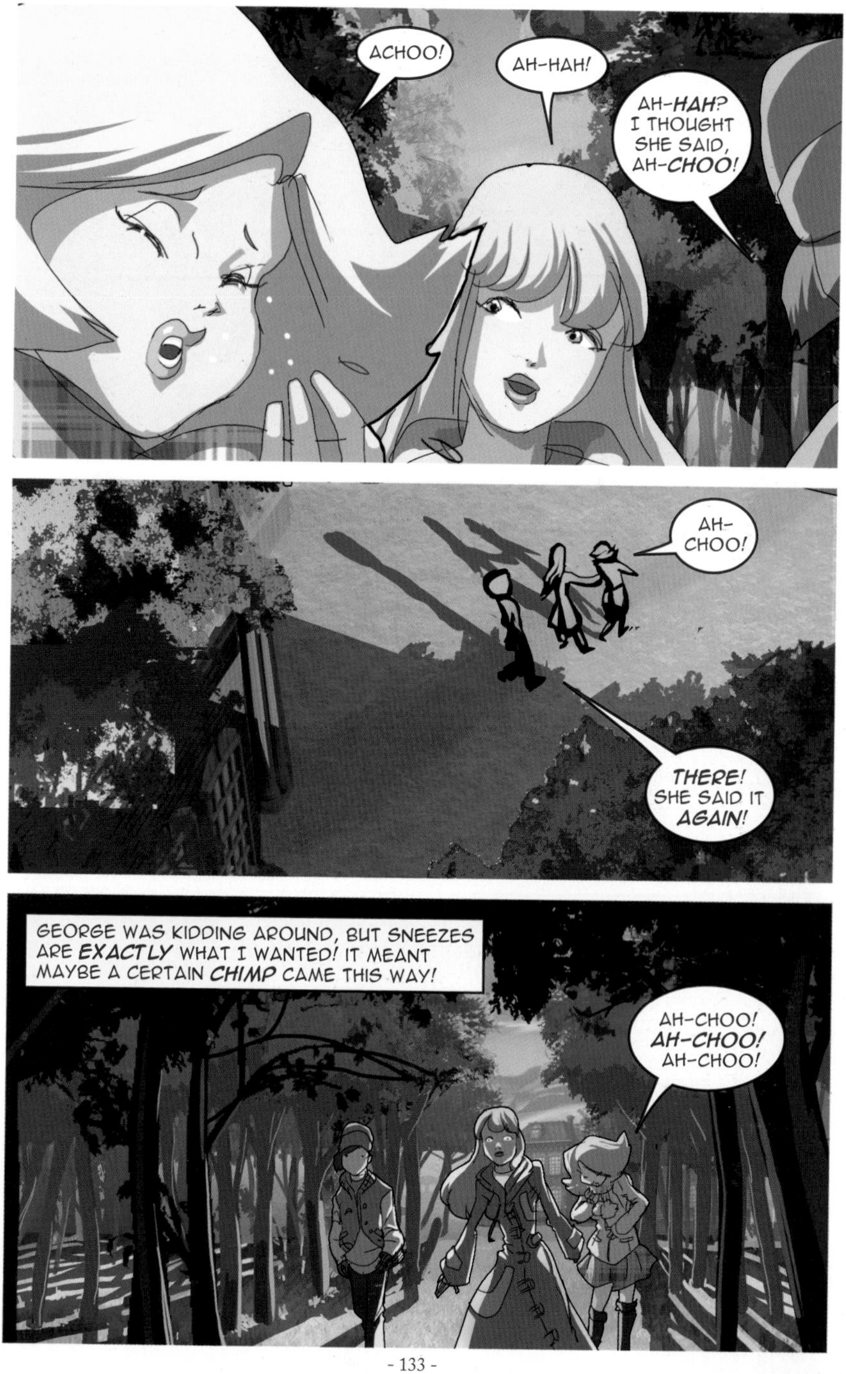

ACHOO!
AH-HAH!
AH-HAH? I THOUGHT SHE SAID, AH-CHOO!
AH-CHOO!
THERE! SHE SAID IT AGAIN!
GEORGE WAS KIDDING AROUND, BUT SNEEZES ARE EXACTLY WHAT I WANTED! IT MEANT MAYBE A CERTAIN CHIMP CAME THIS WAY!
AH-CHOO! AH-CHOO! AH-CHOO!

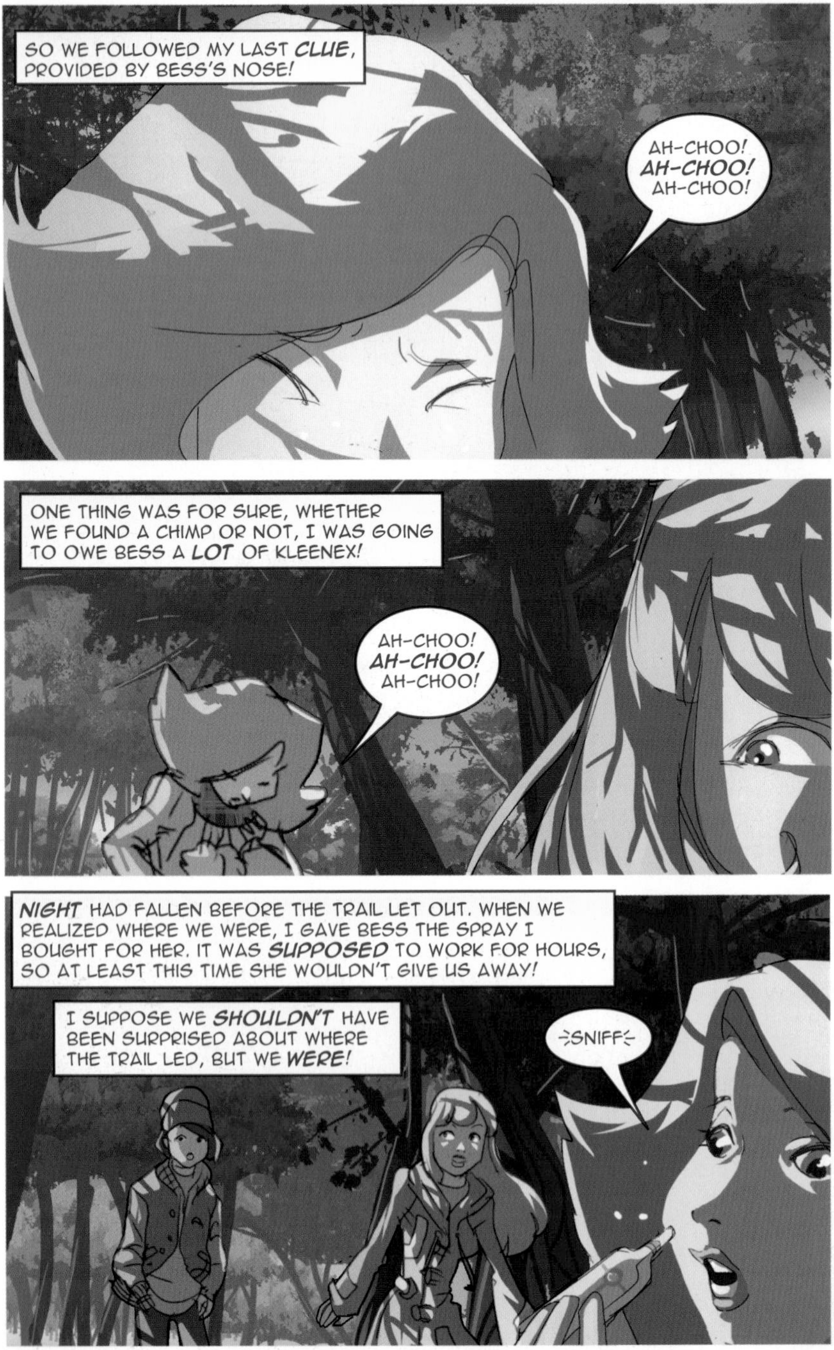
SO WE FOLLOWED MY LAST CLUE, PROVIDED BY BESS'S NOSE!
AH-CHOO! AH-CHOO! AH-CHOO!
ONE THING WAS FOR SURE, WHETHER WE FOUND A CHIMP OR NOT, I WAS GOING TO OWE BESS A LOT OF KLEENEX!
AH-CHOO! AH-CHOO! AH-CHOO!
NIGHT HAD FALLEN BEFORE THE TRAIL LET OUT. WHEN WE REALIZED WHERE WE WERE, I GAVE BESS THE SPRAY I BOUGHT FOR HER. IT WAS SUPPOSED TO WORK FOR HOURS, SO AT LEAST THIS TIME SHE WOULDN'T GIVE US AWAY!
I SUPPOSE WE SHOULDN'T HAVE BEEN SURPRISED ABOUT WHERE THE TRAIL LED, BUT WE WERE!
SNIFF

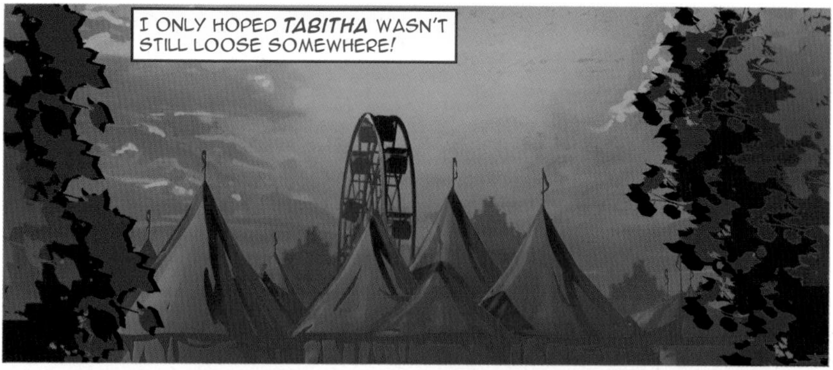
I ONLY HOPED TABITHA WASN'T STILL LOOSE SOMEWHERE!

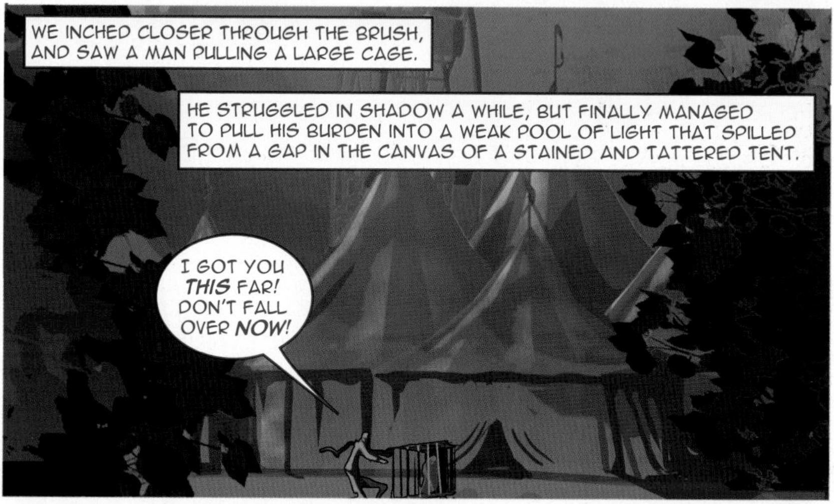
WE INCHED CLOSER THROUGH THE BRUSH, AND SAW A MAN PULLING A LARGE CAGE.
HE STRUGGLED IN SHADOW A WHILE, BUT FINALLY MANAGED TO PULL HIS BURDEN INTO A WEAK POOL OF LIGHT THAT SPILLED FROM A GAP IN THE CANVAS OF A STAINED AND TATTERED TENT.
I GOT YOU THIS FAR! DON'T FALL OVER NOW!

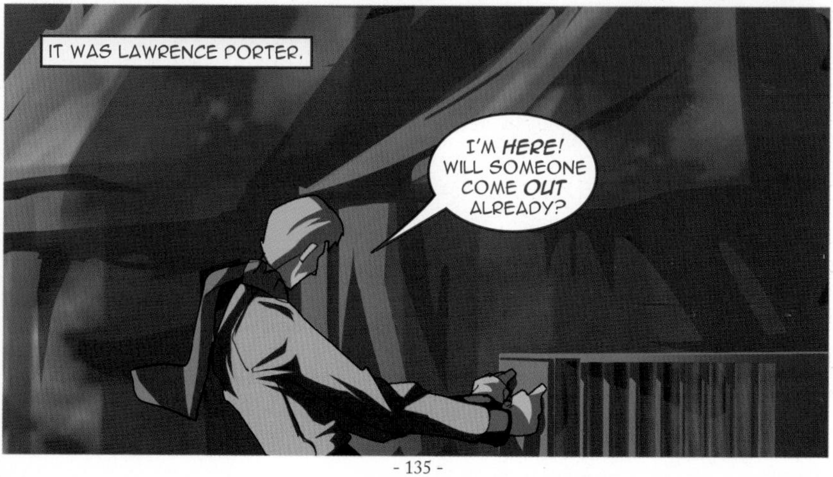
IT WAS LAWRENCE PORTER.
I'M HERE! WILL SOMEONE COME OUT ALREADY?

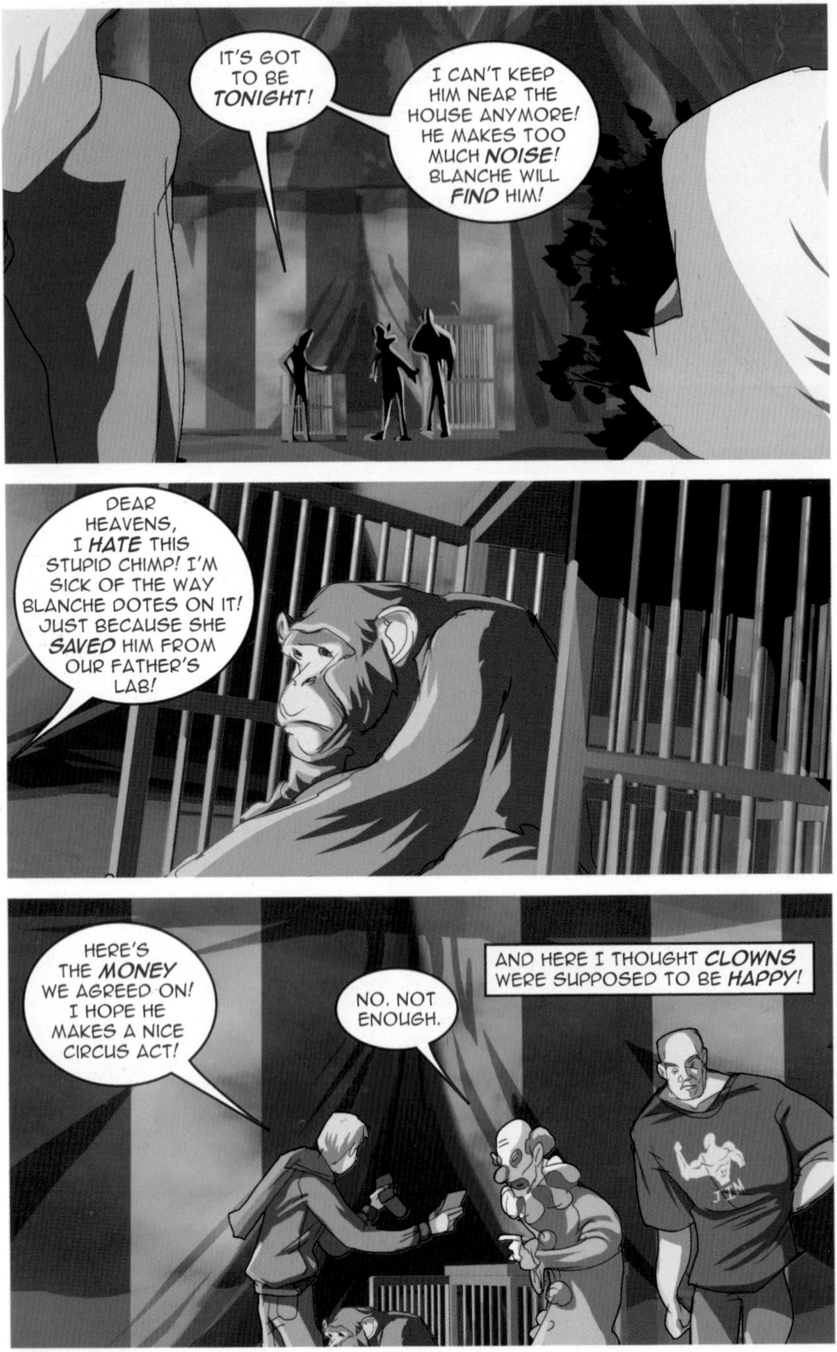
IT'S GOT TO BE **TONIGHT**!
I CAN'T KEEP HIM NEAR THE HOUSE ANYMORE! HE MAKES TOO MUCH **NOISE**! BLANCHE WILL **FIND** HIM!
DEAR HEAVENS, I **HATE** THIS STUPID CHIMP! I'M SICK OF THE WAY BLANCHE DOTES ON IT! JUST BECAUSE SHE **SAVED** HIM FROM OUR FATHER'S LAB!
HERE'S THE **MONEY** WE AGREED ON! I HOPE HE MAKES A NICE CIRCUS ACT!
NO. NOT ENOUGH.
AND HERE I THOUGHT **CLOWNS** WERE SUPPOSED TO BE **HAPPY**!

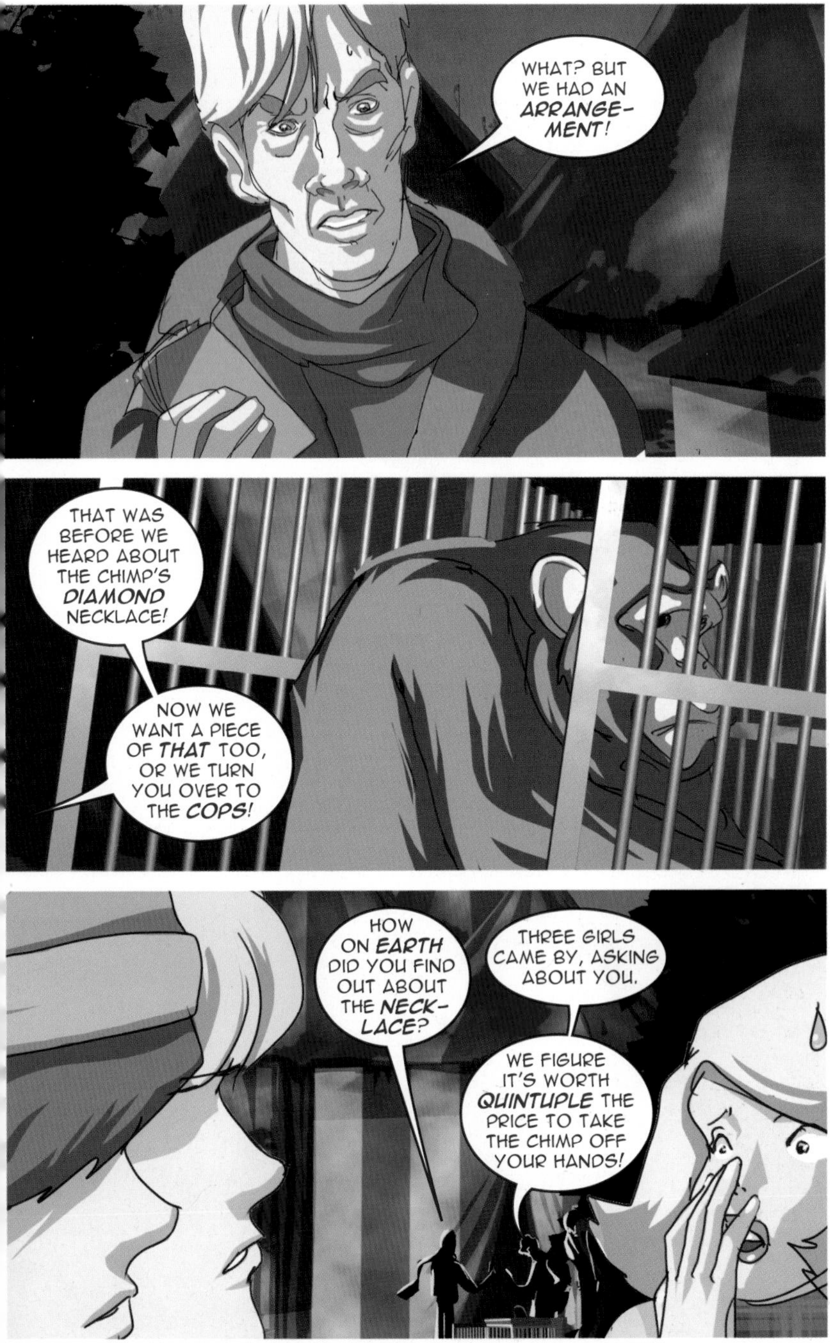
WHAT? BUT WE HAD AN ARRANGE-MENT!
THAT WAS BEFORE WE HEARD ABOUT THE CHIMP'S DIAMOND NECKLACE!
NOW WE WANT A PIECE OF THAT TOO, OR WE TURN YOU OVER TO THE COPS!
HOW ON EARTH DID YOU FIND OUT ABOUT THE NECK-LACE?
THREE GIRLS CAME BY, ASKING ABOUT YOU.
WE FIGURE IT'S WORTH QUINTUPLE THE PRICE TO TAKE THE CHIMP OFF YOUR HANDS!

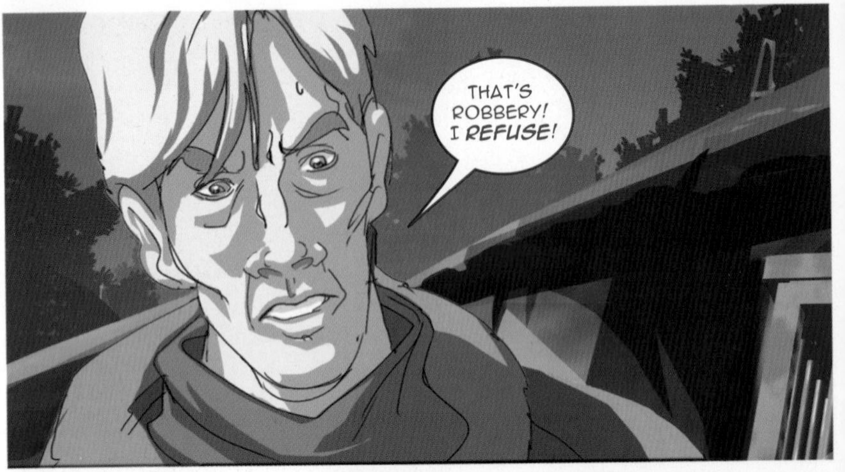
THAT'S ROBBERY! I *REFUSE*!

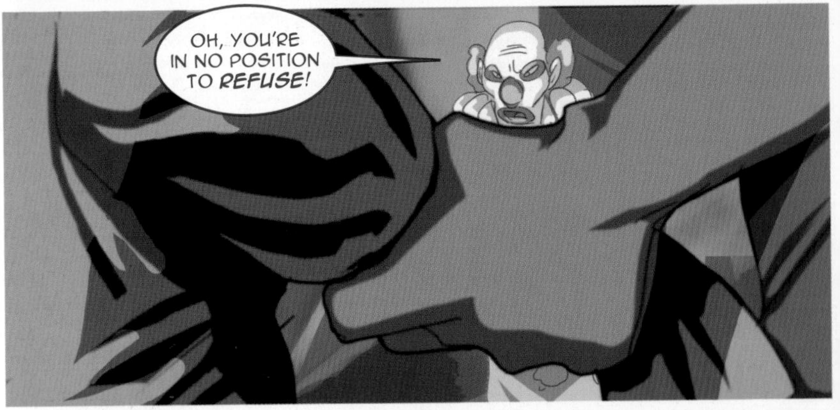
OH, YOU'RE IN NO POSITION TO *REFUSE*!

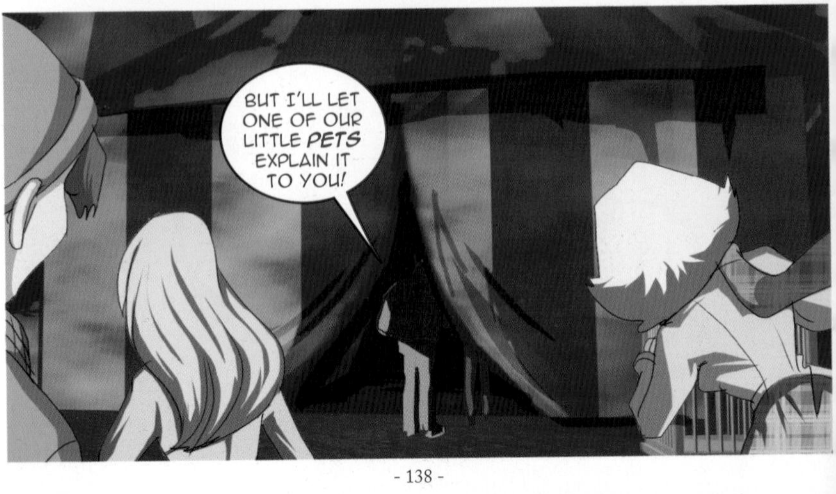
BUT I'LL LET ONE OF OUR LITTLE *PETS* EXPLAIN IT TO YOU!

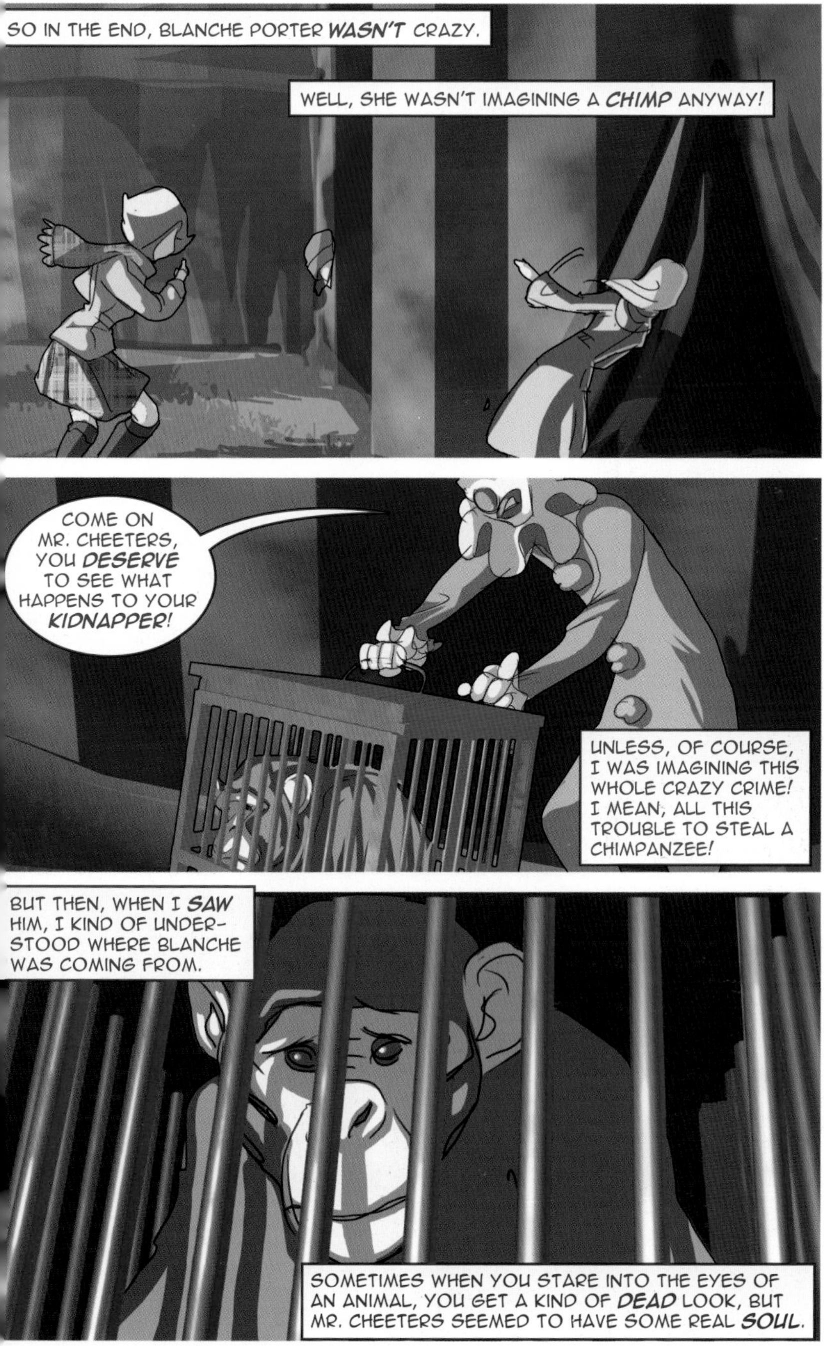
SO IN THE END, BLANCHE PORTER WASN'T CRAZY.
WELL, SHE WASN'T IMAGINING A CHIMP ANYWAY!
COME ON MR. CHEETERS, YOU DESERVE TO SEE WHAT HAPPENS TO YOUR KIDNAPPER!
UNLESS, OF COURSE, I WAS IMAGINING THIS WHOLE CRAZY CRIME! I MEAN, ALL THIS TROUBLE TO STEAL A CHIMPANZEE!
BUT THEN, WHEN I SAW HIM, I KIND OF UNDER-STOOD WHERE BLANCHE WAS COMING FROM.
SOMETIMES WHEN YOU STARE INTO THE EYES OF AN ANIMAL, YOU GET A KIND OF DEAD LOOK, BUT MR. CHEETERS SEEMED TO HAVE SOME REAL SOUL.

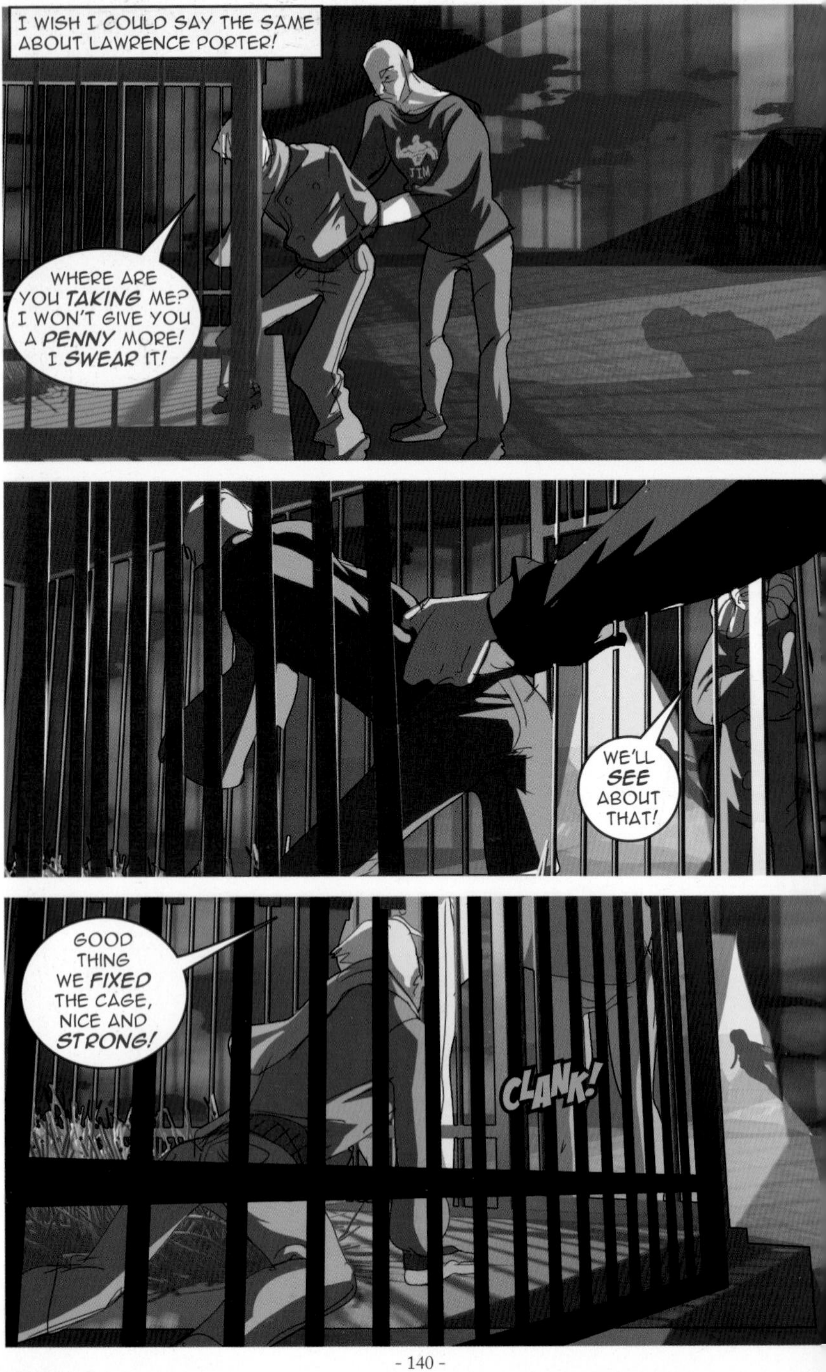
I WISH I COULD SAY THE SAME ABOUT LAWRENCE PORTER!
WHERE ARE YOU *TAKING* ME? I WON'T GIVE YOU A *PENNY* MORE! I *SWEAR* IT!
JIM
WE'LL *SEE* ABOUT THAT!
GOOD THING WE *FIXED* THE CAGE, NICE AND *STRONG!*
CLANK!

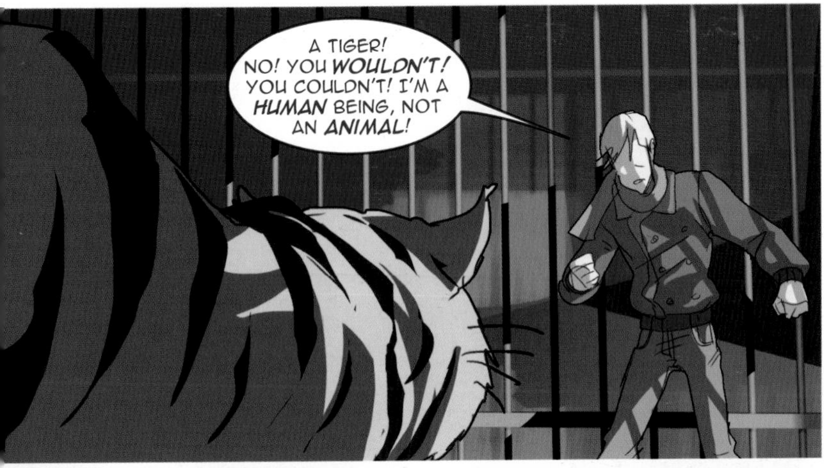
A TIGER! NO! YOU WOULDN'T! YOU COULDN'T! I'M A HUMAN BEING, NOT AN ANIMAL!

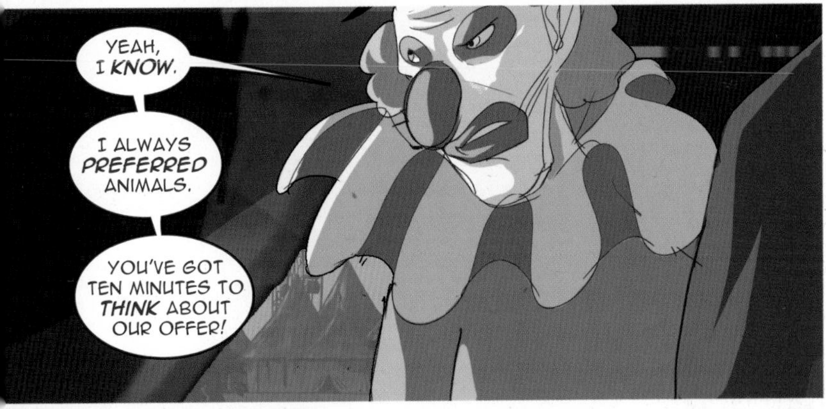
YEAH, I KNOW.
I ALWAYS PREFERRED ANIMALS.
YOU'VE GOT TEN MINUTES TO THINK ABOUT OUR OFFER!

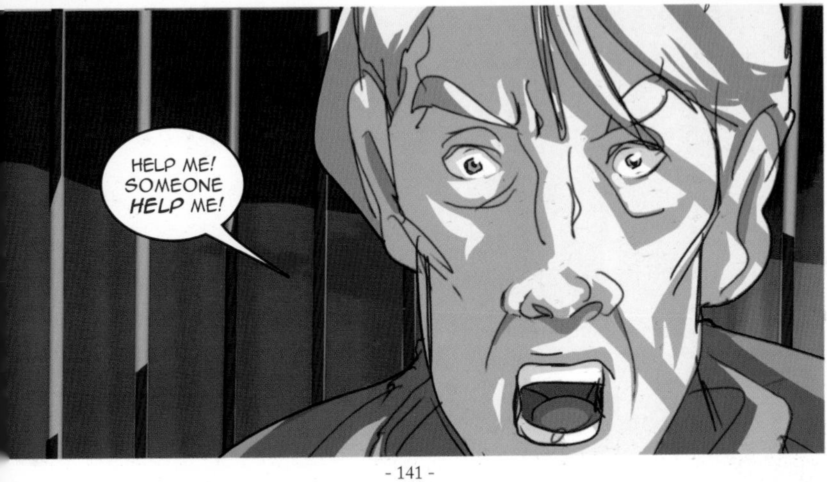
HELP ME! SOMEONE HELP ME!

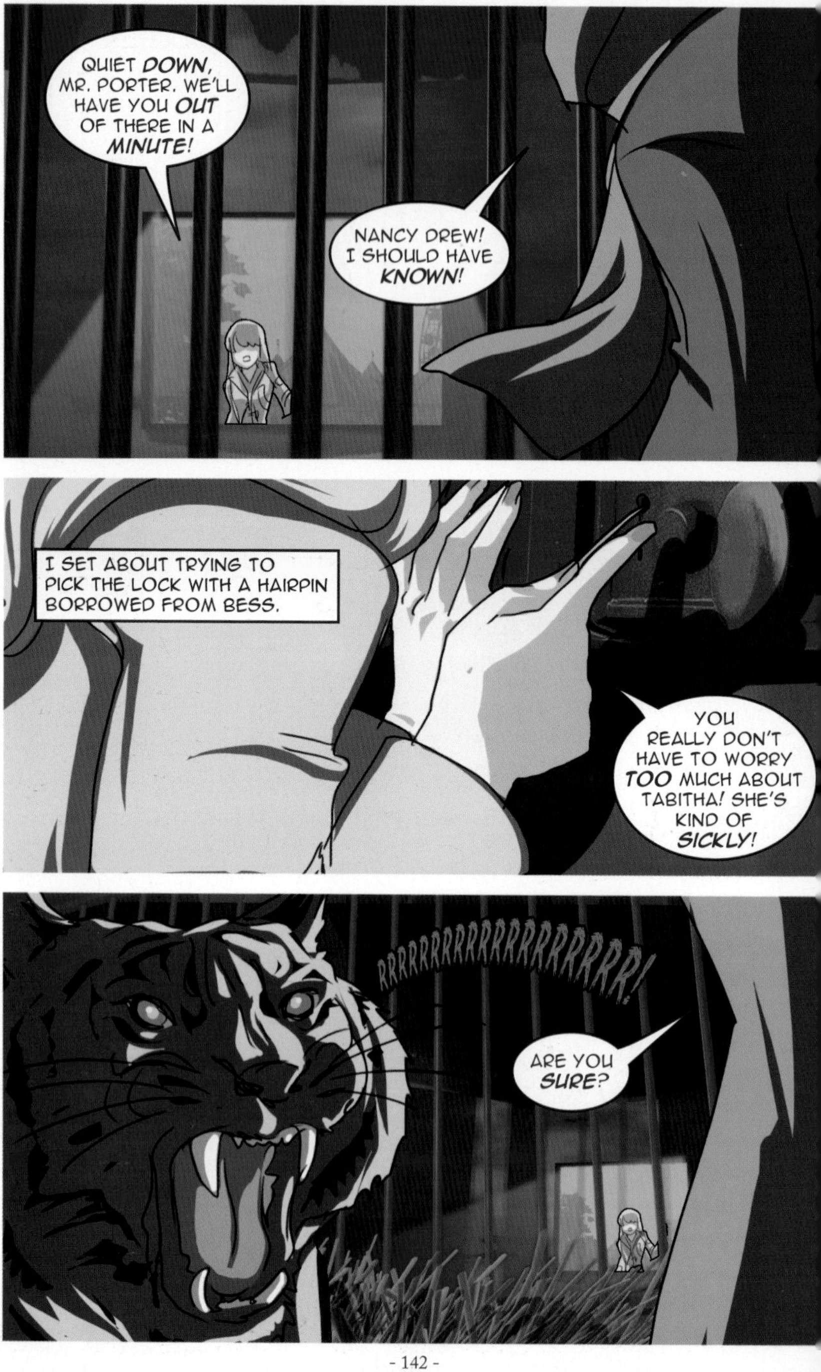
QUIET DOWN, MR. PORTER. WE'LL HAVE YOU OUT OF THERE IN A MINUTE!
NANCY DREW! I SHOULD HAVE KNOWN!
I SET ABOUT TRYING TO PICK THE LOCK WITH A HAIRPIN BORROWED FROM BESS.
YOU REALLY DON'T HAVE TO WORRY TOO MUCH ABOUT TABITHA! SHE'S KIND OF SICKLY!
RRRRRRRRRRRRRRRRRRR!
ARE YOU SURE?

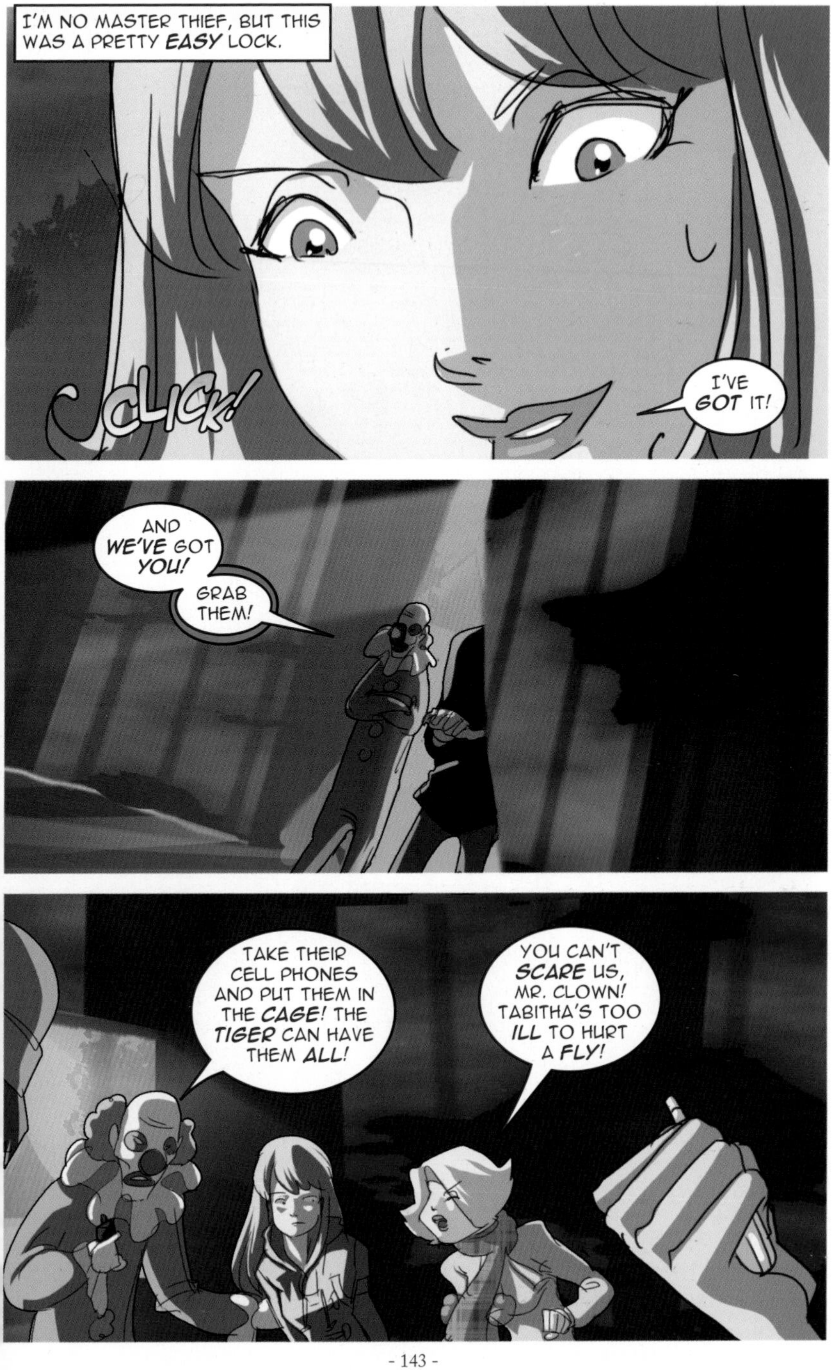
I'M NO MASTER THIEF, BUT THIS WAS A PRETTY EASY LOCK.
CLICK!
I'VE GOT IT!
AND WE'VE GOT YOU!
GRAB THEM!
TAKE THEIR CELL PHONES AND PUT THEM IN THE CAGE! THE TIGER CAN HAVE THEM ALL!
YOU CAN'T SCARE US, MR. CLOWN! TABITHA'S TOO ILL TO HURT A FLY!

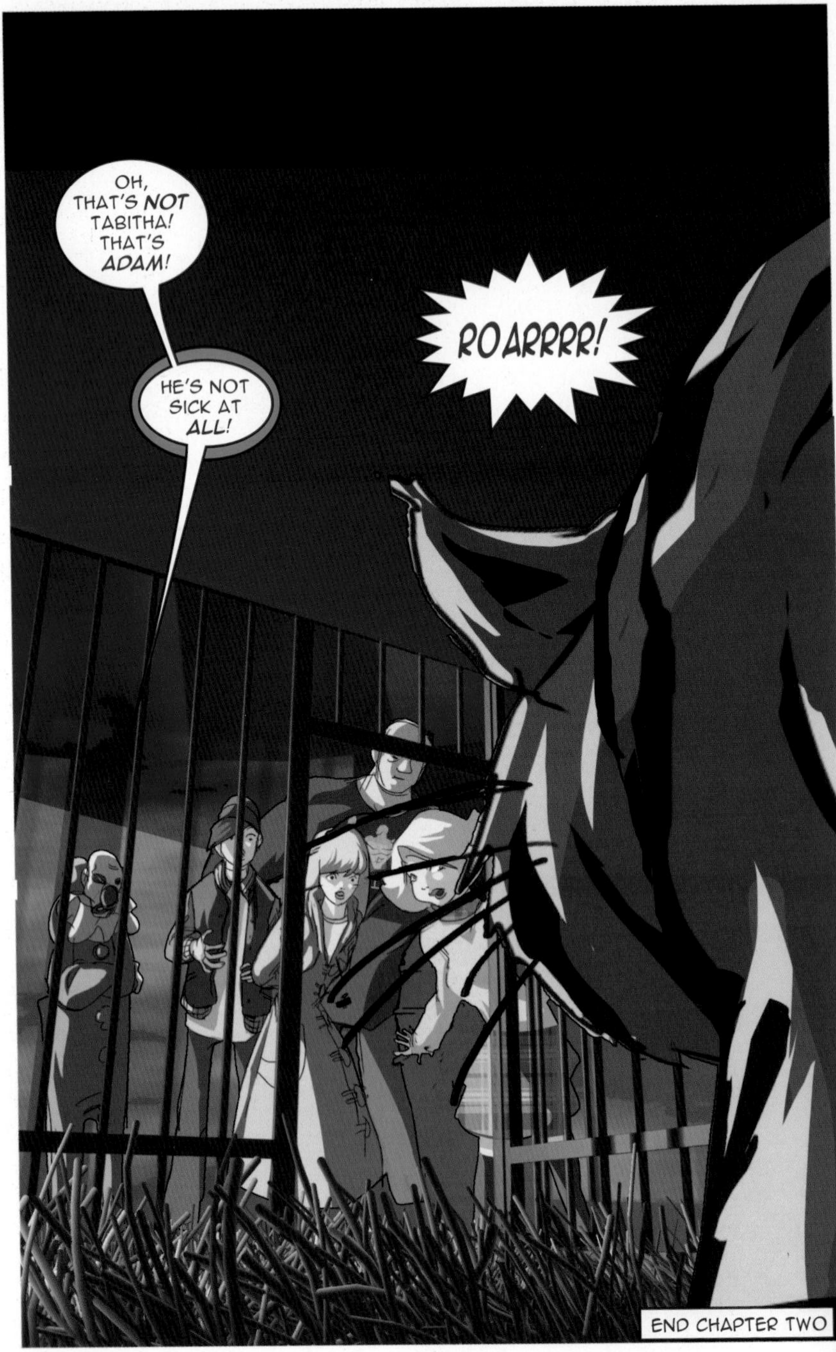
OH, THAT'S **NOT** TABITHA! THAT'S *ADAM*!
HE'S NOT SICK AT *ALL*!
ROARRRR!
END CHAPTER TWO

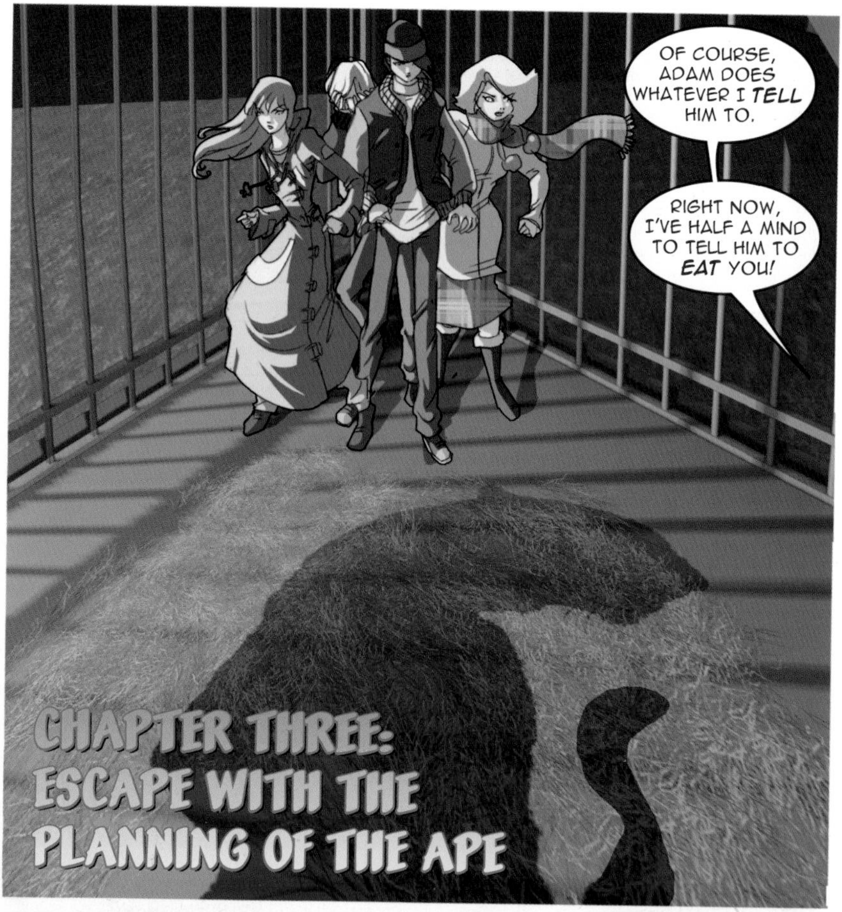
OF COURSE, ADAM DOES WHATEVER I TELL HIM TO.
RIGHT NOW, I'VE HALF A MIND TO TELL HIM TO EAT YOU!
CHAPTER THREE: ESCAPE WITH THE PLANNING OF THE APE

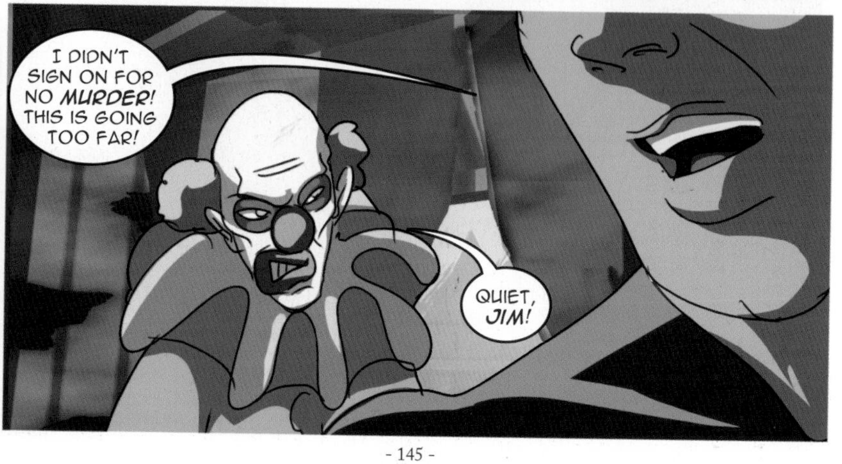
I DIDN'T SIGN ON FOR NO MURDER! THIS IS GOING TOO FAR!
QUIET, JIM!

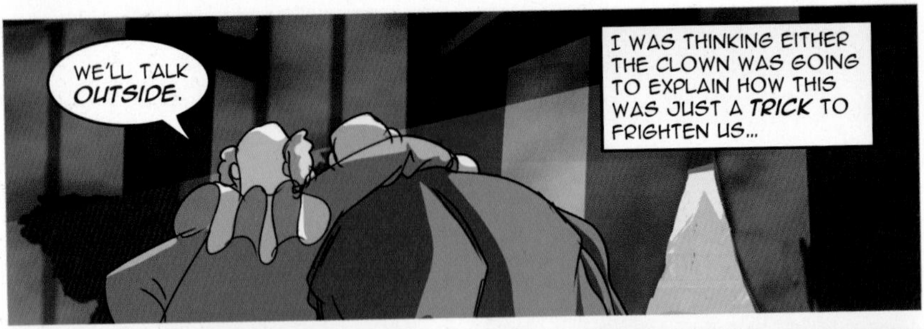
WE'LL TALK OUTSIDE.
I WAS THINKING EITHER THE CLOWN WAS GOING TO EXPLAIN HOW THIS WAS JUST A TRICK TO FRIGHTEN US...

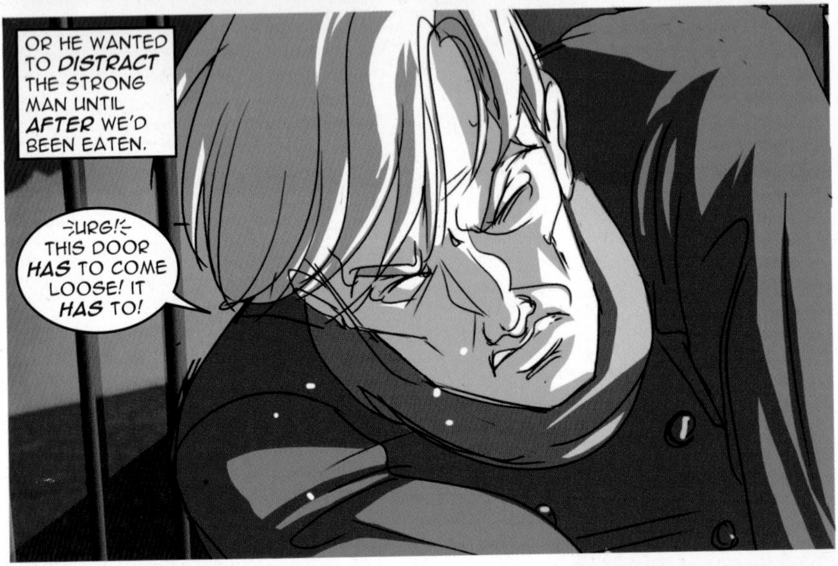
OR HE WANTED TO DISTRACT THE STRONG MAN UNTIL AFTER WE'D BEEN EATEN.
URG!
THIS DOOR HAS TO COME LOOSE! IT HAS TO!

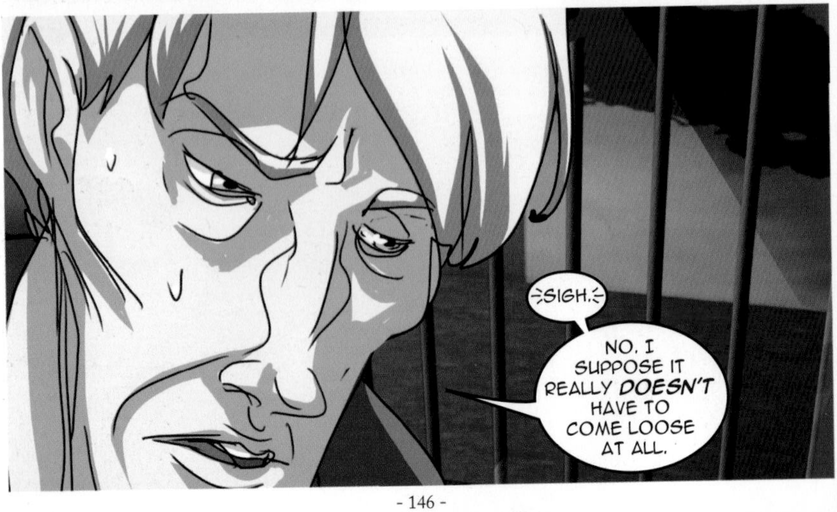
SIGH.
NO. I SUPPOSE IT REALLY DOESN'T HAVE TO COME LOOSE AT ALL.

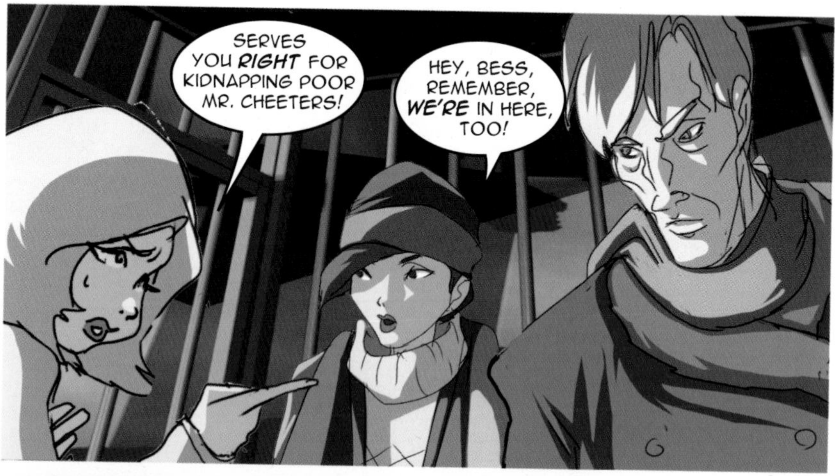
SERVES YOU RIGHT FOR KIDNAPPING POOR MR. CHEETERS!
HEY, BESS, REMEMBER, WE'RE IN HERE, TOO!

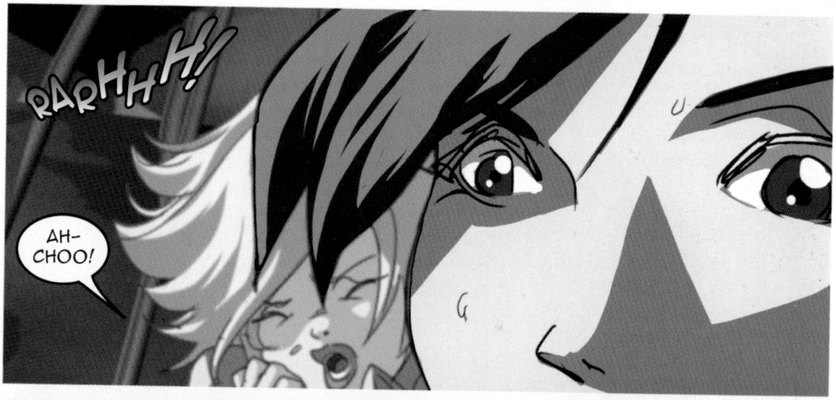
RARHHHH!!
AH-CHOO!

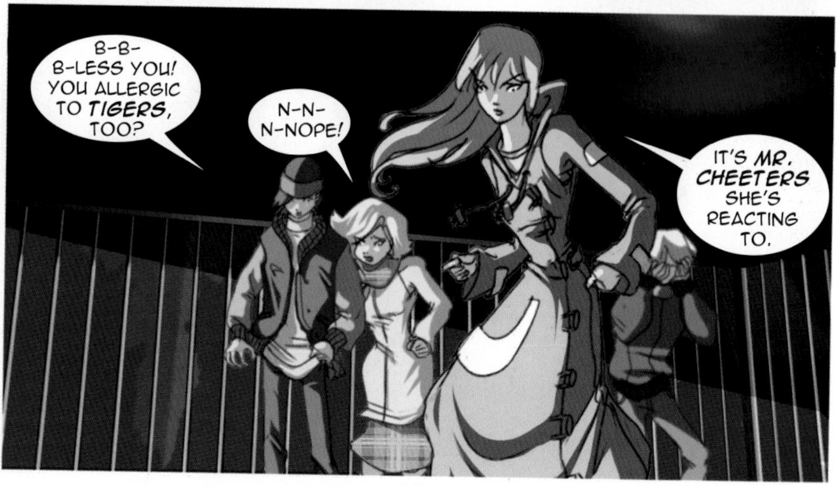
B-B-B-LESS YOU! YOU ALLERGIC TO TIGERS, TOO?
N-N-N-NOPE!
IT'S MR. CHEETERS SHE'S REACTING TO.

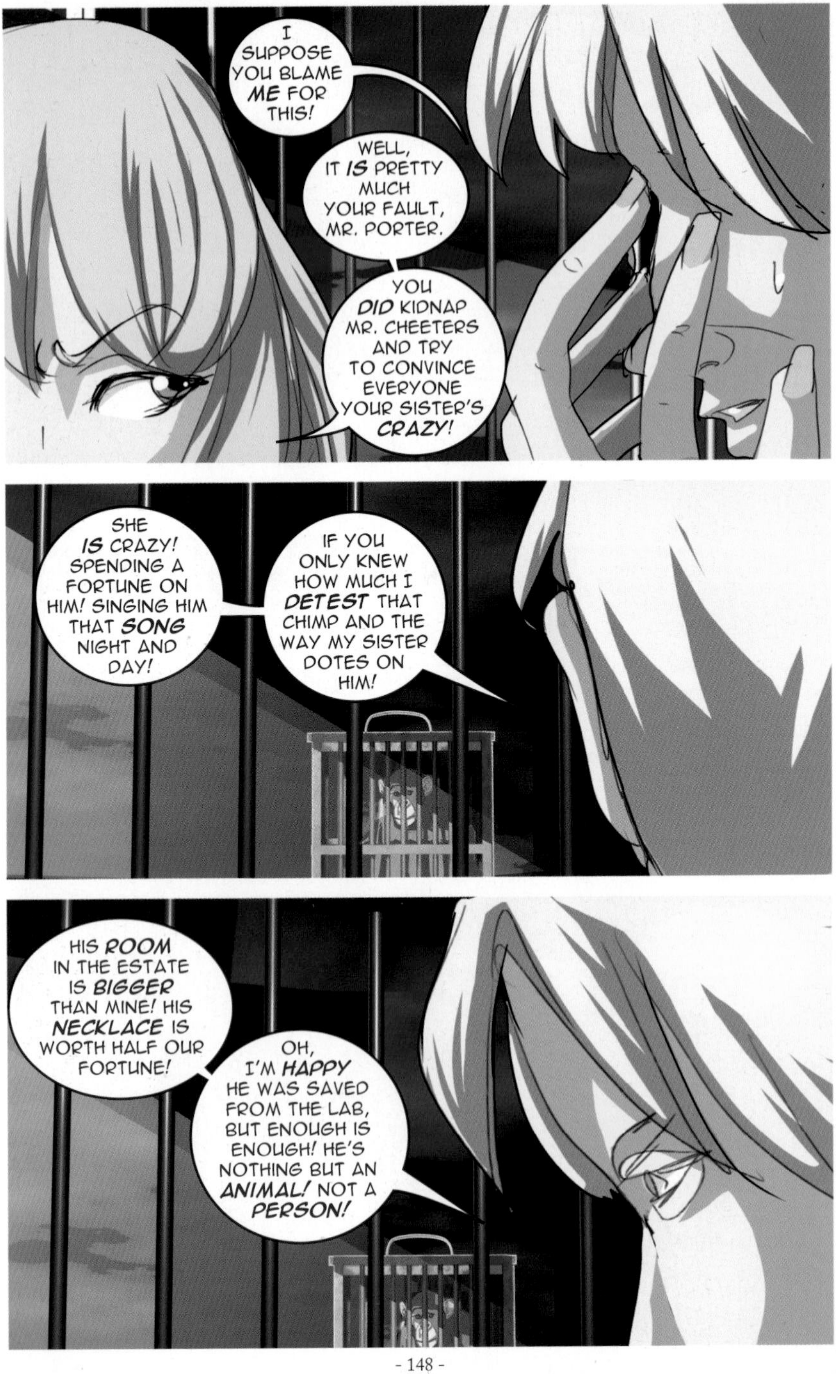
I SUPPOSE YOU BLAME *ME* FOR THIS!
WELL, IT *IS* PRETTY MUCH YOUR FAULT, MR. PORTER.
YOU *DID* KIDNAP MR. CHEETERS AND TRY TO CONVINCE EVERYONE YOUR SISTER'S *CRAZY*!
SHE *IS* CRAZY! SPENDING A FORTUNE ON HIM! SINGING HIM THAT *SONG* NIGHT AND DAY!
IF YOU ONLY KNEW HOW MUCH I *DETEST* THAT CHIMP AND THE WAY MY SISTER DOTES ON HIM!
HIS *ROOM* IN THE ESTATE IS *BIGGER* THAN MINE! HIS *NECKLACE* IS WORTH HALF OUR FORTUNE!
OH, I'M *HAPPY* HE WAS SAVED FROM THE LAB, BUT ENOUGH IS ENOUGH! HE'S NOTHING BUT AN *ANIMAL!* NOT A *PERSON*!

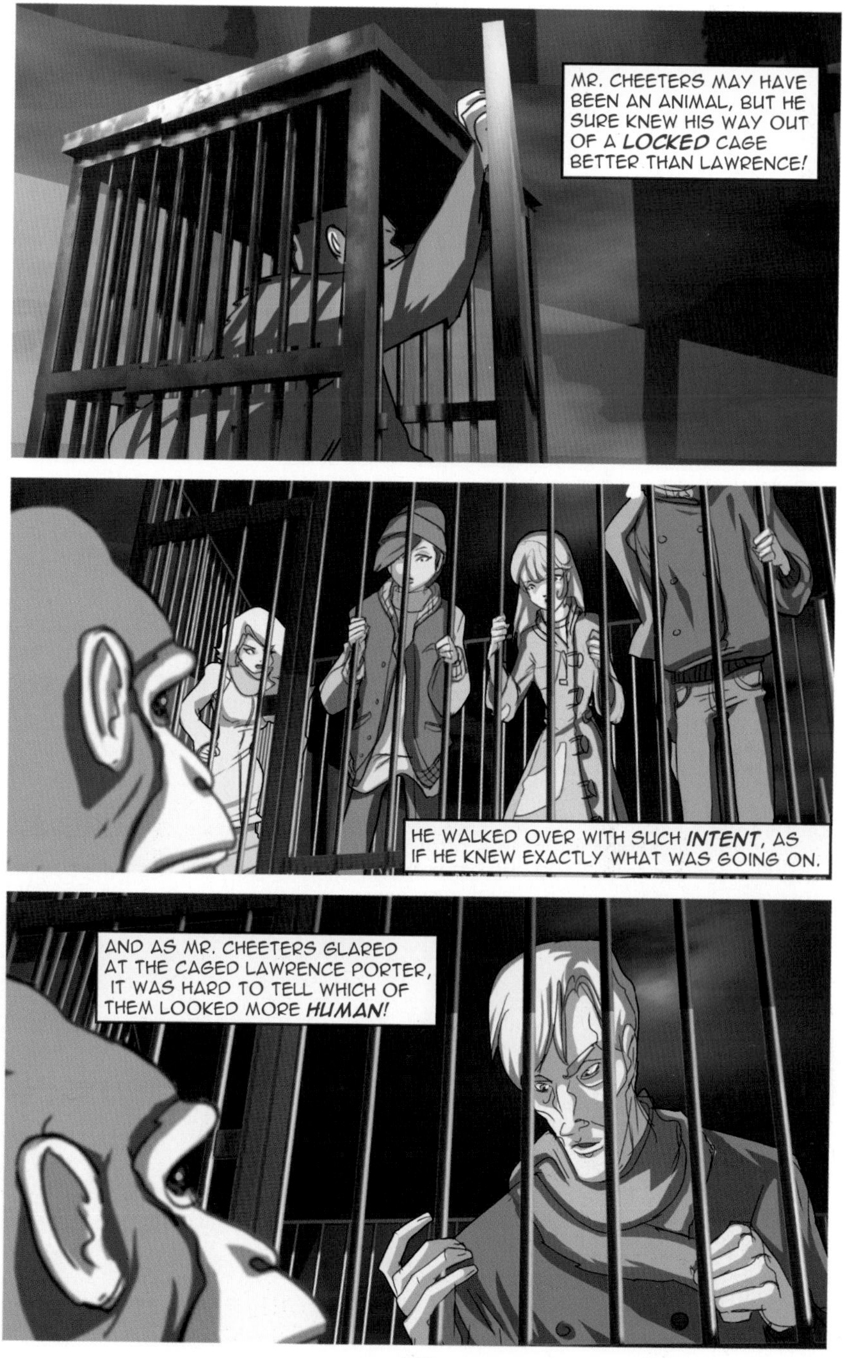
MR. CHEETERS MAY HAVE BEEN AN ANIMAL, BUT HE SURE KNEW HIS WAY OUT OF A LOCKED CAGE BETTER THAN LAWRENCE!
HE WALKED OVER WITH SUCH INTENT, AS IF HE KNEW EXACTLY WHAT WAS GOING ON.
AND AS MR. CHEETERS GLARED AT THE CAGED LAWRENCE PORTER, IT WAS HARD TO TELL WHICH OF THEM LOOKED MORE HUMAN!

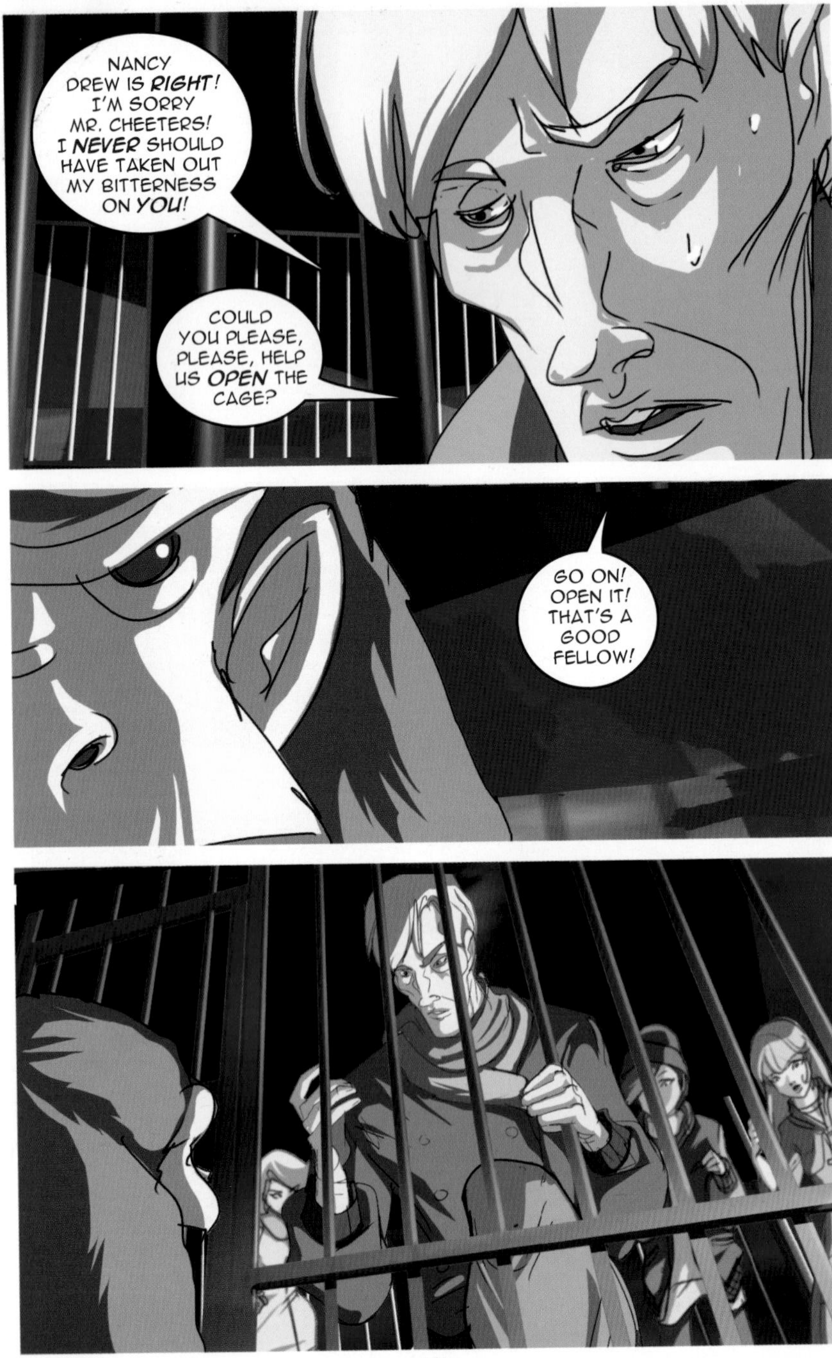
NANCY DREW IS **RIGHT**! I'M SORRY MR. CHEETERS! I **NEVER** SHOULD HAVE TAKEN OUT MY BITTERNESS ON **YOU**!
COULD YOU PLEASE, PLEASE, HELP US **OPEN** THE CAGE?
GO ON! OPEN IT! THAT'S A GOOD FELLOW!

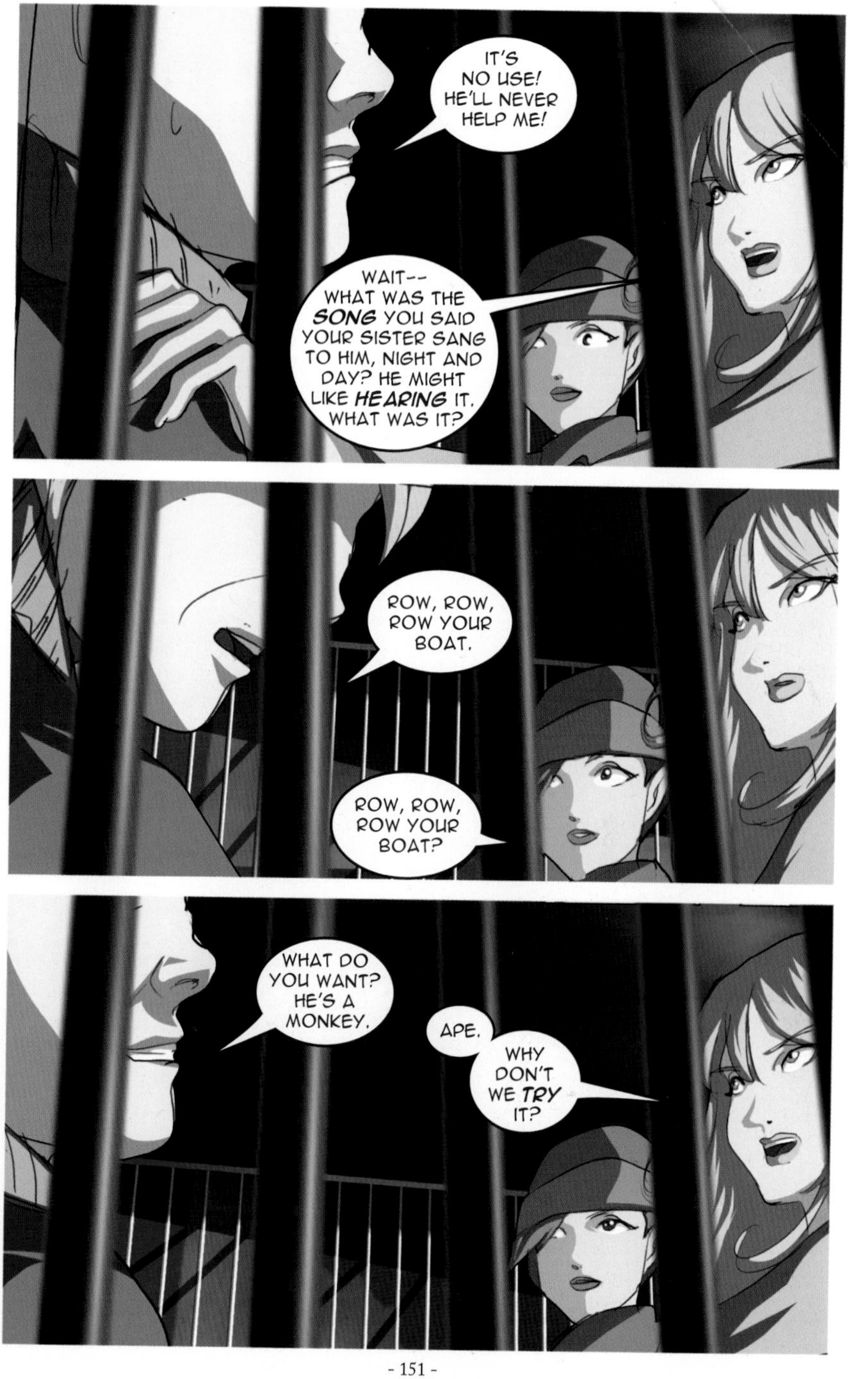
IT'S NO USE! HE'LL NEVER HELP ME!
WAIT-- WHAT WAS THE **SONG** YOU SAID YOUR SISTER SANG TO HIM, NIGHT AND DAY? HE MIGHT LIKE **HEARING** IT. WHAT WAS IT?
ROW, ROW, ROW YOUR BOAT.
ROW, ROW, ROW YOUR BOAT?
WHAT DO YOU WANT? HE'S A MONKEY.
APE.
WHY DON'T WE **TRY** IT?

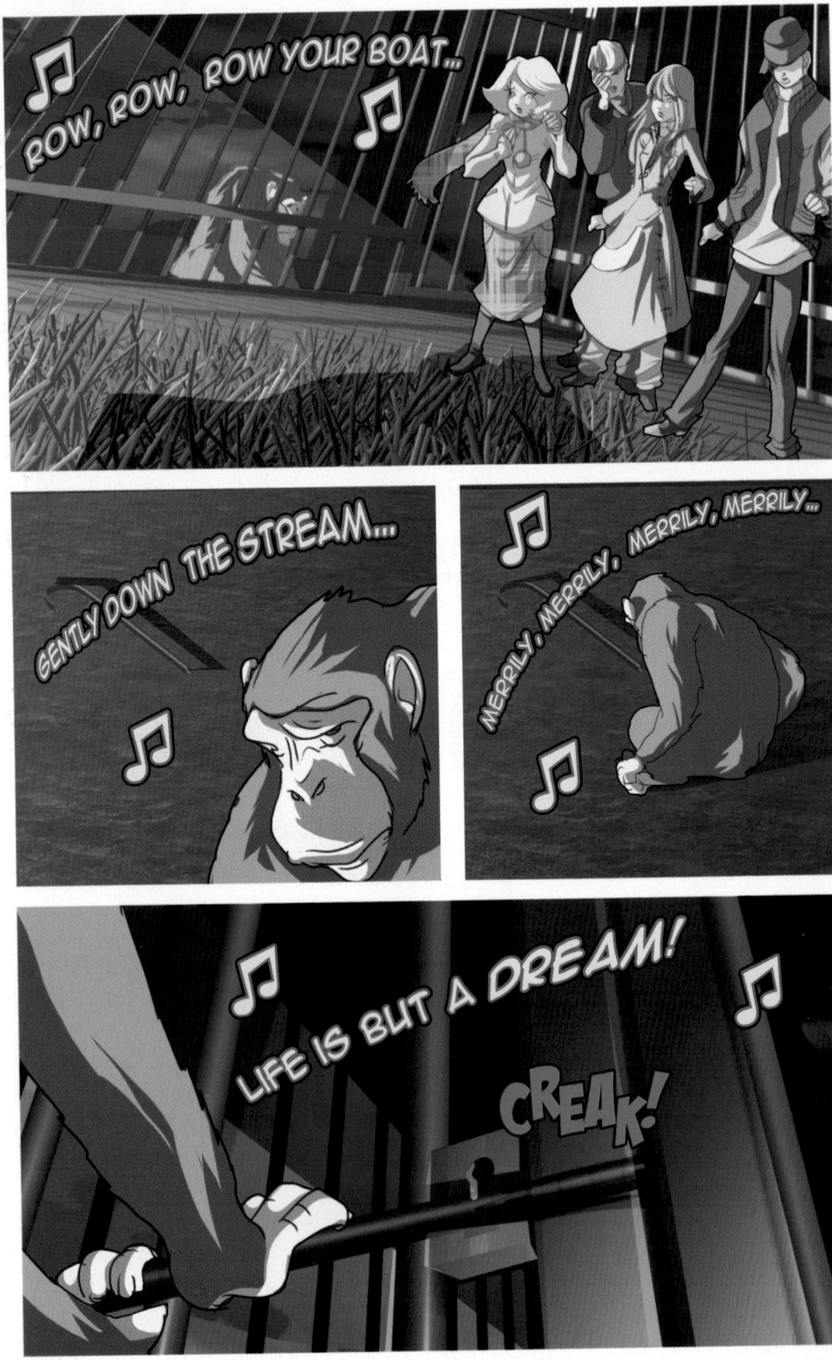
ROW, ROW, ROW YOUR BOAT...
GENTLY DOWN THE STREAM...
MERRILY, MERRILY, MERRILY, MERRILY...
LIFE IS BUT A DREAM!
CREAK!

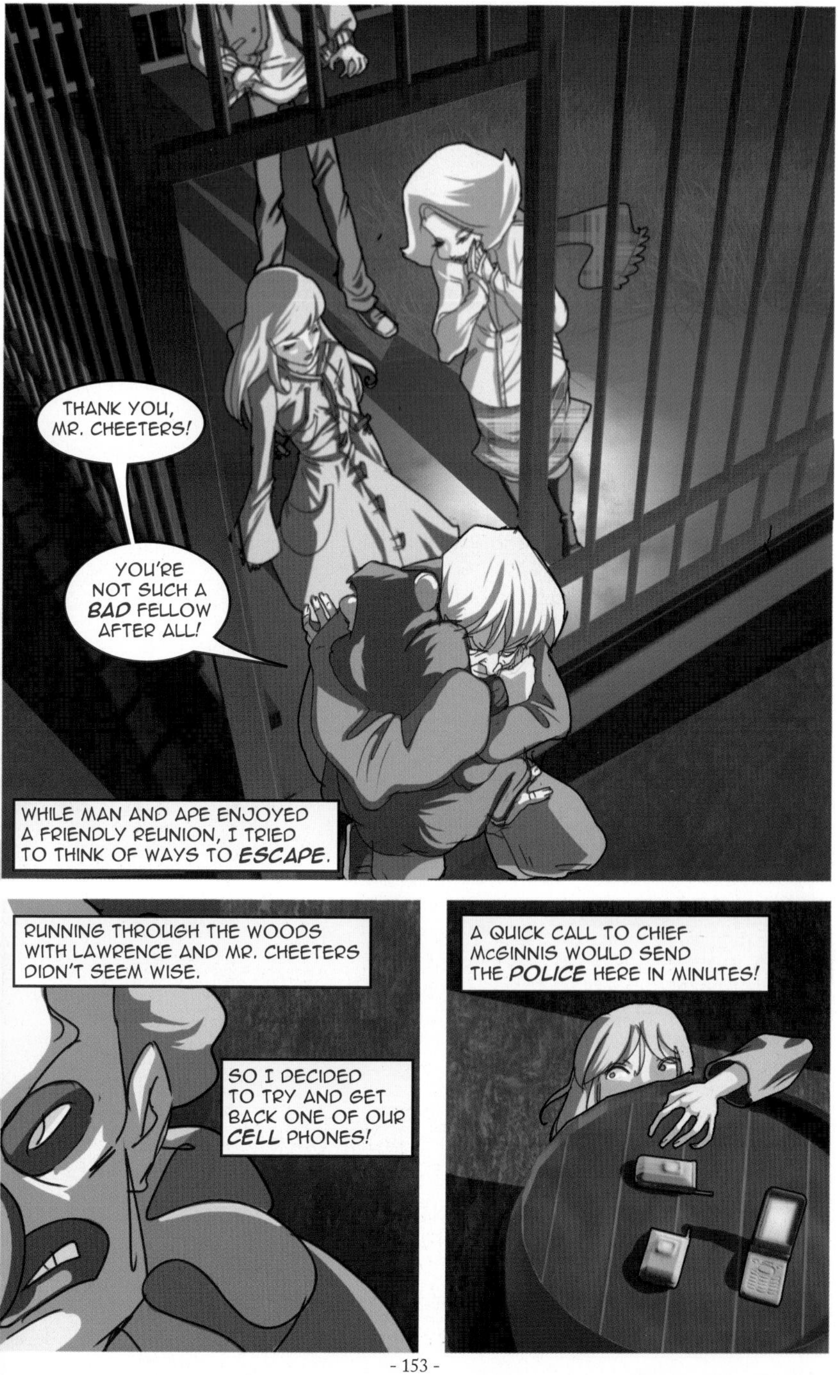
THANK YOU, MR. CHEETERS!
YOU'RE NOT SUCH A BAD FELLOW AFTER ALL!
WHILE MAN AND APE ENJOYED A FRIENDLY REUNION, I TRIED TO THINK OF WAYS TO ESCAPE.
RUNNING THROUGH THE WOODS WITH LAWRENCE AND MR. CHEETERS DIDN'T SEEM WISE.
SO I DECIDED TO TRY AND GET BACK ONE OF OUR CELL PHONES!
A QUICK CALL TO CHIEF McGINNIS WOULD SEND THE POLICE HERE IN MINUTES!

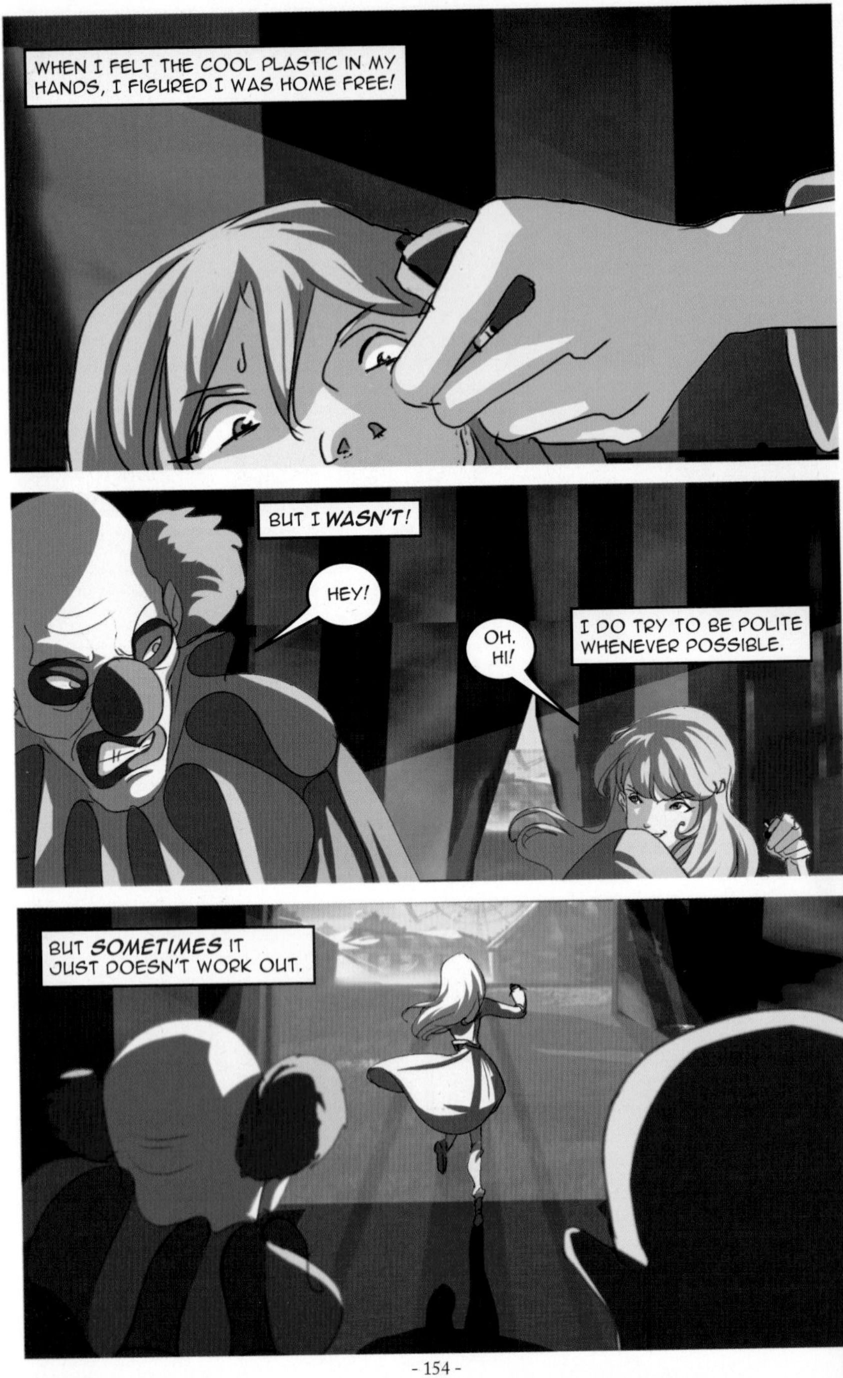
WHEN I FELT THE COOL PLASTIC IN MY HANDS, I FIGURED I WAS HOME FREE!
BUT I WASN'T!
HEY!
OH. HI!
I DO TRY TO BE POLITE WHENEVER POSSIBLE.
BUT SOMETIMES IT JUST DOESN'T WORK OUT.

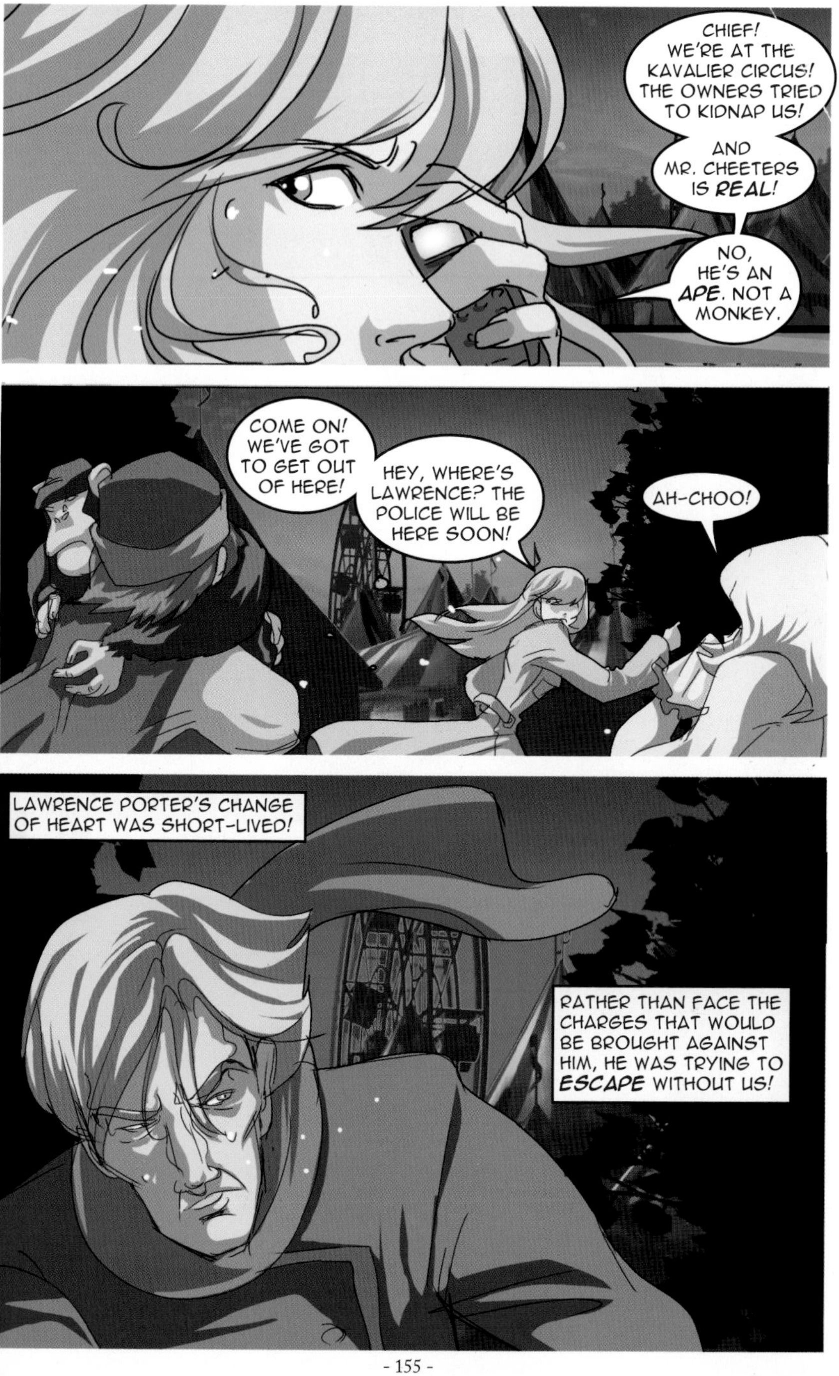
CHIEF! WE'RE AT THE KAVALIER CIRCUS! THE OWNERS TRIED TO KIDNAP US!
AND MR. CHEETERS IS REAL!
NO, HE'S AN APE. NOT A MONKEY.
COME ON! WE'VE GOT TO GET OUT OF HERE!
HEY, WHERE'S LAWRENCE? THE POLICE WILL BE HERE SOON!
AH-CHOO!
LAWRENCE PORTER'S CHANGE OF HEART WAS SHORT-LIVED!
RATHER THAN FACE THE CHARGES THAT WOULD BE BROUGHT AGAINST HIM, HE WAS TRYING TO ESCAPE WITHOUT US!

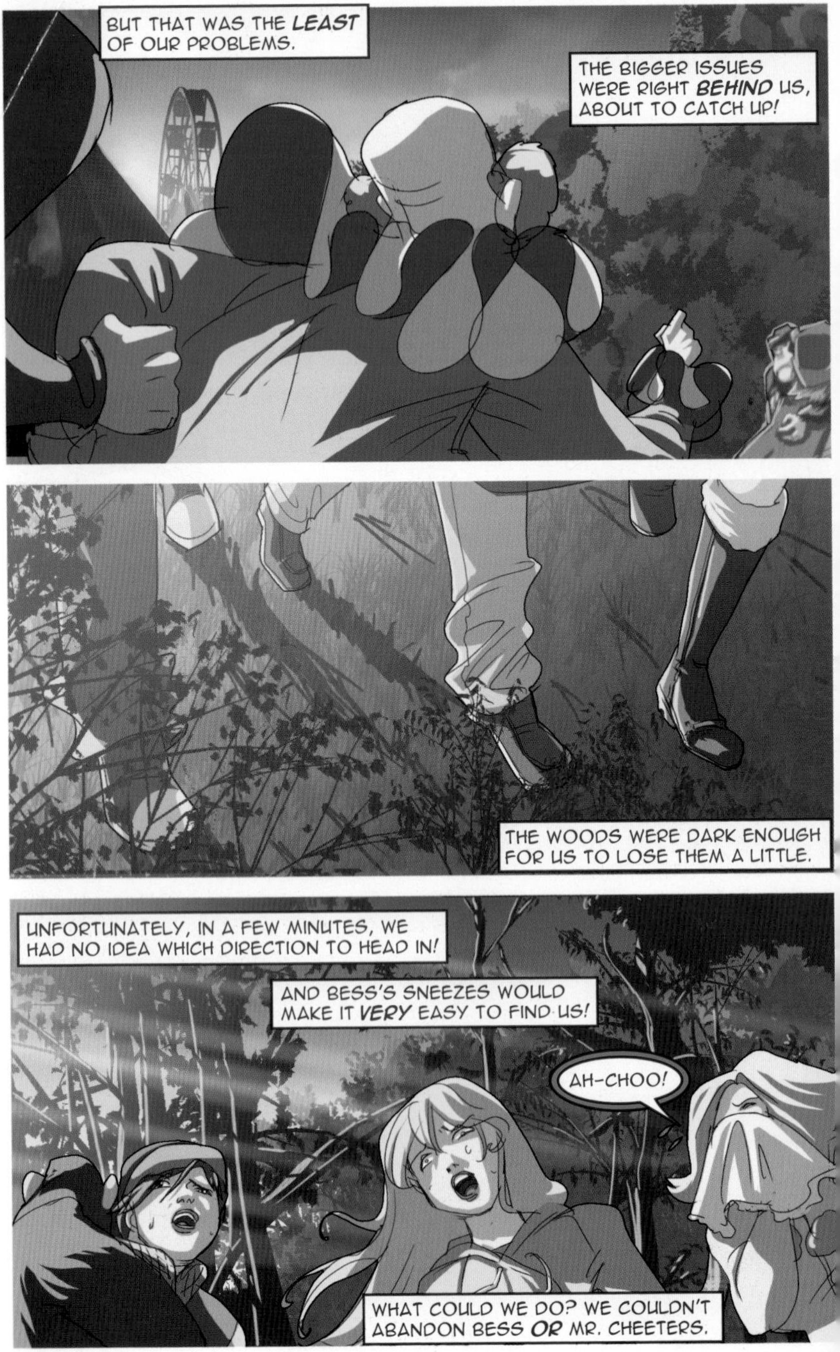
BUT THAT WAS THE LEAST OF OUR PROBLEMS.
THE BIGGER ISSUES WERE RIGHT BEHIND US, ABOUT TO CATCH UP!
THE WOODS WERE DARK ENOUGH FOR US TO LOSE THEM A LITTLE.
UNFORTUNATELY, IN A FEW MINUTES, WE HAD NO IDEA WHICH DIRECTION TO HEAD IN!
AND BESS'S SNEEZES WOULD MAKE IT VERY EASY TO FIND US!
AH-CHOO!
WHAT COULD WE DO? WE COULDN'T ABANDON BESS OR MR. CHEETERS.

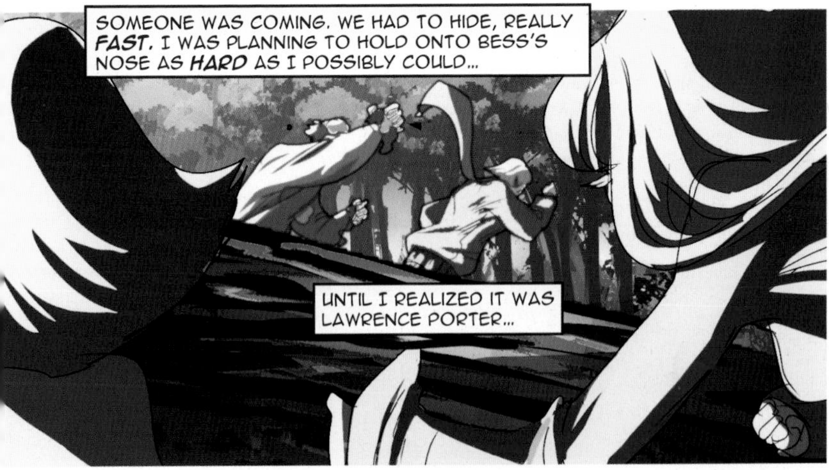
SOMEONE WAS COMING. WE HAD TO HIDE, REALLY FAST. I WAS PLANNING TO HOLD ONTO BESS'S NOSE AS HARD AS I POSSIBLY COULD...
UNTIL I REALIZED IT WAS LAWRENCE PORTER...

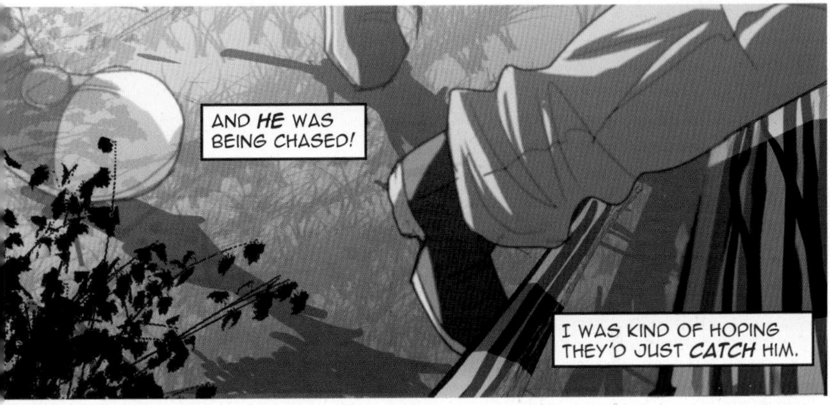
AND HE WAS BEING CHASED!
I WAS KIND OF HOPING THEY'D JUST CATCH HIM.

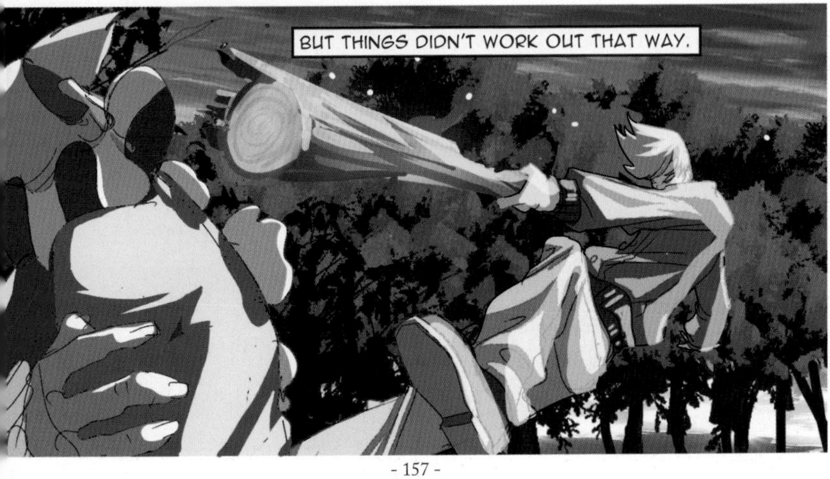
BUT THINGS DIDN'T WORK OUT THAT WAY.

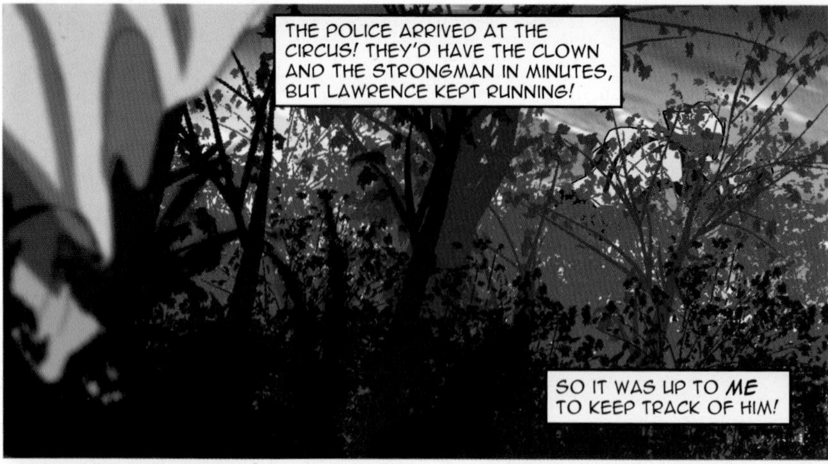
THE POLICE ARRIVED AT THE CIRCUS! THEY'D HAVE THE CLOWN AND THE STRONGMAN IN MINUTES, BUT LAWRENCE KEPT RUNNING!
SO IT WAS UP TO *ME* TO KEEP TRACK OF HIM!

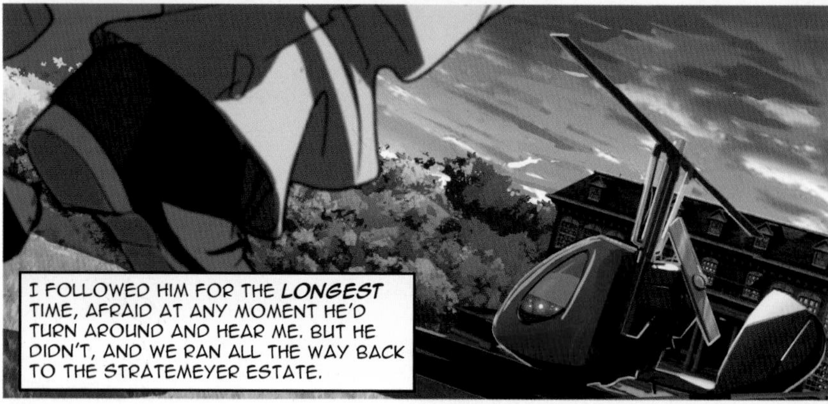
I FOLLOWED HIM FOR THE *LONGEST* TIME, AFRAID AT ANY MOMENT HE'D TURN AROUND AND HEAR ME. BUT HE DIDN'T, AND WE RAN ALL THE WAY BACK TO THE STRATEMEYER ESTATE.

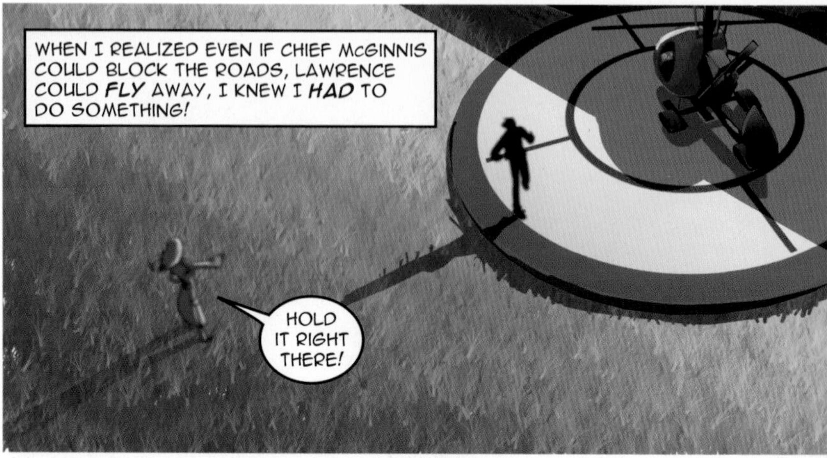
WHEN I REALIZED EVEN IF CHIEF McGINNIS COULD BLOCK THE ROADS, LAWRENCE COULD *FLY* AWAY, I KNEW I *HAD* TO DO SOMETHING!
HOLD IT RIGHT THERE!

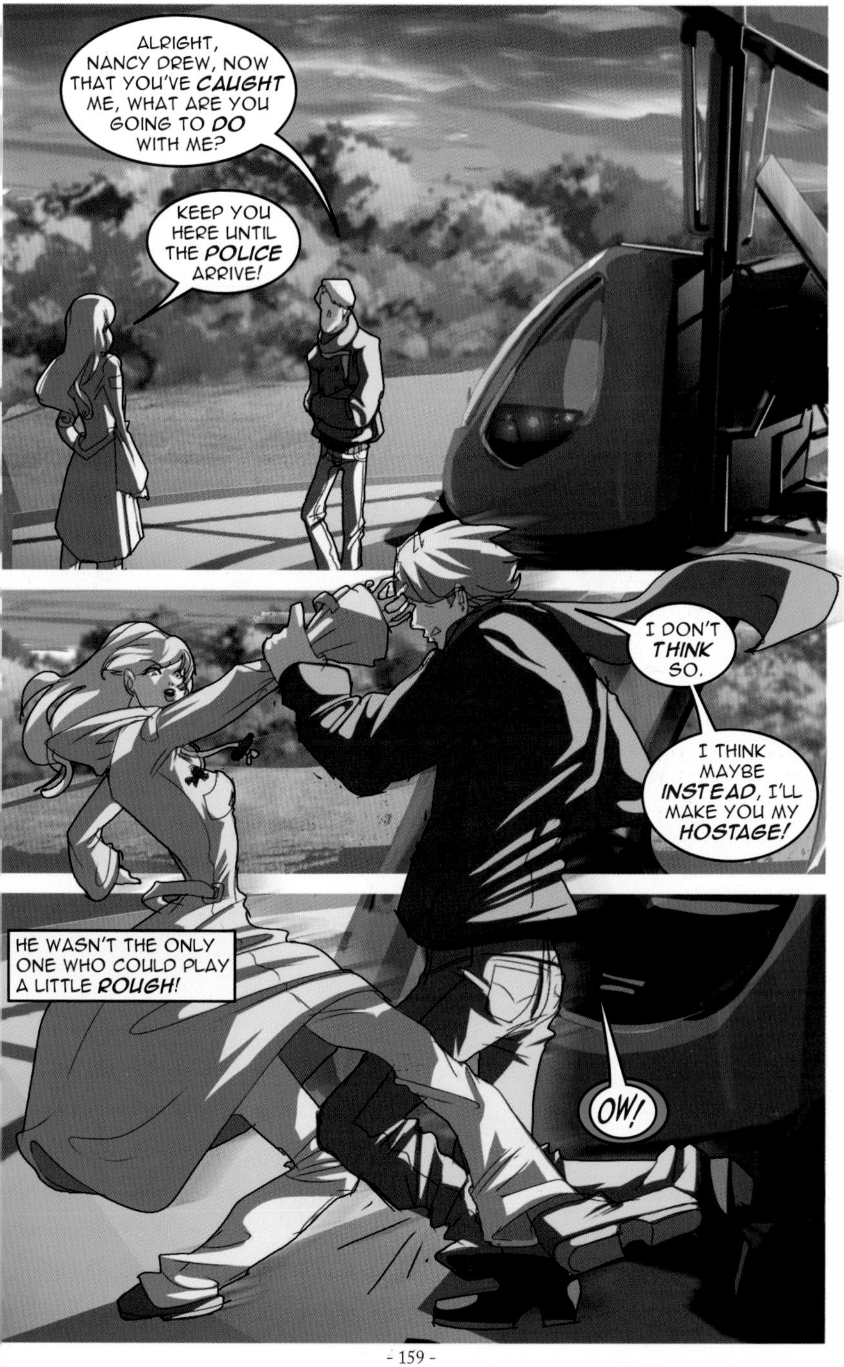
ALRIGHT, NANCY DREW, NOW THAT YOU'VE CAUGHT ME, WHAT ARE YOU GOING TO DO WITH ME?
KEEP YOU HERE UNTIL THE POLICE ARRIVE!
I DON'T THINK SO.
I THINK MAYBE INSTEAD, I'LL MAKE YOU MY HOSTAGE!
HE WASN'T THE ONLY ONE WHO COULD PLAY A LITTLE ROUGH!
OW!

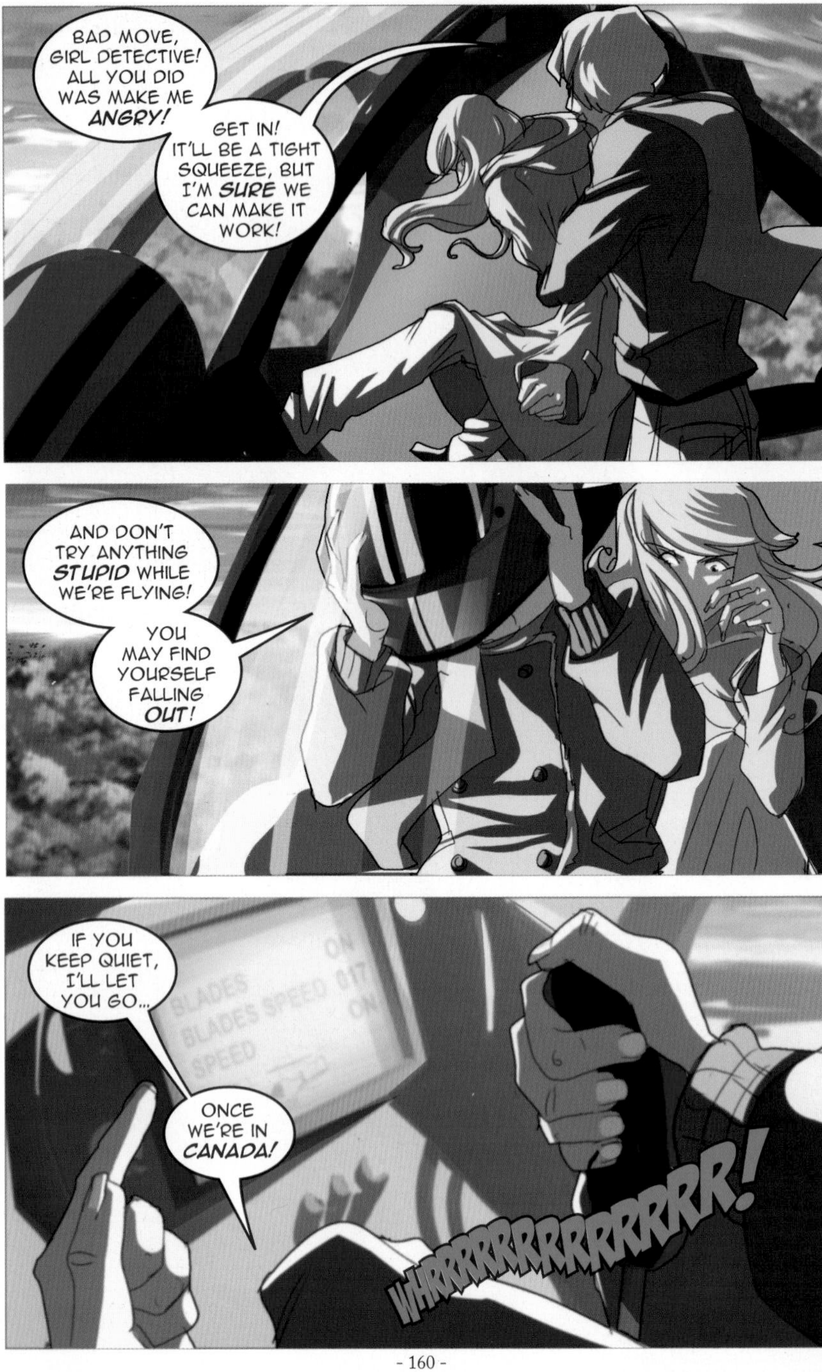
BAD MOVE, GIRL DETECTIVE! ALL YOU DID WAS MAKE ME ANGRY!
GET IN! IT'LL BE A TIGHT SQUEEZE, BUT I'M SURE WE CAN MAKE IT WORK!
AND DON'T TRY ANYTHING STUPID WHILE WE'RE FLYING!
YOU MAY FIND YOURSELF FALLING OUT!
IF YOU KEEP QUIET, I'LL LET YOU GO...
ONCE WE'RE IN CANADA!
WHRRRRRRRRRRRRRRR!

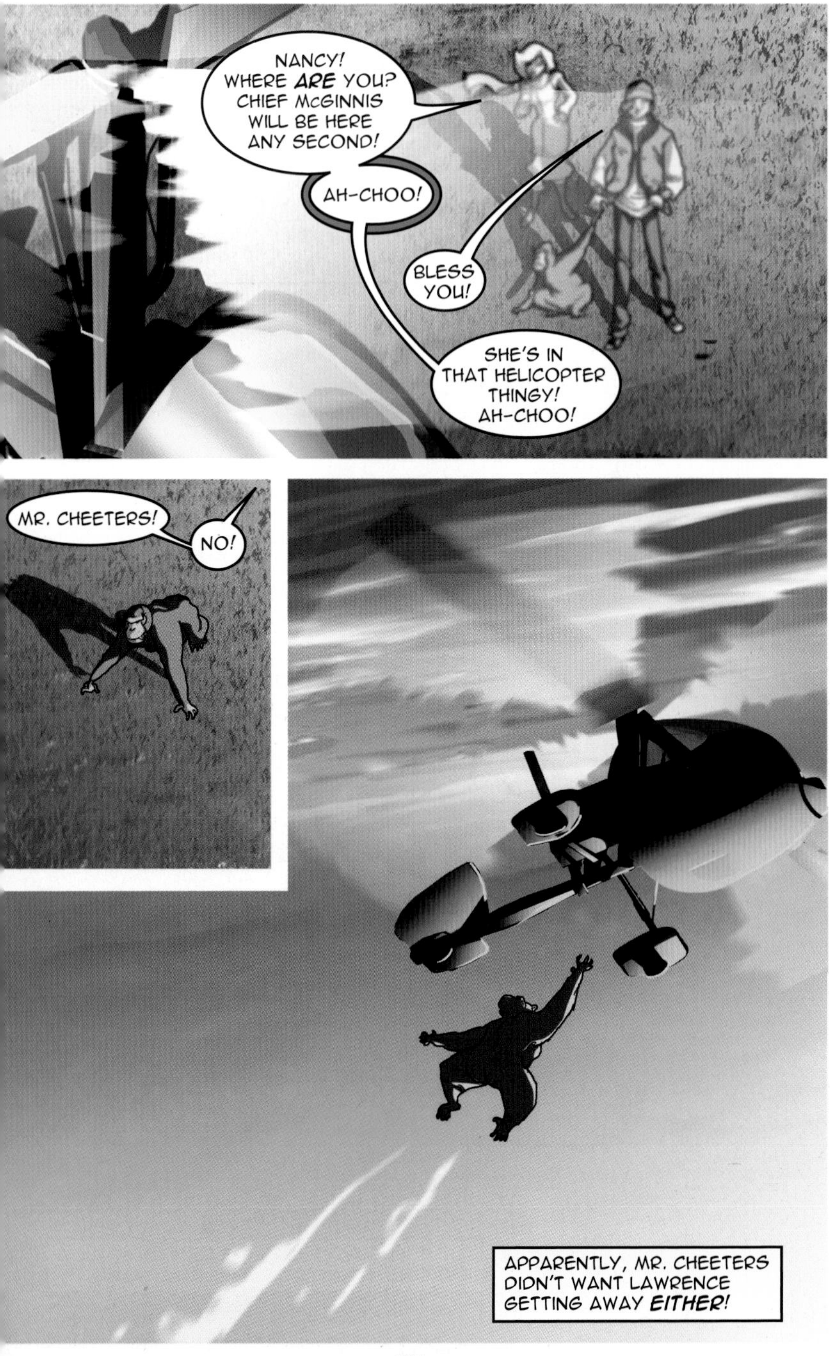
NANCY! WHERE *ARE* YOU? CHIEF McGINNIS WILL BE HERE ANY SECOND!
AH-CHOO!
BLESS YOU!
SHE'S IN THAT HELICOPTER THINGY! AH-CHOO!
MR. CHEETERS!
NO!
APPARENTLY, MR. CHEETERS DIDN'T WANT LAWRENCE GETTING AWAY *EITHER*!

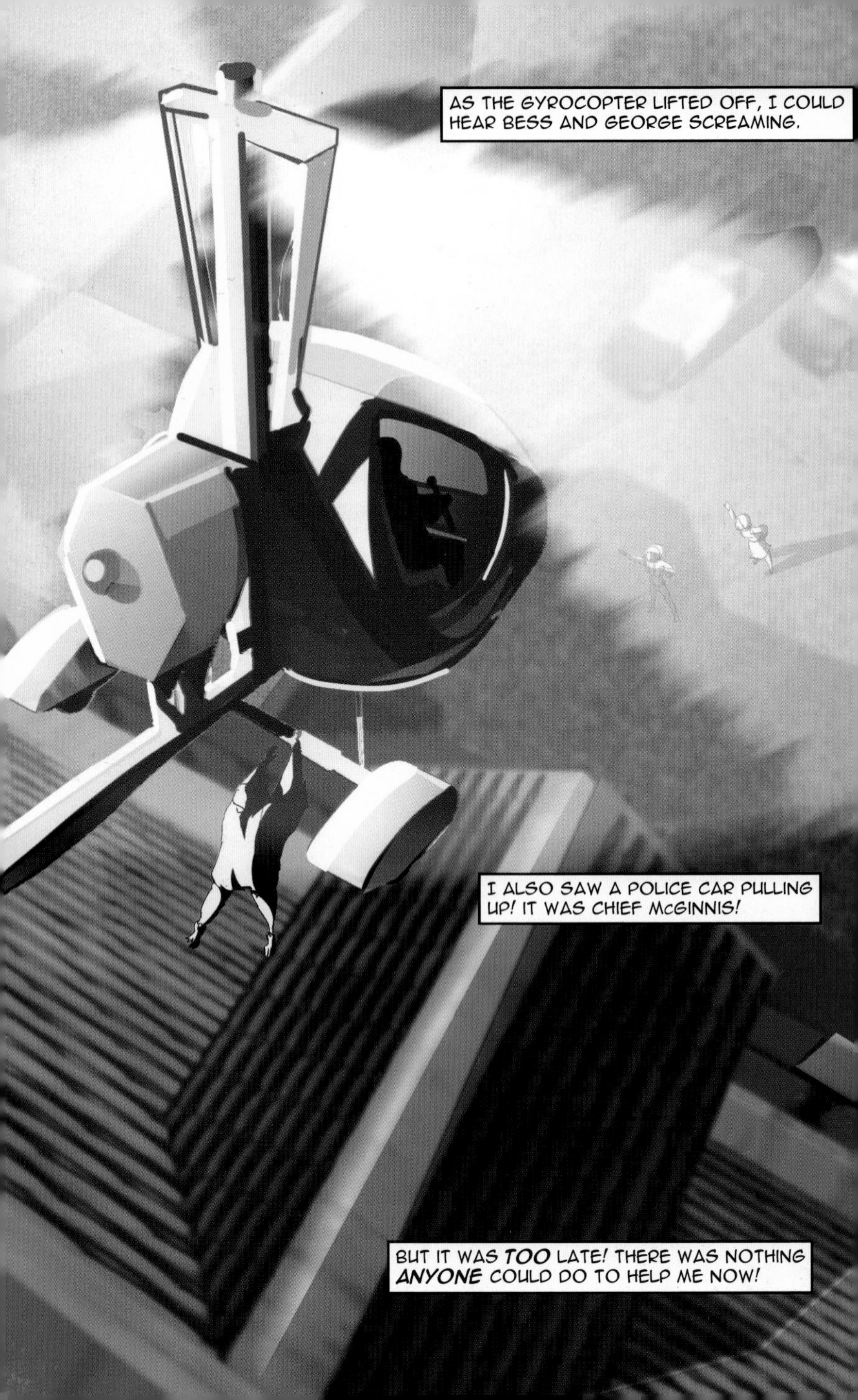
AS THE GYROCOPTER LIFTED OFF, I COULD HEAR BESS AND GEORGE SCREAMING.
I ALSO SAW A POLICE CAR PULLING UP! IT WAS CHIEF McGINNIS!
BUT IT WAS *TOO* LATE! THERE WAS NOTHING *ANYONE* COULD DO TO HELP ME NOW!

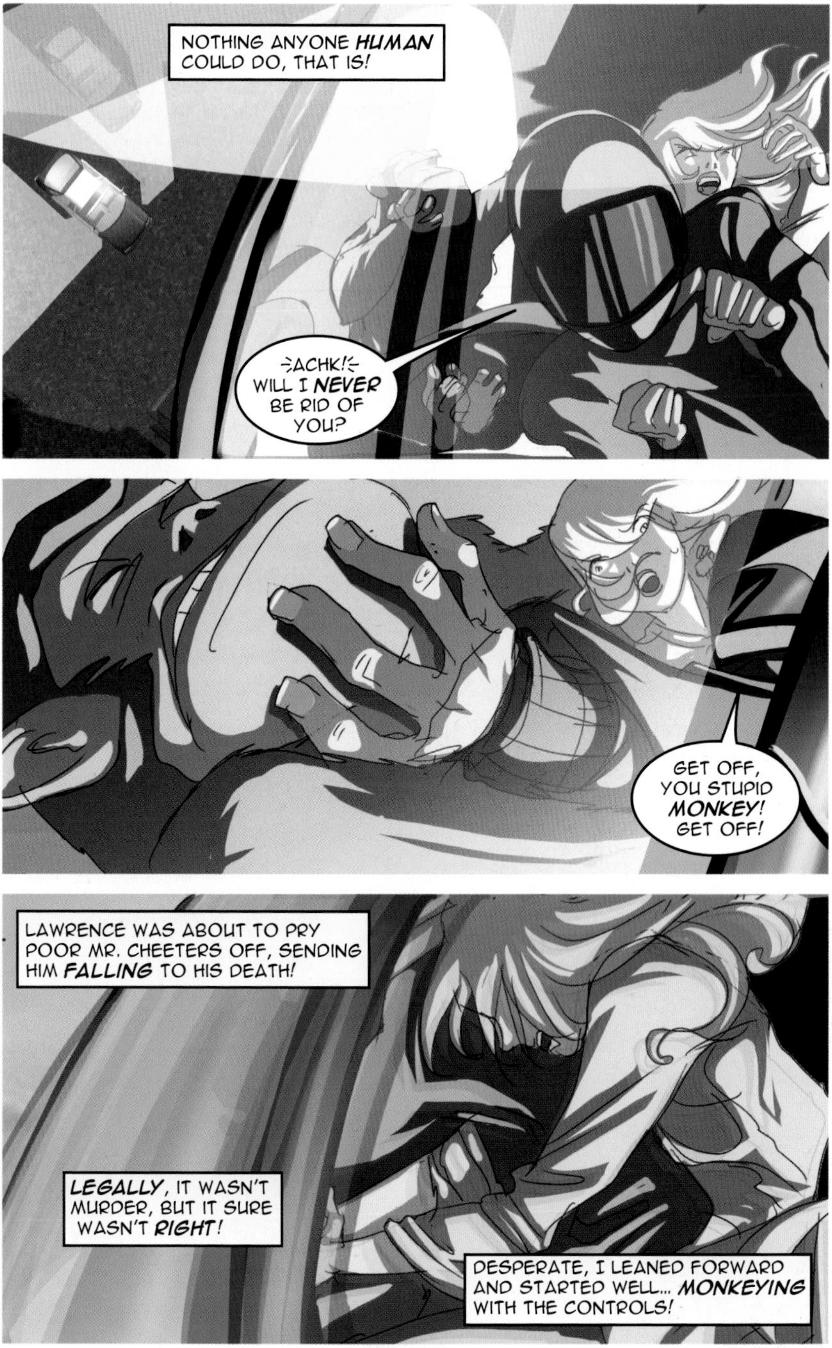
NOTHING ANYONE HUMAN COULD DO, THAT IS!
≈ACHK!≈ WILL I NEVER BE RID OF YOU?
GET OFF, YOU STUPID MONKEY! GET OFF!
LAWRENCE WAS ABOUT TO PRY POOR MR. CHEETERS OFF, SENDING HIM FALLING TO HIS DEATH!
LEGALLY, IT WASN'T MURDER, BUT IT SURE WASN'T RIGHT!
DESPERATE, I LEANED FORWARD AND STARTED WELL... MONKEYING WITH THE CONTROLS!

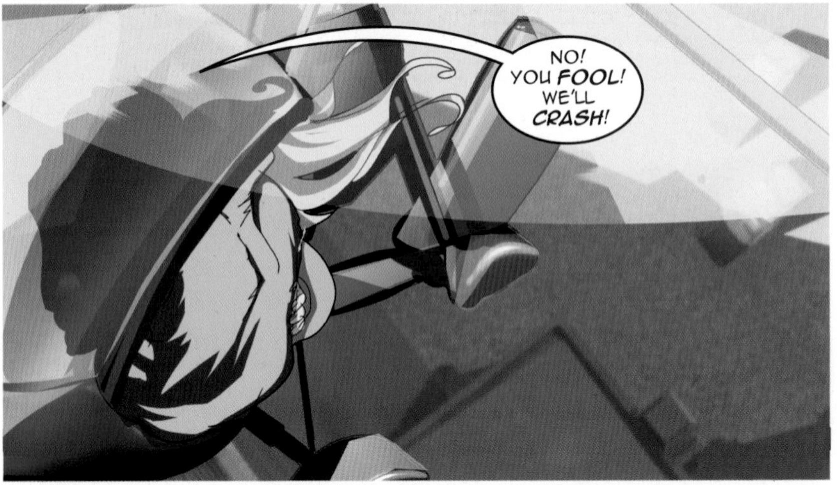
NO! YOU FOOL! WE'LL CRASH!

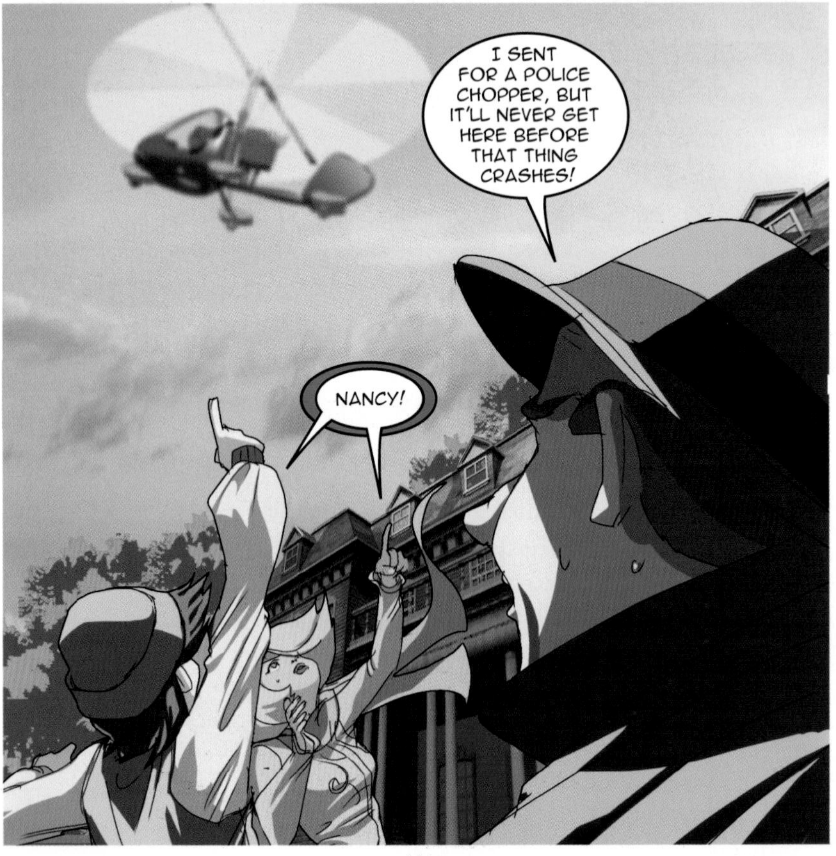
I SENT FOR A POLICE CHOPPER, BUT IT'LL NEVER GET HERE BEFORE THAT THING CRASHES!
NANCY!

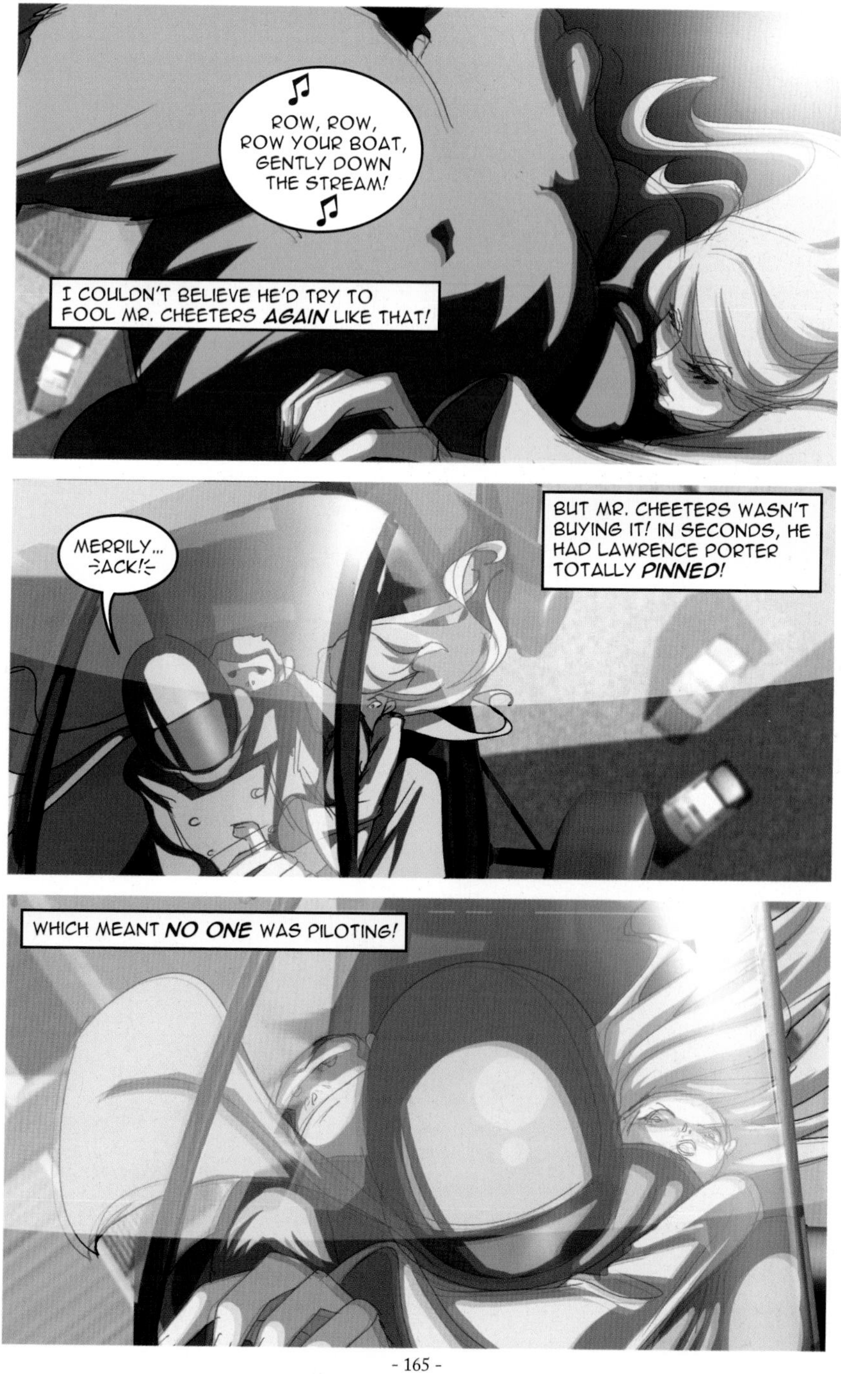
ROW, ROW, ROW YOUR BOAT, GENTLY DOWN THE STREAM!
I COULDN'T BELIEVE HE'D TRY TO FOOL MR. CHEETERS AGAIN LIKE THAT!
MERRILY... ACK!
BUT MR. CHEETERS WASN'T BUYING IT! IN SECONDS, HE HAD LAWRENCE PORTER TOTALLY PINNED!
WHICH MEANT NO ONE WAS PILOTING!

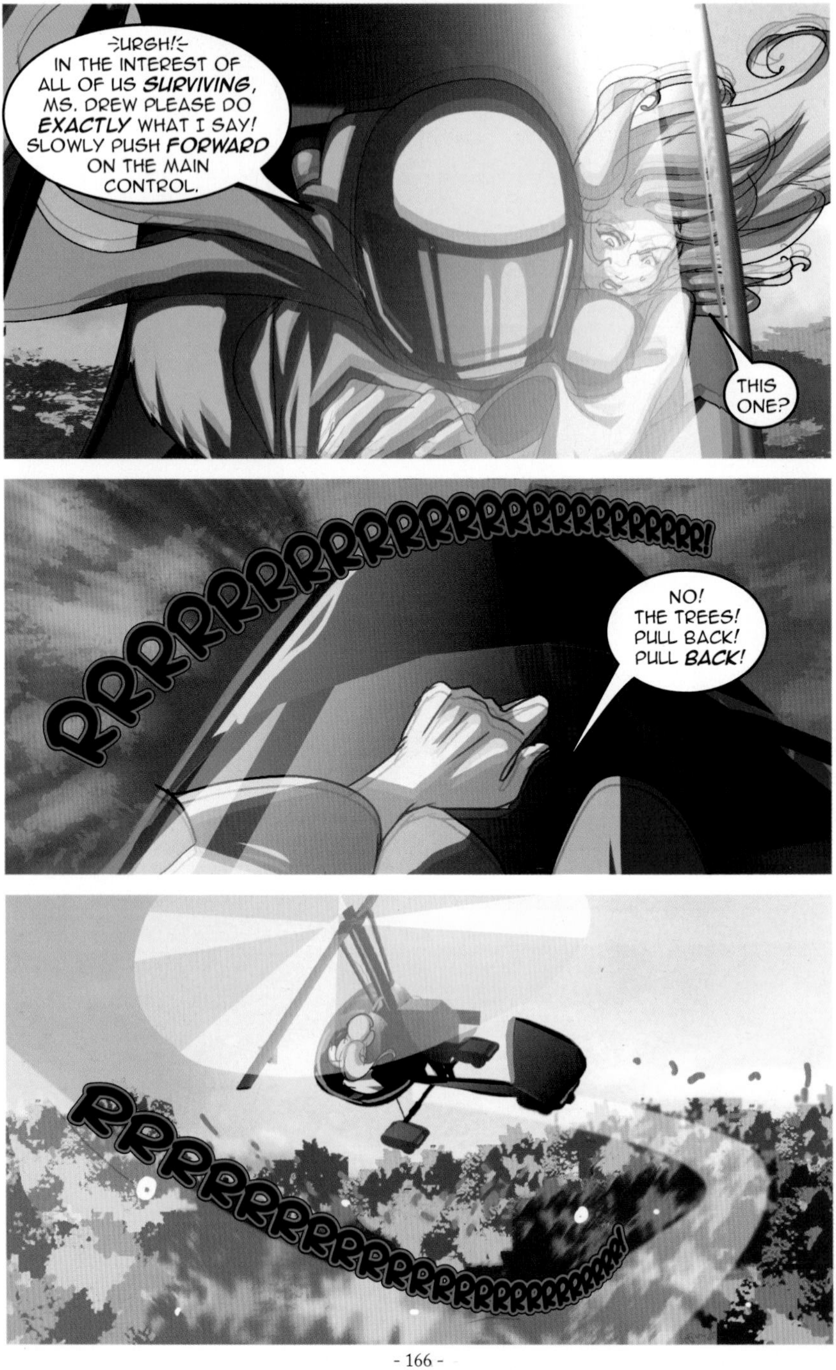
URGH!
IN THE INTEREST OF ALL OF US SURVIVING, MS. DREW PLEASE DO EXACTLY WHAT I SAY! SLOWLY PUSH FORWARD ON THE MAIN CONTROL.
THIS ONE?
RRRRRRRRRRRRRRRRRRRRRRRRRRR!
NO! THE TREES! PULL BACK! PULL BACK!
RRRRRRRRRRRRRRRRRRRRRRRRRRRRR!

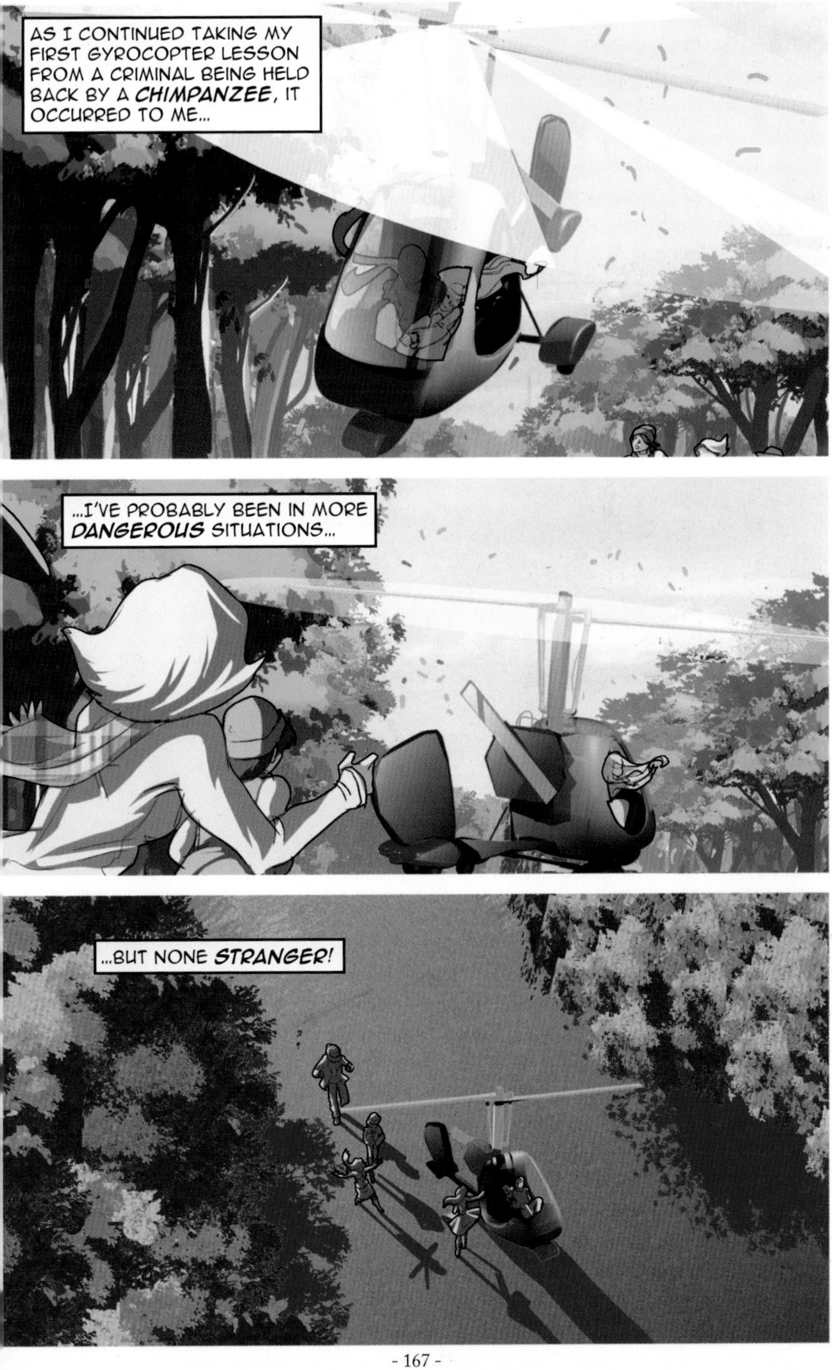
AS I CONTINUED TAKING MY FIRST GYROCOPTER LESSON FROM A CRIMINAL BEING HELD BACK BY A CHIMPANZEE, IT OCCURRED TO ME...
...I'VE PROBABLY BEEN IN MORE DANGEROUS SITUATIONS...
...BUT NONE STRANGER!

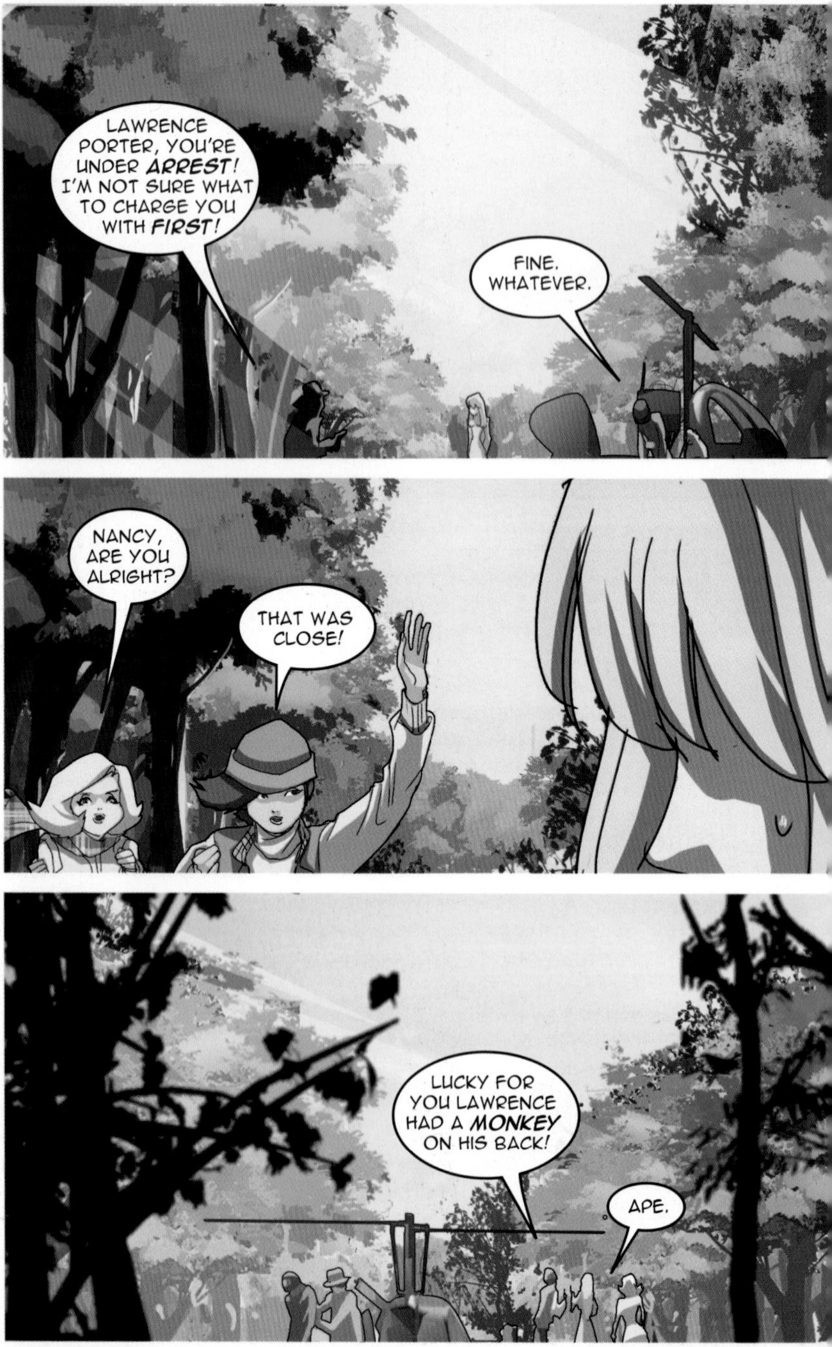
LAWRENCE PORTER, YOU'RE UNDER ARREST! I'M NOT SURE WHAT TO CHARGE YOU WITH FIRST!
FINE. WHATEVER.
NANCY, ARE YOU ALRIGHT?
THAT WAS CLOSE!
LUCKY FOR YOU LAWRENCE HAD A MONKEY ON HIS BACK!
APE.

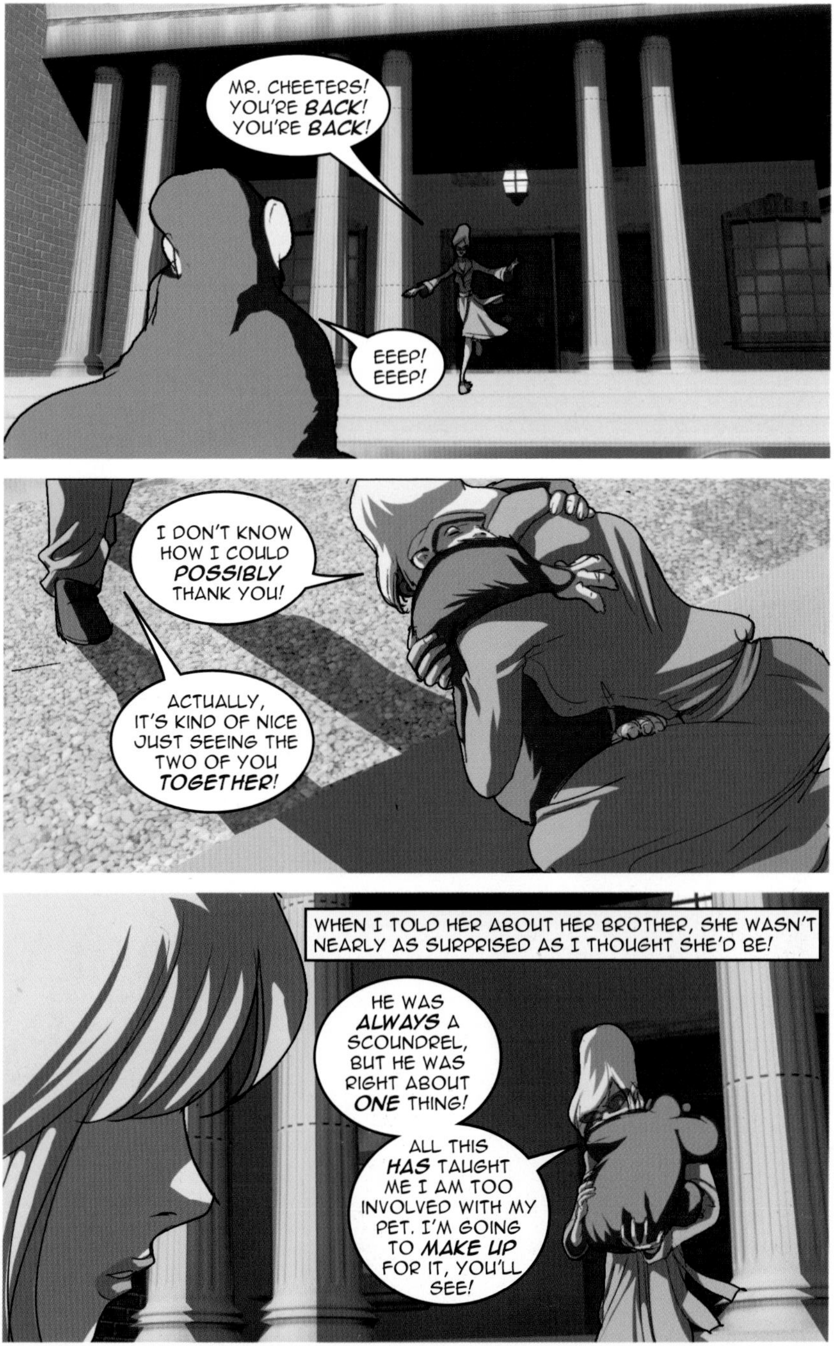
MR. CHEETERS! YOU'RE **BACK**! YOU'RE **BACK**!
EEEP! EEEP!
I DON'T KNOW HOW I COULD **POSSIBLY** THANK YOU!
ACTUALLY, IT'S KIND OF NICE JUST SEEING THE TWO OF YOU **TOGETHER**!
WHEN I TOLD HER ABOUT HER BROTHER, SHE WASN'T NEARLY AS SURPRISED AS I THOUGHT SHE'D BE!
HE WAS **ALWAYS** A SCOUNDREL, BUT HE WAS RIGHT ABOUT **ONE** THING!
ALL THIS **HAS** TAUGHT ME I AM TOO INVOLVED WITH MY PET. I'M GOING TO **MAKE UP** FOR IT, YOU'LL SEE!

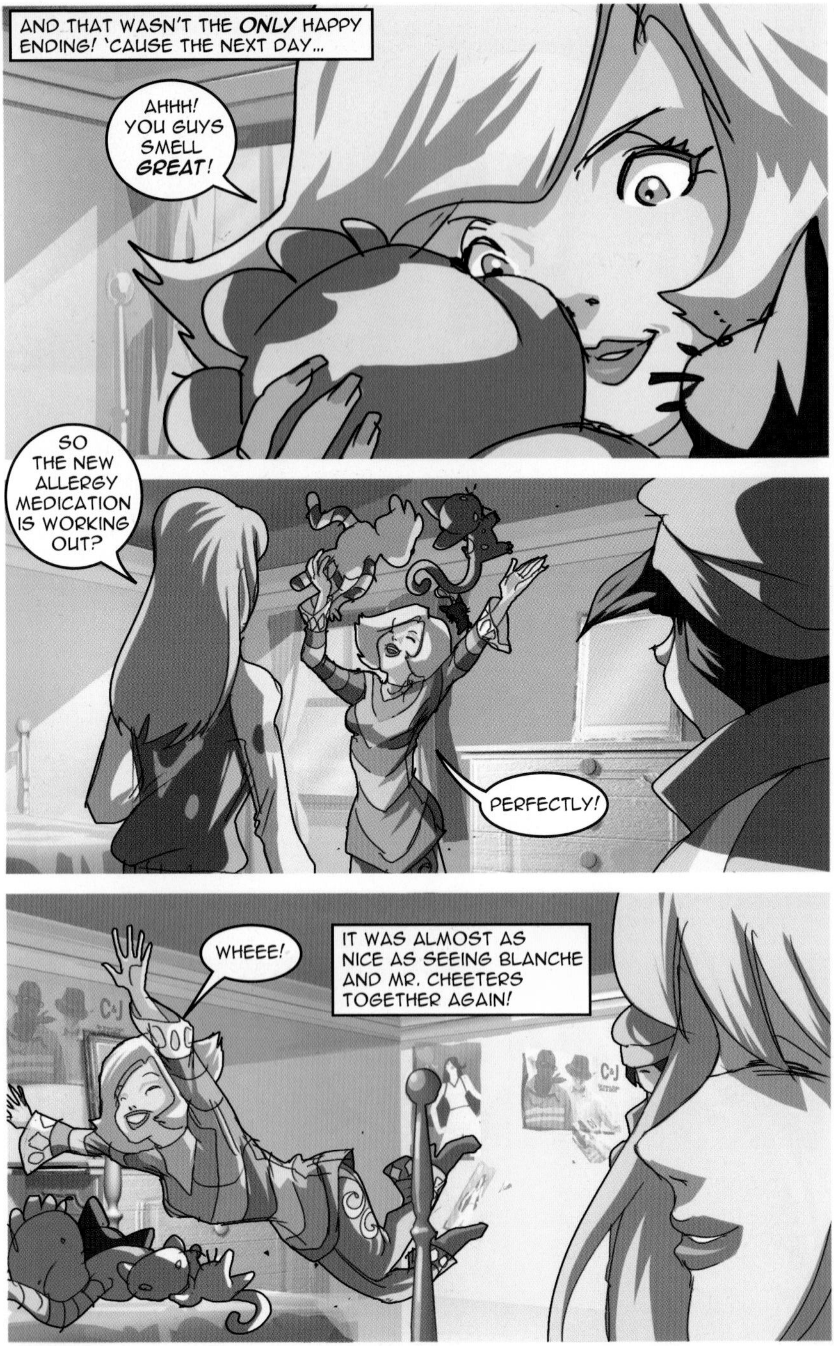
AND THAT WASN'T THE *ONLY* HAPPY ENDING! 'CAUSE THE NEXT DAY...
AHHH! YOU GUYS SMELL **GREAT**!
SO THE NEW ALLERGY MEDICATION IS WORKING OUT?
PERFECTLY!
WHEEE!
IT WAS ALMOST AS NICE AS SEEING BLANCHE AND MR. CHEETERS TOGETHER AGAIN!

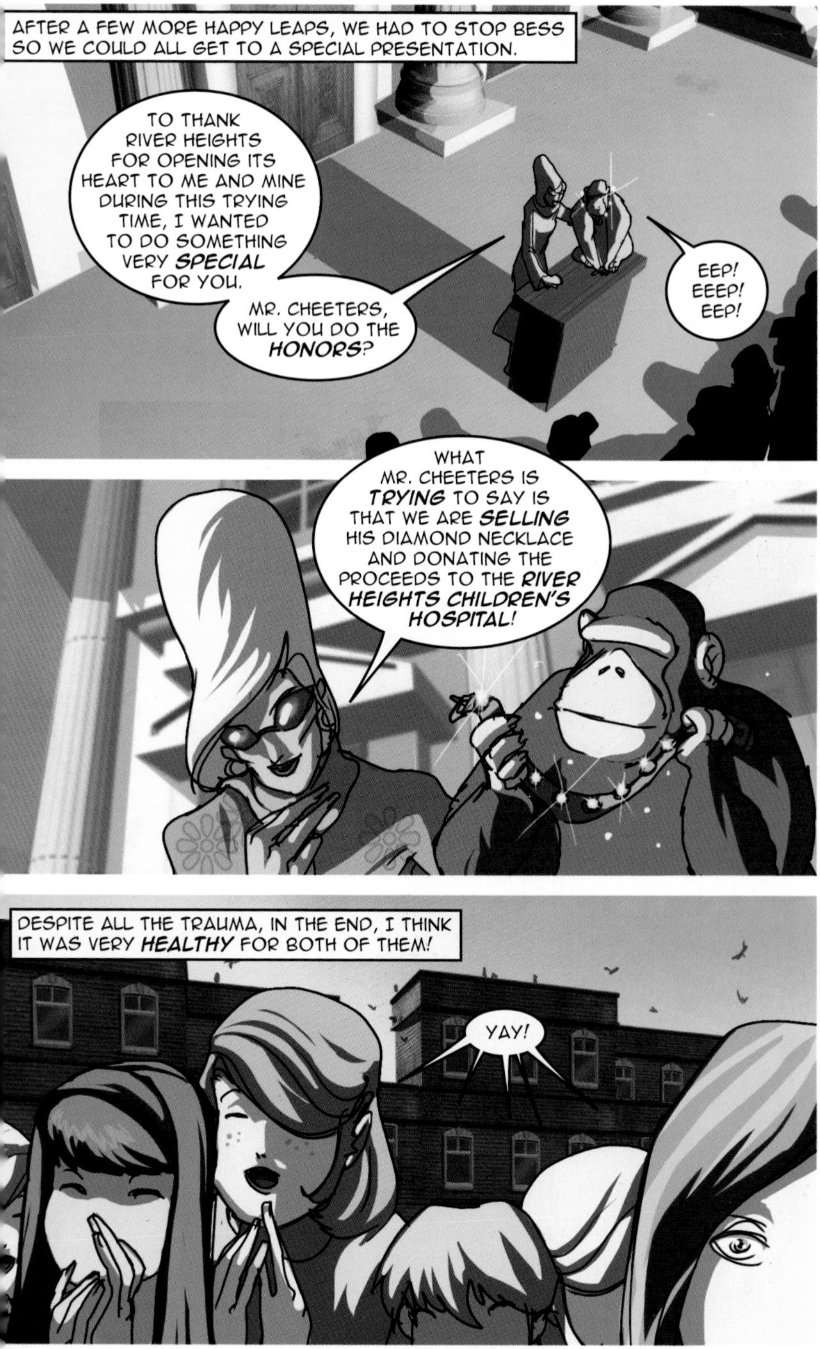
AFTER A FEW MORE HAPPY LEAPS, WE HAD TO STOP BESS SO WE COULD ALL GET TO A SPECIAL PRESENTATION.
TO THANK RIVER HEIGHTS FOR OPENING ITS HEART TO ME AND MINE DURING THIS TRYING TIME, I WANTED TO DO SOMETHING VERY SPECIAL FOR YOU.
MR. CHEETERS, WILL YOU DO THE HONORS?
EEP! EEEP! EEP!
WHAT MR. CHEETERS IS TRYING TO SAY IS THAT WE ARE SELLING HIS DIAMOND NECKLACE AND DONATING THE PROCEEDS TO THE RIVER HEIGHTS CHILDREN'S HOSPITAL!
DESPITE ALL THE TRAUMA, IN THE END, I THINK IT WAS VERY HEALTHY FOR BOTH OF THEM!
YAY!

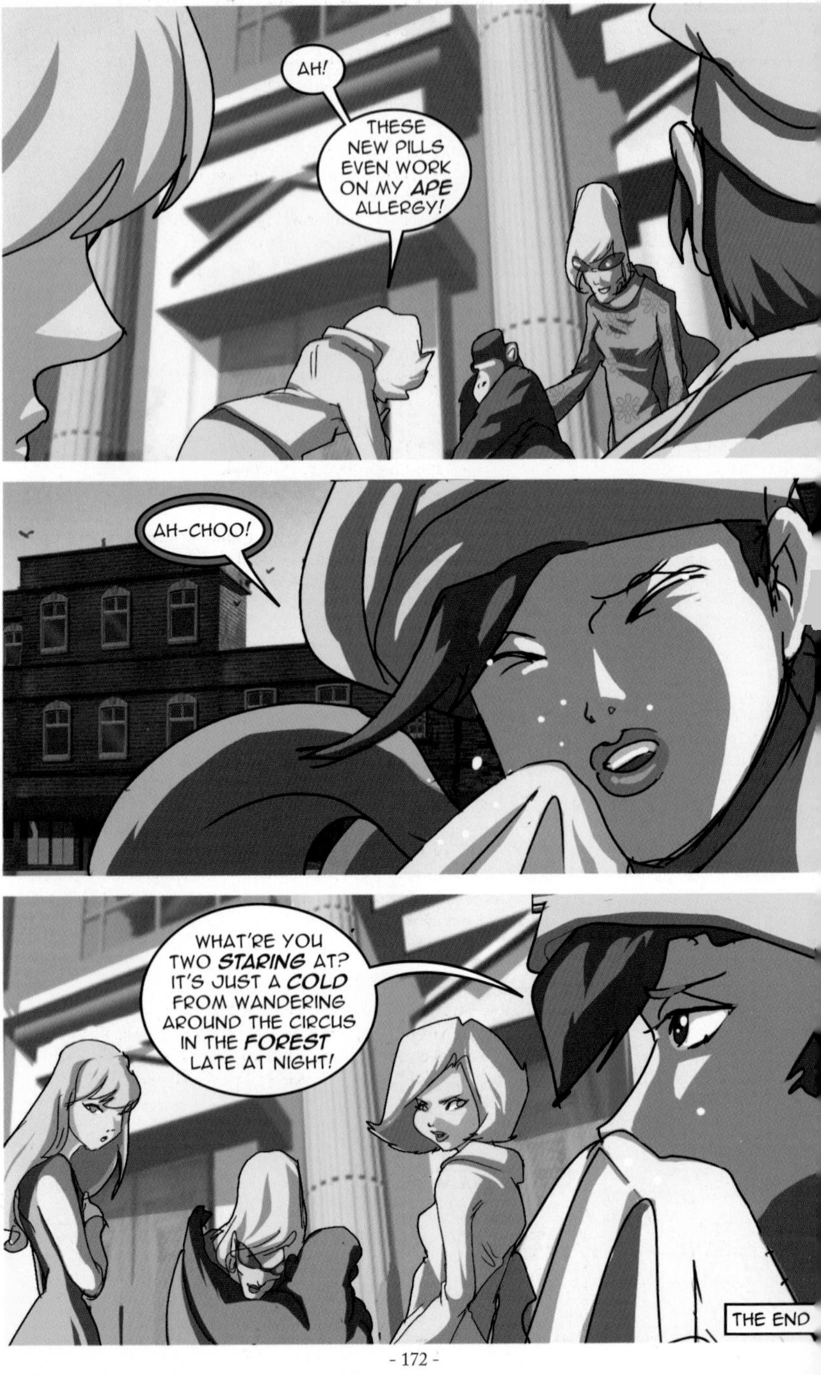
AH!
THESE NEW PILLS EVEN WORK ON MY APE ALLERGY!
AH-CHOO!
WHAT'RE YOU TWO STARING AT? IT'S JUST A COLD FROM WANDERING AROUND THE CIRCUS IN THE FOREST LATE AT NIGHT!
THE END

WATCH OUT FOR PAPERCUTZ ™

Hi, Mystery-lovers! Welcome to the third teen-sleuth-filled NANCY DREW DIARIES graphic novel from Papercutz, those perpetually perplexed people dedicated to publishing great graphic novels for all ages. I'm Jim Salicrup, the Editor-in-Chief and faithful fan of Carolyn Keene.

As you may or may not know, NANCY DREW DIARIES is a new series re-presenting the great NANCY DREW GIRL DETECTIVE graphic novels by Stefan Petrucha and Sho Murase, two at a time. This volume collects "The Fake Heir" and "Mr. Cheeters is Missing." "The Fake Heir" was actually drawn by Vaughn Ross (a fellow member of Maverix Studio, where Sho was working at the time), to help Sho get ahead on deadlines. Vaughn's style seems to divide fans—they either love it or hate it. Probably after after several NANCY DREW GIRL DETECTIVE graphic novels by Sho, fans were expecting Nancy to be in Sho's distinctive art style, and any change would've been upsetting. Ultimately it was a moot point, as Sho returned with the very next graphic novel, better than ever!

Early on in "The Fake Heir," we see Nancy, Bess, and George volunteering for something called Project Sunshine. Unlike the fictional town of River Heights and all its denizens, Project Sunshine is actually real! I had run into Project Sunshine founder, Joseph Weilgus, at a party and he told me all about this awesome organization. As it says on our website, projectsunshine.org, "Project Sunshine is a nonprofit organization that provides free educational, recreational, and social programs to children facing medical challenges and their families.

project sunshine

Project Sunshine empowers a dynamic and dedicated corps of over 15,000 volunteers to bring programming — recreational (arts), educational (tutoring and mentoring) and social service (HIV and nutritional counseling) — to 100,000 children facing medical challenges and their families in 175 cities across the United States and in four international locations: Canada, China, Israel and Kenya.

Volunteers selflessly donate their time to create program materials and deliver programs. Working onsite, our volunteers relieve the anxiety of the young patients and in a context of fun and play, foster in them the courage and coping skills necessary to confront procedures that lie ahead. Project Sunshine volunteers spread sunshine, restoring a crucial sense of normalcy to the pediatric healthcare environment." It sounded exactly like the type of organization Nancy Drew would belong to, so we decided to make Nancy, as well as Bess and George, Project Sunshine volunteers. We didn't want to make too big a deal out of it, we simply wanted to show that this was something Nancy would do just because that's the type of person she is.

Speaking of the type of person Nancy Drew is, allow me to mention a really cool site, run by Jennifer Fisher, that's devoted to everything about our favorite Girl Detective: ndsleuths.com "The Nancy Drew Sleuth Unofficial Website was created for the purpose of bringing together fans, collectors and scholars of Nancy Drew and series books. This website will be useful in rediscovering your favorite characters, stories, themes, issues, and artwork as well as providing information for research and links to other websites and sources for further research. As the premier Nancy Drew site on the web, you will find just about every clue here that you are sleuthing for." They even run an annual Nancy Drew convention, in addition to all sorts of other sleuthy stuff.

Feel free to check the websites for more information on Project Sunshine and The Nancy Drew Sleuths. And while you're surfing the web, be sure to visit papercutz.com for the latest news on NANCY DREW DIARIES and everything else that's going on at Papercutz. And whatever you do, don't miss NANCY DREW DIARIES #4 coming soon, and featuring "The Charmed Bracelet" and "Global Warning."

Thanks,

Jim

STAY IN TOUCH!

EMAIL: salicrup@papercutz.com
WEB: papercutz.com
TWITTER: @papercutzgn
FACEBOOK: PAPERCUTZGRAPHICNOVELS
REGULAR MAIL: Papercutz, 160 Broadway, Suite 700, East Wing, New York, NY 10038

NANCY DREW GRAPHIC NOVELS AVAILABLE FROM PAPERCUTZ

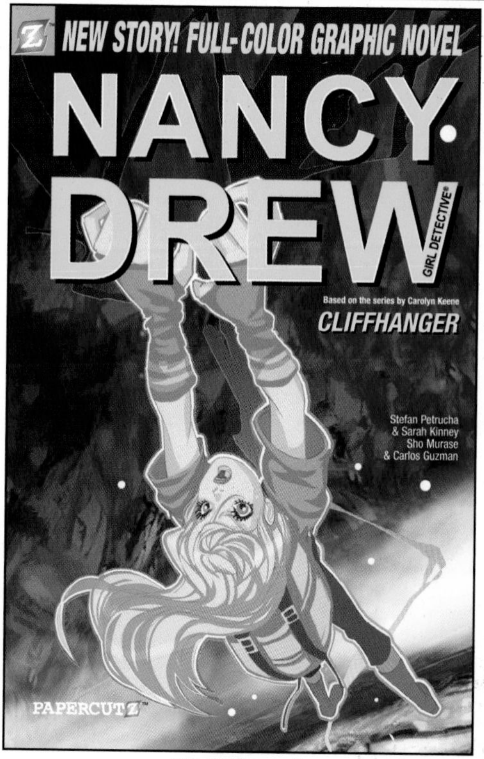
NEW STORY! FULL-COLOR GRAPHIC NOVEL
NANCY
DREW
GIRL DETECTIVE
Based on the series by Carolyn Keene
CLIFFHANGER
Stefan Petrucha
& Sarah Kinney
Sho Murase
& Carlos Guzman
PAPERCUTZ

#19 "Cliffhanger"

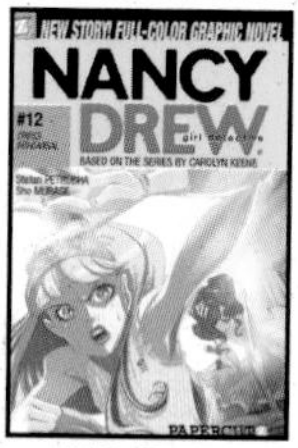
NEW STORY! FULL-COLOR GRAPHIC NOVEL
NANCY
DREW
#12
BASED ON THE SERIES BY CAROLYN KEENE
PAPERCUTZ

#12 "Dress Reversal"

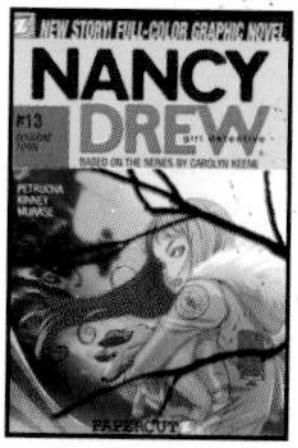
NEW STORY! FULL-COLOR GRAPHIC NOVEL
NANCY
DREW
#13
BASED ON THE SERIES BY CAROLYN KEENE
PAPERCUTZ

#13 "Doggone Town"

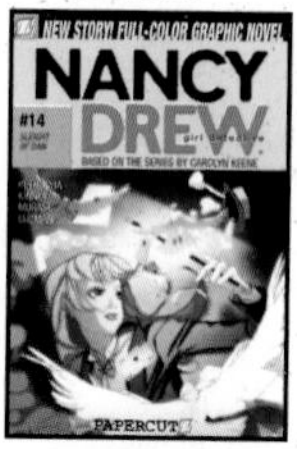
NEW STORY! FULL-COLOR GRAPHIC NOVEL
NANCY
DREW
#14
BASED ON THE SERIES BY CAROLYN KEENE
PAPERCUTZ

#14 "Sleight of Dan"

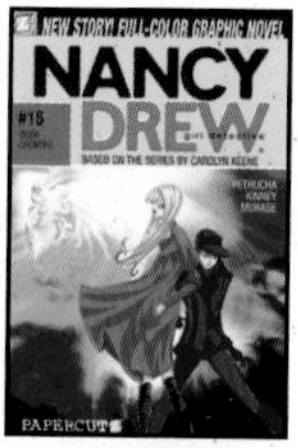
NEW STORY! FULL-COLOR GRAPHIC NOVEL
NANCY
DREW
#15
BASED ON THE SERIES BY CAROLYN KEENE
PAPERCUTZ

#15 "Tiger Counter"

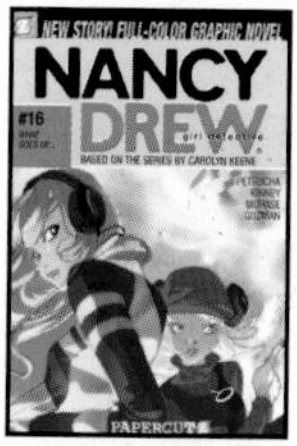
NEW STORY! FULL-COLOR GRAPHIC NOVEL
NANCY
DREW
#16
BASED ON THE SERIES BY CAROLYN KEENE
PAPERCUTZ

#16 "What Goes Up..."

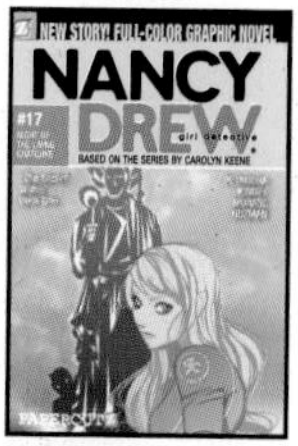
NEW STORY! FULL-COLOR GRAPHIC NOVEL
NANCY
DREW
#17
BASED ON THE SERIES BY CAROLYN KEENE

#17 "Night of the Living Chatchke"

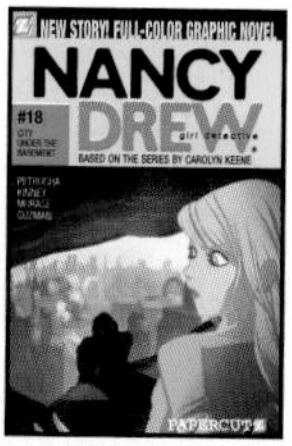
NEW STORY! FULL-COLOR GRAPHIC NOVEL
NANCY
DREW
#18
BASED ON THE SERIES BY CAROLYN KEENE
PAPERCUTZ

#18 "City Under the Basement"

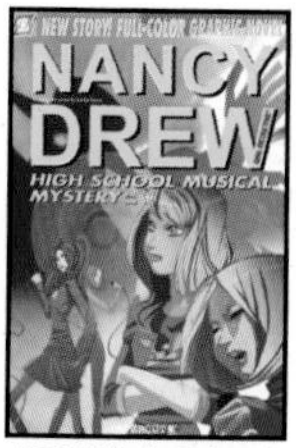
NEW STORY! FULL-COLOR GRAPHIC NOVEL
NANCY
DREW
HIGH SCHOOL MUSICAL MYSTERY

#20 "High School Musical Mystery" 1

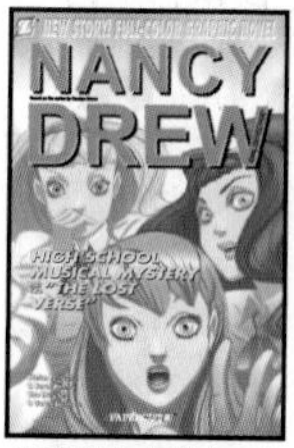
NEW STORY! FULL-COLOR GRAPHIC NOVEL
NANCY
DREW
HIGH SCHOOL MUSICAL MYSTERY 2 "THE LOST VERSE"

#21 "High School Musical Mystery" 2

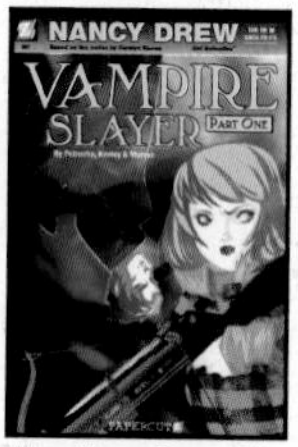
NANCY DREW
VAMPIRE
SLAYER
PART ONE
PAPERCUTZ

The New Case Files #1 "Vampire Slayer" Part 1

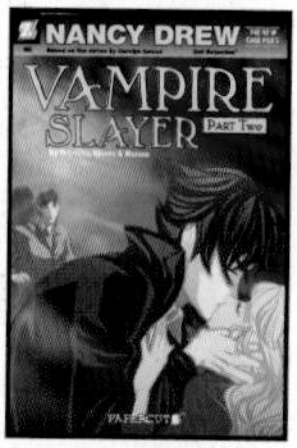
NANCY DREW
VAMPIRE
SLAYER
PART TWO
PAPERCUTZ

The New Case Files #2 "Vampire Slayer" Part 2

NANCY DREW Graphic Novels #12-19 are $7.95 in paperback, $12.95 hardcover. Graphic Novels #20 and #21 are $8.99 paperback, $13.99 hardcover. NANCY DREW The New Case Files #1 and #2 are $6.99 paperback, $10.99 hardcover. Available at booksellers everywhere.

Or order from us. Make check payable to NBM Publishing.
Please add $4.00 for postage and handling for the first book, add $1.00 for each additional book.
Send to: Papercutz, 160 Broadway, Suite 700, East Wing, New York, NY 10038
Or call 800 886 1223 (9-6 EST M-F) MC, Visa, Amex accepted.

papercutz.com